Kim-

I hope you enjoy meeting some new characters and a new story!

MW01717166

Sins of the Fathers

by

Erin K. Pugh

Best,
Erin K Pugh

RED LEAD PRESS
PITTSBURGH, PENNSYLVANIA 15222

The contents of this work including, but not limited to, the accuracy of events, people, and places depicted; opinions expressed; permission to use previously published materials included; and any advice given or actions advocated are solely the responsibility of the author, who assumes all liability for said work and indemnifies the publisher against any claims stemming from publication of the work.

All Rights Reserved
Copyright © 2010 by Erin K. Pugh
No part of this book may be reproduced or transmitted
in any form or by any means, electronic or mechanical,
including photocopying, recording, or by any information
storage and retrieval system without permission in
writing from the publisher.

ISBN: 978-1-4349-6466-3
eISBN: 978-1-4349-4702-4
Printed in the United States of America

First Printing

For more information or to order additional books, please contact:
Red Lead Press
701 Smithfield Street
Pittsburgh, Pennsylvania 15222
U.S.A.
1-800-834-1803
www.redleadbooks.com

Prologue

Leaving Albany, NY
June 17, 2004
9:15 p.m.

Jeremy Beckett bit back on the anger bubbling in his chest as he squinted from the glare of the oncoming headlights. He gripped the steering wheel underneath his tense fingers with a fierce grip, tramped on the accelerator, and put as much space between him and the source of his anger as he could manage, forcing a cleansing breath from his lungs to calm down.

He needed distance from her - and in a hurry, before he lost his resolve and turned the car around, once again returning to the fray of her temper. The need for the quiet solitude that would envelop him when he drove up the long driveway to Cherry Hill throbbed at the base of his skull, pushing him forward. The woman could push his buttons more effectively than any ego-driven businessman he could ever encounter in his day-to-day dealings at the office. Million-dollar deals could be handled with less stress than the woman who held his heart.

He fumed through clenched teeth as the wheels underneath him ate up the highway. Signaling and moving into the passing lane, her face filled his mind. A perfectly reasonable request had turned into an argument, and from that to an all-out screaming match. She'd been spoiling for a fight the moment he walked through the door. He should have known better, but underneath his anger, regret already coiled in the pit of his stomach over his harsh words. He would call her when he arrived because he would know no peace while anger stood between them.

The blaring sound of a horn snapped him back to reality with only a split second to react. He cut the wheel with a violent jerk but was too late to avoid disaster: he saw the telephone pole directly in the path of his out-of-control car, and everything that followed happened in slow motion. The last sounds he heard were metal crushing against metal and metal meeting with wood.

He opened his eyes with tremendous effort. A red haze draped over his eyes, and the most intense pain of his forty-five years invaded every fiber of his being. He struggled to breathe, every attempt feeling like a knife being driven deeper into his chest.

Dizziness flooded his brain, and his stomach lunged and turned from the sudden movement of trying to lift his head. His effort to breathe sapped whatever dwindling strength he had, and he was sure he could feel his life slipping away. He gasped and sucked air into his lungs, only to be dealt a sudden, sharp flash of pain. His head throbbed, leaving any thoughts in his head muddled and confused. He tasted blood.

No matter how hard he tried, he couldn't move. Every muscle in his body felt like water, his arms and legs felt disconnected from his body, and he wondered if he were dying. Off in the distance, a voice was telling him to hold on - but his body and mind wanted to let go.

Shock gave way, and fresh, bright pain erupted through his body as the arriving E.M.T.s began to work on him. A cold wave washed over him, and behind the thin veil separating consciousness from nothingness, he saw her sweet face. The woman who was the love of his life, his destiny. She was just out of reach, hovering before him, and he longed to touch her just one more time. In the distance, more sirens wailed, then an all-consuming blackness took him under.

~ 1 ~

Albany General Hospital
June 17, 2004
11:01 p.m.

Dr. Salvador Montgomery hated this part of his job, but as Chief of Staff at AGH, he had to carry out this duty more often than he cared to think about. He checked his watch and quickened his pace, shoving the door to the stairwell open and bounding down the stairs. It was just after 11 p.m.; he'd been on his feet for the past twenty hours, he was exhausted, and it would be twenty-eight more before he could slip between the comforting sheets of his own bed and surrender to the fatigue settling into his bones. Now he had to tell Christina Wagner that her long-time love, the man she was only a month away from marrying was hanging by a thread between life and death. With a sigh, he knew it never got easier; the ripping away of the false sense of immortality to which we all cling. So, he would offer the comfort he would hope to receive if the situation were reversed.

Though he'd never met her, like everyone else in the city, he knew all about her. He had dined in her restaurants, tasted her fine food, and seen her face in the papers and on TV. The Society Report called her everything from home-wrecker to whore, and The New York Times simply refused to acknowledge her presence by saying anything at all - an act that really spoke volumes. Yes, Christina Wagner was not just famous, but infamous, and for all the wrong reasons.

He took the stairs two at a time and reached the door to the lobby, yanking it open with a force that spoke of his frustration and his wish to be anyone else at that moment. His eyes met with a floor nurse, and she motioned to the window that looked out to the parking lot.

He walked slowly towards her, taking a deep breath as he crossed the distance between them. Even from behind, he could see she was racked by the tension that always came with the unknown. He knew that posture well; her fear radiated into him with every nearing step.

"Ms. Wagner?" he said in a low voice, breaking a silence heavy with fear. When she turned to face him, he couldn't mistake the look on her face for anything other than what it was: absolute terror. He offered his hand and shook hers gently, saying "I'm Dr. Salvador Montgomery. I've been tending to Mr. Beckett's injuries since his arrival here about ninety minutes ago." Over her shoulder through the window, he could see that the media vultures were already circling for their pound of flesh.

"How is he?" Christina's desperate voice struggled for calm. She grasped his arm tightly, and her eyes, frantic and red from crying, bore into him. "Can I see him?" She'd pulled her shoulder length auburn hair into a taut ponytail and left the house without any makeup. She knew she looked awful; five hours of sleep during the past two nights had left her worry lines in full view.

"Of course, but I'd like to bring you up to speed with what we're dealing with first, the most significant being surgery once he stabilizes."

Her unspoken fear, the one she couldn't bear to give voice to, was that Jeremy would die with the last words spoken between them being harsh and angry. "Oh God, how serious is it?"

When the phone woke her with a start, Christina assumed it was Jeremy calling to talk things out. She wasn't prepared for the unfamiliar voice carefully informing her of Jeremy's accident. Terrible thoughts filled her mind as she woke Mrs. Richards and quickly made her way to the hospital. Now, here she stood looking at the man she prayed could save the life of the man she knew she couldn't live without.

"What concerns me most right now is the abdominal injury he suffered on impact, probably from the lap restraint of his seat belt."

"Is it a serious injury?"

"It can be, yes, but we're keeping a close watch," he said, nodding. "The trauma to the abdominal wall is extensive, and there's some internal bleeding. When he's more stable, I'll repair it with surgery." He opened the chart the nurse handed him and flipped through several pages, frowning. "His vital signs could stand some improvement. There are several deep abrasions to his face and one rather substantial wound above his right eye, a severe concussion thanks to an airbag malfunction - which we'll have to keep an eye on through the night - as well as three broken ribs and a compound fracture of his left leg."

Christina steadied herself against the wall behind her as her bones turned to jelly. She was going to pass out; she recognized the feeling well. Taking a deep breath, she got hold of herself and forced herself to focus. "Is his life in danger?" she asked.

Dr. Montgomery put his hand on her shoulder. Her complexion turned white as a sheet, and he was afraid she might drop right in front of him. "He's a strong man, Ms. Wagner, and that's a plus. I'll feel better when he's out of surgery and awake. The next twenty-four hours will determine a lot."

"I need to see him."

"I'll take you to him right now."

~~

The floor of the Intensive Care Unit was eerily quiet. Christina's mind was reeling as Dr. Montgomery guided her down the hallway. She was walking around in a haze. She closed her eyes, and visions of the press swarming outside the hospital waiting for their next sound bite flashed in her mind. Opening her eyes again, she clenched her teeth. *The bastards*, she thought as they came to a stop outside room 311. Christina refocused her attention and followed Dr. Montgomery through the door.

~~

The only light in the room came from the dim tube light above the bed, and the faint light cast shadows on his bruised face. Her gasp surprised her; to see his battered body broke her heart. She went to him and looked down at his face. Cuts and abrasions covered his left cheek, and his right eye was swollen shut and crusted with dried blood.

Her hand shook when she reached out to touch the only part of his face that wasn't puffy and bruised. He felt warm under her clammy fingers; reminding her of how warm and safe she always felt in his arms. Her eyes swept over his body, down to his covered feet and back again, then finally came to rest on his chest. She needed to be sure of his breathing. His chest rose and fell slowly, and relief swept through her in a surging wave. He was alive; it was something to cling to.

"I'm here, Jeremy." Her voice was a whisper in the stillness of the room. Leaning close, she drew in the faint scent of his cologne and whispered, "I'm right here with you." Her voice wavered as his pain shook her. "Wake up for me, sweetheart. Let me see those wonderful eyes."

Dr. Montgomery slid a chair next to the bed. "Why don't you sit down," he suggested. The papers could say whatever they wanted, but there was no doubt in his mind that this woman loved this man, and his heart went out to her. "He probably won't come around for awhile yet, so you should try and get some rest yourself."

Christina sat down in the chair and sighed. This was proving to be the night from hell with no end in sight. She sat, silently berating herself for the fight she'd started with him and decided to do the only thing she could at the moment: protect him and the life they had made together. "The press will be scrounging for details, Dr. Montgomery," she said with steel in her voice. "They're bastards, and this is none of their concern. Don't give them one word more than you have to."

He looked at her and knew she meant every word of what she just said. "Actually, Ms. Wagner, I don't have to tell them anything."

Christina leaned back in the chair and slipped off her heels; her feet were killing her - but then, being on them for ten hours straight, what did she expect? "Don't expect them to let you off that easy. You've heard the rumors." She smirked, revealing the fine laugh lines around her mouth. After so much practice at being the media's number one target, she'd been forced to develop a dry sense of humor. "I'm a gold-digger." Running her fingers through the ends of her long auburn hair, she flashed him an iron stare.

He shifted his weight and searched for something comforting to say. "I tend to ignore gossip of all forms. If I didn't, my brain would turn to mush - and then what good would I be to my profession? Rumors don't interest me. For the likes of them, it is about what sells, and it's unfortunate that lies top the list." A somewhat sheepish grin relaxed the lines in his forehead. "I'll confess, I've enjoyed dining in your restaurants, and your culinary talent is above reproach. Beyond that, I won't speculate. You know your life better than anyone else." He bent over the bed and checked Jeremy's pupils before he moved to the door. "Try to get some rest."

Christina gave him a tired smile. "Thank you." She waited until Dr. Montgomery disappeared through the door while her mind and heart raced. In the answering quiet, she let the pain come and looked at Jeremy with tears in her eyes. "I'm so sorry about our fight. I love you so much." Lifting his hand, she laced her fingers with his and squeezed. "You can't leave me, Jeremy. Wake up and tell me I'm a stubborn fool again."

She leaned back, rested her head, and tried to will herself to relax. Her tension would do him no good. She needed to send him all her energy and strength. He needed her now more than ever before. Before long, though, her eyelids grew heavy. The exhaustion she'd been fighting overtook her. Her mind drifted through a door in the far reaches of her mind where she could see Jeremy, whole and laughing. Younger and as handsome as he remained today...the same as he looked the first day they met, twenty-seven years before.

~ 2 ~

Stanton Island
June 1977

Christina Wagner looked out from the deck of the Stanton Island ferry. She had grown to appreciate the view on her daily trips across the water that separated Stanton Island from the more refined island of Manhattan. It was her daily ritual to take the ferry and walk into the heart of Manhattan, where she worked summers at O'Donnell's Pub, waiting tables. She worked endless hours, scrimping and saving, tucking away most of her pay and tips for her future. She was a young woman with dreams and the drive to make them come true. Some day, she'd have the money to start her own restaurant, and her days of slaving away for someone else would be over.

The ferry docked and Christina, eighteen and fresh out of high school, made her way through the endless streams of people with the long purposeful strides of a woman who knew exactly what she was worth. Her shift tonight would be an exercise in patience for her, but she had only to think of the tips to remind her of why she'd put up with it. Working a private party at O'Donnell's always meant cocky patrons and snide remarks. The only thing that kept her sane was knowing that while their mouths often ran on overflow, so did their wallets.

Paul Wagner had relented two summers before and allowed Christina to leave New Jersey and spend the summers with his younger sister, Bess, on Stanton Island. After much soul searching, he decided that his daughter could use the guidance of a woman in her life, and he knew of no one with a stronger hand on values than his sister. Christina's mother had died three days after her birth, the result of what the doctors diagnosed as a staph infection from a difficult birth. Devastation quickly took a back seat to the endless needs of his infant daughter.

His heartbreak had to be pushed to the far corners of his mind in a hurry. There was no time to mourn when a man was faced with raising a motherless child on his own. So, he raised her the best he could, being both mother and father to the little girl that had so quickly stolen his broken heart. It was hard, sometimes confusing work; harder than any grunt work he'd ever been handed at the packing mill, where he made his living as a supervisor.

And Christina never lacked for anything, especially love. She never realized, at least as a child, how a mother was the center of a home and family. She grew up in an environment of love and laughter. He adored Christina, and letting her out from under his protective wings almost killed him.

Christina loved her freedom and independence and thrived on the chance to fulfill her dreams, dreams that her father, as much as he worried about her, couldn't understand. All he knew was that his daughter had a need to be on her own to spread her wings, away from his constant worrying eye. She was beautiful in a simple way, tall with long legs and even longer auburn hair. Her eyes were the deep sea green of her mother's with a depth that revealed a kindness her father was sure came from his wife. But even he had to admit that his little girl was no pushover; one thing Christina could do was take care of herself. From an early age, she developed a stubborn toughness that Bess swore came directly from him.

~~

Christina swept into O'Donnell's with the air of quiet confidence that others mistook for arrogance. The bartender nodded at her, and her fellow waitresses called out their hellos as Christina walked through the bar into the back room. After she hung up her coat and checked her makeup, Christina tied her apron around her waist and headed out front to her station. The guests for the private party would begin arriving within the hour.

~~

Jeremy Beckett should have been a happy man, but he wasn't - at least not beneath the surface. Under the forced smile and glazed expression in his eyes, he fumed silently. He had turned twenty today and wanted to be out celebrating with his college buddies; or better still, locked away in the attic he had converted into his studio, with a paint brush and a blank canvas in front of him. Instead, he sat slumped in the back seat of his father's stretch limo, going to a birthday party he didn't want to attend. His father sat on the seat across from him with his business partner beside him and permanently attached to his ear. Another business deal potentially worth millions no doubt, he guessed.

He watched his father with a familiar disdain that colored his mood from time to time, but today it took on a whole new meaning. The great Linus Beckett with his fingertips on the verge of yet another legendary deal;

he was a giant in the world of high finance, specializing in corporate takeovers.

His mother, Elise, had become ill, and as a result had an acceptable excuse for missing out on the festivities, but having her there would have been the one thing that would have made it bearable for her son. Jeremy had had no choice but to attend the party his father had put together for him, especially after Elise pleaded with him to go and make his father happy, knowing Jeremy would do anything for her. Jeremy often wondered to himself how two people so mismatched could have fallen in love and shared a marriage that was heading into its twenty-second year.

He watched as Linus gave his partner an impatient look and moved his hand up to pull on his ear; a habit brought on by restlessness, Jeremy knew it well. "Fine," Linus said. A killer headache was beginning to form behind his eyes, and his tolerance for bullshit was running a bit thin. "Christ, Tim, you don't need me to hold your hand through these negotiations," he snapped, shifting in his seat to look Tim in the eye. "Give him the price we've set. If he doesn't like it..." he shrugged and smoothed the knot in his tie, "tough shit. Dennison Electronics isn't the only game in town, and there are other buyers."

"Not at the price we're asking, Linus." Tim Adams leaned back, pinched the bridge of his nose, and huffed out an exasperated breath. He should have known there'd be no talking to him. "It's been a good year; we can afford to be a little generous with Dennison," he continued, lowering the window to rescue his lungs from the strong stream of smoke from his pain-in-the-ass partner's cigar.

"Not if it means taking a ten-million-dollar loss," Linus said through his teeth, puffing on his daily cigar.

Tim Adams slid his eyes from the busy streets of New York back to Linus Beckett. "It's not even a drop in the bucket for us, Linus, and you know it."

The limo came to a stop before Linus could respond - and Tim was already out the door. "Tim, let's leave business alone for awhile." He flashed his million-dollar smile and was rewarded with a grin in return. "It's my boy's birthday. We'll see you at O'Donnell's in about forty-five minutes?"

Tim relaxed and rolled his shoulders, reminding himself that dealing with Linus when he was in one of his moods was like trying to push a tidal wave back with a spoon. "Yeah. Forty-five minutes."

~~

The sound of Jeremy's restless groan attracted his father's vibrant eyes. Linus watched the stiff outline of his son's jaw and knew he was fuming. *So much like his lovely mother and very much different from me*, he thought. But still, Linus smiled; Jeremy was his only son, the apple of his eye, and the future of Beckett International Industries. And as sons went, not too bad - even if they didn't always see eye-to-eye.

Linus knew all too well that Jeremy lacked the killer drive it took to snatch up and devour companies, then break them apart piece by piece, only to resell them at double the profit; to put faceless people out of work without worry or conscience. That he would rather stay in his studio painting and pondering deeper thoughts, working on his latest canvas while the world beyond those walls went on without him, was something he'd come to accept.

While he adored his daughter, Jamie, she had no head for business. The family legacy belonged to Jeremy - whether he liked it or not. The only drawback would be Jeremy's one weakness: unfortunately, the boy had a bleeding heart, a possession that would be a dangerous liability in the business world of "take or be taken."

Studying his son's profile, Linus felt his pride swell. He found it hard to believe that his son was twenty years old, but the undeniable proof was sitting right in front of him - and looking miserable. He was an attractive young man, not unlike himself, Linus mused. With hair the same sandy blond as his mother's and eyes handed down from Linus himself, brown and dark like muddy river water. One look into those eyes, and Linus could see his youth.

The rest of his features mirrored his father's as well: a strong classic nose and forehead, subtle cheekbones - which were perfectly placed on his face - with a chin gifted with the perfect dimple. Some called him a pretty boy, which set Linus on edge; his son was no pretty boy. He wore the face of a handsome, successful future businessman, and it stung that his son had no use for the business he loved so much and wanted one day to hand down to him.

"You look like you're being led to the gas chamber instead of a birthday party," Linus commented, breaking the gate wide open for what would likely turn into an argument.

Jeremy could feel his father staring at him, and he felt like he was under a microscope. He looked at him and forced himself to bite his tongue. "This party's more for you than me," he replied, his tone sharp with edges. "You know I don't like these parties you throw to show yourself off, Dad," he muttered. "I'll bet I don't even know most of the people you invited. I'll no doubt have to hobnob with your business associates." His eyes were full of accusation as he glared at his father. He swallowed the urge to lunge when his father only grinned at him.

"You always think you know so much." Opening the side compartment and lifting out a bottle of brandy, he fixed himself a drink. Offering one to his son, he received the expected response, a terse nod of his head. His son had a taste for many things: young ladies with long legs, fast cars, and fine foods. Brandy was not among them. "I'll have you know, I've spent the better part of a week gathering up all your old college pals," he said matter-of-factly. Linus was determined to keep his tone in check; he wasn't in the mood to fight. He took a gulp of brandy and let it sit on his tongue.

Jeremy studied his father and didn't buy a word of what he'd just been told. "You did?" he asked with a sarcastic edge. "Yeah, right."

Linus opened the sunroof and studied the bright blue sky as if he didn't hear his son's challenging question. After a few seconds of feeding Jeremy's anger, he looked at him and rolled his eyes. "Alright, Eden tracked them down." he confessed. Eden was his ever loyal secretary, and she'd saved his ass on more than one occasion, for both business and personal occasions - just as she had with this party. "But they will be at O'Donnell's nonetheless."

"Is Jamie coming?"

"You know she wouldn't miss it. She adores her big brother."

"She's eighteen and rebellious as hell," Jeremy reminded him. "And completely unreliable."

"She'll be there." Linus promised.

"And Grandpa?"

"He's still at Cherry Hill. That damn cough is driving him mad, so he's decided he will drive the household staff insane instead."

Jeremy rolled his neck, fighting off the urge to leap from the car as thoughts of his grandfather filled his mind. Avery Beckett, his father's father, was all spitfire and fortitude and had well earned his reputation for being stubborn as a mule - and on a bad day, twice as mean. A self-made man with all the pride that came with the distinction, who never backed down from a good fight - especially if he were the underdog. And of all the traits Linus inherited from his father, his stubborn streak was the most legendary.

Avery took no nonsense from anyone and was normally tough as nails, except when it came to his grandchildren. The sun shined on them as if Avery knew God Himself had ordered that the sun be in the sky for no one but them. And it shined brightest on his pride and joy, Jeremy. As far as Jeremy was concerned, the feeling was very mutual.

"Is the doctor with him?" Jeremy asked, stretching out his long legs and crossing them at the ankles.

Linus nodded and took another drink. "And so is the nurse he's driving to the edge of her sanity." He grew quiet and took a sip of brandy. "I wish your mother could have joined us."

Jeremy's face softened. "She's not feeling well again. I think you need to get her to a specialist."

Linus locked eyes with his son. "She has seen specialists on both coasts," he replied seriously. "I'll make some more calls on Monday."

"Good," Jeremy said, shaking his head in agreement. Thoughts of his mother distracted him from complaining about his party.

~~

A half an hour later, Christina was organizing the gift table when the door facing the street opened. She looked up to see Jeremy Beckett walk through the door with his father right behind him. Their smiles showed how alike they looked. They were rarely seen together in public, and it was easy to forget how striking the two of them were in similarity.

Watching them side by side, Christina knew if a person had no idea who the two men were, it would only take one look to know they were father and son. She watched them talk to each other in the clipped shorthand of family while their eyes scanned the room. Always an observant young woman, it was easy to see Jeremy wanted to be somewhere else.

The cynic in her thought him to be a spoiled brat used to getting his own way. The rare picture in the paper didn't do him justice; she could appreciate the fact that he was stunning in person. He didn't want to be there, and it showed in every inch of his face. His eyes were tense and sharp, with his mouth little more than a stiff line.

Linus Beckett threw his arm around his son and squeezed his shoulder, a grin a mile wide splitting his face as he greeted guests warmly as they began coming through the door. Jeremy couldn't control the tension rising in his shoulders and moving into his neck, making him feel like he'd forgotten to remove the hanger from his jacket. He kept the smile on his face and shook hands with everyone who greeted him, trying to match his mood to the brightness of theirs; there would be hell to pay later if he didn't.

Craning his neck, he looked around to see if even one of his promised college buddies were in the growing mass of people. Feeling the subtle pressure from his father's large hand on his shoulder, he attempted to relax and go with the flow of conversation. For the moment, at least, there would be no escape.

Linus pulled Jeremy close and stooped to hear what Jordan Bradford, a fellow tennis player and corporate adversary, boasted over the music. "Ah..." he said a little too loud. He cocked his head to the side and strained to hear. "Yes, of course," he agreed with a grin. "I'm sure he'll become quite an asset to the company."

Jordan laughed a throaty laugh and bobbled his drink on the way to his mouth. Linus bit his tongue hard. Nothing irritated him more than a well educated man in a four-thousand-dollar Italian suit who still couldn't possess the self-control to hold his liquor. "No doubt about that, Linus," Jordan slurred. "The boy's got your genes after all."

Finally, as if God had heard his prayer, Jeremy spotted Jamie standing over by the bar and felt a sense of relief sweep through him. He jumped into the conversation his father was having with a very drunk Jordan Bradford. "Thanks for coming, Jordan," he interrupted, shoving his hand at him. "Dad, Jamie's over by the bar," he said jabbing his thumb in that direction. "I'm going to say hello."

"Fine," Linus replied. "Go have fun, son. It's your night."

Jordan shook Jeremy's hand enthusiastically. "Happy Birthday, Jeremy," he said through a hiccup.

Jeremy shot his father a warning glance and whispered into his ear, "Pour him into a cab when he's ready to leave," he jerked up an eyebrow, "otherwise he'll wrap that pretty little sports car of his around a telephone pole."

"I'll take care of it."

~~

Christina went to the bar and picked up a tray of drinks that she'd ordered. Lou gave her a look that told her to hightail it over to the guest of honor with a drink immediately. Balancing the tray on her palm, she smirked back at Lou and saw Jeremy Beckett heading straight for the bar.

Jeremy slipped up behind the leggy, chocolate brown hair spitfire, put both hands on her waist, and squeezed playfully. She jumped when he pulled her against him and tucked her head under his chin. "Hey, sis," he said, kissing the top of her head. "It's about time you showed up and saved my ass."

Jamie turned around and beamed up at him with her usual know-it-all smile. "Daddy's up to his old tricks again, is he?" She put her palm flat against Jeremy's crisp shirt before jabbing her finger into his chest. "You need to learn how to handle him, that's all."

Jeremy laughed out loud; his little sister never failed to amuse him. "And just how is that, sister dear?" he asked, sure he'd find humor in her answer.

She took a drink from her gin and tonic and winked at a passing waiter before turning her attention back to her brother. "Learn to say what's really on your mind."

"I say what's on my mind - Linus just chooses not to hear me." He slid his hands in his pockets, deciding he needed a stiff drink. "I need a rum and coke."

Jamie rolled her eyes at her brother and turned back to the bar to make eyes at the bartender. She hated when Jeremy changed the subject when it came to their father, but it was nothing new; her big brother hated to talk about Linus.

Christina was making her way to the tables as the place continued to fill, and the orders for drinks came from all directions. The place was packed, and the heat had her feeling like she could melt as quickly as the ice in the drinks she was carrying. After delivering one tray full of drinks, she was heading back to the bar to pick up another. Stuffing another tip into her apron pocket, she felt a hand gently touch her arm.

She stopped and followed the hand to the face, then smiled sweetly. "Can I get you something?" It was Jeremy Beckett, she realized, and she was struck by how tall he was close up - *and very easy to look at, too*, she thought.

Jeremy let go of her arm and looked into what he considered the most striking eyes he'd ever seen. The young woman was quite simply breathtaking. "I'd like a rum and coke, please," he said with an easy smile. He was staring but couldn't seem to help himself.

Christina nodded, smiling back. "I'll take care of it right away." She met his eyes and held them, longer than she should have.

"Thanks," he said and watched her as she backed away and walked behind the bar. *The most intense eyes*, he thought again, watching her give the bartender his order. Thinking back over the past few months, he couldn't remember ever seeing her waiting tables here before. *She must be new*, he mused, *new and very interesting*.

A moment later, Christina came back with his drink. "Rum and coke," she announced.

Jeremy took the glass and sipped, eyeing her thoughtfully over the rim of the glass. "A very good one, too."

Christina nodded and looked back toward the bar. "Well, don't thank me," she said. She had to fight to keep from laughing. No doubt about it, Jeremy Beckett was attractive as hell. "Thank the big guy behind the bar, name's Lou." And with that, she was off into the crowd of people, smiling as she jotted down more orders.

~ 3 ~

Dinner was served at eight o'clock, and it was delicious: lobster and scallops with cornbread and steamed vegetables. As much as Jeremy enjoyed the food and the chance to see his college buddies again, he found his thoughts wondering throughout the evening to the waitress who had so effectively shot him down earlier - leaving him with nothing but a rum and coke and a bruised ego.

He had learned after several rather tricky glances at her blouse that her name was Christina. He was afraid she would catch him looking and think he was ogling her chest. He missed the chance to see her name tag when she had brought him his drink earlier because he'd been too drawn to her eyes. There was just something about her, and the need to know more about her tugged at him.

And it was later, while Jeremy was throwing darts with his college roommate, that a commotion at the rear of the room caught their attention. Angry voices carried over the music, attracting everyone's interest. Jeremy exchanged shrugs, looked out over the heads of his guests, and found Christina giving one of her customers a piece of her mind. He watched her, all fire and rage, holding her own against a man nearly twice her weight and size - and she owned him. Though he wouldn't realize it until much later, she'd taken his heart and earned his respect.

And he might have let her handle it if the guy's hands snaking around her and landing provocatively on her behind hadn't made him see red. The look on her face should have been enough for the guy to get the point, but still he pawed her, pretending her protests were all part of the game. He saw her shove him as he made his way through the gathering crowd, but the guy was too big and too drunk to be held off. Out of the corner of his eye, he saw the bartender coming out from behind the bar with a bat, but he closed the distance first.

Knowing the situation was none of his business didn't stop him. He moved quickly, grabbed as much of the guy's shirt as possible, and yanked him around and away from her. "Hey, asshole, I think the lady'd prefer it if you took your hands off her." And then he realized he knew the creep. "Shit, Freddie!" He rolled his eyes and pulled at his vice-like arms. "What the hell are you doing?"

"Hey, man," he slurred. "Just trying to have some fun."

Christina backed well out of reach, and Jeremy wisely angled himself between her and Freddie. "Doesn't look like she's interested." He shoved him back when he tried to make his way around him for another grab at Christina.

Freddie stumbled, then righted himself and sneered. "What? You the babe's white knight?"

Christina came around and smacked her palm to the Freddie's chest, boring holes in him with her eyes. "I don't need a white knight to knock you on your ass!" She shot a disgusted look at Jeremy and smirked. "Nice guy, this friend of yours."

"I wouldn't exactly call him a friend," Jeremy defended in a huff, successfully ducking Freddie's first wild swing and planting a solid jab to a midsection as big as a football field in defense.

"What would you call him, then?"

"A party crasher." He shoved Freddie again, and the rapid succession of Coors Lights finally got the better of him. Freddie pulled his arm back and drilled Jeremy in the jaw before stumbling back into a vacant chair. The sharpness of the blow had Jeremy seeing stars. He massaged his tender jaw while Christina's eyes fired daggers and picked up the tray she'd dropped when she'd been forced to defend herself.

Christina grunted and straightened her apron. "Look," she said, forcing herself to relax and take a deep breath, "keep him on a leash." She pushed past him and walked off, just as the bartender came up to Jeremy with some ice wrapped in a towel. He watched her go and was surprised when she spun on her heels and glared at him. "Or next time I'll knock that drunken smirk off his face myself." And with that, she was gone; just a blur in the crowd.

Jeremy grinned while she went back to taking orders, smiling and without missing a beat. Jeremy only had to press the ice to his jaw to convince himself he had missed more than a beat. Smiling, he went back to his dart game, impressed and more than a little unsettled at the tight coil of nerves in his gut.

~~

The party went on until ten-thirty with Jeremy catching up with his friends, occasionally trying to keep his sister out of trouble, and dodging his father. Linus wanted to introduce him to the rest of his corporate raiders, no doubt hoping their ruthless finance air would rub off on him. He'd made out like a bandit with all the gifts he'd received but felt were unnecessary; he would donate most of them to charity in the morning. And through it all, Jeremy managed to keep one eye on Christina.

~~

He waited at a table in the corner of O'Donnell's, hidden in the shadows, his face masked in darkness as he worked on his last rum and coke and his wavering courage. His jaw throbbed every now and then, but the rum and coke helped take the edge off. Except for him, the place was empty of patrons. The late hour sent most people home to bed, but not him; he stayed, waiting for another chance to talk to her. Christina Wagner. He finally knew her name and wanted the opportunity to know more. So, he sent his father and sister home with instructions to have the driver wait for his call before he returned.

Linus wasn't happy about it. He replayed their conversation as he was leaving with Jamie. The scene he and Freddie had caused had nearly worked the old man into a fit.

Linus hadn't been pleased with the bruise on his son's face or the fight that had brought it about, but when he mentioned it, Jeremy shrugged it off and said it was nothing. His mother would no doubt feel differently, and Linus wanted nothing to upset her while she was feeling so poorly. He said as much to his son as they walked out to the waiting limo.

"You could have let the bartender handle it, Jeremy," he said in a tone that left no doubt he was annoyed. "I mean, that's part of his job." He helped Jamie into the car and turned back to his son, waiting for a defense.

"It's just a bruise; relax," Jeremy said quietly as Linus dropped into the deep leather seat and tugged at his tie.

"Be sure to tell your mother that when she sees you in the morning."

Growing restless, he glanced at his watch and understood why he felt so damn tired. It was hardly unusual for him to be out until the wee hours of the morning, but even for him, two-thirty in the morning was pushing it. Having Mr. O'Donnell as a family friend came in handy; one phone call from Linus allowed Jeremy to stay long after everyone but his employees had gone home. The chance to see Christina again was worth sitting alone in the dark.

~~

Christina saw him as soon as she walked out from the back room, and for a split second she was startled. She couldn't imagine what he was still doing there at this hour. As she walked slowly towards the front of the bar, she eyed him carefully.

"I was wondering how long you were going to stay in there," Jeremy quipped, relying on his charm and praying his voice didn't sound as thick as his head felt.

She stopped short of the table and looked at him with disinterest. Oh, he was a big on charm alright. He was a man with quite a reputation; one only had to pick up the gossip section of the paper to know that. "I didn't realize I had an audience waiting for me."

She might be all legs and breathtaking in her beauty, but Jeremy knew she was no pushover. Her green eyes, bottomless and bright, revealed wit and intelligence he knew he could take great enjoyment in challenging. The mild annoyance he saw on her face only made her more intriguing. "I'd hardly consider myself an audience."

"You make a habit of lurking around in the shadows, preying on unsuspecting women?" she asked. Most of his face was hidden in the shadows; but for his eyes he was just a voice in the darkness, and it was on those piercing eyes that she now focused.

"Who's lurking?" he asked innocently. He leaned forward and revealed a face lit with a smile. He laughed easily and drained his glass. "I'm not here to attack you." He slid his empty glass across the table and loosened his tie while her vibrant eyes bore into him.

"How's your jaw, Mr. Beckett?" she asked coolly, picking up his glass and taking it to the bar, immune to his charm. "Your party crasher had a pretty mean right."

"He got lucky, caught me off guard."

Her brow lifted, and she wondered if he were either cocky or drunk. "Thanks for coming to my rescue, but it wasn't necessary," Christina said, turning and leaning against the bar. "You don't look like a man who spends much time at the gym. Maybe you're the one who got lucky."

Enjoying this tit-for-tat, he got to his feet and walked to her on unsteady feet, grinning. "I cringe at your faith in me - and you're welcome, Christina."

She was struck off guard by his saying her name.

He took a step closer and leaned against the bar next to her, deciding to go on instinct. "Have dinner with me tomorrow night."

"I don't think so, but thanks for the offer." She was close enough to him now to see the bruise on his face.

"Have to work?" he asked. He already knew she didn't; he'd asked the bartender earlier. "Seems like I rub you the wrong way without even trying."

Stepping back and putting some distance between them, she said, "I don't know you, except what I read in the papers."

"You can't believe everything you read."

"Just the same, no thank you." Her forehead creased, and her eyes mocked him, though she didn't know it. "Rumor has it that you treat women like flavors of the month."

Jeremy nodded and set his jaw; those damn rumors would be the death of him. The truth was far less interesting. He hadn't been with a woman in six months - hardly a card carrying member of the flavor-of-the-month club - but that wouldn't sell nearly as many gossip rags. Anger stiffened his voice when he spoke.

"So, you think I'm after you for a quick toss in bed, is that it?" His eyes flashed, and he took a deep breath. It wasn't as if he didn't hear comments like it on an almost daily basis - so why, then, was her opinion any worse? "Is that all you think men find you good for?" Her eyes went cold, but he continued. "A man asks you to dinner - so it automatically means he wants sex instead of conversation?"

The questions were a surprise, but she found them more of a challenge than an insult. Deciding if she wanted to add to the growing bruise on his face, she took a deep breath of her own. "Men find me good for a number of things, Mr. Beckett."

"Then have dinner with me."

Christina was prepared to tell him to go to hell when impulse stopped her. She'd never been one to back away from a challenge. "Fine."

~ 4 ~

Christina sat in front of her mirror, wondering if she had lost her mind. Wrapped in a towel and applying makeup with a shaky hand, she replayed the conversation with Jeremy Beckett that had led to this very moment. If she had used the good sense she'd been born with, she would have told him to go to hell when he asked her out to dinner. Why she hadn't still puzzled her.

She framed her lips with liner and hummed along with the radio. Before long, she was ready to go and wondering if it was too late to back out. She started downstairs and heard the doorbell. *Maybe it won't be a total loss*, she thought with a smile. At least she'd get a good meal out of it.

Aunt Bess was opening the door when she reached the bottom of the stairs. Christina saw Jeremy on the doorstep and smiled when Bess stood back and invited him inside. She introduced him to her aunt and blushed when Bess said she already knew who he was and that he was as handsome in person as he was in all the papers. Jeremy took all her comments with a sense of humor and looked on with interest when Bess insisted on giving him a tour of the house. She had him cornered by the fireplace, showing him family pictures, when Christina decided it was past the time to leave and went for her coat.

"I've made reservations at Giavonni's," Jeremy said, coming up behind her and helping her with her coat. "I hope that's okay."

"Sounds great." Christina kissed Aunt Bess goodnight and walked out of the house with a smile when Jeremy opened the door and stepped aside to follow her out.

~~

They were seated at the best table in the rear of Giavonni's, private enough for quiet conversation and public enough for Christina to feel comfortable. She'd heard all about Giavonni's: their food, their milieu, and their clientele. If you were someone in Manhattan, you could be found here. In all the time she'd been working in the city, she'd never so much as walked into this place. And now here she was, and with one of the most recognizable men in the city to boot; the absurdity of it almost made her laugh.

She looked across the table and smiled at Jeremy. "I'm sorry about Aunt Bess." Under the lighting, she found Jeremy's straightforward gaze softer than it had appeared last night. His hair was immaculate with its stylish waves, and his smoky eyes held an attraction all their own. He was dressed in a charcoal gray suit, crisp white shirt, and navy blue tie.

"Don't be," he said, smiling. "I'm used to it. Besides, she's a charmer, your aunt." He cut into his veal and took a bite, closing his eyes in approval. It was delicious as always, and the reason he had brought Christina here.

Christina agreed the veal was excellent and sipped her wine. "No one's ever called Aunt Bess charming. You're a good sport, Jeremy."

"Have you lived with her your whole life?"

"No, I grew up with my father raising me. I spent summers with her, and when I graduated, I moved here." She smiled, remembering the first time her father decided to send her to Stanton Island. "I guess as I got older, my father found me impossible to handle and decided I could use Aunt Bess as a guiding hand."

Jeremy sat, content listening to her, drinking his wine and enjoying her company. "You were a real handful, huh?" It didn't come as a surprise after seeing how she handled herself the night before.

Christina laughed now, too. "Afraid so."

They talked for hours, the conversation relaxed and friendly, and Christina was surprised to find she liked him very much. He was more than the opinionated, rich, spoiled man he appeared to be the night before. He was intelligent, thoughtful, and funny.

His eyes came alive when he laughed, and Jeremy found her easy to talk to and confided in her things he'd confided in no one. She was a strong, capable woman, and - except for his mother and sister - so unlike the other women in his life.

They ended their evening dancing, with plans to see each other again the next evening. As Jeremy sat beside her on the ferry back to Stanton Island, he felt more comfortable with her than he had with anyone else he'd ever known.

"I had a great time tonight, Christina," Jeremy said quietly.

He walked her to the door when they reached her house and found that he didn't want to leave. He knew that she was only eighteen and warned himself to go slow, but as she looked at him now with those eyes, he knew she could handle almost anything. The easy feeling of being with her made him reluctant for the night to end.

He told her he would call her in the morning to make plans for the evening, and they said goodnight. Then Jeremy turned, intending to leave, but before he could stop himself he turned and pulled her into his arms, kissing her softly on the mouth. He felt her go limp in his arms and heard her moan softly as she opened her mouth in invitation.

~~

Their relationship blossomed quickly, and soon they were spending their free time with each other. Their evenings together went from the simple to the refined. Whether walking through Central Park eating hot dogs or sharing box seats at the symphony, they were comfortable in each other's company. And before either realized it, a month had gone by.

The passion between them was undeniable, and every kiss they shared drove them closer to the time when their passion would rule. While Jeremy longed to make love to Christina, to become part of her, flesh to flesh and heart to heart, he wanted to be sure she was ready. A smaller part of him wanted to prove to her that he wasn't just out for sex, remembering the accusation from their first conversation.

And then one evening, when they returned to the city after having dinner with her Aunt Bess, Christina kissed him. It was a kiss that said what he'd been waiting to hear. They took a room at the Waldorf Hotel and finally gave in to their passion.

Jeremy ordered wine from room service and disappeared into the bathroom. She was standing across the room when he opened the door, her body silhouetted by the faint moonlight through the window, her falling hair long and lavish over her shoulders. Until the moment he'd met her, he'd spent his life running from the women whom he'd taken to bed. Wanting nothing but their bodies, he had no interest in their hearts.

Filled with love for the first time in his life, he wanted only to get lost in her. His breath thick, his blood warming, he went to her. He came up behind her and pulled her against him, nuzzling her neck, breathing in her perfume. "You sure you want to do this?" he whispered, his voice thick, roughened by desire, his arms wrapping around her waist.

Christina turned in his arms, smiled, ran her fingers through his hair, and gazed into the eyes she'd come to trust. "I'm surer about this than anything I've ever done in my life."

Their lips met softly at first, and that simple touch swept them under. Emotions fought for so long made every caress desperate - and the power was staggering. Everything in the world dimmed, faded until just the simple brush of a hand sent shock waves rippling through them in the darkness. Only touch, taste, and primal need could rule them.

Her skin warming and pliant under his touch banished the cynic in him. Her murmurs and breathless moans made him clamp down on his desires in favor of her own. His hands and mouth worked in tandem, driving them both to heady oblivion, so reckless and wantonly that Jeremy pulled away, struggling to catch his breath. He nearly fell to his knees when her mouth glided along his skin, leaving a wet, blazing trail along his neck.

He filled his hands with her hair, tugged her head back, and, taking his mouth on a journey over the silky skin above her breasts, surrendered. Christina slid her hands over his chest, unbuttoning his shirt and gazing with surprise at his well-toned body. Her palms, warmed by passion, slid down over his taunt stomach, then around to rake her nails along his back.

Desire and need warred in her and cut through, making her gasp. Then, almost painfully, her eyes closed in a surrender she'd have never thought herself capable. She pulled away from his drugging kiss to drop to her knees and press her lips to the quivering skin of his stomach to pleasure him as he was her.

Feeling him shudder beneath her, the firmness of his skin underneath, she yanked at his clothing, wanting the freedom to explore every inch of him. A dull ache building, driving her, she heard him moan her name. She had been with men before, but the sensations pulsing through her now were new. She reached for his belt; she wanted all he had to give - and more.

Jeremy dropped his head and gasped; pulling her against him, he brought her back to her feet. His mouth devoured hers, his tongue plunging deep for the taste of her, and when their tongues met, the heat between them became a fire. He clutched her hair while his mouth consumed hers. Hungrily, his lips slid over her eyelids, down to the nape of her neck while her breathless gasps drove him mad.

They moved across the floor to the bed, their bodies intertwined and their hearts beating in sync. Finally, flesh pressed to flesh, and her hands worked magic to undo him. Her body, battered by sensation after sensation, felt as if it might be consumed by fire. Her touch drove him to oblivion. He groaned and lowered them to the bed.

Slick flesh against slick flesh and heat driving heat, both wanted to teeter on the razor thin edge between control and release. His fingers moved over her body, searching for the sensitive places that would drive her over the edge - and finding them all, he left her pleading for more.

Her breasts molded to his hands perfectly, and he skimmed his thumb over her nipple and groaned approval as her arching, taut body met his hungry touch. When Christina could take no more, she yanked open his pants, reached for him, and guided him into her. They cried out in pleasure together, matching rhythms. In blinding passion, their eyes met and held as they came together, and in that moment they knew they would be linked in every way, forever.

Later, as they drifted off to sleep, Jeremy whispered in her ear, "Oh God, Christina, I love you."

She was already drifting her way to sleep, and she smiled. "Love you, too." She held him close and slept.

~~

Over dinner, Jeremy told Christina about the latest canvas he painted, as well as his father's confusion over his love of painting. She laughed as he described his father's love of breaking up companies and putting people out of work.

"Have you ever told him how you feel about it?" she asked, laying her hand gently over his.

"More times than I can count."

"If you want to paint, then that's what you should do," she said simply with a nod of her head.

Jeremy grinned and lifted her palm to his lips. "Spoken like a woman who's defied her father repeatedly."

Christina smirked and pushed her salad around her plate. "Only about things that really mattered to me. Dad hates that I want to move to Manhattan and open my own place, but I'm standing my ground with him. If painting really matters to you, do it."

~~

The Labor Day weekend arrived, and Jeremy decided it was time for Christina to meet his family. He knew his feelings for her were the kind to build a future on. But, when he mentioned it to Christina, she balked.

"You're not serious?" she asked, tossing her long hair over her shoulder. Jeremy smiled, recognizing the nervous gesture. "I'm sure they'll love your waitress girlfriend."

He pulled her into a kiss and eased back laughing. "My parents aren't snobs, Christina. They'll love you."

"You think so, huh?" She was looking at him with doubts filling her mind. Coming face to face with Jeremy's family terrified her.

"I didn't realize you held such a low opinion of yourself," he teased. "Look, my mother's a lot more like you than you think. Honey, she'll love you as much as I do."

She looked at him for a long time. His eyes said he meant every word. How she had lived this long without him, she'd never know. All she knew was she had never known a love like this before. "I love you for saying that."

The words came from deep in her heart, and he grinned. "I love you, too."

~ 5 ~

Jeremy smiled when he walked into the sun room to find his mother fussing over her beloved roses, her blonde hair tied backed loosely on her head, shoulders hunched in concentration. He walked up behind her to lay his hands on her shoulders. "Morning, Mom." He leaned over her shoulder to kiss her cheek. "You're feeling better today, I see."

Elise reached up and patted his hand, then removed her pruning gloves. "Finally." She turned and smiled warmly. "Well, from the look of you, you don't seem any worse for wear." Pulling him down to her, she kissed him on his stubble-covered cheek. "But how's a mother to know when her son disappears for days at a time?" she chided him.

Jeremy looked sheepish and apologetic. "Sorry," he said genuinely. "I've got some good news, though."

"And you should be," she teased. He looked as if he was about to burst, and it reminded her of when he was a little boy, aching to tell her a secret. "So tell me this good news of yours."

They walked over to the table where she had the morning papers stacked neatly at her chair. It was here where she read the morning papers religiously. He pulled out her chair and sat down across from her. "Well," he began brightly, "I'm not really sure where to start. He took her hand in his, and she smiled at him, giving him the courage to continue. "I've met someone incredible, and I want you and Dad and Jamie to meet her, too."

Elise raised an eyebrow and studied Jeremy's face closely. He hadn't asked to bring someone home to meet the family since Emily Harris, his high school girlfriend, and they were together for five years. This woman must be someone incredible indeed. "I wondered if a young lady was the reason you've been spending so much time away from home. How long have you been seeing her? What does she do?"

"Three months next week. She's a waitress at O'Donnell's," he replied. "Her name's Christina Wagner. She's saving up to open her own restaurant. She's funny and bright, and she completely bowled me over the moment I met her."

Months, Elise thought watching him and seeing how happy he was about it. All you had to do was listen to him to know how much he felt for this girl. This was very serious, and she couldn't have been happier about it, but she doubted her husband would feel the same way. "Why don't you bring her to the cookout tomorrow?"

"I was thinking the same thing, but I wanted to check with you first. What about Dad?"

Elise grinned at the thought; Linus would probably be stunned into silence. "I'll handle your father."

~~

Jeremy arrived with Christina at noon the next day. When they drove up the long driveway leading to the family estate, her stomach dropped as she took in the grounds. The Beckett estate was everything she'd heard it was and more.

Jeremy parked and opened her door to help her out. "Everyone's around back waiting for us." He felt her fingers stiffen in his hand, and he ran his thumb over the back of her hand to calm her. "Relax. They don't bite, I swear." She looked beautiful, the green sun dress and open-toed sandals they'd bought the day before complimented her, and with her hair falling loose over her shoulders, she took his breath away. And he loved that the light breeze blew it around her face.

Christina ran her hand through her hair and gave in. "Let's get this over with."

They walked around the property, past the birdbaths and the Greek sculptures and the towering weeping willows, to the large landscaped back yard. And, just as Jeremy had said, they were all waiting to greet them. His mother smiled warmly when she saw them come around the west side of the house. She was sitting on an overstuffed lounge chair, and Linus stood behind her with a smile that matched his wife's.

Jamie watched them, curious about what drew them to each other in the first place. The girl was tall and leggy, and she made you take notice. But, if Jamie had seen her on her own, she would've been the last woman Jamie thought her brother would go for; yet, here she was for all of them to see.

Jeremy led Christina over to his mother first and grinned. "Christina, I'd like you to meet my mother, Elise Beckett. Mom, this is Christina Wagner."

Elise put her feet to the ground and stood with some help from her husband. "Christina, it's a pleasure to meet you, dear," she said, offering her hand. "I've heard a lot about you. Please make yourself at home."

Christina smiled, "Thank you, Mrs. Beckett, it's nice to meet you, too. Jeremy talks about you all the time."

Elise laughed. "Exaggerations I'm sure. And please call me Elise." She turned to her husband. "I'd like you to meet Jeremy's father, Linus."

"It's a pleasure to meet you, sir," Christina said when Linus wrapped his large hand around hers.

"And you, too, Christina," he said. He'd yet to get over the shock that Jeremy had met someone without him realizing it, and that it had obviously gotten serious. "Call me Linus. I'm sure Jeremy has said as little about me as possible," he quipped, and they all laughed. Linus felt he knew his son less and less by the day.

Jeremy turned to his sister next and pulled her towards him. "And this," he said with a wink, "is my little sister, Jamie."

Jamie smacked him and rolled her eyes. "Being two years younger doesn't make me little, brother dear." Looking at Christina, she smiled easily and stuck out her hand. "It's nice to meet you, Christina. I hope we see more of you here now that my brother has gotten some class."

The uneasiness disappeared in no time, and soon the conversation turned easily from subjects like the war in Vietnam to the stock market, music, Elvis, and the most relaxing vacation spots. Elise wanted to know everything about the woman who had so obviously stolen her son's heart.

Even Linus had to admit they made a striking pair. As he listened to the conversation between her and his wife, he knew that he liked the girl for her spunk and her obvious intelligence. His son was falling hard, and he wasn't sure if it was good news or bad.

The afternoon moved along swiftly, and before anyone realized it, the day had come and gone, leaving in its wake the twilight of the evening, and with it the official end of summer. As Jeremy and Christina said their goodbyes to his family, Elise hugged Christina and kissed her cheek, telling her to come back again soon. Linus shook his son's hand and patted his back warmly, telling him how much he liked Christina. They drove off with smiles of contentment, feeling the day couldn't have gone better.

Linus, however, remained in the driveway long after their leaving. Christina Wagner was a lovely young woman, indeed; yet Linus sensed the potential for much pain in their pairing...trouble on the horizon that as of yet had no face. He went inside, hoping he was wrong.

~~

Winter in New York could be breathtaking one day and a nightmare the next, and that description fit December 1973 like a glove. The streets were packed with last minute shoppers as the final week before Christmas sped by quickly. Christina stole looks out the front window of O'Donnell's while she made her way across the floor, setting up for yet another of their countless Christmas parties. She hated the abuse and grabbing hands drinking brought out in otherwise decent men, but the tips and overtime were too good to pass up.

Christina had so many balls in the air that she wondered how she would do it all. There were a few bright spots this year that hadn't been in her life in the last. For starters, she managed to talk her father into coming to Stanton Island this year for the holiday, and he actually seemed excited about it. He wanted to put a face on the man he'd been hearing so much about over the past six months.

And then, of course, there was the man himself, Jeremy. She found in him a true love she always thought a fairy-tale. The fear of needing someone that much, someone that so defined her was nowhere to be found now. When she thought of him now, only happiness filled her. She felt only warmth and security in his arms, and a passion that grew stronger by the day.

~~

The nervousness rooted in Christina from the moment she knew of her father's impending arrival seemed to be well under control by Christmas Eve, as both Jeremy and her father stood while she took her seat at the kitchen table. She was relieved to find them chatting easily when she walked into the dining room with Bess right behind her. Jeremy was answering her father's questions about his family's business when he caught sight of her out of the corner of his eye.

He stood and went to her, kissing her cheek softly and stepping back to take a quick look at her. "You look stunning," he said quietly.

"Thanks." She smiled at him, then went to her father and took his hand. "So are you two getting to know each other?"

Paul Wagner hugged his daughter and stepped away to look at the two of them. "Yes, I'd say we are," he said, smiling at Christina. "Seems you found yourself a smart young man here."

Jeremy smiled and thanked him for the compliment, and the four of them sat down to dinner. The conversation was light, and Paul found himself liking this young man. He wasn't a stupid man; he could see that Christina was totally enamored with Jeremy Beckett, as he clearly was with her. As he bit into his sister's delicious pot roast, he couldn't help wondering if he were on the road to losing his daughter.

~~

Christmas morning came with three inches of fresh snow and frigid temperatures, thus reminding Christina as she dressed to go downstairs that she had every intention of retiring to a warm, balmy island the minute the opportunity presented itself. She pulled her hair into a high French twist and slipped into the silk blouse Jeremy had given her the night before at the Waldorf. It was the color of copper, and, just as he predicted, it set off her eyes and complimented her hair.

The plan was to spend Christmas morning with her father and aunt and the afternoon with Jeremy and his family at their estate. In the evening they would return to what they now considered to be "their" suite at the Waldorf.

They would spend the night together alone and exchange their gifts to each other in private.

~~

The snow falling made getting to the Waldorf later that night a little complicated, but Jeremy and Christina were in high spirits and didn't seem to mind the long ride. The afternoon with his family had been fun, and they even managed to talk her father into coming to the Beckett's to meet Jeremy's family. As a result, they all shared a wonderful Christmas diner around an opulent dining table overflowing with ham and turkey, turnips, yams, stuffing, and countless deserts.

When at last Jeremy and Christina pulled up in front of the valet outside the hotel, they were still laughing over her father's description of the sad little trees he had to make due with as a little boy. Arm-in-arm, they walked through the lavish lobby to the elevator. Stepping inside, Jeremy wound his arms around her while humor lit his eyes.

"You're looking very pleased with yourself tonight, Mr. Beckett." His hair was wet with snow, but his breath was warm against her cheek when he nuzzled her. She found every inch of him arousing and couldn't wait to get him to the suite. "And just what are you so happy about?" she wondered, smiling and feeling very lucky that she had him. She drew him even closer and sighed when his chilled lips warmed against her neck and had her shuddering.

Pressing his cold cheek to hers, he breathed her scent in and closed his eyes. "Too many things to count," he whispered, nipping at her earlobe and sending a thrill through them both. "There's how happy I've been over the past six months," he continued, working his way down her neck and feeling her shiver in response. He smiled. "Cold?"

Christina sighed and searched for her voice. He knew what he was doing to her, driving her crazy with his passionate assault. Now he wanted her to answer him. "Ah...I don't think cold...is what I'm, oh God, feeling right now."

He laughed against her neck as the elevator stopped at the top floor. "Warm then?" For a second, he thought about ripping her clothes off right there, but the thought vanished when the doors opened and she tugged on his tie and pulled him down the hall.

She wasn't a cheap thrill on some elevator ride; this was the woman he wanted to spend the rest of his life with. Minutes later, behind the closed doors of their suite, he discovered her body all over again - as if for the first time.

~ 6 ~

Spring's arrival was bringing people out of their cars and cabs to crowd the streets and sidewalks in shorter sleeves and sunglasses. Most of them happily squinted against the glint of the sun with purpose in their steps, but a few were too distracted by their busy schedules to notice the warming of the air. The buildings in the heart of the city seemed brighter in the sunlight, perhaps washed anew by the winter's snow.

Away from the city, with work the last thing on his mind, Jeremy stood before the large bay window and looked out over his mother's prized garden. A flood of sunlight had him taking in the scenery with an artist's eye, and the process never failed to inspire him. He stared hard into the distance, trying to drown out his father's voice in his head.

Linus was trying his damnedest to bring him into one business deal after another. He was relentless, and it was driving Jeremy to the end of his rope. The warmth of the sun on his face as he brooded helped to calm him, but he was still mad as hell; he hated being bullied.

The pleasant thought of stealing Christina away from her lunch shift to a sunny spot for a picnic in the park eased the tension in his neck and pushed Linus from his mind. He knew she wouldn't fall for his charms when the chance to earn tips for her nest egg was so important. The woman was driven - and who could blame her? If her dream of owning her own restaurant were to come true, she'd need all the drive she had and more.

He had his pride and a nearly all-consuming love for her, and because he did, he wanted to help her achieve her dreams. But, no matter how many times he wanted to contribute, she turned him down because Christina had her pride, too, and she was a very stubborn woman - but he loved even that about her.

Every day his love for her seemed to grow. *His love for her.* The very thought should have terrified him, and the fact that it didn't should have terrified him even more. After nearly a year together, he couldn't quite remember his life before her - and he didn't want to.

Wasn't it just yesterday that they had their first date? First kiss? The first time they made love? And now they were about to celebrate their first anniversary. For Jeremy, it was a first - and for a guy who seldom committed to anything, it was also a miracle.

He was planning a special weekend at Cherry Hill, his grandfather's Vermont estate and his favorite place on earth. As a boy, he'd romped on the rolling hills, climbed the cherry trees for which his grandfather's home was named, and stuffed himself with not-quite-ripe fruit, earning a bellyache for his greed. Memories of splashing chest-deep through the lake have been recreated on canvas by his hand time and again.

They'd spent her birthday there two weeks before. He wanted to introduce her to his grandfather and couldn't wait another day, hoping they'd hit it off right away.

Avery Beckett bought the property in 1955. Thirty sprawling acres and almost three thousand feet of Lake Frontage added to the estate's beauty and fostered the relaxing atmosphere Jeremy loved so much. The main house, a stunning antique cape of almost forty thousand square feet, twelve rooms, and two full baths, was over one hundred years old, though Avery had it fully restored in 1969 and a large landscaped pond added to the east side of the property.

Wide brown marble steps led from a large rear deck down to a matching circular patio fenced in with waist-high flowers with access to a river front view.

Christina loved the grounds, and they walked along the trails that snaked through the lush Vermont woods. Telling her of his boyhood adventures there made her laugh the rich, throaty laugh he loved to hear. Cherry Hill was an enchanting place where he'd spent many a happy summer as a child, and the fact that Christina loved it there as much as he did made him happier than he thought possible.

He shook himself back to reality and returned to his painting. The woman was a distraction. He studied the canvas with a critical eye. Something was there, hidden in the broad dark strokes and unique shapes. It was speaking to him, and he had to give it its way to the surface to tell its story. It would be dark and foreboding, the colors and depth revealed that much to him. With a knitted brow and fresh concentration, his hands moved over the canvas effortlessly; senses were leading him now, and the task was to create a pathway through which the story can unfold.

~~

"Order's up!" Leo barked from the kitchen. He'd been barking from there all morning and driving everyone crazy. But Christina was going about her routine, letting it roll off her back.

She smiled at a few of the regulars coming through the door and went to get them menus and pick up an order for one of her tables. Leo couldn't help noticing the spring in her step as she got closer. His grimace was a natural defense. "Relax, Leo," she said. "You're gonna work yourself into an early grave with that sour disposition of yours."

"Hey," he said defensively, slapping another burger on the grill and watching it sizzle. "I cook the food, you deliver the food. That's how it works here. If I want my head shrank, I'll pay three C-notes an hour like everybody else." He scooped up an order of fries and slid the plate towards Christina with a wink. "Move your pretty little ass over to table nine, sweetcakes."

~~

Christina slept beside Jeremy, her legs wrapped around his, her warm hands laying on his chest. She slid closer, seeming to sense, even in sleep, that he needed her close. Her warm skin pressed against his, and her soft breath on his neck eased the tension rooted there, but sleep still evaded him. He was preoccupied with his father's latest attempt to manipulate him into Beckett International.

The entire evening, just like the day leading to it, had been a struggle for him. Having a normal conversation with Christina was a chore it shouldn't have been. Asking about her day and planning their upcoming anniversary, unaffected by Linus and his manipulations, had caused the pounding currently in his temples. It never ceased to amaze him the lengths to which his father would go to get what he wanted.

"Just come aboard for this one deal, son. Trust me, you won't regret it. I want you as my right hand on this one."

With his father's voice still playing his head, he squeezed his eyes shut, silently cursing the great Linus Beckett. Damn him. He had his painting and the woman he loved, and it wasn't as if he simply wasted the rest of his time. He volunteered his time in countless ways, and when the mood struck him, he even sold a painting now and then. He had no desire to dissect international companies, to make a fortune from misfortune.

~~

June 1978

Jeremy celebrated another birthday at home with his family and Christina, minus Grandpa Avery. Then he and Christina celebrated their anniversary a day later by escaping to Vermont and Jeremy's much loved Cherry Hill. He longed for peace and quiet and the chance to see his grandpa.

With Linus still pushing for Jeremy to join him in what his father considered the deal of a lifetime, he needed the break. Although he thought he was hiding his conflict from her, Christina watched Jeremy struggle with his decision. It would have been so easy to say yes to Linus; parts of the deal actually appealed to Jeremy, but he knew his father would never let him walk away after just one deal.

Jeremy knew his father too well. He'd fight tooth and nail to keep him in the business once he stuck his foot in the water. To give Linus Beckett an inch was to give him a mile.

Yet, somehow, the long trip and breathtaking scenery helped him relax, so much so that when they arrived at Cherry Hill he was thinking of different, pleasant things. Like the pebbled lane crunching under his tires that would lead to the house, the yellow tulips, and the daises Avery Beckett had lovingly planted himself. The old man himself waved from the porch rocker when the car came into view, making its way up the lane.

Jeremy got out and opened Christina's door as he took in all the scenery and the clean, fresh air. Then his eyes met his grandfather's and softened. The kinship between them was almost palpable, despite the forty-four year age difference. "Hey, Grandpa!" he called out. "How's life in the lush countryside?"

Avery shrugged, tapping his cane in time with the Mozart that could be heard drifting through the open window behind him. "Relaxing, and boring as hell," he replied, squinting against the sun. "I see you've brought your young lady back with you." He grinned from ear to ear as they climbed the stairs to the porch. "Good. I love to be in the company of a beautiful lady."

Christina crossed the porch, laughing as she bent to give him a kiss on the cheek, and then smiling at the mischievous glint she saw in his eyes. "I guess I know where your grandson gets his charm."

"Nonsense." He patted her hand and looked up at his grandson. "I only speak the truth, right lad?"

Jeremy nodded. "Right." Leaning over, he kissed his grandfather's forehead. The two of them sat down on the bench across from him with contented sighs. "So, how are you Grandpa?" He was concerned about his delicate health, and looking at him now, he looked tired.

Avery hated this topic of conversation more than any other, the reminder that he was no longer a young man. It felt like a quick stab to the heart, but he knew his grandson only asked out of love. How could he fault him for that? "It varies from one day to the next," he said truthfully. "The summer air makes it easier to breathe." He watched Jeremy's eyes fill with concern and was quick to reassure him. "Don't worry, Jeremy." Avery said gently, leaning forward and slapping Jeremy's knee to lighten the mood. "I'm not going anywhere anytime soon."

"Better not; I need you to run interference with Dad."

"He called this morning," Avery said. "Says he still hasn't talked you into coming aboard on his latest business deal." He smiled at Jeremy wickedly and folded his arms across his chest.

"He's bound and determined to try," Jeremy replied.

"Would it really be so bad?" Avery thought Jeremy could do a damn good job with the corporate merger Linus had in the works. "Your input might prove valuable, to your father, and to the company." He was stumbling through a minefield, and he knew it.

Jeremy slid a glance to Christina and winked. He was being worked at both ends, but he had enough respect for his grandfather to hear him out, even if it wouldn't change his mind. "So you want me to join Linus at the helm of Beckett International and work this deal?"

Avery slid forward on the rocker, and after some effort, forced himself to stand. "I just want you to consider all your options." He moved across the porch, leaning heavily on the gold-handled ivory cane Linus had given him for Christmas.

Jeremy's eye caught a robin swooping down, landing on the mailbox. He looked at Christina; she'd been sitting quietly, listening and holding his hand. He found himself longing for her objectivity. "And?"

"And what?"

"If you have something more to say, say it, Grandpa."

Avery turned and looked out over his spacious yard. "Has it ever occurred to you that you could be part of the business and still have your freedom?"

"You're joking, right?" Jeremy said, laughing. Freedom and working with his father couldn't co-exist.

Avery shook his head, smirking. "No." he replied. He'd expected this reaction because he knew his grandson so well. "I'm an old man; I want you to share in what I built while I'm still here to see it."

Jeremy pinched the bridge of his nose and sighed. "You're sixty-five, Grandpa. You're acting like you've got one foot in the grave for shit's sake."

"That heart attack in seventy-one opened the grave for me, Jeremy. From that day forward, I've been borrowing time."

"You've got years ahead of you."

"You think you'll have to give up painting, but you won't, if you want it badly enough. I passed the business onto Linus, and someday Linus wants to pass it to you. That's how it's done, passed down father to son."

"And what I want," Jeremy snapped, "does that matter at all?" Why was it that he had to go over this again and again? His irritation rose as his patience came to an end. Setting his jaw, he fought for control, feeling Christina smoothing the back of his hand to calm him. "I'd love to know why the hell this is so important to everyone."

"Not to everyone," Avery said calmly, pausing. It had been a mistake to get into this discussion so soon; he should have picked a better time. "Just to your father and grandfather," he continued, his voice rising.

When the silence fell between them, they only stared at each other. Both of them stubborn and set in their ways, and for the time being, anyway, retreating.

~~

Late in the afternoon, after the nurse insisted Avery take a nap, Jeremy walked beside Christina across the sloping lawns to clear his head. They'd been there less than six hours, and already their celebration had taken a nose dive. He planned to stay at Cherry Hill for the entire weekend, in the room that he had as a child, but now he had second thoughts.

Christina walked beside him quietly, holding his hand, palm to palm, fingers intertwined. He was someplace in his head where she couldn't reach him, but she could see the torment in his eyes. "Where are you?" she whispered, slowing and then stopping at the pond.

He looked down at her, flashed a smile, and quickly averted his eyes. "What'd you mean?"

She touched his cheek with her fingertips and turned him to face her. "What're you thinking?" she asked.

Finally, he looked at her. "I'm thinking about how Grandpa's never really asked me for anything," he brushed her hair back from her face and smiled sadly, "until now."

"So, what does that mean for you?"

"It means a lot," he said through a sigh. Turning away from her, he threw his hands up to the sky and screamed. He listened while the echo of his scream died and turned back to her. "It means I'm about to take a very big leap. He's given me so much, love, acceptance, understanding. How can I deny him this?"

"You're going to work for Beckett Industries?"

He shook his head. "God help me, I think I am."

With dusk, they started back to the house. He drew her close, fighting the fear and uncertainty in his mind. The most influential men in his life had finally gotten what they wanted: Jeremy Beckett in the family business fold.

~ 7 ~

Jeremy spent the two weeks between his return from Cherry Hill and his arrival at Beckett Industries making peace with the new direction his life was taking. He talked with Christina about it constantly. Over the romantic dinners she would make for him in the suite's small kitchen, he reminded himself he hadn't given up his life entirely - just one year of it.

He promised both his father and grandfather twelve months - and only twelve months. As his first day drew nearer, that was all he was prepared to give them. His dreams would lead him down a different path.

When the day arrived, Jeremy woke early with a sense of dread and foreboding no amount of coffee or positive thinking would shake. He slipped out of bed, being careful not to wake Christina, so he could avoid another of her pep talks. Quietly, Jeremy went into the bathroom, shaved, brushed his teeth, and dressed in his favorite pinstriped suit.

Making his way downtown, he saw that the city itself was beginning a new day as well. Newspaper vendors setting up their stands with the morning paper, a few stray joggers with insane amounts of energy were off on their daily workout, and the city transit buses were heading out on their route and would soon be making traffic a nightmare. The city greeted another day while Jeremy Beckett greeted a new avenue in his life.

~~

Linus sat behind his desk, looking over files. He was feeling both triumphant and anxious over the reality of his son joining him at Beckett Industries. He looked around his spacious office like a king surveying his kingdom, waiting for the prince to arrive. He was too nervous to focus on his work, so he stood and began pacing.

His eyes wandered to his watch as he counted off the minutes until Jeremy arrived. Feeling jittery, he rolled up his sleeves and periodically raked his long fingers through his hair. *What could be keeping the boy?* he wondered. Wild, that's what the boy was. Just plain wild.

~~

Jeremy took his time getting out of the car. He was in no particular rush because Linus had chosen to give him space to find his own way and settle in. In life, there were worse things than this, he reminded himself as he crossed the parking garage. His quick pace belied his shaky stature.

He looked very much like a corporate suit on his way to work and the daily trials of high finance. He wished he felt the same. With his briefcase in one hand and an umbrella in the other, he looked prepared for anything.

On the street, the heat, already intense, by noon would be stifling. Jeremy stood on the sidewalk, shading his eyes against the bright sun and staring up at the eighteen story building that boasted his name. *This will probably turn out to be the biggest mistake of my life*, he thought.

It was barely 9 a.m. and already Jeremy could feel the sweat seeping through his shirt, unsure whether the heat or his rolling stomach was to blame. New York's finest professionals passed him, unbothered or immune to the rising temperatures. Everyone had places to go and jobs to do and offices with air conditioning to welcome them when they arrived.

~~

Stepping off the elevator, the first person Jeremy made eye contact with was Eden Carmichael, his father's secretary. Her face bloomed into a smile the minute she saw him, and she wasted no time making him feel welcome.

"Jeremy," she said, all smiles. "Good morning. It's so nice to see you." She offered her hand, and he shook it politely. "Linus said you'd be coming in."

Looking around at all the fast-tracking Beckett employees, he tried not to appear as wary as he felt. "Dad's in his office?" he asked, looking past her to his father's closed door.

"Yes, he's been buzzing me every ten minutes to find out if you've arrived yet."

Jeremy groaned under his breath. "Don't bother buzzing him," he said. "I'll surprise him."

Eden wisely concealed her smile. Stories of father and son Beckett's ability to get under each other's skin were common knowledge. "Go ahead in," she suggested, walking behind her desk and sitting down at her computer.

~~

Jeremy expected to find Linus laying in wait for him, but instead he found him at his desk, his back to the door, and his phone cradled on his ear. He was speaking softly, in a tone he only reserved for his wife. "Honey, I know. Listen, I'm not going to push him, I swear." He ran his finger over the part in his hair, knowing better than to make promises they both knew would be tough to keep.

Silently, Jeremy moved across the floor to the desk, smiling at the thought of his mother bullying his father on his behalf. He sat his briefcase at his feet and leaned, palms down, on the edge of the desk. "You're not going to push?" he said, laughing. "That'll be a first." He spoke a little too loudly, startling Linus and taking a moment's delight when Linus jumped, almost dropping the phone.

Linus spun around in his chair and faced Jeremy with a mixture of annoyance and embarrassment covering his face. "Yes," he spoke to his wife. "He just came in. Right, I know, I promise. I'll see you for lunch later. Good-bye honey." He hung up the phone and grinned at his son.

As if reading his father's mind, Jeremy teased, "Lighten up, Dad." He then walked behind the desk to the window, beneath it, he used to play as a child on the rare occasions when Linus would bring him along to the office.

Looking out over the city, he could see most of the very same buildings he saw as a boy. Some were gone now, replaced by more modern architecture and men with more modern dreams, dreams much like those of his father; dreams different from his own. Dreams he knew instinctively he would never share.

Linus watched Jeremy drift off in his mind and frowned at his son's pensive posture. Joining him at the window, he looked down at the street and the automobiles making their way through the congested streets of the city. "You hate it here already."

"I'm here, Dad, and I plan to do my best for you. Let's not analyze it to death."

"Fine," Linus replied, looking down at his high polished shoes, searching for a safer topic of conversation. "I appreciate this; it means a lot."

Jeremy turned to his father with a smile. "Don't thank me yet, and don't forget our deal," he reminded him.

Their deal was simple: from noon to two every day, Jeremy would be unavailable to the company. Those hours would be sacred, time when he answered to no one, time for personal business like painting at the studio or maybe even in his office. Or time for lunch with Christina or just to clear his head away from the office. He would leave the office no later than six o'clock every evening. The deal was nonnegotiable.

Linus had to laugh when he thought about it. His son drove a hard bargain, it was proof, Linus decided, that his boy was a chip off the old block in some very important ways and an entirely different chip from an entirely different block in others. He pulled Jeremy into a hug before Linus led him to the door. "Let me show you your office."

~~

Christina delivered food and drinks to twelve tables in less than ten minutes. Summers in the city brought customers through the door in droves. Everyone coming and going, in better spirits with the change of weather, eager to feel the vibrant hum of energy the city was known for, and, more importantly, generous with their tips.

Her mind drifted to Jeremy now and again, wondering how his first day at work was going and if he might have been exaggerating when he said he'd stick out like an inept intern. She'd call him when the lunch rush was through and she had a minute to catch her breath.

She woke up long after Jeremy left the suite to find a note on his pillow where he had been. The note said simply that he couldn't sleep and didn't want to wake her, that he was heading to the office early, to get on with it, and that he loved her and would call her later. So Christina lay there without him, knowing that in his heart of hearts he was someplace he didn't want to be.

~~

At four-thirty, Jeremy shut himself in his office, relishing the solitude after three meetings concerning the company's latest buyout attempt and being paraded around the offices of all of the company's underlings. The resentment Jeremy felt in their presence was unmistakable. For them, Jeremy was little more than 'the boss' son,' brought in to be Linus Beckett's right hand man when in reality they were all probably better qualified for the position.

By six, he plowed through the weekly finance projections of a company now in the cross hairs of Beckett International, and the numbers were staggering. The potential for this possible acquisition was endless; there was money to be made, and plenty of it.

Already tired and feeling out of his depth, Jeremy dropped the file he was reading and pushed away from his desk. Every muscle from the base of his neck to the middle of his back ached. He got up and went to the window across from his desk.

His large, handsomely decorated office had all the comforts anyone would need, but Jeremy had seen enough of it for one day. He loosened his tie and sucked in a deep breath. Deciding that for his first day he'd done more than his fair share of the work, Jeremy grabbed his jacket from behind the door and left his office.

His secretary looked up in surprise and smiled when he came out of his office. He told her he was leaving for the day and that he would see her in the morning. With a less than sincere goodnight, he headed for the elevator. When the elevator door closed and he was boxed in its silence, he breathed a sigh of relief.

~ 8 ~

Christina knew the suite would be dark and cool when she arrived dead on her feet, her ears still ringing from customers trying to out shout each other to be heard. The curtains were closed when she opened the door, allowing very little light in the living room and casting a veil throughout. For a moment, she stood motionless, enjoying the silence.

Christina had an armful of Italian takeout, so she pushed the door closed with her hip, squinting in the growing darkness, trying to get her bearings. Setting the food on the coffee table, she kicked off her high heels with a groan. Rolling the kinks out of her neck, she headed for the bedroom, unbuttoning her blouse as she went.

That's where she found him. Sound asleep and stretched across the bed with his tie hanging over his open, limp palm. She smiled at him in the gathering darkness of the bedroom. He looked as tired as she felt. Sympathy and affection warmed her, and she wanted to kiss him hello and see how his first day went.

Instead, she climbed on the bed and lay down beside him, flicking her fingernail gently along his cheek. He was breathing deeply, never stirring under her touch. Softly, she laid her head on Jeremy's chest, watching his even, steady breathing, listening to the steady, slow thud of his heart.

Jeremy opened his eyes just as Christina was closing hers. He felt her snuggle against him and smiled. "Guess I'm not the only one who's wiped out, huh?"

Smiling, with her eyes still closed, Christina inched closer to him. Sliding her hand inside his shirt, she skimmed her fingers down his smooth chest; she skimmed along his stomach and, feeling the warmth there, nearly purred. "It was a long day."

"Tell me about it," he groaned through a yawn.

"So?" she urged. "How'd it go?"

He ran over the day in his mind. "I survived, but not without a pounding headache." He chuckled in spite of himself. "And I'd never admit it to Dad, but it was interesting."

Christina lifted her head and looked at him, laughing. "Sounds like a ringing endorsement for family loyalty." He looked exhausted. "Is the deal with Highland Manufacturing in trouble?"

Pressing his palms to his eyes to clear his vision, he shrugged. "Not really." Leaning forward, he stuffed a folded pillow behind his shoulders without taking his arm from around Christina. "The financial reports are a mess, and Dad wants me to straighten them out," he snapped his fingers for emphasis, "like I've got a magic wand or something."

"He has a lot of faith in you."

"Maybe too much."

"I doubt that," Christina countered, kissing him.

Jeremy rotated his neck, and a sharp pop relieved his pain. "I'm getting a lot of static already. He introduced me around the building today like I was the second-coming."

"They're jealous already?"

"It doesn't take long when you're the boss' son and you're taking away their chance for advancement. Then, add the bonus of not being nearly as qualified and two credits short of your business degree."

"Ah."

He smiled and pulled her against him, closed his eyes, and sighed. "This could be the longest year of my life."

"You'll make it, Jeremy," she murmured, hardly able to stay awake.

"I know." His voice was heavy with sleep. His first day was finally catching up with him.

~~

If time flies when you're having fun, Jeremy was having the time of his life. The days flew, and before he knew it July was gone and August was in full swing. His hours were longer, and the problems he had to deal with grew more and more complicated - but much to his surprise, he loved it all.

His lunches with Christina had become rare reprieves in his otherwise business-driven day. His promises to spend his lunch times with Christina were becoming harder to keep, and the canvas he brought to the office sat in the corner, untouched. The blank canvas taunted him, but there just wasn't time for his passion, not with the potential for millions of dollars riding on his shoulders - taunting as well.

The two things he needed the most were becoming afterthoughts; exceptions, not the rule, and it ate at him. The woman fed his heart, and the painting fed his soul.

Instead, he sat in his air conditioned office, sleeves rolled up to his elbows, numbers running through his head with the speed of a train. Hidden in the maze of Highland Manufacturing financial statements, he felt the weight of his father's expectations. The takeover would be completed soon, and if Jeremy had any say, with as few casualties as possible. If everything went as expected, the company would belong to Beckett International by the end of the month.

Jeremy's biggest headache was figuring out how best to break up Highland in the most effective way and use the capital in the same effective way. Linus was involved in the last minute negotiations with the sitting CEO. Day after day, negotiations concerning the employees and their futures carried on with little or no ground gained on either side.

If Linus had his way, the employees would suffer the same fate as any of the other employees of past acquisitions: immediate termination. But Jeremy hated to think of the names on the employees' records as people with families and obligations; it was easier to see them as objects rather than living, breathing human beings.

Jeremy insisted Linus try to see to the needs of the employees and consider other options besides turning them out on the street with nothing. As a result, the meetings became tedious and frustrating for everyone. Weeks went by, and Linus usually left the conference room swearing about stubborn minds and feeble business sense.

Jeremy's days were running longer and his patience shorter. His days of leaving the office by six o'clock came to an end after the first month. Wanting the deal closed and settled and Linus focused on something else, Jeremy became the go-between for his father and Highland Manufacturing, trying to get Linus to become more flexible.

Eventually, Jeremy joined in the negotiations. His goal was to try and move them along with as little bloodshed as possible. The CEO of Highland Manufacturing was determined to play hardball on behalf of his employees - and Linus was determined to have his way.

Some of the employees had been with the company for twenty-five years and were within two years of retirement. They had their pensions to worry about. While Linus paid no mind to pensions and saving for a rainy day, these men and women thought of little else. Linus gave no thought to when the next paycheck was coming in, while they worked and survived from paycheck to paycheck.

Jeremy listened to demands he thought were completely reasonable, while Linus felt he was being squeezed for revenge. Weeks passed, September gave way to October, and during another marathon negotiation meeting Jeremy excused himself and Linus, pushing his father out of the conference room. Telling Eden to take coffee and rolls inside, Jeremy took Linus into his office and shut the door. Linus went to the desk and looked over his shoulder, surprised to find Jeremy glaring at him.

"What?" Linus snapped, looking at his son as if he were a traitor.

Jeremy sneered, folding his arms across his chest. He'd seen this routine before, and he was hardly in the mood. "You know damn well what!" he barked. He was fed up with Linus refusing to do the right thing. "I was under the impression you wanted this deal closed quickly."

Linus dropped into his chair. He was feeling pressure from all sides, and he loathed pressure from anyone. "I do," he said quickly with a dismissive wave of his hand, "but the man's being totally unreasonable."

Jeremy shook his head, frustrated. He looked at his father with little tolerance. "You're the one being unreasonable, Dad," he pointed out. "He simply wants his employees ready to retire to have their pensions."

"Twenty people," Linus said wearily. "That's a serious headache to deal with."

"We can handle it." Jeremy replied, unmoved by his father's serious face. "It's the right thing to do. Let's do what we wanted to do from the start: get this company." Jeremy sighed, watching his father's mind at work. "If it costs us a little money, so be it. Let's finish this."

"Alright, let's try and find a compromise."

~ 9 ~

In late October, the Highland Manufacturing deal was finally completed to everyone's satisfaction. Linus had agreed that Beckett International would give each of the twenty employees a lump sum payment of two hundred and ninety-five thousand dollars for early retirement with continuing medical coverage. The remaining employees would be given job referrals. Jeremy thought it was a good compromise and readily encouraged Linus in his decision.

Linus was pleased with the outcome and wasted no time in planning a celebration for everyone involved - and no one deserved it more, he felt, than Jeremy himself. His countless hours and tireless effort on behalf of the company filled his father with immeasurable pride. His boy seemed to have the magic touch after all. The company would be in good hands when it came time for Linus to hand over the reins of Beckett International to his son.

There was still much hard work to do, however. The process of breaking up Highland Manufacturing would be complicated and time consuming but challenging in all the ways Linus loved. It was the challenge Linus loved most, and with Jeremy by his side it would mean even more.

~~

Late November
1978

Christina sat in the living room with Bess, going through her mail and catching up with her aunt. It had been ages since she'd been home. She and Jeremy were spending nearly all of their time in the city. And Christina was nursing a bit of a guilty conscience where her aunt was concerned.

She worried about Jeremy more and more; he was distant, overworked, and unhappy. He was unwilling to talk about the growing pressure at work whenever she asked. His schedule was maddening, and his mood swings were becoming more unnerving to them both.

While the man she loved was breaking down, his work at Beckett International flourished. His dealings were impressive and successful, and no one, not even Jeremy himself, could argue he wasn't good at his job. "Like father, like son," was the party line throughout the company - but achievements in the corporate world and a blurb in Time Magazine couldn't fulfill him.

The hours were endless, and there had been entire twenty-four hour periods without her seeing him at all. When she did see him, he was so tired and distracted he could hardly focus on anything other than his lack of sleep and daily dealings with his father.

His eyes were glazed, and dark circles under them scared her. She couldn't remember the last time she'd seen him relaxed enough to take a walk with her through Central Park or with a paintbrush in his hand. The changes in him were subtle, but Christina knew he was slowly becoming a different man from the one she had known for so long and loved so much.

Bess was going on about her weekly bingo game while Christina went through her mail that had piled up during the week. As she flipped through the large stack, she came across an envelope from French Culinary Academy, and the bold lettering caught her attention. She opened it casually, remembering when she sent the application to them eight months before. She was scanning the first paragraph while her Aunt Bess described her daily trip to the fruit market and various other errands she found to occupy her time. This application was just one of three she had sent out.

Christina knew she would do well in school under the expertise of the talented chefs who would be her teachers. She didn't doubt her skills; she knew she was capable, had known it from the age of nine. But, to have experience when it came time to open her restaurant would be crucial for success.

"Oh God," Christina said quietly with a look of stunned surprise. "I don't believe it."

"What's wrong?" Bess asked, fanning herself with the afternoon paper and wishing the air condition were up and running.

"The French Culinary Academy approved a slot for me for their winter session."

Bess thought for a moment and smiled. "Isn't that the school in Napa Valley?"

Christina looked at her aunt in amazement. Her mind spinning with possibilities. This was what she'd been hoping for. "Uh huh."

Bess was stilling smiling. "Well, that's great, isn't it?"

"I...yes...I guess so." Christina answered, wiping her palm over her clammy forehead and pushing her bangs from her eyes, wondering if it were the stifling heat in the house that sucked the breath from her lungs or the realization that one of her goals was about to be laid at her feet.

This was something she thought was unattainable; a dream not to be realized - or at least not this soon. She felt shocked and honored. Her life had changed in some very important ways, and so had the order of her priorities. Having her own restaurant was so important to her, but so was her love for Jeremy. How could she leave him behind to follow her dream?

The very thought of leaving him made her stomach turn. What would she say to him? This would catch him completely by surprise. She hadn't told him about applying to culinary academies in the first place, and now she'd have to tell him she'd been accepted. How would she?

~~

Thanksgiving came and went in a blur, and little about the holiday festivities stuck in Jeremy's mind because his time was no longer his own. He was back in the office the next day, poring over reports while the rest of the city was still working on turkey leftovers, enjoying the long weekend. But not Jeremy; no, he was hunched over his desk, his nose to the grindstone.

Yet, he was refreshed after a rare morning of painting in the corner of his office, and now with his tie hanging loose at his throat, Jeremy listened to the ranting of one of his father's principal cogs, smiling. He was pointing out the negatives of Jeremy's latest project.

"Listen, Tim, I know how Dad can be. I mean, who'd know better, right?" Jeremy said, cutting in, begging for a reprieve from the complaints being flung at him from across his desk.

Tim Adams shook his head, seeing the same stubborn streak in Jeremy that he saw all too often in his father. "Then you also know he won't go for it."

The mere idea of Linus stepping in to get his hands dirty with inner-city youth was almost laughable, and they both knew it. He gave to charities privately all the time, but this idea would require too much hands-on attention. Linus would need to hobnob with people he considered to be beneath him, and Tim could see Linus balking at the mere mention of it.

"But if anyone can talk him into it, it'll be you," Tim added encouragingly. "Just don't get your hopes up."

Jeremy leaned back, propped his feet on the corner of his desk, and tried to think positively. He cursed the warring muscles in his neck, stretching through his pain and wishing for the days when his time was his own and he would make it through an entire day without the need for aspirin. He tugged at his tie and sighed. Tim Adams was right about how Linus would react.

"He'll probably rant and rave, we both know that. That's Linus Beckett. But the bottom line for Dad is money and his reputation. He'll look like a saint if he does this. There won't be any losers in this for chrissake." Jeremy was convinced even if Tim wasn't. "It's good for those kids and good for this company. He'll come around if we put the right spin on it."

Tim shrugged, wishing it would be as easy as Jeremy made it sound. Actually, when he thought about it, he liked the idea and thought it was worth a try. But he was a different kind of man from Linus Beckett. "You really want to do this, don't you?" he asked with interest.

"Yes," he replied with conviction. He was here at the family company, just where his father wanted him to be, but his heart was elsewhere, where he wanted to be. So, if he had to be there, he was going to see that some of his projects were implemented while he had a say in the matter.

The thought of those kids weighed on his mind. Every day, reports came on the news about gang fights and shootings. It would never end, Jeremy thought, unless someone did something to offer a solution. Some of these kids knew of no other way to survive, unless it was through violence. Most were poor and angry at the world, and it made Jeremy's heart ache for them, though he wouldn't admit it out loud to anyone but Christina.

Linus would go on and on about his bleeding heart, about what a terminal flaw it would one day become in business. But, Jeremy wanted to help them in whatever way he could. The realization that the only thing that separated him from those troubled, angry kids on the street, lurking in the shadows, biding their time until the next big score, was luck, hit home for him. Luck that he had been born into a family of independent means and wealth. All those kids needed was someone to give a damn.

And Jeremy Beckett gave a damn.

"Just look over the numbers."

"Sure. Let's do lunch tomorrow," Tim suggested, getting to his feet and shaking Jeremy's hand. He was late for a meeting with Linus and had to get moving. "I'll let you know what I think then," he continued, turning for the door.

"Great," Jeremy said. "Don't say anything to Dad. I will when the time's right."

~~

Just before lunch, Jeremy's phone buzzed, rescuing him from his tunnel vision of eight digit numbers and stock reports. At a glance, he knew who would be on the other end of his private line. Dropping his pen and pinching the bridge of his nose between his thumb and index finger, he picked up the phone and sighed into the mouthpiece.

"You sound tired," Christina said in a low voice she knew would instantly calm him.

"That's because I am," he answered, cradling the phone close to his cheek and opening his briefcase to get out some files. "So," he asked, fanning through the files to find the one he wanted. "Did you just miss me, or are you calling to make sure my head hasn't exploded yet?"

"Yes on both counts," she laughed, though his tone told her he was only half-joking. "Can you get away for lunch?" She wanted to tell him about the school while she still had the nerve.

He was pushing papers around his desk, trying to put some things in order. But the thought of getting away for a quiet lunch with Christina appealed to him a great deal. "Absolutely, I'll be there in twenty minutes."

"Perfect. See you soon," she said warmly. She felt torn, though, caught between wanting to see him and the reality of telling him about going to school across the country.

~~

When Jeremy arrived, they decided to walk to Giavonni's for lunch. The air was cool, but there was time before their table would be ready, and Jeremy thought he could use the time and the fresh air to clear his mind. It was a rarity for them to be out together now without seeing a replay of it in the morning paper. They walked along the sidewalk, holding hands, saying very little to each other, enjoying being together, and ignoring the passing stares.

They strolled along, lost in their own thoughts. Christina knew time was in short supply all too well, and it ate at her just as it has been since she opened the letter two weeks before. Then Jeremy pulled her close, wrapping his arm snug around her waist. They exchanged smiles, and he pressed his lips to her cheek. Her heart filled with an ache unlike she'd ever felt before, knowing she would have to leave him.

~ 10 ~

Their table sat in front of a large floor-to-ceiling window that provided a great view of the Brooklyn Bridge, while the tinting on the glass kept the flood of sunlight unobtrusive. When they were seated, Jeremy reached across the table and covered her hand with his, smiling.

"You're quiet today. Is something bothering you?" Christina asked, rubbing the inside of his hand with her fingers.

He glanced up from his menu and smiled. "I was about to ask you the same thing," he said, sensing since her arrival at the office that she had something on her mind.

Christina had hoped she covered better than that, but he knew her so well by now, she should have known he would pick up on her nervousness. The waiter arrived at the table with a bottle of wine, giving her a minute to stall. She waited while he poured Jeremy a sample and he tasted it, nodding his approval. "I'm that easy to read?"

Jeremy squeezed her hand in his. The waiter poured their wine and took their orders. Jeremy ordered chef salads and breadsticks for both of them and handed the menus back to the waiter, who disappeared with a smile. "Only to me," he said to her when they were alone. "What's on your mind, Christina?"

She took a sip of her wine while his eyes bore into her. "I've got some news," she said simply.

Jeremy watched her eyes dart around the table. She was looking everywhere but into his eyes. He knew whatever she had to tell him was serious. For a minute, he wondered if she might be pregnant, but he knew they were always so careful. His mind spun with possibilities, none of which he wanted to confront. "Well, don't keep me in suspense."

With another sip of wine, Christina waited for her courage to return. Her eyes finally came to rest on his.

"What sort of news?" he asked.

The waiter arrived with the salads and bread sticks before she could say any more. Serving Christina first, she busied herself with tearing a breadstick and pouring dressing on her salad. Jeremy could see she was anxious as he leaned back to give the waiter room to serve him.

There was no easy way to tell him, she decided, watching his intense gaze across the table. "Awhile back I filled out some applications for school."

"School?" He lifted his wine to his lips and paused. "Culinary school?" he asked.

Christina smiled and picked up her fork. "Yes. The French Culinary School, actually," she replied.

"In California? But you're already fabulous in the kitchen." He lifted a fork full of salad to his mouth.

She blushed, watching his eyes shine with pride. "But I need to be even better if I want to succeed in the restaurant business."

He winked and took a large sip of his wine, rolling it around his tongue. "It's hard to improve on perfection."

Christina ripped another breadstick in half, dipping it in the spicy Italian dressing from her salad. "Well, you're biased. I want to be ready when it comes time to open my restaurant."

He knew she'd made up her mind. She was leaving him. "There are great schools to choose from in the city. Why this school, why California?"

"Because it's the best culinary school in the country...and they want to offer me a full scholarship."

He leaned in close to the table, resting his elbows on either side of his empty plate and folding his hands over his mouth, digesting what she just told him. "I wish you would've told me you were applying to school," he said coolly. "I mean, did you think I wouldn't support your decision?" he continued, becoming angry. His eyes hardened. He was waiting for an answer.

Christina looked across the table with surprise. "I knew you'd support me, but I didn't really expect to get in." She felt defensive and took a sip of wine to calm down.

It took a moment to check the anger, but taking her hand, his eyes softened, and he sighed. "I can see you want this." He calmed his voice. "Well, I'm not going to lie; I hate the thought of you being so far away." He looked her squarely in the eye. His voice became a whisper in the lively room. "But," he added after a thoughtful pause, "I want you to do whatever makes you happy, sweetheart."

Tears of relief threatened as she looked at him. Completely in love, and completely torn between her lifelong dreams of fine food and A-list restaurants and a love she knew she could not live without. "We'll make it work," she whispered, the first of her tears falling down her cheeks.

His eyes held a confidence that, deep in his gut, he didn't feel. He lifted her hand and pressed her palm to his cheek. A clear truth filled him. He loved her more than anything. He would do anything to make her happy, no matter what it cost him - though he realized it would cost a great deal. "Yes, we'll make it work," he said firmly when their eyes met and held. "We're meant to be, Christina."

~~

Jeremy sank low on the couch in his office, and his mood dipped lower still. Lunch had taken less time than he'd expected, and he was back in his office long before he planned to be. With more than an hour before his three o'clock meeting with Linus, he sat, replaying the conversation with Christina. Jeremy felt his throat clench shut when she told him about her plans. It came as a surprise to him, but it shouldn't have. Culinary school was the next logical step in Christina's dream, and he wanted her to have her dreams.

He was still thinking about Christina when he arrived at his father's office for their meeting, throughout which Jeremy was elsewhere in his mind. Distracted and preoccupied, he wanted to be alone. He needed to think things over and decide what to do about the sudden detour his life with Christina was taking.

His son's divided attention and obvious discomfort had not gone unnoticed by Linus. So, he cleared his throat, rested his chin on his palm, and bore holes into his son, attempting to gain his attention. After several minutes of silence, though, Linus gave up. "Make an early day of it, Jeremy. Go home."

~~

December 1978

Manhattan's streets were alive with holiday spirit, and Jeremy could see it all from his office high above the busy crowds of people. The city was blanketed in snow, and Santa Claus could be seen on every corner, his nose and cheeks wind-burned, ringing his bell for a charitable cause. Rewarding those passing by with a cheerful, "Ho! Ho! Ho! Merry Christmas!"

Two weeks before Christmas, and Jeremy had yet to finish his shopping or take on the festive mood sweeping through the building. After weeks of badgering, Linus had finally given the green light for Jeremy's inner-city kid's foundation, lending not only the Beckett name but their money for funding as well. The latest figures he worked up for the board were eating up all his time and dampening his mood. The frustration was nothing new, and it always came when there were too many hands out and not enough money to go around.

While Jeremy should have been elbow deep in solving budgetary dilemmas, his desk was cleared of the usual disarray that littered the high-polished oak top desk. Not much business could be conducted with holiday parties on people's minds. The business day was drawing to a close, and he was painfully aware that he'd accomplished very little that day. He sat staring out his window as daylight gave way to the inky blackness of night settling in the sky, and bringing with it a major snowfall.

He had lunch with Jamie earlier in the day, filling her in on Christina's plans for school. Then he spent the rest of lunch complaining about how lonely he would be when she left. So, he was in no hurry to be home alone in the suite while Christina worked the closing shift. A preview of all the nights to come when he would be alone with Christina across the country, he decided. His throat tightened just imagining it.

~~

At Jamie's suggestion, Christina and Jeremy spent the week before Christmas at Cherry Hill. Avery had left for New York the night before they arrived, and they were grateful for the time alone. Though wintertime in Vermont was breathtakingly beautiful, Christina's impending departure loomed over them like a dark cloud. Still, being snowed in with the woman he loved, Jeremy refused to dwell on sad thoughts. They could still enjoy the time left to them before their lives were turned upside down by distance.

Afternoon rides snuggled together in the small buggy Avery kept in outstanding condition, then snowball fights and constructing snowmen. And finally, huddled before a fire inside the cozy house, they might have been the only two people in the world, warming themselves in various, imaginative ways while snow piled up around them.

The icy seasonal winds so notorious in Vermont howled outside to rattle the windows. Late into the evening, they nestled in the large living room, stretched out on the plush deep violet carpet in front of the mahogany fireplace. Romance was a given when in such charming settings. Without distractions, they clung to each other, making love and promises.

Flames, crackling and snapping, fed off the logs, caressing their bodies. The air around them hung sweet, the wooden scent of burning oak. But for their breathing and the pop of burning wood, no other sound could be heard.

They held on and gave in. To each other, to a passion neither could, nor wanted, to deny. Wrapped up in each other and a throw blanket, sensations rocked them. A touch, a sweeping caress of fingertips, each time was new and deeper than before. Finally spent and pleasantly exhausted by each other, when he spoke it was a whisper.

"I've been thinking," Jeremy said softly, running his fingers through Christina long flow of auburn hair, drawing in her scent, praying it would stay imbedded in his senses forever.

Her arms were draped over him, and her long legs tangled with his as he pulled the blanket tighter around them to ward off the chill drifting in from the hallway. "What about?" She studied his face in the firelight.

She drew up and kissed him softly, waiting for him to continue.

"About how much I'm going to miss you."

Her eyes grew sad, and, taking his face in her hands, she said, "Don't think about that yet."

"How can't I think about it?"

"By thinking about how much I love you instead."

"That's easy enough," he agreed, then he spoke the words that broke her heart. "I can't live without you."

Laying her head on his chest, she sighed. "Yes, you can."

"Okay, but I don't want to."

"You'll be so busy with work, you won't even notice I'm gone."

"I'll notice." And then he did what he would never have done before he met her: he led with his heart. "Marry me, Christina."

Hearing himself say the words out loud still surprised him, although he'd been thinking of nothing else for a week. But, saying them to himself and saying them to her was very different matter.

For a moment, her stunned surprise silenced them both.

His heart - and he thought very likely his life - hung in the balance. So, touching her lips with his, he spoke them again, "Will you marry me?"

"Where'd that come from?" She sat up, looking down at him in disbelief. "Jeremy, you know I want nothing more in my life than to marry you."

"So say yes. I know the timing's all wrong, but I'm not asking you to give up school, Christina. I'd never ask you to choose between your dreams and me." Leaning back on his elbows, he lifted a brow and knew this was right. "Just marry me before you leave."

"You're insane."

He grinned up at her, trailing a fingertip along her thigh where the blanket had fallen away. "You love me?"

"Don't be stupid."

"Answer the question."

"Yes, you lunatic, I love you." She laughed, but her eyes were still wary.

"Hey, that's no way to talk to your future husband."

Christina's smile faded and she turned to stare into the flames with her mind racing. She chose her words very carefully; she had to. "What're you thinking? You want to get married, then be apart for over a year and a half?"

"Six months," he corrected, curling the ends of her hair around his finger. "My commitment to the company is through in July. Then I'll fly over, and we'll rent a condo while you finish up your classes."

"You've given this a lot of thought."

"Sure. I'll have the chance to get more involved with my charities in L.A., not to mention all the painting I can do with no one to answer to but myself."

She could see he'd made plans, but she knew very well walking away from his father wouldn't be so easy. Somewhere down deep, he knew it, too. Linus was a powerful presence in his life. "Call me crazy, but when we get married I'd like to be in the same vicinity of my husband, or at the very least, the same state."

"So it's 'no' then?" He ran his hand through his matted hair, struggling to hold his temper in check.

His look of disappointment nearly broke her, and knowing anger was just under the hurt had her reaching out to his stubbly cheek. "It's a 'not right now.'"

When he said nothing, and only looked into the flames with his temper building to match the fire's heat, she leaned in and kissed him, deepening it when he tried to draw away, pushing him flat on the carpet as his pride warred with his passion. He refused to give in, and once again covering his body with her own, she clouded his thoughts and felt his stubborn surrender. A perfect fit as always, she thought, already dazed, already teetering on the edge, found again and again in his arms.

He sighed, and they both knew she'd won. She knew, as she watched his eyes close, that his anger, always a rough and unforgiving force, was no match for the desire she built in him. He knew it when her lips pressed to his chest and he felt his heart stumble.

He couldn't look into those green eyes, feel the heady wave of need, and stay angry. But he wanted to stay angry; damn it, he wanted to. But other wants were having their way, though. With her breasts pressed against him and the feel of their skin sliding against each other, how could they not? And with her penetrating stare drawing his eyes back to hers, how could he fight?

"The second I come back from California, I'm yours. You can have a minister waiting at the airport."

All the fight in him gone, he murmured, "Promise?"

"Promise." Her hands streaked over him, possessing him. He was hard when her hand snaked over him and her fingers wrapped warmly around him. She bolted up, straddled him, and took him deep inside her. His breath caught, hitched, when she took him deeper still, and even in her primal need, it made her smile.

"I love you," she said, breathless now, too, as her hips began to pump with lightning speed, building a dark wave of sensation, even now rolling through her. No more words were needed as she pressed her lips to his, gently first, and then more urgently, sliding her tongue into his mouth, searching and driving them both well over the edge.

~ 11 ~

Christmas came with family and friends wishing Christina well over dinner at the Beckett estate. While gifts were exchanged and pictures of happy faces were taken for scrapbooks, Christina found she was struggling inside. Conflicting emotions distracted her. On one hand she was excited over her coming arrival at the French Culinary Academy, on the other was heartbreak over having to leave Jeremy behind. Just the thought of it could bring on a fresh flow of tears.

He showered her with gifts and affection, resigned now and accepting her leaving. He was determined to support her in every way. The seasonal atmosphere fed both their romantic mood and their underlying melancholy.

On New Year's Eve they made their way through the party scene, dodging the prying eyes of cameras from various news source and gossip outlets. At the stroke of midnight they were walking, hand in hand, through Central Park. With a wonderful view of firecrackers and streamers bursting in vivid colors high in the sky over their heads the night pulsed with energy. Times Square was a virtual sea of the loud, crazed masses and they wanted was privacy. People passed in crowds well on their way to celebrating the New Year, but they only had eyes for each other.

While the ball dropped in Time Square, Jeremy held Christina in his arms and kissed her with unbearable sweetness. Staring into her green eyes, he yearned both for her and for time to stop. In his soul, he buried a building, burning need to go back on an oath he'd made to himself to let her go and instead, beg her to stay.

It would have been so easy to say the words. Too easy, he chided himself, and unfair as hell. By tucking her head beneath his chin and wrapping his arms around her, he comforter himself every bit as much as her. Controlling his urge to be selfish nearly overwhelmed him, but her needs should and would be met before his own.

He pulled away slightly to find her eyes closed, her face turned up to the stars, and her breath making wispy clouds in the frigid night air. He wondered what she was thinking. Was she thinking about Napa Valley or about him? He shifted, drawing her even closer, and pressed his mouth to her ear. "Keep your eyes closed."

"Why?" She laughed and enjoyed the warmth of him. In another moment, she felt something cool slip around her neck, and she reached up in curiosity. "What have you done?"

"Open up and find out."

With a gasp, and a nearly feline purr, Christina was blinded by emeralds and diamonds wound around her neck so brilliant in the chilly moonlight. She turned in his arms with tears once more threatening. "Oh...Jeremy...it's so beautiful."

"I couldn't resist." He pressed his lips to hers and pulled her into his tight embrace. "I was right. The emeralds are the same shade as your eyes. Always remember how much you're loved, Christina," he said, cupping her cheek. "And don't ever forget I can't live my life without you. Happy New Year."

His words, and the emotions behind them, undid her, and the tears spilled down her cheeks as she held him close. "I love you," she murmured into his ear, unashamed to cry.

~~

January 30
1979
Napa Valley, California

Temperatures in Napa Valley were drastically different from those Christina left behind. The sun shining down on the cab as it made its way through the sparse pedestrian traffic was a welcome relief from the frigid winter winds in New York. Napa offered an old village feeling one minute and a modern air the next. Lush greenery burst from the street corners as the cab passed by in no particular hurry.

It was a blessing Christina found herself too busy settling in and preparing for classes to dwell on her heartache. She did miss Jeremy - and she missed him terribly -especially at night when her bed felt so empty without him. Curling next to him or reaching for him in the darkness was one of her greatest pleasures. Hearing his voice on the phone wasn't an acceptable substitute, but they were making the best of their situation by counting the days until they would see each other again.

Remembering the tears she shed at the airport only brought on fresh ones. Determination and force of will put on the brave face she needed to keep from crying then. And it was sheer survival that kept her from crying now. She could still see him from her window seat on the plane, standing at the window, overlooking the tarmac. He stood there, she knew, until he could no longer see her plane in the sky. Just as she had watched him from her window.

~~

Her apartment was a two bedroom walkup with a spacious living room and dining area. The adjoining balcony overlooked the cobblestone street that ran in front of the building. And it boasted a large kitchen and bath with space to spare. The walls were freshly painted a cheery shade of apricot, at Jeremy's insistence and expense. Christina had to admit as she stood taking in her new place that his odd color choice certainly cheered the place up - but it worked no such magic on her.

There was so much to do to make it feel like home, and it would do her good to busy herself. So, she dropped her purse just inside the door, slammed it shut, locked it behind her, and got to work making this place her home. Besides, at week's end her time would no longer be her own. She'd be slave to her goals again, albeit a willing one. After all, that was the reason she was here.

The airy, sunlit space would suit her tastes well, she thought, rolling up her sleeves to get to work, and smiling. There would be plenty of sun to brighten the apartment during the day and ample moonlight to cast a comforting glow at night. Since she had only the basics in the way of furniture, she would have more than enough room to spread out for the next eighteen months.

Despite her loneliness for Jeremy, she felt like this new avenue in her life was the beginning of something exciting. If her heart still yearned for New York, she wouldn't give in to it. She had unpacking and cleaning to do, and was determined to lighten her mood while she waited for Jeremy to call.

~ 12 ~

Jeremy walked off the elevator and headed straight to his office, carrying his briefcase and a canvas covered with a drop cloth. He blew by Joanie's desk with little more than a nod hello and pushed the door to his office closed with his hip. Setting the canvas against the wall and carrying his briefcase to his desk, he picked up his phone and dialed his sister's number. She picked up on the third ring, and Jeremy sighed in relief.

"Free for dinner with your big brother?" He opened his calendar, skimmed the day's page, and ran his hand through his hair in instant frustration. His afternoon was loaded; any hope of painting went out the window.

Jamie tucked the phone between her shoulder and chin and finished applying her makeup. "Depends on where we're eating," she quipped. She'd been expecting to hear from him. Christina had been gone for little more than a week.

He sat down and opened his briefcase, unsure at the moment why he bothered to call his sister at all. He wasn't in the mood for her needling so early in the morning. He had a late night with a scotch bottle and was suffering miserably. "Honestly, Jamie, you can be such a superficial bitch sometimes," he said with mild annoyance.

Jamie smiled at the description. "I think somebody's missing his woman. Sexual deprivation is harder on men than women, so I forgive."

"You have a dirty mind, little sister," he warned. "So, you meeting me for dinner or what?"

"How can I refuse such a lovely invitation? Yeah, but cheer up, or I just might knock you on your ass."

~~

As the first week of classes wore on, Christina found she was learning invaluable things. She took more notes than anyone else in class, determined to excel and get the most out of her classes. The subtle differences in cooking with gas vs. electric were enlightening, and the tricks to shortening cooking times, clever. Dishes were presented for grading and recipes were expected to be memorized after one preparation.

Her days were filled from 9 a.m. to 3 p.m., leaving her very little time for anything but studying and sleeping. Many afternoons, she would stay after class to work on dishes until she got it right. When she got home, she was mentally fried and dead on her feet. She'd fix something to eat and wait for Jeremy's nightly call so she could feel connected to him and the world again.

~~

March 20, 1979
Manhattan, NY
9:35 p.m.

Jeremy moved around on the drop cloth he laid out carefully over the pricey carpeting in his office. Paint smeared his right cheek and forehead, and his attention was most definitely not on takeovers and corporate restructuring. He'd been working on a new painting for over four hours now, studying it with his careful eye and feeling pleased with his progress.

The smock he wore protected his clothing and had several new splashes to add to the rainbow of colors already there. Surgical slippers covered his sock-covered feet. They, too, were sprinkled with the dark blues and blacks he'd been working with for hours.

Wiping his hands on a hand towel moistened with paint thinner, feeling satisfied and less stressed than he had in days, he unzipped the smock content with his progress. The hall outside was dimmed and deserted with only the occasional passing of the overnight security guards to remind him that he was not alone in the world. He rolled his shoulders, groaned, and looked at his watch. Bleary-eyed he scrubbed his hands over his face and allowed his thoughts to turn toward Christina.

He collapsed into his comfortable leather chair and slid closer to the desk. Picking up the phone, he yawned as he dialed her number, slumped back, and propped up his feet. Waiting for the line to connect, he pictured her in his mind and nearly cursed himself for the self-imposed torture.

She answered on the second ring. Her warm, clear voice made him smile. "Hi sweetheart."

"Hey," she said brightly. With a sigh, she pulled her hair free of the ponytail that kept her hair out of the way while she was cooking. "I miss you."

"Good. I like knowing I'm not alone in my misery, I guess." His eyes drifted closed, and he allowed the tension in his body to drain with the sound of her voice.

"You sound beat," she replied in a sympathetic tone, her hair falling down over her shoulders. "You're still at the office aren't you?" She could see him at his desk, brow creased and expletives flying under his breath.

"Mmmm hmmm."

"Jeremy, you should be home; it's late." Christina scolded.

He laughed, opened his eyes, and blinked away sleep. "I was unwinding," he informed her. "I've been working on a new painting all evening. Instant relaxation, promise."

"Really?" The surprise was obvious in her voice. She imagined him locked away in his office with financial sheets and projection reports.

Leaning back on the sofa, Christina relaxed; falling into an easy rhythm with Jeremy made her feel closer to him. "I'm glad you're not working yourself to death while I'm gone. Remember, you have to make an honest woman out of me when I get home."

"Marrying me won't help with that. Don't you read the papers?"

Christina laughed a dark, rich laugh that told him all he needed to know. She'd seen the stories of late about his supposed late night partying in her absence. "Shut up and just tell me how much you miss me."

Jeremy smiled. "Ah, where do I begin?"

~~

April 21, 1979
Manhattan, NY
8:30 p.m.

Thoughts of Christina played through Jeremy's mind while he peered out of the window and focused on the lights of the city. It was not unusual to be caught up in everything he missed about her after their calls. The knock on his door had him spinning around in his chair and glaring at the door because of the interruption.

"Who is it?"

Linus stiffened at Jeremy's tone; experience told him to tread lightly. "Your father."

Jeremy checked his watch; it was late, and he wondered why his father was still at the office. "Come in."

Linus stuck his head in, smiling, his eyes sweeping the office he had redecorated to his son's tastes, his eyes pausing on Jeremy's latest canvas. "I like it," he said, coming into the room and crossing to it for a better look. "It's...vivid." he pronounced, then sat down on the sofa.

Jeremy pushed away from the desk and got to his feet. Knowing what it cost his father to try to understand his artistic work, Jeremy smiled at him. "Thanks." Sliding his hands into his pockets, he came around his desk and leaned on the edge. "Isn't it a little late for you to be haunting the halls?"

"Your mother told me I'd find you here," Linus said, playing with his cufflinks. "She thinks you're spending too much time here, son."

Folding his arms over his chest, Jeremy waited. "And what do you think?"

"I'm tempted to agree."

"That sounds funny coming from you, Dad."

His eyes narrowed. "I'm not that much of a slave driver, son. Anyway, you know your mother. Have you eaten?"

"I'm a big boy," he said. "Tell her not to worry."

Linus sat back, fingering the fringe on the pillows on either side of him, ignoring Jeremy's jabs. "You're worrying your mother. She knows how much you're missing Christina right now, and I don't want her worrying about you. Her health's been up and down again. Added stress won't help."

"I'll go by tomorrow for lunch and try to ease her mind." Rolling up his sleeves, Jeremy crossed the room to the bar and poured a scotch. "What's her doctor say?" He tossed ice chips in his glass, then poured one neat, just the way his father preferred it before turning back to him.

"He wants to run more tests." Linus leveled his eyes on Jeremy. "I don't have to tell you how your mother feels about that." He took the scotch Jeremy offered him and fretted over a loose thread on his cardigan.

Jeremy laughed smoothly, tested his drink, his eyes glittering in amusement. "Mom can be a doctor's worst nightmare."

Linus smiled. "Yes, she can be a handful. So, do me a favor, be home when she calls you in the evenings."

He let a mouthful of scotch sit on his tongue for a moment. "Sure." he agreed, finishing his drink and setting the empty glass on the gray marble surface of the bar.

"Your mother'll be relieved."

"It'll be a break from her having to read about my supposed nightly exploits in the morning paper. Complete with pictures."

Linus grimaced in disgust. "The papers can go to hell."

~ 13 ~

May 2, 1979

Through the window of the lobby of the Beckett building, Jeremy could see the limo pulled to the curb. Then he spotted Edward, their driver, standing by the rear door, rocking on his heels, waiting patiently for him. Jeremy's mouth twitched into a smile as he pushed through the double doors and walked out onto the marble walkway leading to the curb.

A chilly April breeze blew his coat open as he greeted Edward with a wave and watched as he opened the car door automatically, a learned response. But Jeremy sent him home, deciding instead to walk the six blocks to the popular night spot, Puttin' on the Glitz. It was an old stomping ground for him, and where he would be meeting his friends for a night meant for reliving and, no doubt, regressing. They all missed the ease of college days, a time when life was a lot simpler.

The fresh air and brisk walk had the desired effect on Jeremy. A day's worth of tension rolled off his shoulders, and the dull ache behind his eyes was finally subsiding. The solitude cleared his head and stretched the knotted muscles earned throughout a day of back-to-back meetings, outlining, and then dictating four proposals for the Board of Directors.

He covered the six blocks in no time and walked in off the street, ready to let his mind go and have fun. He welcomed the pounding, vibrating music like an old friend. The chill of the night air vanished quickly in the wealth of body heat that assaulted him as he made his way through the crowded club to the back.

He was known and liked by the regulars who squandered their nights with endless partying, flirting, and making general asses of themselves. As the night and booze wore on, they felt like god's gift to women. Under the neon lights of Puttin' on the Glitz, all was expected and forgiven with the sunrise. The drinks were always plentiful, and the waitresses were playful, and in no way shy. Looking around, he saw many familiar faces. Jeremy raked his fingers through his wind-tossed hair and moved into the crowd to mingle.

The music pumped loud enough to make ears bleed, Jeremy decided, crossing the floor. He spotted his pals at a corner table and grinned foolishly. He snagged a waitress and ordered a drink before he headed for their table. For a little while, at least, he would think of something other than work and his loneliness for Christina.

~~

Napa Valley, CA
7:10 p.m.

Christina brought a friend from class back to her apartment for dinner. Her name was Diana Reynolds, and she had a few glasses of wine and some guy talk on her mind - and was more than a little intrigued that Jeremy Beckett was the man who owned Christina's heart.

Diana whistled when they walked into the apartment and Christina flipped on the lights. "Wow!" she said, her eyes wide, taking in everything in sight. "This place is gorgeous, Christina." She walked through the clever maze of furniture and worked her way over to the sliding doors that led to the balcony. "Well, this puts my flat to shame."

"Thanks." Christina set the bag of takeout on the end table by the couch and smiled at the compliment. "I wanted it to feel like home."

Diana opened the sliding doors, breathing in the evening breeze and the scent of jasmine. "You managed."

Tossing her keys on the kitchen table, Christina said, "Come on, I'll give you the rest of the nickel tour before we eat."

~~

Manhattan, NY
May 3, 1979
1:15 a.m.

Jeremy survived his night out with the guys. The heavy drinking and loud music came back to him in bits and pieces; just how he made it back to the suite was a mystery. Now he lay utterly inebriated and dreaming of her. Familiar dreams of Christina formed in his alcohol-soaked mind, and in his dreams he did what he hadn't been able to do in months: he touched her. Jeremy was lost in, and to, her. She was with him again, and she hungered for him, just as much he hungered for her.

While desire and greedy need battled inside him, his vision blurred - even as his tongue glided along the silken skin of her jaw. His body seemed to throb in time with his heart while her moans of pleasure rippled through him. He was hers once more, just as he had always been.

~~

May 3, 1979
9:30 a.m.

Jeremy woke with a vicious, stabbing pain behind his eyes, and a pitiable moan of surrender. His mouth was almost painfully dry and his tongue felt thick as he tried, in vain, to lick his lips. Then the nausea turned his stomach and had him pinching the bridge of his nose to steady the mounting urge to vomit. Swallowing the bitter taste of stale alcohol was hardly the way to save him.

This hangover, he knew, would be the mother of them all. He wanted to curl into a ball and die. But as he assessed the damage done from the night before, he knew without risking it, that his shaky legs wouldn't support him.

His head throbbed viciously, and any attempt to move proved excruciating. Pain was the only proof he had that he was still alive. His tongue was the texture of sandpaper, but he hadn't yet opened his eyes to the punishment of the sun. As far as Jeremy was concerned, death was preferable.

The midmorning light filtered through the partially opened curtains that covered the window to the left of the bed. From where he laid, he felt the warm of sunlight on his face, tormenting him. Behind his swollen eyelids, the comforting darkness was a respite, but he knew he had to grit his teeth and face the day. He rolled onto his side, fisting his hands in his hair. Slowly, he opened one eye to test his vision, then the other to test his resolve.

Cursing, Jeremy forced his legs from the tangled sheets and heaved his body up to slide carefully to the edge of the bed. Burying his face in his hands, Jeremy waited for the room to stop spinning. Deciding this was as close to death as he ever wanted to come, he prepared to stand on liquid legs.

A sudden movement from the other side of the bed startled him and had him turning in confusion. Confusion was to be expected, but finding he wasn't alone in bed was not. He stumbled from the bed, trying to put the pieces together. Through narrowed, bleary eyes he focused on the woman just waking up in his bed.

Pain pounded in his skull like a jackhammer while the fog slowly lifted and he recognized who it was in his bed. Emily Harris, an old high school girlfriend, was stretched out lazily in bed and yawning happily up at him. Clutching the back of his neck, he cursed under his breath. Just what the hell had happened last night?

Slipping out of bed and grinning sheepishly, Emily seemed to prowl over to him. She was very naked and very pleased with herself. Sliding her long, slender arms around his neck, she studied his face. "What's the matter?" She slid her nimble fingers through his mussed hair. "You look a little green, Jeremy."

"Emily..." He pried her arms from around his neck, held her at arms length, and moved away to put distance between them. He had to clear his muddled mind if he had any hope of handling this. "Last night, what happened?" The stupidity of the question hung in the air between them. It was obvious even to his soggy brain exactly what had gone on between them.

Amusement colored her face as she watched him from across the room. She'd never seen a more pitiful drunk. "Nothing that doesn't come quite naturally." She walked over to the nightstand and lit a cigarette. "Just a little sex between friends, that's all."

Rubbing his temples in a feeble attempt to drive the piercing pain from his head, he leaned against his dresser and leveled his grim gaze at her unhappily. "Oh, fuck me."

Emily laughed dryly and inhaled the pungent cigarette smoke. "Already did, thanks."

Swallowing to clear his throat, Jeremy frowned. "I'm ordering up coffee," he muttered, looking himself over, dismayed to find himself in only boxers. "Get dressed." he said flatly. "I'll meet you in the living room."

~~

Emily walked into the living room to find Jeremy nursing his hangover with his first tentative sips of steaming coffee. Dressed haphazardly in sweats and a tee-shirt, he was obviously in pain. She cleared her throat to announce herself and crossed the room to sit on the sofa.

"You want coffee?" he asked, pouring a second cup, sucking a breath in through his clenched teeth.

Emily made note of the stiff tone in his voice and straightened her spine. "Cream, no sugar."

Adding cream, Jeremy lifted his eyes to meet hers. "I won't ask how you got here last night. I've a pretty good idea." He gave the coffee to her and sighed. "I remember you coming into Glitz."

She nodded, waiting for him to get the point.

"I'm sure you know about Christina Wagner and my relationship with her."

"So?" Emily replied crisply. Already, she could see the writing on the wall. "She's in California, for what? The next two years. Are you planning to be a good little boy until she comes back?"

Ignoring the intentional dig, he sat down beside her and drained his cup of coffee. "I'll be joining her in a few months, as soon as my commitment to Beckett International is over."

Emily crossed her legs and folded her hands over her knee. "You've got it all planned out, don't you?" Her voice was ice and her posture ridged.

"I was drunk off my ass last night. I'm sure it seemed like I wanted you last night, but who I want is Christina. I love her too much for this to mean anything."

It cut deep to be pronounced a mistake he already regrets. Anger, then hurt filled her. "You can go to hell, you sonofabitch." she snapped, getting to her feet and storming for the door.

"I'm sorry, Emily. What we had was a long time ago, and it's over. We're friends and we always will be. Why screw that up with……complications?" he said sadly.

Irate, Emily spun around to face him in all her fury. "We're also former lovers," she reminded him. "I was you're first."

Jeremy put his elbows on his knees and dropped his head in his hands. Wanting to die rather than continue this conversation, he sighed. "And Christina will be my last." he said. "You're pissed off, and you have every right to be. But if the tabloids get wind of this, it'll be a nightmare. Other people besides us will be hurt."

"I don't remember smiling for any photographers, Jeremy." She huffed out a breath, pushed her hair back from her face, and struggled with her dignity. "You're afraid to get caught with your hand in the cookie jar, afraid the supposed love of your life'll find out what you were up to last night?" She bit off the words like broken glass and glared at him.

Jeremy shuddered inside, and his sour stomach turned over. Pushing himself off the sofa, he headed for the room service tray. The thought of Christina reading about it in the paper made his knees want to buckle underneath him. He was a son of a bitch, Emily, he decided, was quite right on that score. She could say all those things to him and more - and be right on target. But he owed her the truth, and even if it killed him, he would give it to her.

He poured more coffee and chased three aspirin down his jagged throat. "Actually, I plan to tell her myself." He looked at Emily in all her open rage, then he watched, and winced, as she slammed the door behind her as she left.

~ 14 ~

Two showers and three pots of coffee later, Jeremy finally began to see through the haze that the night of boozing left behind. Dressed in jeans and a black polo shirt, he felt more human as the caffeine did its work. His hair, freshly washed and combed, was still wet from the shower, his teeth were brushed, and he'd used half a bottle of mouth wash.

It was guilt as much as the hangover that gave him the overwhelming sick feeling in the pit of his stomach. He squinted out at the bright skyline, berating himself for the pain he would have to inflict on the woman he loved. He would tell her before the rags and the papers could do it for him - or worse, Emily, in her anger, told Christina for revenge.

He went to the mirror to look himself in the eye. His brown eyes were dull and bloodshot, his face stark white, pale as death. The stubble on his chin made him look every bit as haggard and sluggish and rough around the edges as he felt. He'd forgone shaving for fear he couldn't trust his hands. Miserable, death would be easier than confessing his one-night stand to Christina.

~~

Christina stood in her kitchen, making breakfast. The blueberry pancakes and German link sausages gave off a delicious aroma and would wake Diana before the alarm could. Clad in her robe and slippers with her long wild hair clipped on the top of her head, she hummed pleasantly through the routine.

Happily, her day was free because no classes were scheduled due to an in-service day. It was nice to sleep late, she thought, pouring more batter onto the griddle, listening to the quick sizzle of sausages in the frying pan.

Her night with her new friend had been a relaxing one, and she hadn't realized to just now, how much she needed it.

Diana was coming into the living room when Christina walked into the small dining area with a plate full of pancakes and sausage. "You disgust me," Diana said, putting her palm against her forehead. "I guess you handle alcohol better than me. What was in that stuff anyway?"

Christina added plates to the table and laughed. "Hey, that was top of the line wine from here in Napa Valley." She pulled out a chair and slid a pancake and a couple sausages onto a plate. "Eat." She nodded to the chair. "It'll help with the headache."

Diana rubbed her temples gingerly, looked at the food, then at Christina, and sat. "Who says I have a headache?"

With a raised brow and her tongue tucked in her cheek, Christina cocked her head. "So you don't?"

Picking up her fork and stabbing at the fluffy pancake steaming on her plate, she groaned. "Oh, shut up."

~~

Jamie glided across the lobby of the Waldorf. Dressed in a skimpy, pink sun dress with three-inch heels and her hair piled on top of her head in a twist, she looked like she owned the place. Reaching the elevator, she jabbed the 'Up' button and scanned behind her for the faces of anyone she knew. Winking at a rather well-built bellboy, she reminded herself she was angry and adjusted her posture to fit her mood.

It was rare for her to be truly angry with Jeremy, but there were times when she wanted to throttle him. And this, she decided, as the elevator doors opened and she stepped inside and pressed the button for the penthouse suite, was one of those times. She waited for the second answering buzzer from Jeremy, allowing the elevator to climb to the penthouse. Tapping her foot impatiently, she fumed, as he took his own sweet time answering.

She'd heard all about his night on the town with Emily Harris. What the hell was he thinking? Or more to the point, she mused, what was he thinking with? Friends saw him last night at Puttin' on the Glitz with some college buddies. But before the night was through, Emily Harris sauntered in and took advantage of her idiot brother.

How could he have been so stupid? And the fact that he'd been too drunk to notice the photographers lurking only made a bad situation worse. The pictures, she'd been told by friends, would be worth a thousand rather colorful words. *And just how will he explain this to Christina?* she wondered.

She marched into the suite without knocking, prepared to let him have it with both barrels. "Jeremy, what the hell—" her words broke off when she saw his face.

He turned away from the window when he heard the sharp snap of heels on the marble entryway. He looked at her now, across the large living room, hands in his pockets and his eyes full of pain and regret. "Hold your fire," he said. "It's barely noon."

One look at him, and she knew he was already well aware of the fool he'd made of himself. Taking a deep breath, she crossed the room, tossing her purse on the sofa along the way. "I see you survived." She came up beside him and shifted her eyes to the window. "Goddamn it, Jeremy. What were you thinking?"

He lifted his shoulders and sighed. "Word travels fast." He rubbed the back of his neck, deciding he needed more coffee if he was going to go toe-to-toe with his sister. "I wasn't thinking at all. I had too fucking much to drink last night," he admitted, meeting his sister's cool eyes while he poured more coffee. "But that's no excuse, I know."

"I have friends who saw you last night, Jeremy. You were drunk off your ass." Jamie stated crisply, folding her arms over her chest, resisting the strong urge to shake him. Jamie glared at him. "Climbing all over Emily Harris and telling her to show you a good time. Tell me, why do men think only with their dicks?"

Jeremy walked over, handing her a cup of coffee and muttering under his breath. "Jesus, don't lump me in with all the men you play around with, okay? I'm not like them."

Rolling her eyes, she said, "Right." She sipped her coffee, grimacing at it potency. "This'll make your day: someone called in a tip, and photographers showed up ready. They got plenty of tasteless pictures, big brother. It'll all be in the papers by tonight, tomorrow at the latest."

"I'm flying out tonight to tell Christina." He blew out a ragged breath and swallowed more coffee. "She has to hear it from me, Jamie. I owe her that much." He raked his hand through his hair and started pacing. "I don't know how the hell I could've let this happen. I've been missing her and been too damn busy to do anything about it."

Jamie stepped in front of him to stop him from wearing a hole in the carpet. Taking him by the shoulders, she gave him a small smile. "If that's your defense, she'll flatten you."

Jeremy pulled her into his arms and held on. "I don't know how I'm going to tell her," he said, pulling back and looking at her with a grim face, "but I'll have to find a way."

~~

May 3, 1979
10:00 p.m.
Napa Valley

Christina sat back on her couch with a sigh and closed her eyes. Diana had left to go home. What began as a leisurely day of shopping and lunch in one of the many winery diners in the valley quickly turned sour when a reporter from the Globe ruined her easy going mood. She was ready for a long hot soak in her tub. It would do her muscles, now knotted with tension and frustration, a world of good to be pampered with scented bath oils and steaming hot water.

She opened her eyes to look at the clock: just past 6 p.m. and she was already worn out and worn down by innuendo and solicitous speculation about the now long distance relationship between her and Jeremy. So it was the perfect time, she decided, unfolding her long legs and stretching before standing up, to indulge in some self pity.

She would reheat her leftover lunch when she got out of the tub. With a groan, she turned her stiffening neck in a circle and started for the bathroom, already imagining how deliciously decedent the feel of lavender oil would feel as it worked the tension from every muscle. Halfway down the hall, a quiet knock on the door stopped her.

Frowning, she turned and went to the door. She wasn't expecting anybody and feared for a moment it might be another of those tabloid thugs, pleading for an exclusive about her relationship with Jeremy. Opening the door, she stuck her head out ready to throw a right hook, but she got a jolt of surprise instead.

"Jeremy!" she screamed in surprise and leapt into his arms. Her eyes softened, and she smiled and enjoyed being held in his arms again. Her kisses were fast and hungry on their journey over his face. Christina leaned back, framing his face in her hands. "You said you weren't coming for another week." He was still holding her tight and fell into the kiss without saying a word.

His hands streaked possessively up her back, then fisted in her hair. He pulled away to catch his breath and gather his nerve. "I had to see you."

Running her fingers through his mussed hair, she let him carry her inside and push the door closed with his back before setting her down. "God, you're a sight," she said fiercely, and for the first time noticed the stubble on his chin and his ashen face.

In an endearing habit, Jeremy brushed his knuckles over his chin and smiled. He linked his fingers with hers when she slipped her hand into his and moved over to the sofa. "Just hopped on a plane, and here I am." He let her pull him down on the sofa beside her. "Place looks great," he put in, his gaze roaming around her place and avoiding her eyes altogether.

"You just don't know how badly I needed to see you," she told him. With a lift of her brow, she watched him, curious. "What's wrong?"

"Nothing now." he said, lifting her hand, brushed his lips over her knuckles. He answered her quietly, "There's no place I'd rather be than here with you."

Shrugging, she stretched her legs out in his lap and stared at him, expectantly. Something was wrong, she thought, and her heart quickened. "Something's happened."

He felt her eyes on him and finally turned to face her. She wouldn't buy an evasion, and she didn't deserve it. This woman he so loved deserved the truth, despite his desperate need to cling to the lie.

He wasn't fooling her, and he realized he could no longer try to fool himself. He looked at Christina, watching her furrowed brow, and he sighed deeply. Now was the time to tell her, and it tore at his heart. "I...I have something to tell you." he began, fighting the panic rising in his throat, knowing her look of concern would soon give way to pain. "I was out last night...with some friends and had way too much to drink." he began.

Christina squeezed his hand, smoothed her palm over his cheek. "You flew coast to coast with a hangover? Well, that's devotion." He looked so serious, but he smiled.

"It's no more than I have coming to me." He pushed his hand through his hair and felt nervous sweat trickle down between his shoulder blades. "I ran into an old girlfriend and had a few more drinks..." He met her eyes with his now, held them, and nearly choked on the words that came next. "I...we...." Tears filled his eyes while he watched the truth dawn on her. "I'm so sorry."

He could have struck her, and it wouldn't have shocked her more. Disbelief made her close her eyes, but it was pain that brought her to her feet. When she finally looked at him again, anger was awakening inside her. "You slept with her?" He reached for her, but she pushed his hand aside, and wandered, stunned across the room.

A fist of fear clutched Jeremy's heart as his betrayal, and the weight of it, settled into her eyes, into her soul. He wanted to go to her, but he knew better. "Christina-"

"Don't say another word to me!" She doubted herself and her judgment, and she was already hearing the voice inside telling her she should have known better. Known better than to trust him and ignore her first impression of him. Beckett, the billionaire playboy, she shuddered and turned her back on him. The speed with which he became a stranger shook her to her very core.

"I wouldn't hurt you, not intentionally, not for anything." But as he sat wringing his hands, even he thought he sounded like an idiotic fool.

He watched while she wrapped her arms around herself for warmth, or more likely comfort. Comfort he wanted so badly to give to her himself. Turned away, shoulders stiff, he felt a chasm already forming between them. "It was just a mistake. A stupid, inexcusable mistake."

She spun around, her eyes glinting like steel from pain. She would face him, damn it, and she wouldn't do it cowering in a corner. "Don't bother defending yourself." Her voice was hollow, quiet, and cold, but she wouldn't cry, wouldn't give him the satisfaction.

He got up, started towards her, and froze when he saw the contempt on her face. "I love you," he said quietly. The words were true, but he watched them cut into her like a blade.

Despite her resolve, her eyes filled, and she damned him all over again. Watching him, she wanted the love she had for him to turn to hate, but it wouldn't. "You don't know the meaning of the word. But then, once a cad, always a cad."

Even furious with him, she was breathtaking. That he hurt her so deeply so completely, sickened him. He shook his head, covered his face with his hands, and nearly wept. "Damn it, you know that's not true."

Her bitter laugh broke free, surprising them both, even while her heart was breaking. "Could've fooled me."

"I was drunk." He dropped his hands, blew out a breath, and met her hard, unforgiving eyes. "That's not an excuse, just a fact. It doesn't take away from how much I love you, from how much you mean to me."

"Oh, yes, I mean so much it took you all of what? Three whole months to slide up against someone else? You're such a trooper." She needed to do something with her hands and went into the kitchen.

He heard slamming cabinet doors and the clink of glass against glass. In another minute, she came back with a glass of wine. "You can go, Jeremy - and the sooner the better."

He went instead, opened the balcony doors, and leaned on the frame with his arms spread wide and his palms flat against the wood. He hung his head and entertained the idea of bashing it against the hard oak frame until oblivion took him. There was more to say. So much, too much. "I'll go if that's what you want, but not until you know the rest."

Meeting his gaze, she straightened. "Don't need a play by play, but thanks," she snapped. "And don't bother with the 'I was lonely bullshit', Jeremy; just get out of my sight."

"This'll blow up in the papers, Christina, you have to be prepared. Someone called in a tip." He walked away from the balcony doors, went to the sofa, and sat. "Photographers came out of the woodwork..." he winced, deciding to get to the point "There'll be pictures in the papers, magazines, and on television by morning."

"Ah." Damage control and not conscience was the reason for his brutal honesty. "So, that's what has you falling on your sword, confessing?" Numbness was finally setting in; she felt dead inside. But there was nothing the press could do to her that could be worse than what the man she loved, and who claimed to love her, had already done.

"That's unfair and untrue, Christina. I've told you because I won't let lies stand between us. It'll be nasty; it'll be an invasion of our privacy on an epic level. They'll paint me as a bastard and you as the wronged woman. They'll bait us for a juicy quote, a story, a piece of our pain."

"Pain you've caused."

"I know it."

"It's not enough to make me a fool privately? It has to be done in public for the entire world to see?"

It was a jab that hurt, but he was in no position to defend his actions. "You'll want to prepare your family."

"My family's no longer your concern."

He ached to hold her. Her green eyes were harsh and unforgiving, her body rigid like granite. The wall between them was already solid and unrelenting, and punishment enough for a lifetime.

"We can work through this."

"There is no 'we' anymore. There's you. There's me. Separate." Christina finished her wine, glaring at him. "I don't want to hear your voice, or see your face, Jeremy. Not ever again."

Stunned, broken, Jeremy turned away from her then, and left without another word. She'd made it painfully clear there was nothing more to say. It was over. When the door closed behind him, he couldn't make his legs move. It wasn't until he heard Christina's racking sobs that his heart finally shattered. So, he carried himself down the hall and out of her life.

~ 15 ~

He bought a seat on a red-eye flight and landed at J.F.K before dawn, just in time to see the first of many stories hit print. The first shot fired in what was sure to be a long and ugly war appeared on the front page of The Globe, and they spared him no kindness at all. They even quoted some of the obscene lines he remembered saying to Emily while, according to eye-witnesses, he 'groped her breast with one hand and downed double shots of scotch with the other.'

It was bad; and it was a safe bet that it would get much worse. Jeremy did his best to make it through the airport without any confrontations with rumormongers and press parasites. He squared his shoulders, took his sunglasses out of his shirt pocket, and shoved them on his face. He'd done all of this to himself - and far worse – he done it to Christina as well.

Jeremy turned a corner with his head down and a baseball cop pulled down low on his head. With the paper under his arm, he was heading for a quick exit. When he saw Linus waiting for him at the end of the long corridor, he swore and headed straight for him. He did not look happy, but then Jeremy wasn't exactly thrilled either. His father's presence meant serious business, and Jeremy tightened his jaw. He sucked in a breath and prepared himself.

Linus stood with his hands pushed deep into the pockets of his fine Italian slacks with his face a mirror of Jeremy's. He watched Jeremy striding towards him with mixed feelings. They locked eyes while Linus rolled his tongue around his teeth and checked his temper. A dark pair of sunglasses covered his eyes, but Jeremy didn't need to see them to know they'd be filled with disappointment over his stupidity.

"You didn't need to meet me, Dad," Jeremy said when they were face to face.

"Like hell," he said in a low voice. "God knows what kind of trouble you'd find without proper supervision."

Jeremy rolled his shoulders and walked past Linus. "Let's go, before we attract attention."

"No bags?" Linus wondered, catching up with Jeremy and steering him to the nearest exit.

"It wasn't a pleasure trip."

"How's Christina then?" Linus asked, spotting an exit about twenty feet away and to the left.

"Pissed."

Linus moved aside to let a woman with a stroller pass him. He quickened his pace and took hold of Jeremy's arm to get him to do the same. "So, it didn't go well?"

Jeremy jammed his hands into his pockets and glanced over his shoulder, feeling people's eyes on him. "Don't start."

Pushing past a small crowd, the two of them reached the door, and Linus shoved it open with more force than necessary. The limo appeared out of nowhere. "You can't really blame her, can you?"

Jeremy winced and yanked his arm away from Linus. "No. I can't." Edward came around and opened the door, and Jeremy dropped inside and leaned his head back on the leather seat without another word.

Linus settled beside him and removed his sunglasses, grateful to be out of public view. "Why in the hell you sent Edward home the other night, I'll never know." He grabbed a glass from the cabinet under the seat and poured himself a brandy. "If you'd let him drive you to that dive you're so damn determined to hang out in, he could've saved your ass."

Jeremy would have argued, but his father was painfully right. Edward would never have let him slink up to his suite with Emily Harris or anyone else. The man could spot trouble a mile away and had spent the better part of the last twenty-five years fixing Beckett messes. In all those years he'd had plenty of practice problem-solving. "I've told myself that about a million times, but it doesn't change anything."

"No, it doesn't," Linus readily agreed. "Your mother is beside herself," he continued lecturing as he sipped the brandy and closed his eyes. A migraine was working its way through his skull. "Take the eighteenth street exit, Edward." He pulled out a cigar and bit off the tip. "She's used to the lies and exaggerations printed about you, but not the awful truth. You'll have to face her next, my boy, and let me tell you, it's going to make what happened with Christina seem like stroll in the park."

Jeremy lowered the window, tipped his glasses down. "I know I fucked up, okay? This is a long-ass route to the Waldorf."

"We're not going to the Waldorf."

"Why?"

"Because at this very moment, journalistic leeches of every variety have the Waldorf surrounded. I'm taking you home." Linus informed him, lighting the end of the cigar and puffing it to life. "They're under the impression you're hiding out in your penthouse to avoid the press - and that's just what we're going to let them think."

"This is ridiculous."

"This may perk you up a bit," Linus said, puffing out a mouthful of smoke. "Tim's found a building to house your inner-city youth project." He gave him a quick smile.

Jeremy sighed, slumped back in the seat, and looked at his father. "Good." Grateful to focus on something other than his misery, his thoughts shifted. "What kind of renovations are we looking at? Can we open the doors in a month?"

"Depends." Linus puffed on his cigar, considering, and flicked ash out the window. "This fiasco of yours shows poor judgment. Poor judgment and financial responsibility don't mesh when you're asking for other people's money. The organizations you're going to hit up for donations might want distance from you."

"Damn."

"Damn, indeed."

~ 16 ~

July
1979

The Beckett Foundation for Inner-city Children opened it doors on schedule, and despite the bad press, with much acclaim. Dozens of prominent families attended the gala with curious minds and, graciously, open checkbooks. Journalists from every major paper in New York attended, crowding the red carpet with microphones, cameras, and questions, some appropriate, but most not, at the ready.

And while the buzz of his one-night stand with Emily Harris was still a hot topic, few people apart from the press were actually rude enough to talk about it openly. Jeremy Beckett, though still thought to be a playboy at heart, was a man who was driven to help those less fortunate than himself.

And Jeremy, surrounded by his family, heard the rumors and whispers daily, and fought to ignore them. He was thankful to have his attention diverted in preparation for the opening. Preoccupation to the point that there was no time to think about the pain eating him up a little bit more every day, and no time to torment himself over how the press were hounding Christina across the country – and knowing he could do nothing to protect her because she wanted nothing more to do with him.

There was no time to wallow when the painting he'd sent for her birthday, 'Central Park at Twilight', came back refused. It wounded him, just as she knew it would, because his heart had been in each and every stroke. Behind the smile plastered on his face, he bled. But in the end, the night proved to be a success, leaving the entire Beckett family breathing a collective sigh of relief.

Early August
1979

Thirty children came through the doors in as many days. Each of them came with his or her own scars. And each and every one of them was carrying chips on their shoulders too enormous to fight. In the paperwork that crossed his desk, each child's history was described in brutal detail. Horror stories of physical and sexual abuse, abandonment, drug addiction, and drug dealing.

The weight of their misery weighed heavily on Jeremy's conscience from day to day. How dare he whine about his problems? Not when children three miles from where he sat were going hungry, suffering rape and the abyss of drugs. His troubles were small in comparison - and self-inflicted.

~~

An afternoon of meetings and conference calls did little to improve his sour mood. He and Linus were butting heads over a buyout nearing completion. The last thing Jeremy wanted to find when he got back to his office was a pile of urgent messages on his desk. Swallowing a groan, he slammed his door shut and crossed to his desk, frowning as he scanned the mess covering it. He picked through the messages, tugging his tie free and praying someone would show up to fix his air conditioning before he melted. He saw her name on more than six of the messages he'd thumbed through, and his stomach dropped even while he dropped into his chair.

All six said the same thing:

"I have to talk with you right away. Please, call me to arrange a time and place. Emily."

His stomach turned sour while his hands raked through his hair. A nervous habit, and hearing from Emily Harris made him very nervous. As their story broke and gained momentum, Emily became a media darling and loved every minute of the attention. She courted the papers and television like a queen addressing her subjects.

Damned if she didn't declare her long-time love for Jeremy and paint their ancient past as effectively as he painted a canvas. She and Jeremy had been lovers in school, convenient sex whenever the mood struck them. But Emily had played them as Romeo and Juliet, and in doing so reduced Christina to nothing more than a mere fling to make her jealous.

Jeremy glanced at his watch and considered his options. Ignoring her would only prolong the inevitable. So he placed the call and held his breath.

"Hello?"

Her tone was soft and polite, but he wasn't in the mood for soft or polite and got to the point. "I got your messages," he said formally. Holding the phone with his chin, Jeremy picked up the files his father sent over and began going through them.

"We need to talk."

"We are."

She closed her eyes, working to keep her voice light. "We've got a problem."

Jeremy bit the inside of his cheek, drummed his fingers on the desk. "I'm the one with the smeared reputation, Emily. I mean, let's just get honest for one damn minute and admit you're sitting pretty right now." His anger surprised him, but he wouldn't apologize for it.

"You'd like it to be that simple," she argued, remembering how he made her feel the morning after, making excuses, professing his love for Christina Wagner. She took a calming breath. Another argument would solve nothing. "But it's a lot more complicated."

He wasn't about to listen to the 'woman scorned' routine. He turned his attention to the paperwork on his desk requiring his signature and picked up a pen. "Fiction often can be. Get to the point."

"Not over the phone. I'll come to your office."

Jeremy had had enough. "No," he paused in his signature. "I don't want more pictures of us in the paper."

"Fine," she said, ignoring his stinging words. "I'm pregnant."

The news dropped like a bomb. "Excuse me?" Jeremy managed while his insides turned to liquid.

"I said I'm pregnant," she repeated. "Eight weeks."

"Eight weeks?" Jeremy's mouth went dry as a cool sweat broke out on his skin. "You're sure it's mine?"

"You're a real prick. The doctor confirmed the pregnancy, Jeremy," she said. "And it's yours, so you better get used to it."

Jeremy cursed under his breath and squeezed his eyes shut. Disbelief, then despair seeped into every pore.

His life as he knew it was over.

~ 17 ~

"I won't do it, Dad," Jeremy blurted out, stalking around the living room unhappily, his shoulders pushed forward and his eyes red from lack of sleep and misery.

Linus felt bad for his son, but there was no room for discussion, and just now he felt a rising sense of frustration and anger to mix with his sympathy. "There's nothing else to do."

Jeremy stopped at the fireplace and leaned on the mantle. With his pride eating away at him, he met his father's eyes. "It's a disaster waiting to happen."

Linus looked away and folded his hands behind his back. He couldn't agree more. But he could see no other way to deal with this crisis. "You'll make it work," he said on an exhale. I won't have my first grandchild being called a bastard, son. Owen's livid, threatening to go to the papers. Your mother's in bed, sick with this whole situation." He went to his son and placed a steady hand on Jeremy's shoulder. "Marry Emily Harris and make this child legitimate. It's the right thing to do."

Jeremy stood up straight, set his jaw, and rolled his shoulders. "Except I don't love her," he said simply. "We're not talking about a business deal, Dad. We're talking about my life - or doesn't that matter to you?"

Linus shook his head. "What matters now is the child," he said reasonably. He looked at Jeremy, sighing at his dejected look. "This baby didn't ask to be brought into this world, so why should he suffer for it? It's time to put this child first - your child, Jeremy, and as your mother has so keenly pointed out, he deserves your name."

Jeremy's heart sank at the mention of his mother. "She supports this? How could she? After always drilling home the importance of love in any marriage, she wants me to marry a one-night stand whom I was stupid enough to get pregnant?"

Linus shrugged and went to the bar to fix a drink. "She's heartbroken about this. We all are, but she's thinking about how to make the best out of a bad situation. And Emily is more than that to you, or at least she was in the past."

Brushing his palm across his cheek, Jeremy realized he was alone with no one to support him. "Emily'll never agree to it. She knows I love Christina."

"She already has, son. And this isn't about love, it's about responsibility." he said, downing his drink in one gulp and slamming the empty highball glass on the bar.

"I'll never love Emily. We're two different people."

"Time works wonders," Linus said quietly. "As for Christina, it's a shame because she's a wonderful girl, but you've burned that bridge. She won't speak to you, and she returned your birthday gift without as much as a word."

"I didn't burn any bridges," Jeremy argued, sliding eyes full of steel to his father. "After some time has passed, she'll forgive me."

"I'm sorry," Linus said, and he meant it. "But think about the press and the damage to your reputation as a respectable businessman. They'll destroy you. And it'll be a nightmare - for no one more than your child." He stood toe-to-toe with his son, and tears dampened his eyes as he took his sons' face in his hands, love filling him. "Cameras with zoom lenses, gossip columns, sound bites...I know you want more for your child."

What could he say to that? He looked into his father's eyes and realized his fate was determined. He'd ruined so much in his life already.

He'd ruined his dreams of a life in the galleries of New York and traded it instead for a life in its boardrooms. Ruined a relationship he knew would have brought him a lifetime of happiness. Ruined the trust and the heart of a woman he loved more than anything. So how could he risk ruining a defenseless child as well? His defenseless child.

Covering his father's hands with his own, the enormity of what was to come settled on his shoulders. He choked back everything that told him what dangerous ground he'd be treading if he married a woman he didn't love, but he knew what would happen to his child if he didn't make the right, and awful, choice. "Okay, Dad...okay."

Late August
1979

The wedding took place one week later in the backyard of the Harris estate. And father of the bride, Owen Harris, always mindful of appearances, made sure both families and hand-picked members of the bona fide press were in attendance. It was hardly the celebration the pictures and accompanying article portrayed. The story would run in the Times society page the following day. Everyone present managed their way through the festivities with forced smiles, stilted laughter, and brave faces.

Jeremy spent the morning trying to get Christina on the phone to tell her about the marriage before she read about it, but she was either not home or not picking up the phone.

Underneath his fixed smile, regret - not joy - coiled in Jeremy's gut. While he watched Emily walk down the aisle toward him, he watched his future slip away. Emily stood beside him, knowing all too well that Jeremy didn't love her and never would, and that, were it not for the baby, the wedding would not be taking place.

Their marriage was a duty; nothing more. Despite that, Emily tried to be hopeful that in time Jeremy would remember their long forgotten love. Jeremy, arm-in-arm with his new wife, smiling for the press and pictures, harbored no such illusions.

On a secluded private island in Greece, Emily chose to pretend her new husband wasn't as miserable as he looked; instead, she relaxed by wading in the ocean and waited for Jeremy to decide to make the best of their life together. She enjoyed the quaint villa and the picturesque scenery and ignored the ghost of the woman her husband truly loved and longed for. It bothered her that Christina, a woman who had shut him out of her life forever, was all Jeremy could think about.

How could he still want her? How could he want her even though she so clearly didn't want him?

To be fair, Jeremy did his best to put Christina out of his mind, and accept that she was no longer a part of his life. To come to terms with the fact that she did not want him anymore. His life had changed whether he liked it or not, and he was still left feeling shell-shocked. And the blue skies, sun, and sand couldn't pull his thoughts away from the past to a future with his new wife.

Walks together on the beach helped in getting to know his wife again, but the closeness of a husband and wife was missing, and they both knew it might never come. While Emily was ready and willing to commit to her marriage in every way, making love was the last thing on Jeremy's mind. No matter how much Emily wanted him, making love with Emily, he felt, would be another betrayal of Christina.

From time to time, she stole a kiss or a warm hug from her husband, but pushing for anything more physical proved humiliating for them both. She did everything short of rape to get him aroused, but nothing worked, and it left them both frustrated. As a result, they returned home to a twelve-room home in Manhattan without consummating their marriage.

~~

Napa Valley

Christina read about the wedding in the society column of The New York Times. Gathering the courage to read the in-depth article took willpower she wasn't sure she possessed, but three glasses of wine gave her the push she needed to choke down every last word.

Christina read through it twice, angry with him and with herself for her tears. The picture of husband and wife felt like a slap in the face. They made an attractive couple, though it pained her to admit it. How could he sleep with Emily Harris, profess his remorse, beg her forgiveness, only to turn around and marry the slut weeks later? She stumbled into the bedroom to sleep off the wine and her churning emotions.

The dark room spun around her while she convinced herself anger would make it easier to let go. Sleep crept in and she knew it was time to move on. It was time to leave him and their past in the past, where it belonged.

Manhattan
September 7, 1979

While the last of the boxes were unpacked at the new Beckett family home, Jeremy and Emily were dealing with awkward silences and struggling to find a comfortable way to co-exist. They'd gone from individuals to a couple within a span of mere months. The differences were conspicuous, and as if to complicate matters further, news of Emily's pregnancy broke in the gossip columns before they were prepared to handle it.

Speculation over the timing of their marriage ran amuck, and wild rumors soon took on a life of their own. In the midst of it all, Jeremy and Emily adjusted to the shocking news that she was carrying twins. In the hopes of riding out the worst of the storm, and keeping Emily's pregnancy as stress-free as possible, Jeremy kept them both out of the public view while things settled down.

Linus and Owen handled the press with a prepared statement on behalf of both families. The statement itself was a work of art, announcing the joy over the impending arrival of the combined family's first grandchildren. Of course, leaving out the hesitation with which the groom entered into his marriage and the doubts of the bride that her husband would ever come to love her, prettied up the new family picture.

In public, they were the perfect couple; in private, perfection was harder to come by. They were tied together by a marriage neither felt ready to handle, two bound people who wanted very different things out of life.

~ 18 ~

His name was Sam Radcliff. He was a promising law student, friend, and neighbor of Christina's, and he was totally besotted with her. He'd walked into that little bar-grill down the street from their apartment building and been taken with her the moment he saw her across the smoke-hazed bar.

Now, months later, they were walking into that same bar and grill, a budding relationship between them, wanting an escape from law books and egg timers. So when the whispering started before they even reached their table, they tried to ignore it and regretted their decision to come. She felt the eyes in the dim light focus on her and made sure to hold her head high, seemingly oblivious to the stares.

Sam wanted to tell them all to mind their own business, but he pulled out her chair for her instead. He slid her closer to the table with her back to the room to protect her. It grated on his patience, the unending invasion of her privacy. The open gawking and hushed, childish whispers of strangers, providing a constant supply of grist for the rumor mill, and there wasn't a damn thing he could do about it.

Sam sat across from Christina in awe. He marveled at her composure while grabbing the bowl of peanuts on the table. "You look cool as a cucumber," he winked, smiled, and said, "and amazing."

Christina smiled defiantly. "Well, it took awhile to achieve coolness. I had to learn not to give in, not to scurry away like a helpless little girl."

Sam grinned and helped himself to more nuts. "Good for you." He scanned the specials on the board above the bar. "How about the fish and chips special?"

"Sounds good to me."

He motioned for a waitress and ordered the specials and two house drafts. "Boy, you sure attract a lot of attention, lady."

She smiled at his teasing. "I hate being put under a damn microscope."

Sam covered her hand with his. "No one can blame you for getting fed up, Chris. Even when you and Beckett were together, they were in your face."

"Even then it was tough to take...but I let Jeremy take the brunt of it. It was just easier."

"Always is when they're rooting for you instead of throwing your problems in your face."

The waitress came with their beer and Sam took a long, satisfying pull. He smiled a little too wide at her when he saw she was staring at Christina. She got the message and went on her way. "If it's any consolation, they're not cutting your ex any breaks either. The party line is he married his wife because he knocked her up."

Christina drank her beer slowly, thoughtfully. "I should want him to suffer, but I don't," she admitted, sliding her fingertip along the edge of the glass. "He might have done a shitty thing to me, but he loved me."

Their food arrived, and they wasted no time digging in. Their waitress didn't make the same mistake twice and left as soon as she put their plates in front of them.

Sam watched her and knew she meant what she said. "That's big of you, Chris," he said, cutting a piece of fish and putting it in his mouth. "Not wanting him to suffer, I mean."

She shrugged her shoulders and stabbed another piece of fish with her fork. "It wasn't totally selfless on my part." She swallowed her fish and popped a few chips in her mouth. "You'd be surprised how much energy it takes to hate someone. I just want to put it all behind me and move on with my life."

Sam licked the salt from his fingertips and lifted a brow. "Really?" He wondered if it was really that simple.

Christina laughed at the serious look on his face. "Don't you believe me?"

"I don't know if you're bullshitting me or not. It's a body language thing. If he hadn't married her, would you've taken him back?"

"Burned those bridges; he hurt me too much."

He finished the last of his fish and pushed his plate to the middle of the table. "I'm just sorry I wasn't here when the shit hit the fan for you all over again. I know the marriage thing hit you pretty hard, so the pregnancy must've been even more of a kick in the gut. You still love him?"

Her eyes narrowed. "You're starting to sound like all those fucking reporters," she said with a look of disdain. "I've moved on - or at least I would if the press would let me. Jeremy has his hands pretty full right now; I'm probably the last thing on his mind."

~~

His desk was piled with files of proposals, and his hand worked at a quick pace, signing off on memos and contracts needing his approval. He glanced at his watch and squeezed his eyes shut. He guessed that he had at least two more hours of work before he could leave for the night.

His eyes wandered to the painting of Central Park, a gift returned, hanging on his wall; an unending punishment for hurting the woman he'd painted it for. He thought about her still, though not as constantly as he had in the beginning. The ache was still there in the quiet moments.

He dropped his pen, forcing his thoughts back to the present. He picked up the phone and dialed home. Emily answered, sounding out of breath.

"It's me," he said, turning to the window to look out over the city. "You alright? You sound tired."

"I'm okay," she answered. "Burning the midnight oil?"

Jeremy closed his eyes at the slight edge in her voice. The last thing he wanted was to fight with her. "Yeah, but I'll be home soon."

Emily sighed. "Will you?"

Jeremy sighed, too. "Emily, please. I just wanted to let you know you shouldn't hold dinner for me."

"I ate hours ago, Jeremy," she replied, impatience ringing through every word. "It's after eight already. You need to decide how long this hide-and-seek game of yours is going to continue, because I'm getting pretty tired of having a husband who is missing in action." And with that final barb, she hung up the phone.

His year-long commitment to Beckett Industries had come and gone. When he stayed, no one was more surprised than he. That he needed the escape to make life with a woman he didn't love tolerable only made him sad. Denial, he discovered, could be a wonderful thing.

Lately, he was feeling guilty about all the time he stayed away from home, but he just couldn't be the husband Emily thought he could be. His heart wasn't in it, and he doubted it ever would be. That made him a son of a bitch, but at least it was honest.

So Emily Beckett battled back the only way she knew how: by settling into her fifth month of pregnancy and putting the finishing touches on the nursery. It had doubled in size from the blueprints with the news of twins. A home would be provided for her children, and if she had to bully her husband until he stopped fighting and gave them the chance they deserved at real happiness, she would do exactly that.

~~

Jeremy was determined to keep things cordial and comfortable with Emily. For their children and for himself there needed to be at least contentment in the absence of love or passion. A secure home, if not a happy one.

Spending late hours at his office and maintaining a distance between he and his wife was far easier than forcing himself to feel things he just couldn't. Hiding was easier than trying to pretend. How, he wondered miserably, was he supposed to love someone who he hardly even liked?

An escape was needed, so he handled the more complicated negotiations for his father. His hands were in all aspects of Beckett Industries, and he was able to do it all with an ease that, little more than a year ago, he would never have imagined possessing.

Linus raved about his business finesse, and there could be no doubt within the hierarchy of the company that he had become an extremely talented asset in the family empire. Jeremy wouldn't argue, but he wouldn't celebrate either. His passion still lay in his painting, but it had been months since he'd picked up a brush.

~~

Months passed, and Jeremy's feelings about his marriage gradually began to change. He was tired of being miserable and feeling like an intruder in his own home, not to mention weary of seeing pain in Emily's eyes when she looked at him. The time for self pity was over; God knows Linus drilled that into his head at every opportunity.

But it needed to be his choice, and late one night when he slipped into bed beside Emily and felt the sure kick of his babies under his palm that he made his decision. It was time to make the best of the life he had before him. He made an effort to be a support to the mother of his children, to get to know her again and forge some kind of a bond.

He started coming home from the office early so they could have dinner together. He freed up a few of his busier evenings to attend birthing classes with Emily. And without being asked, he cleared his schedule to go to her checkups with her.

Maybe it was impending fatherhood or the talks he had with Emily in their bedroom after a long tedious day at the office. Or maybe it was finally acceptance from both of them that fitting into a marriage that was less than blissful required a sense of humor. He'd make his marriage as successful as possible, for his children, for his wife, and for himself.

Emily loved him, and he slowly came to realize she always had. She went out of her way to make him happy in their new home and with their new life together. She wore her feelings for him close to the surface and made no apologies - feelings he hadn't returned, and guilt became a weight on his heart.

When he finally gave in and made love to her as her husband, it was six months after their wedding night. She wasn't Christina, the woman he couldn't find a way to stop loving; yet, he cared for Emily. Maybe not as intensely or as deeply, but his feelings for his wife were becoming meaningful and important to him nonetheless.

~~

After another long day in meetings, Jeremy pulled into the circular driveway and stopped in front of the steps. He shut off the car on a sigh and looked at his home through the car window. It hid the turmoil going on inside very well, he thought. It lacked warmth, feelings always present in his home when he was a little boy. But, warmth came with time, and so did love. He wondered, thinking of Emily, if there were enough time in the world.

He thought about her often, hoping passion and need for her would come eventually. Money and standing mattered to her. She laughed, but rarely at herself. A quiet evening at home felt more like a punishment to her than a pleasure. So they were different - shouldn't they enjoy the differences?

Getting out of the car, he couldn't help noticing the light in their bedroom window. She was frustrated with him, and he couldn't blame her, really. He put up emotional walls the moment they married, walls Emily Beckett had grown tired of trying to climb.

He leaned back into the car to grab his briefcase, then frowned at the house. Emily was miserable, and with her swollen feet and back spasms, Jeremy grew more concerned with each passing day. Her back pain grew more severe with every pound she gained, and her doctor had ordered complete bed rest for the remainder of her pregnancy.

~ 19 ~

He walked up the staircase and down the hall. When he pushed open the door, Emily glanced up from the book she was reading, and for a moment their eyes met. Jeremy smiled and came in, closing the door behind him and dropped his briefcase on the plush carpet.

"I was beginning to wonder if you'd ever get home." The condition of their marriage had improved over the past two months. The holiday helped, even though they were not yet beaming newlyweds.

One look at her, and Jeremy knew Emily wasn't having a comfortable night. Propped up on pillows with her feet elevated to relieve the swelling, it was hard to miss the misery in her voice. He loosened his tie, and, trying to read her mood, went to the bed to lean down and kiss her. "I was hoping you'd be asleep."

Emily laughed, putting her book aside and looked closely at Jeremy. "I'm seven and a half months pregnant. Sleep is no longer an option."

He chuckled and dropped down on the bed with a sigh, kicking off his shoes. "Just keep reminding yourself, you're in the home stretch."

Emily smiled ruefully, shaking her head. "If you think either of us will ever sleep again once these babies come, you're dreaming." She began kneading the tight muscles in his shoulders when he leaned back against her.

He groaned, enjoying the soothing massage of his tired knotted muscles. Thankful she wasn't spoiling for a fight tonight, he relaxed into the warmth of her hands on his skin. "We'll grab a few minutes here and there."

~~

Christina had other things on her mind besides the drive into wine country with Sam. The permanent crease in her forehead told Sam who was on her mind. She was thinking about Beckett again. If he'd only be honest with himself, he'd admit he'd come to expect the faraway look in her eyes when she thought he wasn't looking. Expecting it, however, didn't mean he had to accept it. "Earth to Christina."

She looked at him blankly. "Did you say something?"

Sighing, he rolled down his window for some air. "Forget it."

Christina realized she'd been ignoring him. "Sam."

Sam looked at her and cleared his throat, squinting in the afternoon sun. "Don't you ever get tired of tying yourself up in knots?"

"I'm not doing that," she said, annoyed.

"Yes, Chris, you are, like it or not." He pinned her with his intense blue eyes and kept pushing, even when he knew better. "Here I am trying to get you out from behind cookbooks and locked doors, and you still pine for him."

Her temper strained; this wasn't something she wanted to examine too closely. "You're being an ass."

He slammed on the brakes and glared at her, matching temper to temper. "Get your head outta the sand and wake up. The man has a wife, and in a month he's gonna have two kids, as you keeping pointing out to every goddamn reporter who corners you. If you're so angry with him, let him go!"

Stunned into silence, she could only gape at him, her eyes bright with tears. She hadn't been fair to Sam, and it had taken his explosion to see it. Turning to the window, she looked out at the woods that lined the road and said nothing at all.

~~

January 4, 1980
Manhattan, NY

Emily's keeling moan woke Jeremy, and he found the sheets wet underneath him. For a few disoriented seconds, he wondered why. Two breaths later, though, the explanation hit him like a sucker punch. He turned to Emily, threw back the sheets, and found that her nightgown was soaked. He bolted up in bed and turned on the light with his heart pounding.

He leaned close and tried to keep them both from panicking. He wasn't sure how, but her water had broken, but it had. He heard her sharp intake of breath and pressed the back of his hand to her cheek. "It's going to be alright."

Emily only moaned and clutched at his hand in desperation. She knew something was wrong, but she couldn't give voice to her fear before a contraction stole her breath. Unbearable pressure seemed to pin her to the bed, and a dull pain centered in her stomach. She clutched at the soaked sheets, and through a ragged pant, cried, "Jeremy, something's wrong!" Emily looked at him with terror in her eyes.

Jeremy eased her up to the headboard and got out of bed, yanking the blankets to the floor as he did. "Just try to stay calm." He grabbed her hand

and squeezed it reassuringly. "Your water broke." The fear in her eyes matched his. "I'm calling an ambulance, and then Dr. Riker."

January 4, 1980
5:07 a.m.
Manhattan General Hospital

Freezing rain slowed the ambulance considerably. The contractions were five minutes apart by the time they pulled up to the emergency entrance. Emily was screaming through her breathing techniques. Jeremy jumped out and followed as the EMTs rolled her into the ER.

"I'm right here, Emily." He took her hand, running beside her as they rushed her down the hall into maternity.

Her face was wet with perspiration as another contraction sliced through her. "Jeremy, God, it hurts!" She twisted and contorted while Jeremy stroked her cheek and tried to keep her still. Panic was all over her face, and fear shone in her eyes.

The senior EMT rattled off her vitals to the nurse. "Twenty-two years old, thirty-two weeks pregnant, water broke, contractions progressing in route, about five minutes apart."

Jeremy's eyes swept the hall, frantic to see the familiar face. "Where the hell's Riker?" he demanded as a nurse came around and slipped a blood pressure cuff on Emily's arm.

"He's on his way, Mr. Beckett," the nurse said calmly, frowning at the pressure dial. "Let's get her into a labor room now."

Moments later, they were wheeling her into a private room and hooking up a fetal monitor. Two more nurses rushed into the room and put her feet in stirrups to check her dilation. Jeremy heard them, but he was focused on Emily. He was berating himself, thinking that Emily's premature labor was his fault.

"She's almost completely dilated."

"It's too early," Jeremy blurted out.

"Tell that to the babies," the nurse said smiling, trying to reassure him. She'd seen many first-time fathers look the same. "Don't worry, Mr. Beckett. Dr. Riker will take care of them all."

Jeremy braced himself for another contraction as Emily gasped and grabbed the front of his shirt. He tossed a glance back at the nurse. "Where the hell is he?"

As if on cue, Dr. Riker walked swiftly into the room. "Right here," he replied, grabbing the chart from the nurse. He sat down on the stool, snapped on a pair of surgical gloves, and lifted the drape that covered Emily, checking her progress.

"Can't you do something?" Jeremy asked as another contraction sent Emily rearing up off the bed. He did his best to calm her, pushing her back against the pillows and trying to pant with her through the contraction.

"Yes, deliver your babies. She's ready, nine centimeters," he replied, rolling over to read the monitor. "We play the cards we get, Jeremy." He ripped off the readout tape and nodded for Jeremy to follow him out the door.

In the hall, Dr. Riker looked Jeremy squarely in the eye as the soon to be father demanded, "Just say it. She's a month premature, and there'll be problems."

Dr. Riker put a hand on Jeremy's shoulder. "Take it easy. This doesn't have to be a disaster. It's not the best situation to be in with twins, but we've got her pressure under control, that's something. Her contractions are four minutes apart. It's time."

Riker went back in the room and told the nurse to get incubators ready and get the neonatal attending right away.

~~

7:30 am

Jeremy paced across the waiting room floor, his hair askew and his shirt loose and wrinkled. He hadn't wanted to leave Emily's side, but Dr. Riker needed room to work. He called his parents and Owen Harris. With any luck, there would be something to tell them when they arrived.

The first hour crept by with Jeremy feeling helpless and frustrated. Emily's pressure went from one extreme to the other, and exhaustion left her drained and delirious. Dr. Riker's face was taut with concern. Precious seconds were lost while her pressure nosedived, and she lost consciousness. The next thing Jeremy knew, he was being ushered out of the delivery room against his will.

He hadn't heard anything in thirty minutes. The last time he was updated, he was told Dr. Riker was preparing to take the babies by Caesarian Section. He would have to be patient - but his patience was wearing thin.

~~

10:30 am
Manhattan General Hospital

Five hours of labor with no news put everyone's nerves on edge. Linus and Elise flanked Jeremy on one sofa while Owen sat wringing his hands in a chair across the room. Tensions between them were obvious, and the uncomfortable silence only made the strain worse. Jeremy stood and was about to pace off nervous energy when he noticed Dr. Riker coming down the hall.

Desperate for news, Jeremy met him in the doorway and stammered, "Is she alright?" The question hung in the air, with all eyes in the room on Riker.

Dr. Riker wiped his forehead with his palm and nodded. "She lost a lot of blood, but she pulled through." Riker pulled off his surgical cap and met Jeremy's hopeful eyes. "She's in recovery; you can see her in a bit.

Congratulations, you have a daughter and a son." He waited while there was back-slapping all around.

Jeremy blew out a breath, feeling like he hadn't breathed in hours, then grabbed his father's shoulder in relief. "Can I see them?"

"We need to talk first," Dr. Riker cautioned.

Jeremy read the serious look in Riker's eyes and leveled his shoulders. "What is it?"

"There's a problem." Riker led them all over to the sofa and waited while they all got settled. "The twins are in remarkable condition, considering their weight and prematurity, but right now they're having some trouble breathing, particularly your son." He watched as their collective faces fell.

"So what can you do to help them?" Jeremy fought the sinking feeling in his stomach and focused on Riker's face.

"We've put them on respirators and given them antibiotics to stabilize them and fight off any infections."

Jeremy stiffened. "I want to see them."

"Of course." Riker pushed himself to his feet and turned to the family. "The rest of you are welcome to look in through the hall window."

"Let's go." Jeremy made a beeline for the door with Dr. Riker trailing behind him.

~ 20 ~

One Week Later

Seven days. Seven days since the birth of little Debra Ann and Nathaniel Avery Beckett. Small gifts, Elise Beckett had gushed when she first saw them. Small and fragile, with their father's noses and cleft in their chins.

Debra weighed in at four pounds and one half ounce, and her brother weighed in at four pounds even. Their arrival might have been early and dramatic, but they seemed content as they lay in the incubators, no doubt wondering about their new surroundings. Seeing their father for the first time they started wailing mightily. Jeremy wondered as he touched their tiny hands, if they could already feel how much they were loved.

He had never seen anything so tiny and vulnerable before. It humbled and frightened him to imagine the battle they would have to wage for these two precious lives. The cynical vein in him hadn't thought it possible. To love so quickly and completely, but standing there, wanting so desperately to breathe for them, he knew his love for his children was an instantaneous and powerful thing.

There was light at the end of the tunnel and he was grateful for it. Little Debra made progress with each passing day. Gaining an ounce or two, her lungs growing stronger with every passing hour (if her fussy cry was any indication), she had her father wrapped around her tiny little finger.

Nathaniel, though, was a constant worry for them. His irregular heart rhythms, and the narrowing of his nasal cavity, weren't his only problems. One of his tiny lungs kept collapsing. His son, with hair the color of his father's, clung to life by the thinnest of threads, but Jeremy saw in him a tiny warrior with a will to survive; he could only pray he was right.

Linus flew in the country's best pediatric specialist, Dr. Simon Jones. He arrived, taking over the care of the Beckett twins less than forty-eight hours after their birth. He met with Emily and Jeremy in her hospital room after his examination of Debra and Nathaniel. He pulled no punches while he delivered his diagnosis.

"Your children have under-developed lungs that steroids have yet to help." He sat on the edge of Emily's bed and met their troubled eyes straight on. "They're having difficulty breathing on their own, Nathaniel much more so than Debra."

"Will they survive?" It was Jeremy who asked the wrenching question.

"Their odds improve daily." He patted Emily's hand and stood. "I'll do everything in my power to help them." Shaking Jeremy's hand, he turned for the door. "Get some rest. Your children need you both to be strong for them."

~~

Emily, so emotionally undone over the condition of the children, couldn't look at them without breaking down. Dr. Riker said she was most likely suffering from depression brought on by a hormone imbalance. Then came the news that she would never be able to become pregnant again - the result of the emergency hysterectomy performed to save her from bleeding to death - only made her all the more inconsolable. So it fell to Jeremy to pick up the pieces and be the strength for his children and his wife.

He stayed with the twins for hours at a time, rarely leaving the N.I.C.U. His place was with his children and Emily, who was now sedated and unable to nurture them herself. From the moment they drew their first difficult breath, they were his to soothe, his to encourage. He had no intention of letting his son or daughter go without a fight.

Jamie spent as much time at the hospital as Emily's wild mood swings and crying would allow. It was a sacrifice she was willing to make so Jeremy could focus on the twins. Linus would come every afternoon to drag him outside for fresh air. Until the press crawled out from under their rocks and went on the attack, father and son could look up into the bright crisp sky and talk around the fears that haunted them both.

"Has the doctor seen the babies today?" Linus asked, strolling along beside his son. His heart was twisting in his chest over the grief he saw on Jeremy's face.

Jeremy stopped, tipped his head back, and sucked in a deep, fresh breath. "Early this morning," he finally said. "There hasn't been much positive change for Nathan. But Debra's vital signs are getting better."

Linus thinned his lips and looked hard at the pavement under his feet. "They're stronger than we give them credit for. Babies, I mean," he said thoughtfully. "And they're Becketts, don't forget. Tough as nails by nature." He gave his son a small smile, trying to comfort him.

"Please...don't, Dad." Jeremy said, pained, dark circles beneath his eyes, turning away. "Don't stand here and tell me this is just a bump in the road." Shoving his hands in his pockets, he blinked back tears, focusing on a big cloud in the crisp blue sky above him. "We're talking about little babies who should still be in their mother's womb thriving, still getting ready for life."

"I know, son," Linus said quietly, wrapping his arm around the broad shoulders of his firstborn. "But we've just got to hang in there, ride it out."

~~

Jeremy would have stayed with his children around the clock, if only the staff would leave him in peace. The constant beeping of the machines helping his children survive were a comfort to him. Sometimes, he felt like he was a drowning man, struggling to break through to the surface to draw air. Day would turn into night before the nurses could convince him to go stretch his legs, or to go eat something more solid than the crackers and soda from the hallway vending machines.

He would go to Emily and sit with her, holding her hand, trying to be a source of strength. He tried to get her to talk about their babies' futures, tried to get her to connect with them as the living children they were and not children already lost to them. Bright futures and big dreams awaited them, and he wouldn't accept anything less.

~~

"Maybe we're getting what we deserve," Emily mumbled on her first night home from the hospital. She and Jeremy were sitting at the dining room table picking at their food in silence.

As they so often were now, her cheeks were wet from fresh tears. She was a young mother haunted by the thought that this was God's way of punishing her; of saying she was incapable of being a good mother. With her face drawn and pale and her eyes glassy from medication, she murmured on, "We kind've stumbled into this, and now our kids are paying for it."

Jeremy sighed deeply, trying to work all the knots in his neck loose. "Don't, Emily." He leaned over toward her and waited for her to look at him. His head was pounding, and he wanted to get back to the hospital. "What's going on has nothing to do with punishment. You need to focus on the positive. Debra's getting stronger, so will Nathan."

Emily shook her head and fought back more tears. She could swear she has cried a river of tears, but tears wouldn't help her little boy. "He's so sick," she sobbed, pushing herself away from the table. "I'm afraid, Jeremy. I'm afraid we're going to lose him."

"No." he snapped, getting up from the table to go to her. "You can't let yourself think like that, we have to fight for him and pray he gets stronger, Emily. And we have to be grateful Debra's doing so well."

She pulled away from him to pace, and he worried about her, watching her shadow move along the wall as she passed by him again and again. He could see her nerves were warring away inside her. Lately, she seemed as fragile as their children. He wondered if she came home too soon, and if she would ever be the strong, willful woman he married again.

~ 21 ~

Debra's steady improvement buoyed everyone's hopes, and smiles transformed the faces of those who loved her most, as they marveled at her progress. Her color was better now that and she was finally able to breathe on her own. She had her mother's eyes and her father's sandy hair, and she stole the heart of everyone on the N.I.C.U floor.

But the celebration was short lived.

Nathaniel took a sudden turn for the worse as his temperature spiked and an infection further compromised his lungs. Emergency surgery was performed, and tubes were inserted into his lungs to drain fluid caused by the rapidly moving infection. Doctor Jones considered his survival thus far a miracle. Together, Jeremy and Emily stood at the window of the N.I.C.U., watching their son wage his fight to live, and prayed for a miracle to save him.

~~

When the phone rang at the Beckett home, Jeremy was fresh from the shower and heading for a cup of coffee. "Hello," he said, apprehension moving up his spine while he held his breath. When the phone rang these days, fear moved through him, nearly suffocating him.

His worst fear was finally, painfully, recognized as Dr. Jones told him to return to the hospital right away. Nathan had stopped breathing when both of his lungs collapsed. He and Emily raced to the hospital, running red lights and nearly causing two accidents along the way. They left the car at the emergency entrance and ran to N.I.C.U.

Jeremy was terrified and out of breath as he spoke with the doctor. "Is he..." he risked meeting the somber eyes of Dr. Jones. Dread twisted in his gut as he stole a glance at Nathan through the window. "He's not..."

"We've got him breathing again." Dr. Jones quickly replied, taking Emily, whose fear was a palpable presence, by the arm and walking her to the window overlooking Nathaniel's incubator. He waited as Jeremy came up beside him. "But I'm afraid his condition is deteriorating, despite everything we're doing for him."

Jeremy stared at his son, a lump growing in his throat. *Such a small boy*, he thought, looking down at his tiny featured face. Tape that had been protecting his sensitive eyes from the harsh florescent lights in the unit had finally been removed. How much Jeremy wanted to look into his son's eyes. His impossibly small chest rose and fell with so much effort.

"What're you saying, Dr. Jones?" He went to Emily, folding her in his arms. "Are you telling us our son's going to die?"

Simon Jones looked every bit as worn and tired as he felt. He was dressed in wrinkled scrubs and a white physician's coat. His hair was a mess, and his eyes sagged from too many hours without sleep. The day had been a long and frustrating one.

It frustrated him beyond measure to not be able to help the tiny boy on the other side of the window, but there was just too much going against Nathaniel Beckett to save him. After a telling look at his parents, he needed to decide if false hope was better than no hope at all.

"The infection breaking down his lungs is spreading," he said quietly, knowing the devastating blow he was delivering. "Both his liver and his spleen are now infected as well. His respiration's shallow and becoming more labored. I'm afraid it's only a matter of time."

Emily's broken moan as she collapsed against Jeremy brought the rest of the family out of the waiting room across the hall. As sobs racked her body and tears left tracks down her cheeks, Jeremy was choking on tears of his own when he tucked her head firmly under his chin and sank with her to the floor. Shutting his eyes to the pain, he refused to believe it.

"There has to be something more we can do for him." His voice was desperate, his miserable brown eyes pleading.

Dr. Jones only shook his head. "I'm afraid it's up to God now."

~~

Jeremy looked at his watch and then at Emily sleeping in a rocker next to Nathan's incubator. It was nearly one in the morning, and they had been sitting with Nathan for hours now, watching him fight for every breath. Aching for him, and praying God would let them keep their son, both he and Emily were exhausted. So he draped a cover over her and kissed her softly on her forehead. Then he went to Debra's incubator to see his little girl.

He smiled at her, surprised and delighted to find her awake and looking him right in the eye. "Hey, sweet girl." His voice was whisper soft as he lifted her into his arms and cradled her, careful of the tubes in her arms and nose.

"How's my little one doing?" He held her until she fell asleep and kissed her softly before laying her back in the incubator. "Sleep, little one." He brushed his fingers over her cheeks. "Dream big dreams."

His head jerked up in surprise when the door opened and Simon Jones stepped quietly inside. He nodded and walked to Nathaniel's incubator. He checked his color, his vitals, and his breathing before opening his chart.

Meeting Jeremy's penetrating gaze, he shook his head to the silent question. "It's good she finally getting some rest," he said quietly, noticing Emily asleep in the rocking chair. "You could use some, too."

Jeremy laced his fingers behind his neck and stretched, taking a deep breath. "Is he suffering?" he asked. But one look at his son, and he knew the answer.

"I don't think so, Jeremy. His organs are shutting down, his heart rate's dropping. I honestly don't know what's kept him hanging on this long." At the pained expression on Jeremy's face, he laid a strong hand on his shoulder in support. It was the worst kind of pain to lose a child. "I'm very sorry."

"Can I hold him?"

"I think that's a good idea." He smiled and squeezed Jeremy's shoulder. "Babies respond well to the touch of their parents. They feel secure."

Jeremy picked his son up carefully and eased himself into the nearest rocker. He wondered, as his eyes filled with tears, if his son felt the waves of love surrounding him as he lay struggling for breath in his arms. He lowered his cheek to Nathan's warm forehead. "How's my boy, huh?"

Simon Jones had witnessed many bittersweet moments with families over the years. Too much empathy could be a liability in his profession, but watching this father take his dying son in his arms touched him deeply. "I've called your family. They'll be here shortly." He walked silently to the door. "I'll give you some time alone."

~~

The neonatal unit filled with family as precious minutes passed and Nathan grew weaker. Jeremy's parents stood at his shoulders while Owen Harris smoothed his palm over Emily's hair as she wept. Jeremy held his son close, whispering sweet, gentle words in his ear while Jamie sat at his feet, a comforting hand on his knee.

When more tears came, he let them fall. With Nathaniel's tiny hand squeezing his little finger, his heart broke. His son's tiny head lay nestled into the warm crook of his neck, his labored breaths fluttering against Jeremy's skin for the briefest of seconds. As he felt his son's last breath and the sudden stillness of his body, Jeremy closed his eyes, biting back on a sob. He knew he'd remember this moment forever. The monitor flat lined, the wheezing stopped. The only sound in the room when the machines were turned off was the weeping of those left behind.

Nathaniel Avery Beckett died at four-twenty in the morning. He lived ten short days. Emily and Jeremy kissed him goodbye and wept openly. Their family changed forever the moment their son left this life for the next.

~ 22 ~

Ten Years Later
February 1990
Long Island, NY

The Avenue would be filling up for the noon crunch, and Christina's day, already impossible and getting worse, began well before the sun. The fresh produce she was counting on was late. The delivery truck was caught in a major traffic jam, leaving the kitchen staff, and her afternoon chef in particular, in an uproar.

Salads were popular with her lunch-time regulars, and without fresh romaine, loose-leaf lettuce, and fresh spinach, the only lettuce left to serve would be the less popular, and harder to move, iceberg. She had a splitting headache, and her staff was acting like brats. This, she mused while pressing her thumbs to her temples, must be what it's like to have disagreeable children.

The Avenue, the second of her small but modest restaurants, had only been open six months, the success or failure of which was hanging by the thinnest of threads. The last thing she needed was to disappoint a new and growing clientele.

Her first love was the restaurant that started it all, Manhattan Special. She'd opened its doors on her twenty-fourth birthday with her seed money, socked away after years of waiting tables, pushing drinks, and smiling at the right men, laughing at their jokes, and tolerating the rare drunken backside slap. Her building success at fulfilling her dream made every drink served and every nerve frayed well worth it.

Her savings, coupled with the wisely invested insurance money from her mother's policy, provided her the means to take her shot at her dream. The first year had been a struggle, and everyone who was anyone in the restaurant business thought she was a bad joke risking financial ruin. Too young, they said. Too immature, too inexperienced, they said. But top quality cuisine couldn't be denied, and word of mouth had been swift. The proof lay in the dishes she prepared and served, the atmosphere she provided, and the inviting and friendly service. And now, a handful of years later, it remained one of the hottest spots in Manhattan.

The decision to open its sister restaurant, The Avenue, was a risk no one thought she should take, though. If it had been a financial risk to open one restaurant, it could very well be financial suicide to open two. Sam had been the voice of calm and reason that she needed to take the chance. After over a decade of friendship and love, Christina trusted him above everyone else.

At her desk in the back office, she dropped her head into her hands as her head waitress complained about the afternoon chef. "Lucy, do me a favor and try to get along with Henry, please?" It was a plea of desperation as her head pounded and more problems closed in. She'd been fighting a cold for over a week and right at the moment she felt miserable. "Today, of all days, I can't have him leaving in a huff, threatening to quit."

Lucy was a petite blonde, all curves and charm, heavy with her makeup and light on patience. Her hands on her slim hips, chin lifted in defiance, she looked less than forgiving. "He's in the kitchen right now, throwing a fit about no fresh tomatoes for his red sauces, no greens for salads, no peppers to stuff or use for garnish." She cracked her gum loudly and blew out a breath, causing her bangs to flutter on her forehead. "He's a pain in my ass."

Christina nodded, sighing. Henry could be a handful. He was old-world and set in his ways and still coming to terms with having a woman for a boss. Laying her palms flat on the desk, she pushed herself to her feet. "Yours and everyone else's, Lucy, trust me." She moved over to the window, rubbing her temples and frowning out at the falling snow. "This snow keeps up, and we won't have to worry about fresh produce because no one in their right mind would come out and face a mess like this."

"Oh, we'll get a full load," Lucy said as if it were a certainty, "and that's why we need our fearless leader in her kitchen. Henry'll be drivin' us crazy, bitchin' and moanin' when people bark out orders he won't be able to fill since the damn truck never showed."

Christina lifted a shoulder and turned to Lucy. "I wish I could. I'll talk to him, calm him down," she promised, already thinking about how to smooth things over with Henry and handle the produce shortage. "Push the chowder and the pasta with the white sauces. Soup of the day is long grain rice and chicken. Really talk them up."

With one problem solved, she made her way to the kitchen to deal with Henry. She wished for two more sets of hands, ten more hours in her day as her head throbbed, and her throat grew sorer with every swallow. The dining room was already filling up. Any other day that would have thrilled her; today, it just added pressure.

~~

Linus watched her from the doorway in silence, scrutinizing every move, every minute detail of her expression. His wife was tired, weak, and pale more often than not. His worry for her consumed him. She hadn't been sleeping, and when she didn't sleep, he certainly didn't. They'd consulted more specialists who ran more tests and advised rest and a strict vitamin regimen.

This woman he had loved for more than thirty-five years was in pain but willing to suffer in silence just to keep him from worrying. She was having her lunch where she felt most at ease. He remembered when he first showed her the blue prints of this sun room when they broke ground on the house. Pure delight had warmed her eyes all those years ago, and she had favored this room from the day they moved in.

One look at her pensive face as she studied her food told him her appetite had not returned. He'd seen her strength depleted to the point of being unable to stand. Seen her bedridden for days at a time, too exhausted for even a simple, soaking bath.

And all he could do was sit helplessly by do nothing. A man at the helm of an international company, able to divide and devour any weaker company at will, was not a man used to doing nothing. He crossed the sunlit room, carefully covering his growing concern on the way.

"So, here you are," Linus said brightly, coming up behind her chair to press a kiss to her cheek. "I was beginning to think you ran off with that gardener you hired and left me behind."

Elise chuckled and touched her fingers to his chin. "Afraid not, dear."

Linus sat down across from her and began untying his tie. He wouldn't be going back into the office today. He needed to be close to her for his own peace of mind. "Just as well, I'd be useless without you."

She smiled, picking up half of her sandwich. "That's why I'm still around," she said, taking her first bite.

He pulled his tie from around his neck and watched her pecking at her food. "You're feeling poorly again."

"What else is new?"

"We should reconsider the clinic in Sweden."

Elise looked over at him warily. "I'm too tired to go to the mailbox, let alone Sweden."

Linus sighed. "You need the best possible care."

She took his hand and pulled it to her lips. She loved him more and more every day. And knowing him as she did, she knew he hated that he couldn't fix this for her after a lifetime of fixing anything in business. "You're far too busy for an extended trip."

"I'm never too busy for you," he countered.

She picked up her fork and stabbed at her salad. "Jeremy called earlier. He's dropping Debra off for a sleepover so he and Emily can go to the charity guild dinner."

"Sounds like fun. I'll tell the cook to break out the hamburgers and fries."

"I'm worried about him."

"Jeremy?" Linus asked, leaning back in his chair and lifting his wife's feet into his lap.

"Yes." She lifted a fork full of chives to her mouth and looked at Linus. "I think he and Emily are having problems."

Linus sighed, beginning to massage her feet. "She's been difficult to handle lately."

~ 23 ~

Summer
1990

Linus rapped on the door and stuck his head in to find Jeremy behind his desk, elbow deep in financial projections and mumbling under his breath. His son, he decided, was a chip off the old block, but wouldn't appreciate hearing it. He strolled in, looking around at Jeremy's paintings on the walls; some, he noticed, were new. "Hey, son. Looks like you've got your hands full."

Jeremy spared his father a brief glance before turning his attention back to his work. "It's been a busy day." He scribbled his initials on a report and moved it over to the finished pile. "What's up?"

"Just wanted to let you know I've scheduled a lunch with Hancock's board chairman for tomorrow," he replied, looking at his son's latest painting. It was vivid with colors and details. "Tim and I want you to join us."

"I haven't had much to do with the Hancock deal, and it's about wrapped up anyway, Dad," he pointed out, looking up at his father. He'd spotted Jeremy's latest painting. The man was completely out of his element in the face of art of any kind. "I call it 'Hidden Within.'"

Linus pulled his attention away from the engrossing painting, interest and confusion warring in his eyes.

Jeremy got up and came around the desk, pointed to the painting. Careful to hide his amusement, he studied it himself for a second and could understand his father's confusion. "It's my latest, and my most unusual."

Linus nodded, sliding his hands into his pockets. He angled his head, knowing nothing of abstract art, though he would never admit that to his son. "I'd say so. Certainly is an eye-catcher though."

Jeremy, realizing this was a compliment, grabbed it. "Yes, it is that." They looked at the painting together for a moment. "So, anyway, why the in-person invitation?"

Linus shifted his eyes from the painting to Jeremy again, went to the couch, and sat down. "Because we'll be having lunch at Manhattan Special," he said, preparing for the onslaught, "and I wanted to warn you."

He felt his chest tighten and a quick, sharp pain at the suggestion. "There are plenty of places in this city to have lunch."

Well, Linus thought, reading the rigid glint in Jeremy eyes, *he took that much better than expected*. "This is business, son. Nothing says it has to be personal; in fact, it shouldn't be. Hancock's chairman heard the food's great, not a bad place for networking, and after tomorrow he'll need to be doing just that. I want to coddle him, keep him happy. Until he signs those papers, it could go either way. I want this deal pushed through."

~~

His annoyance with Linus propelled Jeremy through the rest of his day. He finished his paperwork and left his office before six for the first time in over a month. He arrived home in time to sit down to dinner. As distracted as he was, it faded away the moment his little girl greeted him by wrapping her arms around his waist and kissing him hello.

With a smile, he lifted her into his arms. "Where's Mama?" he asked, hugging Debra and stooping to set his briefcase inside the hallway entrance. He walked into the dining room with her still in his arms and inhaled the aroma coming from the kitchen.

"Upstairs, getting dressed."

Thoughts of Christina shifted to the background as he thought of Emily and the familiar worry coursed through him. He knew what 'getting dressed' meant. It meant she had spent the day in bed while their daughter was left to amuse herself. He tugged at his daughter's pigtail. "I think I'll go up and tell her dinner's ready."

"Okay, hurry up though, Frannie made pot roast." Her eyes gleamed as she licked her lips. Pot roast was one of her favorite meals.

He grinned, stooped to set her on her feet and felt the tension ease as he watched her head off down the hall. Turning to the stairs, he took them two at a time; loosening his tie on the way. A sigh escaped when he looked down the carpeted hallway at their closed bedroom door. Slowly but deliberately, he walked down the hall, preparing himself for whatever mood his wife might be in.

He found her in front of the full-length mirror brushing her hair. And, he thought, even with the deep crease in her brow and dark circles under her eyes, she looked lovely. He stood for a moment, watching the smooth steady strokes of her brushing, in silence. Finally he closed the door behind him, mindful that most of their conversations over the past weeks had turned into screaming matches.

"You're home early," she said. Her head was throbbing. She could cover how much pain she was in if she applied herself. She convinced herself that he didn't need to know. The last thing she wanted was pity to cover the absence of his love.

He came up behind her, slipped his arms around her waist, and pulled her back against him. Pressing his face to her blonde hair, he breathed in the scent of her jasmine shampoo. "Your hair always smells so good, Em." He pressed his lips to the nape of her neck, kissing her softly.

She felt the jolt that always came with his touch. "Debra told you I spent the day in here again, and you came up to scold me." His hands slid up to her breasts, her eyes closed, her will slipped. She sucked in a breath. Her hand reached up, cupping his cheek as he worked his way down her neck with his mouth.

Turning her around, she slid into his embrace easily, meeting his intense gaze with her own. "Actually, I came up to tell you dinner's ready." When her eyes shifted and she lowered her head, he lifted her chin, forcing her eyes back to his. "You need to see someone, Em. This depression's gone on for too long. This can't be how you want to spend your days." His fingers squeezed her waist. "I can't reach you, you won't let me."

Her eyes filled, and, though it felt like a kick in the gut, she knew he was only saying what should have been said long before now. She dropped her head onto his shoulder. "Maybe I'll call someone tomorrow."

Maybe Jeremy was right, Emily thought, turning her face into his neck. Maybe it was time to deal with the grief and pain always threatening to choke the life from her at any moment. She had to stay in control. For her husband and her daughter, she had to take back control of her life.

He squeezed her tight in his arms, grateful. "Call Michael. I'm sure you can get some referrals from him," he suggested, kissing the top of her head.

"I'll call him in the morning," she said softly, her thoughts drifting briefly to the past. Promising herself that this would be the only secret she would have from her husband, Emily let herself slip into the moment of closeness with him.

These moments of closeness between them were rare and fleeting. Emily preferred the distance to Jeremy's dissection of her behavior. But she wanted him, and in a sudden flash that surprised even her, she had his jacket off and his shirt open, feeling his flesh under her palms.

Forgetting their dinner downstairs, they moved together, wanting the same thing now. In a haze that was more primal need than desire, he yanked her robe open and brought her against him. She met his eyes, searching them for a trace of the boy who once craved her as desperately as she craved him.

She saw nothing of the boy, only the physical needs of a man who, after a decade of marriage, still couldn't love her. Resigned, she unzipped his pants and guided him to her. They fell on the bed desperate for a connection that never came.

~ 24 ~

Owen Harris was a busy man with a lot of priorities. He was in his office every morning by nine, and he worked his ass off until well after five every evening. He had built himself a thriving business which afforded him a lavish lifestyle. When his wife died nearly twenty years ago, he was left with a broken heart and a seven-year-old daughter.

He'd done his best by her, but there were problems that nearly destroyed them. When he allowed himself to look back, he could admit that he should have seen the changes in Emily from the start. The quiet, sullen looks, the sadness that clouded her eyes. He had misinterpreted it all as a young girl missing her mother, but it was more than that, and it rooted itself in her more deeply than he realized.

He did all he could for Emily because he loved her more than anything in the world. He had lost her mother, and it very nearly killed him. He would not lose his daughter. He dreamed more for her than an out-of-wedlock pregnancy and an unsettling marriage.

He adored her, but he couldn't ignore the disappointing reality that she possessed weaknesses. One of her worst was her neediness, and it was pure and simple neediness that derailed her well-planned life. She had done what she'd always done: let her heart lead her, instead of her head. Now she had to live with the consequences.

Jeremy Beckett. The boy had been trouble in high school, and it was a disappointment to see that so many years later, he hadn't changed. He had proven that when he took advantage of his vulnerable young daughter. And now they would be bound for the rest of their lives.

But to his utter amazement, the marriage was lasting and seemed solid. And for all his faults, Jeremy was proving himself to be a capable husband. He seemed to care for Emily, and she loved him without doubt and more than Owen thought he deserved. All in all, he was grateful his daughter seemed content in a stable environment.

Until now, he thought warily. Now Emily seemed to be faltering again. The emotional pain and torment had returned, and her eyes were troubled again. She wanted to tell Jeremy about her past. A past, Owen knew, that was best left alone. She was feeling at loose ends again, out of control, and Jeremy was suggesting she talk to someone.

He was lost in his thoughts of his daughter when he looked up to find her standing in his doorway. "Emily." He wasn't used to unannounced visitors at his door. "You startled me." But shock gave way to happiness with this chance to see his little girl.

Emily closed the door behind her. "I didn't mean to," she said, walking over to press a kiss to his cheek. "I need to talk to you, Daddy."

He folded his hands together and laid them on the desk in front of him. "What's happened?" he asked quickly. It was rare for Emily to come to his office, and the look on her face was anything but serene.

She sat down and fidgeted with her purse. "I know you don't like to talk about it, and you don't agree, but I've decided to tell Jeremy everything."

Owen shook his head at her. "We've been through this all before, Emily. You're in a better place in your life now, why dig up the past? He doesn't need to know."

Emily met his eyes, straightened her shoulders. It was long past time that she stood up for herself. "He deserves to know what could be in the future."

"Just talk to Michael, and everything will settle down again." Owen came around the desk and took her in his arms. "Besides, do you really think you can handle his reaction right now? Don't do anything rash, sweetheart. It could all be as simple as an adjustment to your medication."

Emily closed her eyes. "I've already made up my mind. I'm only telling you in case Jeremy comes to you with questions."

~~

Manhattan Special always made quite an impression on Jeremy. No matter how many times he walked through its doors, he found it impossible to resist being sucked into the atmosphere that spoke so definitely of the woman who created it. He'd seen the layout in Manhattan Magazine, read all the rave reviews, and followed every blurb printed about it.

Much like the owner herself, the restaurant was one of the loveliest in all of New York. Christina's flare for design and atmosphere could only be matched by her business savvy and smarts. His eyes swept over the décor and its energy shot through him like a surge of errant electricity. He followed his father to the back of the restaurant to the table reserved for them.

He felt her presence in everything around him. From the deep plush violet carpeting, to the seemingly delicate tables draped in shadows and moody candlelight, even in the middle of a hot summer day. Everything from the lighting fixtures to the art on the walls spoke of, and came from, Italy. Class, he thought with a sense of bewildering pride, as he slid into his chair and ran his hand over his tie. Pure class.

The cream-colored walls accentuated the soft lighting and created a cozy atmosphere. He sipped from his glass of chilled water, tuning out his father's idle small-talk. He felt at home here - and it scared the hell out of him.

~~

Michael Lessinger's parlor brought back old memories for Emily. Not all of them were good, and as a result her heart had raced as she paced back and forth in the small, stifling space. And now, after finally being shown into his private study, her skin felt like ice as she fought to calm herself. The décor of his private space had changed and should have been relaxing; instead it sent panic skittering up her spine to clutch at her throat. Relax, she told herself in a soothing voice, until it played as a chant inside her head.

Lingering doubts crowded her mind as she waited for Michael to arrive for their session. An old habit, she thought with a sad smile. She'd seen him at Christmas, but that had been for a family celebration. Then there had been no pressure, no feeling of being under a microscope. Coming to his office under these circumstances changed everything, she knew, staring out the window, trying to reign in her nerves.

Michael was an old family friend of her father's and someone she had counted on her entire life. He had been her father's college roommate and remained his oldest friend. When her mother died, he stayed at the house for more than a month, offering constant support and a strong shoulder to lean on. She clung to that memory now, just as she'd clung to him as a child.

It calmed her, remembering that he was a good and caring man with her best interests at heart. He was also one of the country's top psychiatrists. If she had to bare her soul, there was comfort in knowing it would be to him. He had thrown her a lifeline in the past, and she hoped he could do the same again.

To her, he had always looked like Santa Claus. Short, but carrying himself like a man who stood six-feet-tall. His hair had been snow white for as long as she could remember, and he always kept it a little long but well-groomed. His cheeks were rosy and full, and he hid his face behind a closely cropped beard. And when he laughed, it was full-bodied; he'd throw his head back, and his laugh would be rich and deep.

She was standing at the window, lost in thought, when Michael came in and closed the door. "Hello, Emily." his voice, as always, was soft and soothing. He crossed the room with her file tucked under his arm and a smile spreading across his face. He kissed her. "How are you?"

She kissed his whiskered cheek and smiled. "I'm not sure." She let him take her hand and walk her over to a chair. In any other place, she would have felt totally at ease with him, but here in his professional environment her nerves betrayed her.

Michael smiled, remembering the little girl, once all mischief and curls. But, the woman before him now was in trouble. He had seen her in pain before. "Take a deep breath and relax." He leaned against his desk, folding his arms across his chest. She smoothed her silk pants and crossed her legs to get comfortable. "Owen called, told me I might be seeing you professionally again. I'm surprised you've waited this long."

Emily knew the meaning behind his words. She looked at him and rolled her shoulders. Tension began to tie a knot in the pit of her stomach "Why?" Maybe she really did look like a woman coming apart at the seams.

Michael angled his head and shrugged. He then pushed himself off the desk and went around to the other side. "I figured you'd come by when...Nathaniel..." Her body language told him all he needed to know. He lowered himself into his chair, making eye contact with Emily.

The mention of her son's name nearly made her wince. Looking away, she spoke in a soft voice. "Debra took all my time, kept me focused." Emily looked at Michael with a steady gaze. "And I wasn't ready. Maybe I'm still not."

"You're taking the first step."

"I'm afraid."

"Fear can be a constructive emotion," he said. "This isn't like before. You're taking control now."

"I'm not sure I can go through this again."

"That's why I'm here. You won't be going through anything alone," Michael promised. He saw her unmistakable fear. Read it in her posture; saw it all but consuming her. He opened her file, put on his glasses. "Let's get started." He smiled with a confidence he knew she didn't share. He would make sure she got it all back. Her strength, her courage, and most importantly, her own self-worth.

~~

Just when Jeremy was finally convinced he was content with his life, a near tragedy revealed the truth to him. The newspaper brought him face-to-face with his past and his buried feelings. The headline on the society page nearly undid him.

The half page article reported, 'Former flame of Jeremy Beckett and successful restaurateur, Christina Wagner, had been the victim of a vicious mugging while leaving her restaurant, Manhattan Special, two nights ago.' His heart tripped in his chest as he continued reading. The bastard violated her by 'holding a blade to her throat.'

When he thought of what might have happened to her, his blood ran cold. She could have been raped, murdered, or sliced up for the twenty dollar bill she probably still carried behind her driver's license in her wallet. It explained why he hadn't seen even a glimpse of her when he'd gone there for the business lunch with his father. Anger misplaced, but consuming, put him behind the wheel of his car just after midnight, in a direction best left alone.

And yet Jeremy drove on. Quietly envisioning wrapping his hands around the punk's throat and choking the life out of him, he drove on. Weaving in and out of the sparse late night traffic, he envisioned Christina's lifeless body lying in the alley behind the restaurant and his throat nearly closed in panic. If he had any sense, he would be in bed next to his wife instead of heading into a past that, up until five minutes ago, he thought was behind him.

He ignored the voice in his head, telling him to go home, and reasoned with himself instead. He had to be sure she was alright to have any peace at all. He was asking for trouble, he told himself, moving into the far right lane. But even knowing it, he drove on. This was just something he had to do.

Despite knowing he belonged with the woman he married, he couldn't turn back. His wife, who at that very moment, he thought, while turning into the rear parking lot of his destination, lay in their bed sound asleep. Despite knowing she had had a difficult and emotional day and needed the security of knowing he was beside her; still, he was here.

Emily had her first appointment with her psychiatrist earlier in the afternoon. It had to have been hard to expose herself, to open up. He berated himself for being unable to provide her with the security of his love, even as he was crossing the parking lot asking for more trouble than any one man needed.

She had been downstairs, dressed and spending time with Debra when he came home from work, and that was a real improvement. Michael had prescribed mild sleeping pills to help her sleep, but other than that she shared nothing about the details of her first session.

And yet, while he worried about his wife, he worried about Christina as well. The difference between them was simple. One woman he cared for deeply. She was his responsibility and someone he'd come to have great affection for, even love to a degree. But the other woman knew and claimed his heart in a way his wife never could.

It didn't matter that she had shut him out of her life years ago. His heart belonged to her, beat for her, and yearned for the passion only she could ignite. His mind drifted to Christina now and how close she had come to a violent end, but she wouldn't see it that way, he knew. Her pride and her strength, and her unwillingness to submit could have been disastrous.

With the success of her restaurants, they often moved in the same circles. Attending some of the same parties forced them into the same environment, and sometimes the tongues of the city's elite would wag about their past. A few even suggested their past wasn't in the past at all.

But they were aware of the lingering gossip - and they weren't the only ones. Emily knew and hated any suggestion that romantic feelings still existed between her husband and Christina Wagner. He and Christina were nothing more than polite when they were forced to mingle and eventually crossed paths.

Through design and effort, they were sure to never be alone. The pain he caused them both still lay very near the surface. Too near, for being alone to be anything but uncomfortable. Because of that, they kept their distance from each other whenever possible.

Yet, here he sat in the rear parking lot of Manhattan Special, torn between what was wise and what might bring him some real happiness. He could stay in his car, content to see her only from a distance. Or he could walk inside and find a table in the back. He could order a cup of coffee, slip a waiter a fifty, and ask to see her.

He came only to talk to her. To see for himself that she was unharmed. What was the harm? Maybe he wanted to bridge the gap he put between them, which had only widened throughout more than a decade of staying out of each other's lives? To make amends perhaps? Taking a deep breath, he gathered his nerve. He could handle this, he whispered to the empty car and his wavering ego.

He opened the car door and climbed out. He straightened his shirt and stooped to check himself in the door mirror. He swallowed the lump in his throat and almost changed his mind, but he crossed the lot because he wanted to see her damn it - and Christina was just on the other side of the approaching door.

~ 25 ~

It went as he expected it to. Well, almost. Fifty dollars wasn't enough for the privilege of sitting at a table while the staff cleaned and closed the restaurant. The price turned out to be a cool hundred, but Jeremy considered himself lucky. It was obvious the kid recognized him and could have easily gouged him for more.

Then the kid showed him to a back table and brought him a cup of coffee while he waited. He didn't know when Ms. Wagner would be coming out of her office. But she was there, of course, just like he knew she would be, and it was no surprise to find it was against her doctor's orders.

So he sat at a table in the back of Manhattan Special, sipping coffee, thinking about what he would say when he saw Christina. Thinking about a night more than a dozen years ago when he sat waiting for her, just like this, until very late in the night. He smiled. It made him ridiculously proud that the restaurant he sat in tonight belonged to her. That the kitchen she cooked in was managed under her careful eye.

These were her waiters and waitresses busy with the routine of closing down a city hot spot for the night. But that didn't stop them from stealing glimpses of him. They recognized him - and why wouldn't they? With his face forever splashed over the financial and society pages, he was a living, breathing train wreck in a tailored suit.

A half hour, then forty-five minutes passed, with him beginning to wonder whether he'd wasted a hundred bucks. Then he heard the click of a door behind him, and he froze. He drained his coffee cup, feeling it burn its way down his throat and used the sensation to steel his courage.

When he got to his feet, weak in his knees, he turned and saw her standing with an employee who was pointing to his table. He held his breath, wondering if the same tangle of nerves gripped her. Then he watched her look his way, and his pulse quickened as their eyes met.

He watched her body stiffen as her shock registered. And watching, a million sensations coursed through his body. Was she happy to see him? Was she angry at the intrusion of him showing up at all? Would she greet him with her legendary temper, or would she smile and be happy to see him?

Then she started toward him with confidence in her stride and without hesitation, and he knew he would have his answer in seconds. Except for the wariness in her eyes, he might have thought her unaffected. And with the distance closing between them, he knew something else. He'd never seen another woman more breathtakingly beautiful.

As for Christina, she betrayed none of her feelings on her way to Jeremy's table. Exhausted and shaken to find him here, she drew in a steadying breath and put a look of unconcern on her face. So what if the intensity in his eyes quickened her heartbeat? And so what if the pull she felt threatened to break her heart all over again?

But the complete, unvarnished truth she saw in his eyes put her on guard and on unsure footing. Why was he here? What did he want? Did he know just seeing him like this could undo her resolve?

Unable to look away from her, Jeremy stumbled, knocking his chair over in the process. Because his hands were aching to touch her, he stuffed them in his pockets and managed to smile while his mouth went dry. He swallowed, hoping to sound clever. "Hello, Christina."

"Still hiding in shadows?" A snappy introduction, but her voice betrayed her. She was certain she was screaming over the buzzing in her ears.

Nervously, he lifted his shoulders in a careless shrug. "Old habits," he quipped, then he got honest. "I'm not sure why I'm here." Then he added a brutally honest confession. "But I just had to see you."

"Why?"

Jeremy pulled out another chair. "Sit down. Just for a minute, please?"

While logic sounded in her head, she had the option to turn around and walk away. But her pride wouldn't give him the satisfaction of knowing he'd rattled her. So she sat with her disinterested gaze pinning him, and with her heart hammering in her chest.

"What is it you want, Jeremy?" she asked, her tone polite but guarded, her carefully folded hands on the table in front of her to keep them from shaking.

"I read about the mugging," he said. "My heart stopped dead in my chest when I saw the article in the paper. I had to make sure you're okay." His fingers worked themselves into fists. "I would've kept my distance...Dad said you were fine, but I had to see for myself. Old habits, like I said."

He looked into her eyes and wondered what she was thinking as she sat looking at him. He saw coolness, confusion, and feared coming might have been a mistake. Was she happy to see him?

Christina lifted her hands and rolled her shoulders, before flicking her glinting emerald eyes back to Jeremy. "I'm still in one piece."

"You might've been killed, Christina, for chrissake. You need to be more careful."

"You left your wife, drove twenty-five minutes across town at this hour, to what? Lecture me?" Anger seeped in, but it was tempered by dark humor. "Well...you haven't lost your nerve, I'll say that for you." She glanced down at her watch. "But, in case you've forgotten, I'm no longer your concern."

Jeremy remembered the tone. He'd come face to face with it too many times not to. "That came out wrong," he said in defense, wishing he could start over. "I'll always be concerned about you."

Christina arched a brow, and chuckling, pulled the pin holding her hair on top of her head. Long, lush, and auburn, it fell unkempt to her shoulders. "Thanks." She raked her fingers through it to keep it from knotting up later. "Anything else?"

It was a move that arrowed straight to his gut. Jeremy straightened his shoulders and wisely tucked his tongue in his cheek. "Well, since you asked: your parking lot could use better lighting. No wonder the sonofabitch had the balls to grab you. You have to be aware of your surroundings, especially in the wee hours."

"Feel better getting that off your chest?" She stood; she'd had her limit of men telling her how careless she had been. "It's nice to see you can still be a self-important ass. I can't believe I'm having this conversation," she said, shaking her head and heading for the bar. "But as long as I am, I'm having a drink. Want one?"

Blowing out a breath of frustration, he slumped back in his chair. Watching her walk around the bar, he found the years hadn't touched her. Her beauty couldn't be hidden under fatigue or the white cotton chef's uniform she was wearing. "Better make it a double."

She reached over her head and took down two glasses from the ceiling rack. "Rum and coke?"

"You remember."

"Good memory." She filled a glass half full with coke and topped it off with rum. "Comes with the job."

If she meant that as a statement of warning, he'd regard it as one. She came back to the table with his drink and wine for herself. Years of distance hadn't affected her ability to read him.

"Thanks." Picking up the glass she'd put in front of him, he took a drink and smiled. "You still make a pretty mean drink."

"Again, part of the job."

"Where were we?"

"My stupidity." Her eyes smiled. "Sorry to interrupt."

"Sorry," he said, chagrined. "Guess I should think before I open my mouth." He tapped his finger on the rim of his glass. Every nerve ending in his body hummed. "I don't have any business getting upset, do I?"

Christina sat back down and crossed her legs. Sipping her chilled wine, she watched him over the rim of her glass. He was nervous, thinking she still hated him, but she didn't. Those wounds took a long time to heal, and when they finally did she let go her hate. "It's your nature, always has been," she said simply, setting her glass down.

The tension slowly lifted. Jeremy could finally feel himself relaxing; and Christina's eyes were softer, kinder.

"You've been in the kitchen."

"I try to spend at least two nights a week here handling the cooking," she said. "Between here and the Avenue, I manage to spend the majority of my time in one kitchen or the other. That's really what I love anyway."

"I know," Jeremy said, looking around the darkened restaurant, nodding and smiling. "Well, this is quite a place. You're a hit."

"I'm coming into my own," she agreed. "But it was luck more than anything that made this place a success. I couldn't count the number of people who told me I was risking my shirt opening my own place." She shrugged, tipped her wine glass to her lips. "Too young. I had to learn fast. When I started, I knew next to nothing about running a business, and what I did know, I picked up at O'Reilly's."

"You don't give yourself enough credit." Drumming his fingers on the table, he wasn't sure he should, but he had to say what was on his mind. "I've missed you."

"Jeremy-" She held her breath, shudders rippling in her stomach and her heart. She feared the conversation might come to this. Dangerous ground for both of them.

He held up his hands to stop her. "I didn't say that to make you uncomfortable, Christina. I said it because it's true, and because how I let things end between us is probably my biggest regret in life."

She shook her head, gulped down the rest of her wine. "That was a lifetime ago, Jeremy." She pushed away from the table. "We were kids; neither of us handled it very well."

He stood, cramming his hands in his pockets. "It never should've happened. And that one-night stand changed my life – our lives - forever. Letting you push me away was stupid. If I'd've fought, we'd be together right now."

"You know that's not true," she said evenly, giving her hair a careless toss turning away. "There were extenuating circumstances. I threw you out of my life that night, and by the time I was able to see past the hurt - it was too late. I found out Emily was pregnant and you were getting married."

He came closer, ran his hand through his hair, because he couldn't run it through hers. "You should've heard it from me. About the pregnancy and the marriage, I owed you that much. Then maybe we could've ended as friends."

He was blaming himself, but she shared in the blame, and it was time to take responsibility for her part. "I wouldn't take your calls or read your letters. How could you tell me anything? And friendship was never an option. Not then. Especially not then, you know that."

"No, I guess not," Jeremy said with resignation. He remembered all too well how the press had hounded Christina. Painted him as a careless playboy caught with his pants down. How they tried to prove that he was marrying Emily out of duty and nothing more.

"How is Emily?" Christina asked. She knew the gossip as well as anyone else. The party line was that Emily never really recovered from the death of their son.

"She's depressed and unhappy most of the time."

"I'm sorry," Christina said, and meant it. His frankness surprised her, and she could only imagine the pain of losing a child. Was that the reason for the sadness in his eyes? And why did she care?

"I try to be supportive, but there's always been a wall between us," he said. "Emily keeps her pain to herself. It's like she locks it away the minute I walk into the room. But she's finally agreed to see someone about it. She had her first appointment today." He felt hopeful, but why was he telling her? These were his problems, not hers.

"It can't be easy for either of you."

"Nothing's ever been easy for us."

"And your daughter?"

"She's a bundle of energy." He grinned as any proud father would. "And she has me wrapped around her little finger."

Christina laughed at the image in her mind. "I'll bet. Bring her in for a sundae sometime. I'd love to meet her."

He smiled. "I'd like that."

~ 26 ~

Emily's depression took a turn for the worse while Jeremy was on an overnight business trip. A frantic phone call in the middle of the night had him waking his pilot and flying home mere hours after landing. She had shut herself away in the bedroom ranting about being watched. The flight home seemed to take forever, with him dreading what he would find when he got there.

The cars parked haphazardly in the driveway told Jeremy that whatever was going on inside the house was far from a simple mood swing. Michael and her father must have arrived in a panic, if their still opened driver side doors were any indication. Dread brought the bitter taste of bile to his mouth. The limo hadn't fully stopped before he'd thrown open his door and jumped out, bounding up the stairs to the door.

He walked into the darkened foyer with the distinct sound of shattering glass over his head. The sun had yet to rise, but the house was chaotic. Debra ran to him, crying, and Jeremy dropped to his knees to wrap her in his arms for comfort. "It's okay, sweetheart, Daddy's here." More glass shattered overhead, and Debra flinched in his embrace and began to cry even harder. "Shhh, don't be afraid."

"Mommy's so scared. Help her, Daddy! She's even scared of Grandpa Owen." Debra sobbed, clutching his neck.

"I will, sweetie, don't worry."

The bright light over the foyer came on, and he looked up to see the housekeeper hurrying down the staircase in her bathrobe. "Mr. Beckett, thank goodness you're home. Mrs. Beckett..." she trailed off when Jeremy's quick nod silenced her.

"Please take Debra up to her room and stay with her. I'll see to my wife." He kissed his daughter's wet cheeks and soothed. "Go on, I'll be up in awhile."

With the fright on her face breaking his heart, he watched his daughter walk up the stairs and disappear down the hall before he pushed himself to his feet and ran up the stairs. He found Owen and Michael preparing to take the bedroom door off its hinges, so he pounded on the door, hoping she might open it for him.

"Em!" he shouted, then bit back an oath, forcing the panic out of his voice. "Emily, open the door for me."

The voice that replied was shrill and incoherent. "I can't, they won't let me, and they're all around me. They want to hurt me."

When she started to sob uncontrollably, Jeremy rattled the knob and cursed under his breath in frustration.

Owen shoved him out of his way and started to pry the pins out of the hinges. "Good God, you think we haven't tried that already?!!" His wild eyes and demeanor almost mirrored his daughter's.

Jeremy stepped away to give Michael room to help Owen. The sobbing grew louder and made his heart race. "What the hell's happened?" He wanted to know, needed to know. "She's never sounded...unglued before."

Michael exchanged a hurried look with Owen before he went back to work on the bottom pin. "Let's just get her out of there." His troubled eyes met Jeremy's. "Then we'll talk."

"Michael, I don't think-"

He cut Owen off as more glass shattered against the door. "First things first, I'll examine Emily. And then, Jeremy, I'll tell you everything."

~ 27 ~

Jeremy waited in the study alone, with no choice but to relive the utter destruction he'd found when he rushed into the bedroom. He stopped short when Emily, hysterical in the middle of the floor, cried out and slid away from him until her back was against the bed and she could go no further. Her eyes, red, puffy from crying, and frantic, were pleading.

Jeremy went to her. Slowly, cautiously so he didn't frighten her. "Emily, it's okay. It's me, Jeremy. I'm not going to hurt you, sweetie."

Once he was next to her, he waited until recognition took the place of the terror in her eyes. She blinked, and he watched her eyes clear as she reached for him. Gathering her close, he slid down to the floor and rested his back against the bed, as he tightened his arms around her. Her hands, covered in blood, clutched at his white shirt.

Clutch, release. Clutch, release. Bringing her head to rest on his chest, Jeremy smoothed her hair away from her face, murmuring comfort with his wife's blood all over him. He did the only thing he could. He held her tight.

Once Jeremy had her calm, Michael came in, preparing a sedative injection while Owen disappeared into the bathroom for towels to wrap around her wounded hands. When he was ready, Michael crouched down in front of her and spoke softly. "Emily, it's Uncle Michael." He lifted the hand she had resting in her lap and with two fingers checked her pulse. Frowning at Jeremy, he shook his head. "She's in shock."

Owen came back with the towels and dropped to his knees to tend to his daughter's mangled hands. "I called downstairs. Someone's bringing up warm water and a first aid kit."

Michael turned her face away from Jeremy's chest to examine her pupils with a penlight. "Good." When at last she met his eyes with hers, they filled with tears.

"Uncle Michael?"

He smiled at her. "Right here, honey. I'm going to give you something to help you sleep."

She yanked her arm away. "No, they'll take me!"

"No, Emily," Jeremy said, fighting to keep his panic at bay. "They won't, I swear. Trust me. Let Michael help you."

Michael slipped the needle in her arm and slowly administered the sedative. When she was asleep, Jeremy stood with her in his arms. Their bed was covered in broken glass, torn sheets, and blood, so he grimly turned for the door.

"I'm taking her down the hall to the guestroom," he said in a hollow voice. Crusted blood smeared on his cheek, his eyes bleak, he glared at Michael. "Then I want to know what the hell you've been keeping from me."

~~

Michael found Jeremy staring out the window. It was not quite 8 a.m., and the night had been long, but the sun's bright rays shined into the study, slanting light on the binds of books on the shelf across the room. He closed the door behind him and cleared his throat to let his presence be known.

Jeremy didn't turn around, but instead asked the question that had been running through his mind from the moment he'd seen Emily crumpled on their bedroom floor. "What's really wrong with her?"

Michael considered, and then jumped right in on the long journey toward truth. "How much do you know about her summers during high school?"

"Just that she spent most of her time in Paris."

An uncomfortable realization set in, and Michael knew Jeremy was still in the dark. That he didn't know a vital truth about his wife. "Nothing more?"

When at last Jeremy turned away from the window, he fixed Michael with a ridged stare. "Just spit it out," he snapped, devoid of patience.

"Perhaps we should sit down." Michael moved to sofa.

Jeremy didn't move at all. "Perhaps not."

Michael decided in that instant, that the time for full disclosure had come. "Emily's battling a chronic, degenerative mental illness, and has been for the last twenty years."

Feeling as if he'd just slammed into another wall between himself and his wife, Jeremy dropped into a leather chair, shaking his head. Anger replaced helplessness. He knew without being told that Owen Harris was to blame for keeping him in the dark.

The urge to slam his fist into something was strong. "I want to know everything." he demanded. "I think it's long past time, don't you?"

~ 28 ~

For the third day in a row, he'd neglected to shave. The thickening stubble on his drawn, hollowed out face, combined with the tired, broken gaze in his eyes, gave him the appearance of a man adrift, unrecognizable even to himself. At a table for two in the back of a diner in the upper eastside, Jeremy Beckett scratched his itchy cheek and motioned to a waitress for a refill of his strong black coffee. If his hand shook when he picked up his cup, he pretended not to notice.

Jamie zeroed in on her brother the moment she came in the door. Of course, he would choose to wait for her in the far back, out of any passerby's line of sight. As she got closer to the table and took in Jeremy's haggard appearance, she understood why. If their mother could see him, Jamie knew she would be beside herself.

As casually as she could, Jamie dropped her bag onto the table and bent to kiss Jeremy's cheek. "I suppose I don't need to point out you look like hell?" she teased, dropping herself into the only other chair at the small table.

Jeremy smirked, lifting his coffee to his mouth for a sip before he spoke. "I told you when you called and nagged me into breakfast. I'm not fit company."

"Well, you weren't kidding." Their waitress came and turned her coffee cup upright on her saucer, filled it with fresh coffee and, sliding menus in front of both her and Jeremy before moving to her next station, smiled in greeting.

"Give me a break, Jamie. Things haven't exactly been a breeze lately." he replied. And that was putting it mildly, she knew. Her sympathy and love had her covering his hand with hers.

In the week following Emily's breakdown, Jeremy felt broken down, too. To find out his wife is mentally ill, and has been the entire time they'd known each other was a revelation he wasn't prepared to handle. Learning the medication keeping her inner demons at bay was suspended during her pregnancy and never resumed after had left him reeling.

Was he married to a stranger? He'd asked himself that question again and again. There was enough guilt to choke him if he let it. Guilt over the absence of real love for her in his heart. And, still more guilt knowing he'd done nothing to hide that harsh truth from her. Maybe now that cruel fact made a certain sort of sense. How could he love someone he so clearly didn't know?

"How's Emily?" Jamie asked over her eggs Benedict.

"Better." Jeremy said around a mouthful of French toast. "Lucid finally, thank god."

"Well, Debra was frightened by the whole episode. I'm worried about her."

"No more than me." he agreed. "But I've been keeping an eye on her, and she's much better after having dinner with her mother last night in her bedroom." A yawn took him by surprise.

"When was the last time you slept more than a couple hours in a row?"

"A week, give or take."

"You need to take care of yourself so you can come to terms with your new reality."

"I'm wrapping my mind around my reality a little more every day." A rueful laugh bubbled out of him. "And let me tell ya, little sister, reality sucks."

~ 29 ~

Summer
1991

A smile spread across her face when Christina walked into her office and spotted the vase with the single long-stemmed red rose on the corner of her desk. It was an acknowledgment that she was another year older whether she liked it or not. She gave in, walking over to take in its sweet scent. Sam obviously felt last night's dinner and diamond-studded tennis bracelet wasn't enough.

Clicking her tongue, she pulled the card free, and then the blood drained from her cheeks as she read the note.

Happy Birthday - for old time's sake, Jeremy.

She read the card again as the breath began to clog in her lungs. Her heart was in her throat, as first happiness, then confusion overwhelmed her. He'd sent her a rose.

For old times sake. It cut deep, hearing from him in this intimate way. He'd eaten in her restaurants and passed on rave reviews to friends and associates. He'd spoken highly of her in those rare interviews when a reporter was tactless enough to mention their past. But not once since that night a year ago, when he came to her to take the first tenuous steps toward healing and friendship, had he been so overt - or so intimate.

She walked to the window and pressed her forehead to the cool glass to gather herself. That he still, after all this time, could find a way into her heart worried her. That time and distance couldn't kill the longing from a lifetime ago, heated her blood.

Stepping back, she looked at her reflection in the glass and brought her fingers to her cheek. More than a decade's passing. The changes were subtle, but telling. The young girl she had been had matured into an intelligent, competent woman - but the young girl's heart remained.

The pain of losing Jeremy remained as well, and what memories time had been kind enough to bury returned with her shaky breath. Her vivid green eyes mirrored the same misery now that they had then. Then sadness dulled them, and sleepless nights added dark shadows underneath them. And a long time passed before the long buried light in her eyes returned.

She couldn't forget the man who helped her heal. Sam. *Such a good man*, she thought, as her heart warmed. She pressed her thumb to the crease in the middle of her forehead where a headache was forming. In her mind she began damning Jeremy, all the while missing his embrace and feeling disloyal to Sam.

He would react predictably. His jealousy of Jeremy might be his only flaw, she thought, and he'd never made a secret of his feelings. But Jeremy's rose sitting on her desk, an echo of a past with her lost love, would infuriate him.

Refocusing on what her day would entail, Christina sat down at her desk and began reviewing the previous night's receipts. She pushed her bothersome bangs out of her eyes with the heel of her hand and reached up to tighten her ponytail. Turning on the adding machine, she started crunching numbers. After all, she did have a business to run.

~ 30 ~

Jeremy walked into Manhattan Special and found it packed table for table over the lunch hour. Professional and blue collar people alike kept the waiters and waitresses busy, mulling over their menus or digging into their meals. Many of the faces were familiar to Jeremy, some were business associates and others personal acquaintances. He smiled and waved hello, before he loosened his tie, and drifted over to the bar to slide onto the only stool available.

Delicious scents tempted him as he decided to order the special for lunch. He knew coming here like this wasn't wise. Just like he knew that if Christina knew he were there, he might be wearing his lunch instead of eating it. Still, he liked the idea of treating his palate to her culinary genius and gathering his courage at the same time. But he also knew he was biding his time, because sooner or later he would have to face her.

Settled at the bar, he ordered a single-malt scotch, deciding it was better to face her with the nervous edge smoothed. A quick belt would calm the nerves coiled like a snake in the pit of his stomach. Word would drift to Christina that he was here, as it always did. More grease for the gossip mill, he knew, that pulsed in this city and thrived like a wild fire out of control. He could practically already hear the tongues wagging as he tested his drink.

~~

Emily lay on the bed, still and repentant and swearing she would never again drink wine at thirty-thousand feet. Her head had been pounding since she and Debra landed at J.F.K the night before, but at least she could be thankful that the trip accomplished what she hoped it would. Time together was bridging the distance between she and her young daughter. Jeremy had been right after all.

At eight years old, Debra was blessed with a quick, easy smile, much like her father's. Her daughter's early wisdom, though, humbled her mother time and again. Her mother's episodes of illness had left her wary and withdrawn, and she knew far too much of her mother's pain. And Emily knew her days locked in the darkness and silence of her illness damaged her daughter in ways not easily seen by the casual observer. But Emily could see each and every subtle sign of the damage she had done.

How could she explain her grief to a child? How could she explain that looking at her and being with her was a double-edged sword, a constant reminder that her son was gone? Her eyes fluttered opened on that thought as the pills did their work and she wrestled with the questions that always haunted her. How could she explain her grief to her daughter when she couldn't understand it herself?

Jeremy handled his pain over the loss of Nathan much better than she. His grief ran deep and fed his guilt. From the moment she went into premature labor, he blamed himself. They suffered through the loss of their son together and separately, carefully masking their grief from Debra as she grew older. Jeremy was better at shielding her from his pain. He was able to smile, tickle and play, to give her his undivided attention and affection.

While Emily envied Jeremy's ability, she couldn't emulate it. The ache was as constant as the beat of her heart, and was etched deeply in her soul. Could such a palpable grief be the root of her physical pain? Michael seemed to think so.

The thumping pain rooted behind her eyes lessened, so she sat up, bringing her feet to the floor with a sigh. The pain sure as hell felt very real, she reasoned. But it was time to put a smile on her face and play the part of a happy, contented wife.

~~

He didn't hear her walk up behind him, and he nearly choked on the last of his scotch when he felt a slap on his shoulder. In an instant, he was looking into a pair of angry, green eyes. He tried to ignore that her hair was cascading over her shoulders like a curtain of silk. And that the dangerous glint in her eyes warned him and left him speechless.

Christina came out of the kitchen with the mouthwatering scents of her cooking still clinging to her. She was breathtaking. With his heart in his throat, he decided with a careful look that she looked ready for a fight.

"Christina," he managed to come off nonchalant. "I can tell by the look on your face you're happy to see me." He rolled the joke off to dull the sting of her glare.

She glanced around to be sure they didn't have an audience. "What were you thinking?"

"I was thinking about wishing you a happy birthday." Even he wasn't buying it.

Her spine stiffened. "Bullshit."

Jeremy bit his tongue to keep from adding fuel to her fire. Under her penetrating gaze, he shrugged his shoulders innocently. "I remembered your birthday and wanted to give you some measure of a gift. A token of friendship, that's all. I mean, hasn't that been what we've been working towards this past year? Friendship?"

Christina wanted to maintain the edge of anger she'd been riding on since she came out of the kitchen, but she was feeling more unnerved than angry at the moment, and decided that was something best kept to herself. "Friendship?" She had to check her temper and mind her tone. Even if she didn't believe him for a minute, her restaurant was packed with people who would love a free show with their meals. "Daisies say friendship, Jeremy. A rose says.......something else entirely."

"I think you're being a little overly sensitive."

"You think!" her whisper came out more like a hiss. "Would you like to know what I think?"

Jeremy gave her a slight smile. "I think I can guess. Listen, I meant it as nothing more than a gesture. I swear."

Damn it, he sounded genuine. "Well...thanks."

He wondered if Sam Radcliff was at the root of her reaction. He found it interesting, very interesting, just how much his simple gesture had shaken her. "If I'd known one rose would upset you so much, I wouldn't have sent it." And then his common sense abandoned him. "Or is this about Sam?"

"This doesn't have anything to do with Sam. He's out of town on a case. It's about boundaries."

Jeremy stood up and slid his empty glass across to the bartender. "Boundaries?"

"Yes." She glanced warily around them. As she expected, they were beginning to attract attention. "You'd better go."

"I ordered lunch."

"I'll have it delivered to your office."

Jeremy shrugged and walked with her to the door. She was annoyed but no longer angry. He'd touched a nerve in her and in himself.

Christina watched him walk down the street. The deep breath she'd been holding escaped her. Then she went back to the kitchen, leaving her rattled nerves and a fresh dose of gossip behind in her wake.

~~

Just home from the office, Jeremy was surprised to see Jamie sitting on the living room floor, engrossed in what looked to be a very lively game of monopoly. Debra was celebrating Aunt Jamie's landing on one of her properties. And Aunt Jamie was retaliating by tickling her niece's tummy. Her innocent laughter erupted through the house.

"Well, this is a productive way to spend the afternoon."

Jamie released her niece and turned with a smile to her brother. "For your daughter, the shark, it is, anyway. Emily had a last minute meeting with one of her charities, so I said I'd stay with squirt here until you got home," she said, playfully poking Debra and bringing about another fit of laughter.

He tossed his suit jacket over the back of the sofa and crossed the room, dropping onto the floor next to his sister. "Guess that means her headache's better, then."

"Guess so."

They finished the game, and to Debra's delight, Jamie stayed for dinner. She tuned into her brother's mood, sensing his restlessness. From the beginning, Jamie had been vocal about her disapproval over Jeremy's marriage. And with the uncertainty of mental illness to contend with on a daily basis, Jamie could see nothing ahead for him but misery and a life spent with a woman whom he no longer knew.

But when Emily came home later with armloads of packages and a smile, Jamie saw an ease between them that spoke of true affection. The conversation over veal with parsnips and endive salad was light and relaxed. Underneath, Jamie sensed that, though Jeremy was unsettled, he was attentive and kind to his wife.

After dinner, they had coffee in the living room while Debra went off with the maid for her bath. Jamie wasn't blind. Closeness lay between them, her brother and his wife. There was love here, too, she supposed, watching the two of them share a private joke. But there were many kinds of love, and not all of them were the kind to build on or maintain a marriage.

The love between them for their daughter held a depth she envied as well. But their ease as a couple revealed more friendship than passion. Friends. Close enough and comfortable enough to sleep with each other and share a life together.

Not a bad component in any marriage, to be sure. But, alone it was hardly a strong enough foundation to share a lifetime together. Besides, another person altogether, knowingly or not, pulled at the fibers of this relationship. A relationship that had its beginnings in anything but love. Jamie wondered about that and many other things as she drove away from house later on that evening. And she worried.

~~

Sam shuffled into the bedroom without turning on the light. It was late, and he was dead on his feet, but he won his case. An innocent man was free to get on with his life. And Sam could be thankful for the half-million dollar fee he'd collected along with the not guilty verdict.

In the darkness of the bedroom he shared with Christina, he heard her breathing deeply in sleep. Lowering himself onto the bed, he slipped off his socks before standing and dropping his pants, removing his shirt, and slipping into bed beside her. He kissed Christina's cheek and rolled onto his side. His eyes adjusted to the darkness, and he could see that, as they often were, the blinds on the bedroom windows were drawn tight.

Christina hated prying eyes looking in on her, privacy meant everything to her. It was bad enough that out on the streets she was an open target for zoom lenses from the tabloids and society pages. But here, in her home, her haven, they wouldn't catch her in an unguarded moment.

His eyes grew heavy and all the legal knowledge crowding his mind began to drift away as exhaustion crept in. She turned to him, murmuring, snuggled in close to feel his warmth against her, and relaxed. He felt the warmth of her body, too, pressing against him. Even sleeping, Christina could always find a way to soothe.

Her breath on his cheek was a comfort. He pulled her closer to him and kissed her brow. She sighed softly, and he let his eyes close and sleep take him over. Breathing in her scent, he ached for her, but his body and mind needed rest more. In moments, fatigue won, and he gave in to his favorite dreams.

Six Months Later

Jeremy walked into his office with a sour expression on his face and guilt eating away at his conscience. He spoke to no one. Distraction colored his mood as he tried to begin his day. His mind was drifting from Christina to his wife and back again, and he couldn't focus on anything else.

The night he reunited with Christina, he slipped into bed beside his wife without waking her, and without a second thought. When Emily woke up in the morning never realizing he'd been gone till the wee hours of the morning, he'd said nothing and felt like a coward. His late night drive to Manhattan Special had nothing to do with her.

But it was a lie of omission, and she wouldn't understand. So, he kept it to himself, like a secret, he thought grimly, realizing it, and slammed his door shut.

Wasn't honesty the one thing he always gave Emily? But he had to hide this from her because she was fragile, he told himself in the beginning. And now wasn't the time to upset her, considering her recent collapse.

Irritated with himself, Jeremy flipped through the day's itinerary to see his schedule. Countless meetings awaited him, some over lunch or coffee; this was not the day for distraction.

He flipped open his briefcase and began pulling out files needing his attention, but his mind wasn't on his work, and couldn't be with thoughts of Emily and Christina pulling at him. Business was no place for personal problems, and there was business to tend to, damn it. There were contracts to sign and benefits to structure, hands to shake and his word to keep.

But he was a husband, although not a good one. And he was a man conflicted, pulled in two different directions, by two very different women. One sparked his passion, the other his loyalty. One had a fierce grip on his heart, the other was the mother of his child and his confidant in a shared unspeakable grief.

Watching Emily's mental state wither away day by day was torture. Little by little, her grasp with reality was weakening. She was lucid one moment, then ranting the next. And the helplessness he felt wasn't easy to endure.

For months now, the symptoms of her mental illness were taking their toll and having physical connotations. Her face was thinner, her skin paler, and she always seemed to be in physical pain. Light made her head hurt. Loud noise could make her flinch.

At least her depression was under control with antidepressants. He reminded himself of that and was thankful. But her physical health grew more and more tenuous. The weight loss, the chills, and the crushing fatigue were mysteries.

Grimacing, he smoothed his fingers over his forehead. Another headache. He pressed his fingers to his eyes until he focused. He opened his eyes, and, blinking until his vision cleared, opened his drawer to find aspirin. He found the bottle in the back and swallowed three tablets dry.

He slumped back in his chair. He would be no use to anyone until the pain behind his eyes abated. He was putting in ten-hour days, and all these years later, still taking shit from those who still resented his presence in the company.

In generous moments, Jeremy could understand their feelings. They all had what Jeremy did not: a passion for the corporate game. He understood passion, and he missed it in his own life.

He did what was expected of him. Made the million-dollar deals Linus was too crass to manage on his own. Worked straight through lunch more days than not, signing off on memos and drawing up projection reports, updating files, and dictating letters to his secretary. His days were long and never-ending.

He played the game well, but his mind was forever preoccupied. Whether with his sick wife, his lingering feelings for Christina, or the pull to paint to quiet his mind, he had no drive or ambition for the corporate world.

Yet he stayed. And worse, every morning he returned for more. When he really wanted two uninterrupted hours closed up in his studio, he drafted contracts and dictated letters to his secretary instead. It was amazing what love for his father could drive him to do.

By 2 o'clock, he'd had enough and was headed out the door for the day. By 3, he was safely enclosed in his studio in the attic of his home. He relished his time alone here and welcomed the silence and fresh paint under his fingernails. Allowing what was inside him to come alive on the canvas under his skilled brushstrokes revived him.

The time in his painter smock with paint-covered hands calmed his soul. The aroma of paint fumes eased his busy mind. It felt good to get back to the simple joy of mixing colors and stretching canvas across a wooden frame, letting his emotions guide the brush wherever it wanted to go. No pressure. No deadlines. Just his canvas and his passion.

Within the four walls of his haven, the businessman crafted over the years would disappear, freeing him. In this place, he wasn't a cut-throat businessman or heir to a billion-dollar business dynasty. Here, surrounded by his art, Jeremy Beckett was a man driven by nothing more than his own creativity.

His brush flew furiously over the next few hours, and what began as a blank canvas turned into an ocean view at dusk. Sand dunes appeared on the right, a rustic little beach shack on the left. Sea cranes swooped across the purple tinted sky. Every stroke worked its magic on Jeremy, relaxing him and releasing the tension from his body.

He stood back to admire his work when he put in the finishing touches. He smiled slowly, scrutinizing every stroke, appreciating how well the colors blended together. He wiped his hands off on a paint rag and dipped his brushes in the paint thinner solution to clean them. He looked at his painting, and felt like a new man.

~~

He was still in his paint smock when he walked into his study that afternoon. He needed to call the art supply store, have more canvas delivered, and replace some of the paint he was running low on. He was enjoying a rare afternoon with no demands on his time.

But Jeremy's solitude was short lived. He was rifling through his desk for the number when the phone rang. He picked it up, absentmindedly. "Yeah."

Jeremy assumed it would be Linus calling to complain about his leaving the office in the middle of the day, but instead he was greeted by an unexpected but familiar voice.

"Jeremy? It's Michael Lessinger. I called your office; your secretary told me you left the office early."

Jeremy laughed, hunting up the missing store number up and finding it. He hadn't talked to Michael since having dinner weeks ago. "Hi, Michael. If you're looking for Emily, she's out right now."

"I called to talk with you. I was wondering if you could stop by the office."

"When?"

"Tonight. How's seven sound?"

"Fine. Anything wrong?" Jeremy asked with concern.

Michael was quiet for a moment. "It's important."

Jeremy's brow peaked at Michael's tone, and he straightened in his chair. "Okay, sure."

"Don't say anything to Emily," he paused, "until after we talk."

~ 31 ~

Jeremy pulled the car into the garage and shut it off with a long sigh. Torn between anger and desolation, he sat unmoving, drumming his fingers on the steering wheel. Trying to sort out the chaos in his mind, trying and failing to understand why Emily would shut him out again.

Michael had just turned his world upside down, but he'd done the right thing. He'd done what Emily should have. The truth, as awful and dismal as it was, was necessary. Yes, this news was ugly, unacceptable and too much to process, he decided, raking a hand through his hair.

He noticed his hand was trembling and knew he had to pull himself together. He had been taken completely by surprise, but he still had to face his wife. He couldn't fathom it, couldn't wrap his weary mind around it.

Every fiber of his being wanted to storm inside and demand an explanation, to vent his anger over a situation completely out of control. To rage against fate. But there was Debra to consider. She didn't need to wake up to the arguing of her parents. And Emily, as angry as he was with her, needed his support much more than his anger.

Secrets and lies, he thought miserably, thinning his lips and wishing like hell Owen had been home when he arrived at the enormous, pillared estate of his father-in-law. Damn secrets and lies. His own, and now hers. And the mastermind behind it all was Owen Harris. Listening to the pinging of the cooling engine, Jeremy fumed.

Owen Harris would have plenty to answer for, Jeremy decided, stepping out of the car with the howling wind slapping the garage windows behind him. Jeremy closed his eyes and blew out a cleansing breath. Owen was a problem for tomorrow because there were more than enough problems for tonight.

~~

The house was dark but for the moonlight cascading through the skylights in the kitchen and breakfast room. Gentle light played through the panes of glass and cast slanted shadows on the walls. He unbuttoned his coat and took off his gloves on his way into the foyer. He was chilled too deep in his bones to blame the bite in the air. He recognized the cause as shock over what he learned only hours ago, and prepared himself for what was to come.

From the middle of the foyer, he looked up the staircase and thought of his daughter. He missed her bedtime kiss and felt deprived of it. Tonight their precious ritual of stories and banishing the boogie man wasn't to be. He imagined Debra probably pouted herself to sleep and hated letting her down.

The shadows dancing on the living room wall caught his attention. He walked into the living room wary and cautious and found a cozy fire burning in the fireplace. Then he saw her. In the firelight he watched her, tucked into the sofa, flipping through a magazine, with tension eating its way up his spine.

With a quiet breath, he saw her true beauty in this moment. That he couldn't love her the way she deserved to be was his loss. That he stood there, watching her in this unguarded moment, and realizing this was a woman he couldn't possibly know, pained him.

His sad eyes scanned the spacious room, and memories played through his mind. He remembered moving in to this house, their home. Emily had been every bit as happy as he had been miserable. She had thrown herself into decorating without delay; while he had been too busy looking for a way out. And confessing that, even to himself, cost him.

There were two opposing sofas in muted fabric and antique end tables, angled, at the arms of each one. English Tudor arm chairs sat, one on each side of the fireplace. The polished oak floor, dressed with large area rugs of maroon and midnight blue imported from England, shined in the firelight. Tall, brass floor lamps stood in each corner of the room, complementing a large brass chandelier that dropped down from the center of ceiling.

He ached for the woman who had made this wonderful house their home. And he ached for himself, standing there frozen, unable to move. He shuddered now to realize that after ten years of marriage his wife had no real trust in him. A log rolled in the fireplace, sending sparks flying, and brought him back to the here and now.

"Quite a fire you've built there," he muttered, slipping out of his coat and tossing it onto the antique oak chair Emily gave him for their last anniversary. He sat there every morning with the paper and a last cup of coffee before leaving for the day. "It's late. I thought you'd be in bed."

She glanced up and noticed taut lines of tension in his face when he passed to warm his hands by the fire. She could see the hard of his jaw and the stiffness in his posture. "Or hoped."

His hands fisted, he turned to her, and then away. Seeing her with her face drawn and thin, most of his temper drained. Until he could trust his voice, he watched the flames flicker in silence.

She was probably in no shape to defend her choices. So he stamped down on his anger and decided to wait for morning to get into it. "Go ahead on up, I'll be along."

"Should I bother asking where you've been?" she asked, already thinking she knew the answer. She had been sitting there for hours, letting vivid images play out in her mind. The thought of him doing what she'd been imagining in such vivid detail, stole her breath.

"I left a note, I had a meeting," he said.

"And how did your meeting go?" Emily said with sarcasm.

"The details aren't important."

She slid off the couch to her feet with her blonde hair sweeping along her cheeks. A strength she rarely felt these days buoyed her. "I think they are." Her tone was icy and sharp as she took a few, cautious steps towards him.

He finally looked at her in the firelight. He saw the same tiredness he had seen for so long now. Why hadn't he questioned it before? He cursed his own stupidity, looking at her. Surprised to see anger in her stark blue, sunken eyes, he waited, saying nothing as her lips set in a frustrated, tight line.

"I don't think you want to get into this right now, Emily," he warned, shifting his eyes to glare into the flames, his jaw twitching with tension.

"Oh, I do." She moved closer, placing herself between him and the flames.

A long moment passed, their eyes met, held. He was quiet, considering. "Fine, then," he relented, stepping close enough to feel her breath on his skin. "Michael wanted to see me." He paused, watching closely for her reaction. This was her chance to come clean. *Tell me before I tell you*. He begged silently, watching her, and saw the dread in her eyes before she could bury it.

Her head drummed, and her throat went dry, then bitter. She watched his eyes pleading with her and growing dark with anger. Michael was her confidant, she reminded herself. He wouldn't betray her. "What did he want?"

She was backing away before he could take hold of her so he turned on his heels and put even more distance between them. "I think you already know." He bit the words off one by one.

Emily wanted to run, the pressure in her chest was too much, her heart was beating wildly, but she had forced this. There was no way to stop it now. "I...I...don't understand."

Jeremy grunted, pinning her with his hard, doubtful stare. "Like hell." He went to her then, his eyes hard as steel, cutting into her. He took hold of her shoulders and yanked her roughly to him. "Why didn't you tell me, goddamn it!" At her stricken expression, he let her go and raked his hands through his hair. "Didn't you think I had a right to know?"

The fury in his eyes answered her unspoken question. And her worst fears were coming true. "Oh...god...Jeremy." She took his face in her hands as tears filled her eyes and spilled over. "I can only imagine what you're thinking."

This was all part of it, he knew. One minute she would rage, and the next she would soften, love taking the place of anger in her eyes. He pushed her away and covered his face with his hands. "Don't worry, Emily. Michael told me everything." Now it was his turn to back away. When she reached for him, he shook his head to warn her to stay away.

Emily felt her carefully constructed world shifting. "He shouldn't have. He's bound by ethics, for God's sake." Desperate, she sobbed into the back of her hand.

Jeremy sank into the chair she had given him and laughed dryly. "Let's keep ethics out of this. He did it for your own good, whether you know it or not. And don't think he came to the decision to tell me easily." He scrubbed his hand over his face, now wet with tears of his own. Borne out of pain and frustration, he let them fall. "He said I needed to know. To be prepared." He met her eyes with accusation. "But you should've told me."

"I didn't know how." The words came out in a rush, and she only needed to see his eyes to know how weak those words were.

She dropped her hands limply to her side. Devastation seemed to be all they could offer each other. Seeing Jeremy devastated was killing her. She crossed the room, wanting to reach out and hold him, but sat down beside him instead.

"Maybe I didn't want to face telling you because telling you made it too real."

"Were you just going to let me wonder what the hell was happening to you?"

"He told you everything?"

Jeremy sighed deep, dried his eyes, and cleared his throat. "God, I hope so. I don't think I could take any more." He turned to face her. "I knew about the manic depression but not the underlying cause, the neurological disease they discovered months ago...and the prognosis."

Emily blew out a deep breath. It was my responsibility to tell you and no one else's."

He got to his feet and crossed the room. "Then why didn't you?" he said, whirling on her, fresh anger in his eyes. "All these fucking secrets and lies. And don't think I don't know your father's part in this."

He didn't give her the chance to answer; instead, he just plowed ahead. "What? Let's see, he told you I'd leave you if I found out? Our marriage would crumble, right? And God, Emily, you believed him. What kind of man do you think I am?" he asked, fixing his bleak eyes on hers.

She sat watching him, a stunned expression on her face, then shook her head sadly. In an instant her fragility was gone, and in its place was incredulity. "That's quite a question coming from you, Jeremy."

He picked up the poker and stabbed at the logs, sending sparks flying. "What the hell're you talking about?"

Emily stood, folding her arms across her and rubbing them for warmth. She watched anger contort his face and the quick thrusts of his arm to punish the burning logs because he wouldn't punish her. "Funny, you attack me for my secrets - what about yours?"

Jeremy stopped poking the fire and straightened, angling his head to look at her "What?"

Emily lifted a brow, walking over to him. "You treat me like a fool, but I'm not one." She found herself laughing at his baffled expression. Tired of the pretense, she decided to spell it out for him. "You know where I thought you were tonight?" She watched his eyes narrow. "I thought you were with Christina Wagner again. Gone out for another roll in her bed, or whatever it is you do when you're with her."

For an instant, he could only stare at her. "You're way off base," he managed, after his shock wore off. "I'm not sleeping with her."

She looked at him and smiled sadly. "Well, let's give you a prize, okay?" she sighed. "That's hardly the point anyway. You love her. I remember wishing, not too long ago, that just once in our marriage you would want me, love me as much as you love her."

"I hurt her," he said simply, squeezing the back of his neck, with sweaty palms. He wasn't ready to defend himself.

"You hurt me!" she shouted, and surprised them both. "Don't you think I know your breakup had nothing to do with you? You'd still be with her if I hadn't gotten pregnant, if you hadn't been forced to marry me. Every time you go to her, you hurt me."

"You're jumping to conclusions," he said impatiently.

"Oh, please, Jeremy, be honest with me. I was pregnant, and your back was against the wall."

"It ended because I was unfaithful to her," he said, defensively.

"With me." Turning away, she walked back to the couch, feeling a wave of fatigue wash over her. "I guess she's forgiven you then. If you're not having sex yet, you will be."

Hearing the resigned tone in her hollowed voice, he could see he had hurt her. "Christ, Emily, we're talking, not shacking up for a quickie."

"I wonder how Sam Radcliff feels about your talks, your lunches, your intimate walks in the park."

Jeremy turned around, surprised.

"Don't look so shocked," she said, leaning back and closing her eyes. "This city's too damn small for people like us. Do you really think anything illicit goes unnoticed in our circles? You're easily recognized, and so is she. Did you really think I wouldn't find out?"

"I didn't keep it from you because I thought I was doing anything wrong."

"Oh, I'm well aware of that."

He came and sat beside her, his anger draining away so he could really listen to her. "You had enough to deal with. Christina and I are friends, and that's all."

"So, now you know my dark secret, and I know yours." She opened her eyes on a sigh. "I'm going to bed; brutal honesty's exhausting." She tensed, and the lines deepened around her eyes. "If you're going to leave me, do it now."

He shook his head and took a breath as a pang of pain rang through him. "I can't believe..." he started to defend himself but realized it was an acceptable question. "You're my wife, Emily, and maybe I didn't come into this marriage happily, but you seem to forget, neither did you. But we're here, and we are a family."

"You haven't said you don't love her."

He could have lied, he knew. And sometime, perhaps long into the future, he'd come to realize he should have. "No, I haven't." Whatever else lay between them, be it a longing for a love more fulfilled, a sometime apathy, and early into their union, resentment, he had never been anything less than honest with her. "I've never lied to you, and I won't start now."

"I don't want your pity."

He grasped her hand when she turned away. "I love you too, Emily. And we'll fight this together, but I can't help you fight if you keep me in the dark."

"It's going to get bad." She pressed her palm to his cheek. There may not be passion in his eyes for her, but there was love. Not as deep as hers for him, but love just the same. "Worse than you can imagine."

He pulled her to him, wrapped his arms around her, and kissed her. "Em, you need to start the treatments and the medication."

"I want to be clear headed with the time I have left. However long that is, I want to be a participant in my life, not a bystander."

Jeremy drew away and looked at her. "Michael said it could be years before your symptoms progress."

Emily hugged him and wished she could share his hope. "I know what's coming. I'm terminal. Why prolong it?"

Part of her wanted to scream at the cruelty of fate and what the future held for her. Another, deeper part, wanted to fight what was coming with every fiber of her being. But the largest part of her was too scared to do either.

He smoothed his hands through her hair, pushing images of what might come out of his mind. "The specialists are hopeful, and so is Michael. At least your father did that much for you. You're being treated by the best in the field."

"I'm going to lose my mind; I won't even be allowed my dignity before I die."

"You can't think like that."

"There's no way to stop it," she said quietly.

"We might not be able to stop it, Em, but we can fight it." He tucked her head under his chin and sighed.

And this was the Jeremy she couldn't help loving. And hearing him say 'we' meant the world to her, but she still couldn't trust it. "You're staying with me because I'm sick," Emily said, pushing away from him.

He stood, cupped her cheek with his palm. "I'm staying because I love you. And I'm not going anywhere."

~~

Jeremy walked back into the master bedroom after having kissed Debra goodnight. He felt better having stolen a few moments watching his child sleeping. He looked up from unbuttoning his shirt cuff to see Emily sitting on the bed with her head in her hands. He went to her first, and then he went for the pills she'd been taking for months.

It humbled him knowing his wife felt the need to hide from him. And it lessened him as a man to know that the deception was so easily pulled off. He found her pills in the medicine cabinet - in reasonably plain view, if one were so inclined to take an interest. He felt like an ass.

He took the pills and a glass of water into the bedroom and watched as Emily choked them down, a ritual that up until now took place behind the closed door of their bathroom, and one that was no longer necessary. She crawled into bed, and he covered her with the over-stuffed comforter. He watched her drift into a fitful sleep, cursing himself and the man who shaped this woman with agony etched on her face.

And Owen Harris would have to pay.

~ 32 ~

Jeremy was disappointed to storm through the door of Owen's office and find it empty. Maybe it was better, he decided, to lay in wait for his father-in-law; the element of surprise gave him the advantage.

While he waited, Jeremy took in the disgusting display of opulence around him. *Only the finest for Owen Harris*, Jeremy thought with a bitterness he already felt spreading. Behind the massive oak desk were French doors that opened onto a terrace overlooking Park Avenue. The chairs and sofa at the far end of the room were Victorian in style with walls painted a pale blue, and the art hanging on them was stale, lifeless, and very much like the man who occupied this office.

The man was an unqualified jackass and pretentious as the day was long, Jeremy thought with a wry smile, and clueless when it came to recognizing fine art. With a sigh, he shouldered out of his coat and tossed it over the back of the nearest chair. He then paced, replaying the conversation he and Emily had had the night before.

It tore him up inside. The pain in her eyes, both physical and emotional, made him feel inadequate and unable to protect her. He'd sworn to Emily he would stay calm and keep his temper in check - but, sliding his fisted hands into his pockets, he wasn't sure he could keep his promise.

He wanted to choke the life out of Owen Harris; his unmitigated gall fed the temper Jeremy was trying so hard to keep under control. A master manipulator, that's what his father-in-law was, and without a doubt, he excelled at it.

Jeremy heard Owen's arrival before he saw him, giving him the chance to move behind the door and take him by surprise. Concealed, Jeremy watched him walk through the door straight to his desk. To say the least, Owen was surprised when Jeremy revealed himself by slamming the door with a shove.

The momentary flicker of uncertainty that passed through Owens' eyes gave Jeremy a moment of great satisfaction. "Owen," he said in a measured tone.

"Jeremy," Owen replied, moving the files he was carrying from one hand to the other; this was hardly how he wanted to spend his lunch hour. "I wasn't expecting you," he said, taking notice of his son-in-law's posture. "Something I can do for you?"

Jeremy angled his head, considering. It was no surprise to find the bastard practically oozing his own particular kind of smugness. Meddling in other lives besides his own comes to him so naturally. "Well, I'm trying to decide if you're worth the effort it would take to break your neck...decisions, decisions."

Owen straightened and narrowed his eyes. "Excuse me?"

"You heard me." Jeremy began rubbing his palms together briskly.

"I don't know what the hell you're talking about," Owen snapped. "What's gotten into you?"

"See, I'm trying to figure out just what kind of man tells his daughter to lie to her husband?" Jeremy said, crossing the room and jamming his finger into Owen's chest. "Convincing her telling me the truth would mean I'd leave her."

Owen shoved Jeremy's hand away. "Now just a damn minute." He stepped up toe-to-toe with his son-in-law. "Don't get holier-than-thou with me. We both know you're just biding your time in this marriage. You might be able to snow my daughter with your smile and charm, but I know you. Little piss ants like you are a dime a dozen."

"Takes one to know one, I guess." Jeremy bit down on the inside of his cheek and tasted blood, and for an instant he thought about going for Owen's throat. Worthless or not, it might do him wonders to ruffle his pretentious feathers, to slap utter disarray into his well placed hair. When he spoke, there was a dangerous edge in his voice. "You know nothing about me, I'm well aware of my responsibilities. And I'd never leave my dying wife."

Owen scoffed, brushing off the statement with a dismissive flick of his hand. "Oh please, don't play a player. Dying or not, Emily's not who you wanted to marry, was she? It was one damn miserable sperm with a good sense of direction that put you back in my daughter's life. Responsibilities? Please. You don't love her - you only tolerate her."

"You're one selfish sonofabitch," Jeremy snapped, grinding his teeth. "Don't stand there and tell me how I feel about my wife. Emily's sick, mentally and physically. She's dying, for God's sake, and you manipulate her, play on her insecurities."

Owen propped himself on the corner of his desk and smiled smugly. "You're weak, Beckett; always have been, so I told her to keep her mouth shut. Because you don't have the stomach to stick around when things get ugly. You don't have the guts to watch her suffer, so you'll leave. And when you do, you'll break her heart."

"Go to hell, you twisted bastard."

"You'll make her feel she owes you for doing the decent thing, you little prick. And you'll make her grovel and crawl with appreciation, won't you? So be warned, humiliate her - and I'll destroy you. Understand?"

Jeremy narrowed his eyes. "Emily owes me nothing, and I'll stay because she's my family and I love her. So you be warned, come between me and my wife again - and I'll destroy you."

Owen lifted a brow and watched Jeremy turn to leave. He couldn't resist one more jab. "Oh, and son," he waited as Jeremy looked over his shoulder, "if I were you, I'd keep my distance from Christina Wagner."

Jeremy turned around, his hands fisted at his sides. "Be careful, old man."

Owen grinned, folding his arms across his chest. "I can make her life very unpleasant if she becomes a...distraction for you."

Something in him snapped, and before he could stop himself he was across the room with Owen's shirt collar gripped in his hands, yanking him forward, hatred gleaming in his eyes. "There'll come a time when Emily won't be between us, protecting you, old man." He tightened his hold and watched Owen's face turn purple. "Then I'll deal with you." He shoved him out at arms length, drew back, and drove a hard right into his father-in-law's glass jaw. In disgust, he let go of Owen's shirt and watched him crumple to the floor.

Owen blinked his wild-like, watery eyes and struggled to sit up. Blood dribbled down the front of his shirt as embarrassment rose inside him. He covered it with anger. "Get the hell out before I have you arrested for assault."

Jeremy bowed dramatically as a laugh tickled his throat. "With pleasure," he said, then turned and headed for the door. Stopping with his hand on the brass knob, he glanced over his shoulder to find Owen pulling himself to his feet. "Consider the fact that you're still breathing a favor to my wife." He then left, slamming the door behind him.

~~

Jeremy paced in the living room of the home where he grew up; his face was pinched with anger and fear and his hands were fisted in his pockets while his parents and sister watched him with growing concern.

Elise slid a look out of the corner of her eye as Jamie came to sit beside her and took her hand. "Jeremy. Sweetheart, please sit down and explain all of this."

Jeremy stopped abruptly and looked at his mother. His face softened. "Mom, I don't know what I'm supposed to do."

Linus had had enough of his son bouncing off the walls and stood up to take him by the shoulders. He held him in place and looked into his eyes. "How bad is it?"

Jeremy shrugged and went to sit on the other side of his mother. "Emily's stable now, but Michael says it's going to get worse as the disease progresses." He raked an unsteady hand through his hair and sighed.

Linus needed to keep his son focused. "Tell me more about it. Surely, there's treatment of some kind?"

Jeremy shifted, then exhaled another frustrated breath. "There's a malformation of some kind in her brain. A tumor - and it's a nasty one. It's aggressive and breaking down her cerebral cortex bit by bit every day. Surgery's not an option, it's impossible actually, because any sort of attempt at removal would devastate her brain function. The damage is ongoing, and any treatment's experimental with unknown side effects."

~~

Christina stood in the kitchen of Manhattan Special with her hands on her hips and her patience running thin. *If it isn't one thing, it's another*, she thought. Visions of slapping the plumber - who at that very moment was hunched under her sink, humming a horribly out of tune version of Billy Joel's "Piano Man" - came to mind. She looked down at the shallow water she was standing in and sighed.

The plumber, whose shirt pocket said "Bill," popped out from under the sink, chuckling, deciding he was looking at one unhappy lady. "Hey, don't sweat it, hon," he said, pushing himself up from the floor. "Pipe's corroded. I can fix it toot sweet." He flashed what he thought was a million-dollar smile while he pulled a rag from his back pocket and wiped his hands clean. "Not a problem."

Christina held back a laugh. His illusion of being a sex symbol was way off the mark, but why crush his dream, she decided. "Great," she said, careful to hide the irritation in her voice.

Later, when the crisis seemed to be under control, Lucy came through the swinging doors with 'pissed off' written all over her face. "You've got a visitor," she informed her boss, grimacing at the mess in front of the sink. Sighing, she shook her head, sending the hoops in her ears dangling. "I don't want to be anywhere near this place when Henry sees this."

Nodding her agreement, Christina said, "That's why it'll be fixed by the time he gets here. Who is it?"

"Billionaire Beckett himself," Lucy said before leaning over and peering cautiously under the sink. The mess underneath it made her wince.

Grateful for an excuse to get away from the disaster happening before her, Christina was relieved for the chance to escape. "He's here for a table?" she asked with her heels snapping as she walked to the door. "Do me a favor, make sure lover boy doesn't leave until the job's done; the last thing we need is a flood for the dinner crowd."

"I'll handle it," Lucy said, "but I think a table's the last thing on Beckett's mind."

Christina winced and turned around. "Please, Lucy, don't get into the gutter with the rest of the gossips. We're friends - and nothing more," she said, and with that she disappeared through the door.

~~

She saw Jeremy standing at the bar, making small talk with the bartender, and she wondered why he was here in the middle of a working day. She walked towards him, and their eyes met; somehow, just looking at him, she felt more at ease with the chaos going on around her. If she were smart, though, she would turn around and walk away from temptation.

~ 33 ~

He watched her walk towards him and knew it had been a mistake to come here at this time of day; his presence would look suspicious and could send the society reporters and their slimy camera-toting sidekicks off to stop the presses. It made all the difference in the world knowing he was here in friendship and nothing more.

"Thanks for seeing me," Jeremy said, keeping his voice low. "Can we grab a table for a minute?"

Christina looked at Jeremy with concern as they made their way to a table in the back. Worry lines were set deep in his forehead, and his eyes were dull, tired, and troubled. "What's wrong?"

He took a deep breath and was momentarily thrown, realizing she still wore the same perfume he remembered. "I'm that transparent?" he said, settling back in his chair and shrugging.

"Something's on your mind," she said, fingering the corner of a sugar packet on a small tray in the middle of the table between them.

He scrubbed his hands over his stubbly chin and closed his eyes; his tongue didn't want to form the words. "Emily's sick," he said, pausing to gather his nerve; his eyes were serious. "She's terminal - and she's known for months and kept it from me." His eyes closed, he pressed his palms together, shifted uncomfortably in his seat, and said, "She's dying."

~~

Christina sat, absorbing Jeremy's news over strong black coffee and a warring conscience. Her heart ached for him, and she felt the old familiar need to comfort him. It was strong, the need to be a strength and a shoulder for him to lean on. The urge to reach out pulled viciously at her, and compassion swelled inside her as if trying to fill the void of sudden silence. There were too many reasons why she shouldn't let her heart lead her. So she sat, feeling the flutter of nerves and doubt in her chest, feeling her heart thudding, pounding in her ears, and her resolve weakens.

Jeremy was a changed man. He had changed in ways she would never have thought possible since his marriage to Emily Harris. He was a good husband to her and a good father to his daughter - but he was anything but happy, and it shouldn't take loving him to see it.

Over the past years, it would have pained her too much to admit such things to herself but she could do so freely now. The misery in his eyes left her unsettled and wanting to help - but what could she do for him when being with him caused as many stirrings as being without him?

She saw through his troubled veiled eyes to his soul. Jeremy was a man struggling with misery too palpable to hide, and his pain caused her pain and nearly broke her. Was she waiting for absolution? she wondered. Was she waiting for a sign that she wasn't an awful person, about to overstep?

He sat with his shoulders hunched forward, elbows resting on the table, so she did what she thought anyone would have and, reaching out, took his hand - damning the consequences.

With the intimate contact, Christina realized why Sam had tried to warn her. With the touch, she also realized something else. It was more than jealousy fueling his constant need to remind her of what a dangerous game she could be playing; it was simply truth - and it was a truth she didn't want to face.

This was a line she shouldn't cross, but she was already stepping over the line and deep down knew she didn't want it any other way. This man, a man she knew and loved so well and for so long, was another woman's husband - and still she felt a claim on him, despite it. It was not her place to offer him the comfort he so desperately needed, but in her heart, feeling every twinge of his pain, she couldn't turn him away.

When she reached across the table to lay her hand over his, it felt right; it felt like a connection, and any and all doubt faded. When she looked at him with her eyes mirroring his grief and so filled with compassion, he recognized the tug-of-war going on inside her because the same war was raging inside him.

All reason and sense failed them both. The passage of time hadn't weakened their bond, or their love. Love; he saw it in her unwavering gaze and felt it stir in his heart. When their eyes held, unblinking and tearful, nearly a decade's time disappeared, and he found comfort in those beautiful, green depths once again.

Christina felt it, too. The connection. Looking into his deep, muddy brown eyes was like returning home. As shaken as it left her, she couldn't deny it. She wouldn't. Their fingers laced together, and they felt both the urge swelling between them and the surrender to something stronger than them both.

When in the dark, desolate corner he lifted her hand to his lips and pressed his lips into her warm palm, he felt the jolt of a memory. When she shuddered and her eyes closed, he knew she felt it, too. Warmth cruised up his spine as he remembered and tasted her skin again, and her quiet sigh told him she remembered, too.

~~

Still shaken by what passed between her and Jeremy at the restaurant, she was hoping for some time alone to gather herself. She walked into the living room with her mind on Jeremy - and there he was with his feet propped up on the edge of the coffee table, tie askew, reading over the files in his lap: Sam; preoccupied, charming, easy to love, Sam.

His latest case occupied all his time, but for the few hours of sleep he stole a night. This case was in town and didn't have him jetting across the country like so many of his others did, so it was an improvement. Any other day, she would be thrilled to have him home before nine o'clock, but he could read her too well, and with one close look he would know the trouble brewing in her heart.

Sam looked up from his file just as she considered slipping out unnoticed. Instantly, the pensive, agitated expression on his face changed at the sight of her. "Well, it's about time you get home," he said, pushing the file off his lap and holding his arms out to her. "Lucy mentioned something about Henry and a sex-starved plumber." Smiling, he lifted a brow when she slid into his lap. "Care to elaborate? I'm intrigued."

Christina smiled too as she settled into his arms. "I should call her."

Sam pulled her into a kiss and said, "No need. She said everything's fixed, and Henry's none the wiser." He kissed her softly on the cheek and drew her closer. "You're all mine for the rest of the night."

Christina fidgeted nervously, suddenly uncomfortable with a man she loved for so long now. "You looked pretty busy when I came in."

"Not that busy, I swear."

She smiled at his sweetness and felt disloyal for her time with Jeremy that afternoon. "What'd you have in mind?"

"Takeout and anything else we can think to do."

Christina kissed him then, hard, deep, and with all the love she felt for him. This was the man that belonged to her, the one she could have without question. "I've missed you, Sam," she whispered.

He slid his hand up her smooth nylon-covered leg and sighed. "Me, too, Chris; me, too."

~~

Emily leaned into Jeremy's kiss hello when he walked into their bedroom and found her laying back on the bed. "You looked tired," she said, watching him move heavy-footedly around the room, undressing.

First, he tossed aside his jacket and tie, then he removed his cufflinks and tossed them carelessly onto his dresser top. When he turned his full attention to her, he forced his thoughts of Christina aside. Emily was pale and chilled and tired. Concern for his wife brought him across the room, unbuttoning his shirt on the way. His eyes were heavy, his jaw was set and his shoulders hunched forward as he dropped down beside her.

"I am tired," he said with a sigh. The knot that guilt had twisted in his gut on his drive home let go. "There could be trouble coming with one of the deals Dad has his heart set on." He took a long look at Emily then and wondered how much pain she was hiding. Why his heart pulled him in another direction when the eyes looking back at him were filled with love left him confused. "How're you?"

"Weaker than yesterday. I figured I'd get some rest so I could join you and Debra downstairs for dinner tonight."

He cupped her cheek and moved in for another kiss. "Great. If you're sure you're up to it."

"I am." He seemed preoccupied with something and wasn't in the mood to share it with her. She might not want to know the cause of his turmoil. "Grab a shower and unwind before dinner."

"Sounds like a good idea, wanna wash my back?" Inwardly, he cringed before the words were out of his mouth, feeling like he was offering a consolation prize.

Emily smiled and ran her fingers through his hair. "Go, I want to dress for dinner. It's time our daughter sees me in something other than a robe."

He kissed her and pushed himself off the bed with a grunt. She watched him disappear into the bathroom and heard the shower start and saw steam waft out through the open door. The look she'd seen in his eyes left her wondering. As she got up to dress, she thought that business might have been part of what was bothering him - but there was more to it...maybe much more.

~ 34 ~

He was expecting Emily for lunch, but as time got away from him and paperwork landed on his desk, his date with his wife temporarily slipped from his mind. It was the subtle scent of her perfume that stilled his pen and had him looking up into her smiling face. The paleness in her coloring was common now, but it was the slight wobble in her walk that alarmed him.

He came out of his chair and went to her. "Em, you okay?" he said, wrapping his arm around her waist to support her.

Through bleary eyes, she smiled up at him, but she was unable to focus on his face. Her legs went out from under her, and her eyes rolled back in her head. Dread sent him into action and had him sweeping her up into his arms as he called out for his secretary to call 911.

The last clear thought in his head became a chant.

Please God, don't let her die. Don't let her die.

~~

It was like a replay of the worst time in his life: another endless night in a hospital waiting room.

Same hospital waiting room where the first goddamn nightmare happened.

That thought had tormented him since he'd arrived and gotten a good look at his surroundings three hours ago. So what if there was a new coat of paint on the walls and new carpeting under his feet? Or new cushioned chairs designed for comfort against new chair molding on the walls? Bad news lived here, he thought, and misery, too.

He dragged his trembling hand through his disheveled hair. With his tie pulled loose and shirt tail half-tucked, Jeremy paced across the plush floor, just as he had been for over an hour. His mother and father watched him in silence, wringing their hands and fearing the worst while Jamie did her best to distract Debra.

"Jeremy." Elise Beckett's voice was little more than a whisper as she watched him make another pass in front of her. "Jeremy, please sit down. You're making me nervous."

He stopped mid-stride to lock eyes with her. "It's been hours. No one's come to let us know what the hell's going on."

Linus sighed and decided to join the conversation. "Son, when there's something to say, they'll talk your ear off, believe me."

Jeremy paid no attention and plowed through the next thought in his head. "And where the hell's Owen?"

"I only tracked him down an hour ago," Linus reminded his son. "He's taking the next flight out of Chicago."

"Daddy?"

Jeremy turned at the sound of Debra's voice and offered her a smile. "Hey, sweetie." He closed the distance between them and wrapped his arms around her.

Debra let her father hold her; her fear was stronger than her other more confusing feelings concerning him. "When can I see Momma?"

His eyes closed as he picked her up into his arms, and tucked her head under his chin. He smoothed the hair that was so much like her mother's. "Soon," he whispered and prayed it wasn't a lie.

A family was in crisis as the media circus got underway outside the doors of the hospital. *God, spare us all*, Jeremy thought miserably while hugging Debra tighter.

~~

A stroke. He sat in the bar, replaying the word over in his head. Stroke. Someone as vibrant as Emily had had a stroke. Her neurologist delivered the news, and it felt like a blow to the stomach. For the moment at least, she'd been rendered speechless and partially paralyzed on her right side.

An incredibly hard week after that terrifying night in the waiting room - waiting to hear if his wife was going to live or die - Jeremy was questioning fate again, as he had done so many times in his life. The first time was over losing Christina; the second time had been over the loss of his son.

Somehow, though, Emily rallied, and she was hanging on, clinging to life. *For Debra*, he told himself. He ordered another scotch to wash the guilt down his throat, then let the truth slip in under his defenses; she was clinging tightest to him.

His father and daughter remained at the hospital by Emily's side. In her weakened condition, she spent most of her time sleeping, and Jeremy sought some time to himself. With his wife sleeping twenty-two hours out of the day, he couldn't take the hospital's bleakness and the constant prying eyes of the media.

~ 35 ~

1995
Cherry Hill

Emily was in New York, undergoing more experimental treatments, and she insisted that Jeremy go on to Cherry Hill. His grandfather wanted to see him, and his age was finally getting the better of him. Now he spent his time in a state-of-the-art motorized wheelchair, zipping around the property like a madman on wheels.

The stresses of work and her failing health weighed heavily on his shoulders. She knew her husband well enough to know he needed the peace and solitude he always found at Cherry Hill. He left her in the care of her home nurse and Debra, relenting only after Emily convinced him that not having to worry about him would help her deal with the treatments.

Arriving mid-afternoon, he wasted no time saddling his horse and setting off for an easy ride to unwind from the long drive. He made his way over the trails that wound their way through the property and greedily drew the fresh air into his lungs; there was no air as clean as this in the city.

He hadn't realized how much he'd missed the feel of a horse under him. He sent his horse into an easy gallop down his favorite trail; here in this place, there was no room for his ever-present guilt.

Jeremy still couldn't contain his excitement.

Christina had actually agreed to come.

~~

Christina had missed her time at Cherry Hill. The long drive brought memories flooding back from a lifetime ago. It had taken much soul searching for her to make the decision to come back. She thought of Sam during the drive and wished her guilt had been enough for her to tell Jeremy no. Sam was a good man, and a man she loved, but she couldn't keep up the lie, even to herself. It was Jeremy who held claim on her heart.

Rounding the last curve, the charming house atop the hill came into view. As she turned up the long, winding drive, she smiled, realizing how little had changed here. She parked her Lexus next to Jeremy's Range Rover and shut off the engine.

Nerves caused her hand to shake, so she inhaled deeply and willed herself to relax. She was doing nothing wrong. It helped to remind herself of that, as Christina got out of the car with her eyes scanning the familiar surroundings. She took in all the country charm, her eyes searching before coming to rest on a face she hadn't seen in many years.

Avery's doubts about insisting that his grandson invite her vanished in that moment when their eyes met. She came to him without hesitation, and the old man was pleased as she stepped onto the porch with a warm smile lighting her face. "Well, time's been a friend to you, Christina."

Christina bent down and pressed her lips to his weathered cheeks. His legs may have given out, but one look at Avery Beckett proved his mind and his charm were as sharp as ever. "I see you still have your silver tongue."

"Guilty." He took her hand and motioned to the swing beside him. "Come sit with me awhile; Jeremy's down tending to the horses."

Part of her wanted to turn around and run - but only part of her, the part that knew that being here with Jeremy - in this place where they had spent so much time planning for the future - would only be asking for trouble.

The rest of her wanted this time and this place - and the man who was waiting for her here; without the prying eyes of media, the pulse of the city, or the heavy burden of her conscience.

With a deep, cleansing breath, she took in the peaceful surroundings and worked to settle her nerves, then she allowed herself to do what she hadn't done in many years: she remembered. Memories washed over her, warming her and bringing a flush to her cheeks.

Memories of nights locked away here with only Jeremy and a fire to keep her warm. Of the young woman she had been. Before Emily Harris and Sam Radcliff. Before she became a little too bitter and jaded. Before sneaking away with a married man became acceptable behavior.

These feelings where easier to fight in the city; where their lives pulled them in different directions, but here they were so strong and close to the surface. This was the last place she should be, but this was where she found she wanted to be.

~~

She sat with Avery, listening to his stories of new horses and breeding, pushing away thoughts of leaving. He told her of the latest acquisitions Beckett International made and of how he was considering retiring from the board of directors. His eyes were as warm and welcoming as she remembered, and his humor put her at ease.

They were sharing tea a half-hour later when the sound of barking dogs and muttered curses had Christina looking out across the lawn. Her first impulse to laugh was overpowered by the sudden turn of her heart when their eyes locked across the distance - but there was much more than friendship in the long look between them, and they both could feel it.

"Your damn horses can be as stubborn as you, Grandpa," Jeremy bellowed as he crossed the lawn with his eyes still on Christina.

Avery laughed heartily, slapping his knee as he got a look of Jeremy's dirty shirt and messed hair. "They know their mind." He watched his grandson's attention shift to Christina. "Christina's been kind enough to keep an old man company."

"You made good time." Jeremy held out his hand, and she took it without hesitation. "Wanna stretch your legs?"

She nodded, then stood to come down the steps to join him.

"We'll be back in time for dinner, Grandpa."

Avery Beckett smiled as he watched two of his favorite people make their way across the manicured lawn for the trails beyond, and the old man wondered. Despite his grandson's love for the woman walking beside him, he remained a devoted father and husband - but there had been a cost. Sadness always threatened because Emily was unable to be an active participant in their life together, or in some case life at all.

Avery had watched Jeremy become increasingly quiet over the years. There was unhappiness in him that took the light from his eyes and the excitement from his spirit. Even his love of painting had suffered; he knew from Jamie that it had been more than a year since Jeremy had picked up a brush.

His life now revolved around Emily's illness, and his determination was to care for the woman who was the mother of his child. He was a man caught between two women, both of whom he loved - but only one truly knew what it was to have his passion and all of his heart. He loved his grandson and wanted to give him a place to be at peace and whole with the woman with whom he was in love and who had captured his heart long ago.

~~

They walked together in a companionable silence, holding hands with an ease that their separate lives in New York would never afford them. A weight lifted off Jeremy as he stopped and did what he had been wanting to do for so long now: he pulled Christina into his arms. "I'm glad you came," he said, letting his fingers play with the ends of her hair.

She let his warm eyes pull her in. "I almost didn't."

Her admission didn't surprise him, but he looked over at her for a long moment before he spoke. "You were always stronger than me. Pretending I'm not still in love you is too hard; all these years without you, and I still can't manage it."

"Jeremy..." Christina released a deep breath that became a sigh. The truth in his words shone in his eyes; she loved him, too, so why should she deny it anymore? If she couldn't tell the truth here, where could she? But there was another truth as well, and she couldn't help but speak it. "Just because this feels right, doesn't mean it is."

"Maybe, but it doesn't feel wrong to me either." He drew her closer and caught the scent of perfume at the nape of her neck. A low groan tickled his throat. "Kiss me, Christina." He risked brushing his lips over hers and felt her tremble in his arms. "Aren't you tired of being noble yet?"

She should pull away from him, from this, but she didn't. She couldn't. "I've never been noble," she whispered, letting her fingers slide into his hair, letting her heart have its way, "but I'm tired of pretending, too." Then he kissed her, truly kissed her, with passion and longing pent up for too long, and she simply surrendered.

~~

He didn't plan for this and cursed himself for his lack of finesse, but he couldn't have known that one kiss would unleash a torrent of feeling and pent-up emotions. He wanted her - right there on a dusty horse trail, he wanted her.

Nearly mad with need, nearly desperate, and before he could stop himself, his hands were moving over her, groping, caressing. Searching, sliding, gliding over her breasts, his hands molding to them through her clothing. Their bodies still fit together, and he wanted her flesh damp and heating beneath his.

As she fell into the kiss, her lips parted and invited, and from deep in her throat she murmured that she wanted him, too. When her tongue slipped into his mouth and found his, the where, the how, and the when hardly mattered. Christina wound her arms around, then, pressing her body into his, took the kiss deeper.

He swept her up into his arms, carried her off with their lips still locked together in need, so much need he couldn't think; he needed to touch her or burn up from their combined heat and die. When they finally drew apart from the heady kiss to catch their breath, they found themselves in the stables.

He lowered her back to her feet, cupped her cheek, then let his hand slide into her hair. "I'm sorry," he managed, his chest heaving. "Please don't think I asked you to come here so I could maul you."

A little dizzy, she clutched at his shirt to steady herself. "I don't."

Taking her face in his hands, he waited while her dazed eyes met his. "But I want you," he said, simply, quietly. "I want this." As if to prove it, he dragged her against him and crushed his mouth to hers again.

When she moaned, her hands slid up to his broad shoulders and gripped them tightly as she tilted her head and he took the kiss deeper. Then she broke away, dragged air into her lungs, and murmured, "I want you, too."

It left a foul taste in her mouth, though. "It's wrong, I know it is, but I love you - and I want to make love to you."

"But?" Jeremy muttered, feeling her conflict and nearly choking on his own.

"But there are other people to consider," she sighed and turned away. "People we love."

Jeremy grimaced and stared at her back. "Sam."

"And Emily." She turned back and despite her words, reached for him, clutching his shirt. "And your daughter."

"Debra has nothing to do with this," he countered, laying his palm against her cheek, "and I do love Emily, Christina, but I'm ***in*** love with you. Just like you love Sam, but you're ***in*** love with me."

"Yes." Her hands slid up his neck and into his hair. "But I'm not made for this; I'm not cut out to be the other woman. I deserve more."

"You deserve much more," he agreed, wrapping his arms around her, "and you could never be the other woman. You're the only woman who has my heart."

"And Sam thinks he has mine." She dropped her head to his chest. "But you have it now, maybe you always have," she murmured.

Dropping his chin to rest on her hair, he spoke desperately, "Then we should allow ourselves this." He lifted his head and tipped up her chin to look at him. "God knows, you deserve more than stolen moments. I know it's selfish, but it's all I can give you right now. I know you need more. But let's just give ourselves this. Let me make love with you, Christina."

"I do need more, but, God help me, I ache for you; I ache to feel your touch again." She pulled his mouth to hers and kissed him for what felt like forever. She wanted him, and for once she'd let this heady feeling whirling throughout her body be enough. "I ache to have you inside me again."

~~

He looked around the stables and sighed. He'd have to improvise because a horse stall was hardly the surroundings he'd envisioned when he fantasized about making love with Christina again; so blankets from the tack room and an empty stall would have to set the mood of being hidden away in the countryside.

Even the pungent aroma of fresh hay was lost in her scent. It clouded his senses as he lay her down on a bed of soft blankets and hay and covered her face with kisses. His heart began to thud in his ears when she dragged his mouth to hers. As she wrapped herself around him, the hay beneath them gave under their weight.

Her eyes fluttered closed, and she sighed as his mouth skimmed from her lips to make the slow, delicious journey to her throat where her pulse pounded wildly. For him. His tongue left behind a searing trail to her lips, then he fisted his hand in her hair and gave a seductive tug to tip her head back, giving him even more of her to feast on. The taste of her made his heart pound, and his mouth slid hungrily along the sensitive line of her throat to the creamy, moist skin beyond.

Her purr of pleasure blinded him, stoking a fire in him that threatened to devour them both, driving him past reason. He tore her blouse open while his tongue glided greedily along the valley of skin between her breasts. Silk and lace covered her, but he didn't waste time delighting in the sexy barrier when she pressed him to her and arched maddeningly beneath him.

Heated blood pounded in his veins, his muscles strained as her clever touch became a wondrous assault to his battered senses, and he knew he was losing his grip on control. He wanted all of her and knew he was about to have her as she tugged desperately at the denim covering his broad chest.

Drifting on wave after wave of pleasure, she was desperate to touch him. Skin to skin in an intimate way, without barriers, without shame. She fumbled with buttons and hurriedly opened his shirt to let her hands streak over his chest and roam to his back. With a shuddering moan of pleasure, she reveled in his body. He nipped at her ear and heard her gasp. His heart beat wildly, and her sigh made him respond with a rough sigh of his own.

With a flick of his finger, her bra opened, and he could only groan over the feel of her creamy, full breasts in his hands. He closed his mouth over her nipple and felt her breath shudder through trembling lips and then he felt her whole body trembling in response.

His hands then went on a slow journey of her long, lean body - which he remembered well. Lost in sensations, she gasped at his avid hands thorough assault on her body, and raked her nails down his back until his gasp matched her own. When he cupped her, he felt the moist, inviting heat at her center, and felt as if he were finally where he belonged. His simple, familiar touch bucked her wildly over the first sweet edge, and she cried out as the orgasm whipped through her with the force of a raging storm.

He wanted to drive her as ruthlessly as she was driving him. Her tongue glided along his as she moved against him, pulling at the snap of his jeans as she reached for him. As his fingers dipped under the lacy waistband of her panties, her eyes flew open.

Her glazed eyes met his, heavy with mounting passion. "Don't you dare." She stilled his hand and used her own to wrap around him. "I want to feel you inside me."

Jeremy's breath caught. "You're killing me."

Nipping at his chin, she chuckled seductively, tugging his jeans down over his hips. "Hurry, I want you fast," she panted, then her breath caught and she clung to him, holding him close when his mouth closed over her taunt nipple. "I want to feel everything, Jeremy. I want to lose my mind."

"And I want you to scream my name."

Christina reached for him, and he was hard and ready when she tightened her hold on him. With a vicious oath, he moved over her, letting her guide him, wrapping her other arm around his neck. There was no guilt as he plunged into her. The glory of it stilled him. He couldn't say if she lost her mind, but his was already blank from the all-encompassing pleasure. Neither moved as sensations - ripple after ripple of them - rocked them until they could do nothing but tremble.

Desperate and nearly mad, Christina's hips lifted to meet Jeremy desperate to set the rhythm they both remembered well. Breathless and weeping, her eyes fluttered open to lock on his. "Please, Jeremy."

It was a plea and the look in her eyes; the blinding desire he saw there made him weak. "I love you," he gasped, finally beginning to move inside her. "Look at me."

And she did. With their eyes locked on each other, their lips met. Every thrust, every stroke dragged them closer and closer to the edge. He stared into her green eyes, dazed, clouded, half open and blinded. Her lips parted, her breath trembling out with each thrust of his hips.

Love overwhelmed him, he whispered her name. "Christina. I want to watch you fall." Her eyes finally focused on his, and they held.

Their breath quickened. Her hips moved in a feverish pace, and a fire stoked by passion nearly consumed them. They came together, crying out as he buried his face in her hair and she clung to him; there was no turning back.

~ 36 ~

May 1996

She came to the ocean just as she knew she would when she stepped off the plane. Somehow, when things seemed darkest to her, Christina felt drawn to the water; it had been that way her entire life. It was to the sea that she'd escaped after her father's death, and then again when she'd allowed Jeremy back into her heart and her bed.

She'd never bothered to question why she found solace in the water and the waves, and she didn't now. Not with her feet tucked into the warm sand, not with the salty air stinging her skin. Because, for all its vastness and depth, the ocean could mirror human emotion so completely; understanding and comfort could always be found there.

Christina needed understanding now, and the beach she chose off the main land on Hawaii's Maui Island seemed as good a place as any to find it. She knew she was far from home, but distance was necessary to ensure that the prying eyes of the tabloids couldn't find her, couldn't stalk her like a hunter does his prey. She rolled her aching shoulders and sighed with relief. Here, at least, she would have the privacy she needed to sort out the latest change in her life.

She was pregnant.

The tension gripping and crowding her since she'd learned of her pregnancy was already beginning to loosen. Tipping her head back and closing her eyes, she let the early morning breeze coming in off the water feather its way over her skin to soothe. It bathed her, it clung to her, in a whispery, salty mist smelling of the sea. Her body and soul needed this quiet contemplation before the bottom fell out of her life once more. And she had no one to blame but herself.

For a moment, she let the wind toss her hair and massage her tension-riddled body into submission. She knew what her next move had to be, and it would not be an easy one. Opening her eyes and focusing on the vivid hue of the morning sky, Christina began to worry over the details. She would have to tell Jeremy. And then, her queasy stomach pitched at the thought, she would have to tell Sam.

The word reverberated in her head over and over. *Pregnant*. Thirty-seven years old and pregnant - and scared - and for the most part, alone. She couldn't imagine being more frightened if she were seventeen and alone. They'd taken every precaution, hadn't expected it, and hadn't planned for it; even so, she couldn't pretend she didn't want this baby. She walked into the surf knowing she could not ignore or deny the current of joy she felt under the fear.

The breeze picked up, and she pulled her hair into a knot on top of her head. A baby. As dismal as the situation was, Christina smiled at the thought. Her child was coming into the world. Granted, it would have been better for everyone if the baby could have a home with the mother and father married, happy, and settled, but this baby had been created in love - and sometimes events were beyond control.

She could understand that more than anyone. She pushed the negative thoughts aside and focused on the positive. As shocked as she was to find herself pregnant, she already loved this baby and was excited about impending motherhood - when she could battle back the guilt long enough.

On top of all else, the father of her baby was a man she loved more than anything, and - right or wrong - he had always been the man she wanted to be the father of her children.

Stolen moments with Jeremy had redefined her life, as they had all those years before in the darkened bar of O'Donnell's. He was a charmer then and remained one now. And, he loved her, and she him. She denied it for too long to bother denying it now, so she had to think that, somehow, all this was happening for a reason.

Would Jeremy be happy about their baby? How could he not be when many times, as they lay in each other's arms, he would dream out loud about what a child of theirs might look like? And his dream was becoming a reality.

She walked further into the waves as they broke over her knees and looked out into vast, endless blue. The water, though crystal blue and seeming to go on forever, was as restless and unsettled as she. Foam-edged waves rolled in, heading for the shore, and matched the emotions churning inside her.

The waves whooshed in fury as they crashed into shore, and yet she felt comforted - but there was a storm moving in to bring havoc into her life, and she prayed she would find the strength to do what was right.

Sam deserved the truth, she knew, as the call of a tropical bird flying over head pulled her gaze up and away. The morning sun was growing brighter, and she squinted as the bird disappeared into a nearby palm. Pulling her sunglasses from her shirt pocket, she pushed them on her face.

She'd told many lies and half-truths to Sam for more than a year, and it was hard to know where to begin; but she had to find a way, although she had an uneasy feeling that he may have already suspected a change.

With his firm up and running smoothly, he had regular hours and was spending more time at home. Christina thought about the growing distance between them and hated that she was the cause. He knew something was wrong, but she'd always denied it when he asked her. He deserved honesty, and time was of the essence.

Christina had to tell him soon. Already six weeks along in her term, it wouldn't be long before she would begin to show. The gossip columns would go crazy, assuming the baby was Sam's and that the long speculated marriage between them would be a foregone conclusion. The thought of hurting Sam brought her physical and unimaginable pain, but the truth had to come from her.

She pulled off her sunglasses and squeezed her eyes shut against the bright rays of the sun. She'd betrayed a wonderful man who had done nothing but love her, and she loathed herself. When she began to weep, she felt every tear deep within her soul.

Christina didn't deserve the pity she allowed herself, shoving the tinted glasses back on her face and turning to walk up the beach. Emotions overwhelmed her most of the time now, the hormones and guilt were quite a combination. Those first days after learning she was about to be a mother, the tears fell unabated. Somehow, she would find the strength to do what was best for everyone, but for no one more than the baby growing inside her.

For now, though, she was tired and needing to get off her feet. She'd promised to call Jeremy first thing this morning, and he'd worry if he didn't hear from her soon. He knew where she was but had no idea the real reason why, no idea his life was about to change forever. For the time being she wanted to be by herself, and he wouldn't be able to understand why. She felt her stomach churn and realized she'd forgotten breakfast and chided herself. She needed to take better care of herself; she was eating for two now.

~ 37 ~

New York City

It was nearly nine p.m., but Jeremy was back in his office after rushing home for the doctor's home visit to examine Emily earlier in the evening. The disease attacking her brain had found a new way to torment her. Now, seizures racked her frail body for minutes or sometimes hours at a time, leaving her arms and legs stiff and her unable to speak or even focus her eyes.

Michael and her neurologist finally advised a radical course of treatment: a drug-induced coma, to allow her fragile system to recuperate. He wanted to weep for the pain Emily was suffering, but found he could only be grateful that the coma would put an end to the seizures.

Frustration gnawed away at him, but at least Emily was finally resting comfortably as her coma entered its third hour now. He stayed with her as evening turned to night and tried to get some paperwork finished at the foot of her bed. That proved to be a waste of time, though, as he sat and constantly watched for the slightest change in her condition.

The night nurse was with her now, and he was too restless and edgy to be of any use to her. Her pain had become intolerable, and her only relief was a morphine haze before the deep sedation her doctors had prescribed had given her total relief. She would hate what was happening to her if she were aware or even a shadow of her former self.

It was late and growing later, but he couldn't make himself get up out of his chair to leave. Home was hardly the refuge it had once been. With his wife a prisoner in her own body and their daughter growing into a teenage rebel, he was overwhelmed. And as night closed in around him, he was also feeling bitter.

The building was deserted except for the security staff as he stood glaring out his window at the street lights along Madison Avenue. If Christina were home, he could call her and talk his way out of his dark mood - but she was on an island paradise and pushing him away.

He stood and stretched, wondering if the distance he felt between them was real or imagined. What was eating her up inside? Fighting off a yawn and raking his fingers through his disheveled hair, he crossed to the sofa and collapsed into the overstuffed cushions with a groan. He could have used some time on an island himself, but there was no time for fun in the sun.

He wanted to go to Christina and find out what was going on. He wanted to snap his fingers and eradicate the disease that was slowly and cruelly killing his wife with chilling efficiency. When he talked to Christina that morning, she'd sounded distracted and edgy when what he needed was a shoulder to lean on.

Maybe, he thought with another yawn, that that was the problem. Had he been leaning on her too much lately? Maybe sharing Emily's setbacks with her only added to the guilt Christina already battled. He battled it, too, although it had been a long time since Emily recognized him as anyone other than a stranger.

He needed Christina.

It was difficult to watch Emily lying motionless in the bed they once shared, and when she looked at him and didn't recognize him - it broke his heart. To hear her laugh silenced and the special lilt in her step stilled made him miss her more than he would have thought possible.

He needed Christina, like it or not, selfish or not. The decision made, he left his office in a rush before he could change his mind.

~~

Jamie watched him throw his suitcase in the back seat of his car, his mouth a thin line of frustration, his shoulders pushed forward and stiff. "You look like hell."

Jeremy turned around and sneered at his sister as he checked his wallet to make sure he had enough cash on hand. "Thanks." He hated the judgment he saw in her eyes, but he'd seen it too many times to be affected by it anymore. "I need to get some distance, that's all."

She folded her arms across her chest and angled her chin. "Do you even know if Christina wants to see you?"

He sucked in a breath. The last thing he had time for was another fight. "It's none of your business, Jamie."

"It's four o'clock in the fucking morning, and you drag me out of bed to babysit so you can catch a plane with a clear conscience." She huffed out a breath, realizing she was getting loud. "That makes it my business."

As quickly as his anger flared, it died. Sweet god he was tired. His hard eyes softened, and he climbed the steps on his rubbery legs to take her hands in his. "Sorry," he said quietly. "I'm useless here anyway, and I'm worried something's wrong with Christina. I can't help Em, but Christina's a different story."

"What about Debra?" Jamie asked, softening as she saw the pain in her brother's eyes for the first time since she'd arrived hell bent on giving him a piece of her mind.

Jeremy sighed and shrugged. "Right now, she doesn't want to be anywhere near me. She's sixteen and wild, a lot like someone else I know," he said, pinching his sister's nose between his thumb and forefinger.

She pushed his hand away and feigned ignorance. "I don't know who you're talking about." She walked him down the steps and opened his car door for him. "She's scared."

Dropping into the car, his face grew sad. "So am I."

Jamie leaned into the open window and touched her brother's face. "She just needs someone to blame."

"I know," he sighed and grinned lopsidedly, "happy to oblige." The grin disappeared. "Tell her I love her."

"I will. Tell Christina I said hello."

"I will." He kissed her cheek and started the engine. "Call me if there's any change."

"Of course."

~~

He found her on the beach, just where the manager of the hotel said she'd be. He could see her in the distance, sitting on the sand with a colorful sheer gabardine covering her shoulders to ward off the early morning chill coming in from the ocean. With her lush bronze hair flying free, the sight of her stole his breath. For a moment, he just enjoyed the rare chance to watch her without her knowing.

Her stomach rolled, and she took a few deep breaths before the morning sickness could overtake her again. Christina woke up with the dawn that morning and spent the next hour vomiting; still, she could smile because the payoff was worth any annoyance.

The cry of a tropical bird made her turn and follow its path, and it was then that she saw him. He was coming closer, closing the distance between them, with that easy, unhurried stride that could only belong to one man.

His hair was as sandy in color as the sand at his feet, his eyes were shaded by sunglasses, and the sleeves of his powder blue lightweight sweater were pulled up to his elbows. His light brown shorts showed off the well-formed muscles in his legs. Dressed to his own impeccable standards, Jeremy Beckett could simply be a woman's dream come true.

When their eyes locked, his mouth curved into an easy smile. Christina wanted to stand but couldn't; she felt too struck to see him, too moved that their connection could be felt so strongly between them. Then, time seemed to stop, and before she knew it he was right there in front of her.

He stood, his hands tucked into his pockets, gazing down at her, his eyes searching, intense on her face. She knew his hands were fisting - a habit he used to relieve tension - and she felt his dark eyes taking their fill of her. Neither of them spoke; it was unnecessary because both felt the familiar, subtle pull that always drew them together, and in that recognized current of emotion they found enough.

In the weighty silence, Jeremy pulled his hand out of his pocket and held it out to her. When she took it, she felt the same jolt, the same charge between them. He lifted her to her feet and simply embraced her.

Christina broke the silence. "I asked you not to come," she murmured, but she clung to him fiercely.

With a deep breath of relief, he clung tightly, too. Her scent mixed with the salty, ocean air was enthralling. He looked out over the ocean and knew why she would pick this beautiful spot for escape. He drew away and pulled off his sunglasses, then wrapped her in his embrace again.

He could see she was tired, and if he weren't mistaken, she looked a little green. "But I never agreed."

The breeze blew Christina's gabardine off her shoulders as she looked away to the water. When she felt him press his lips to her skin, her breath caught and she sighed; this wasn't how she was planning to tell him, and now she would have to summon the courage to tell Jeremy the truth before she was ready. His arrival, though, left her little choice to do otherwise.

Christina finally looked at him; his face was so close, she felt his breath on her skin and almost smiled. She should have known he wouldn't be patient. It was just like him to take matters into his own hands.

"I just needed some time, Jeremy. I'm trying to sort a few things out on my own." Apart from each other, she might have been able to hold him off, but face-to-face her resolve would crumble. He could always pull everything inside her, her passion, her anger, to the surface.

With his arm around her, Jeremy eased them down to sit on the sand. This wouldn't be the romantic reunion it should be, he knew, because he still felt distant from her even though she sat right beside him. So they sat in silence with, to his way of thinking, an undefined tension between them; a sort of third companion on the sand. He pulled his knees up and planted his sandaled feet in the sand, stamping down hard on his urge to drag what was bothering her out.

With control tightening his jaw, he decided to wait and give her the chance to tell him on her own. The time it might take hardly mattered now that he was here with her. He could give her his patience, even if it was a virtue he usually found hard to come by. But he didn't know for how long. So, he did as she was doing, he looked out to the mesmerizing waves without demands.

If ever there were a place where time might stop, this stunningly beautiful paradise was it. He'd looked into her eyes and saw they were pained, and he felt his own stomach twisting into knots. And still he waited. One minute, then two. After five minutes of continued silence, his patience, always a fragile thing, and despite his best efforts - snapped.

"Damn it," he mutters. "Are you going to tell me what's going on?" Trying to keep the tightness in his chest out of his voice was a struggle. When he risked looking at her, he cursed again under his breath. "It's damn hard knowing you ran away from me, so can you at least tell me why? Is this your way of telling me it's over?"

She looked at him, into him, and saw the love for her fueling his anger; it helped to hear it, to *know* it. It soothed and calmed her, and she nearly sighed with relief. "No, but you may want it to be when I tell you what I'm about to."

"You're scaring me."

"Good," she laughed nervously. "I'd hate to be the only one scared here."

Jeremy tried to shrug off the weight he felt settling on his chest. "Goddamn it, Christina," he snapped, frustrated.

She stared at him, watched the hard line of his jaw twitch. He was losing his patience, and surprisingly, she found so was she. "Don't push me, Jeremy." Annoyance had her tossing her hair over her shoulder, trying to control her temper; she'd come here to avoid pressure, damn it. "This isn't a business deal you can control with a tantrum. I won't let you bully me either."

"Tell me, or by Christ, I'll shake it out of you."

His famous temper unleashed. Under different circumstances, she would have found his temper sexy as hell, but she didn't like being pushed. So, giving in to a bit of her own temper, she decided to push back. "I'm pregnant." The words hung in the air between them, and her heart froze. "God...say something, would you?"

He gaped at her in stunned silence. He opened his mouth, then, at a loss, managed, "I....a baby." His mind was spinning. His heart was thudding, one beat utter joy, the next numbing fear. His smile, though, was wide, foolish, and genuine. "When?" He cupped her cheek in his palm. "You're alright?"

As easily as that, her anger drained away - how could it not, seeing his boyish grin, the delight on his face? There was comfort in that. That, and finding he wasn't making a beeline down the beach away from her. She tossed her glasses aside, touched his cheek, and then went into his arms.

"I'm six weeks along." Her eyes leveled on his as she swallowed another twinge of nausea. "My stomach's churning worse than that water out there, but otherwise I'm fine."

"I'm shocked," he said quietly. "Shocked and happy." He leaned in and kissed her, loving her more in this moment than ever before. Then, he understood her turmoil. "Sam." His face turned grim. "What'd you tell him?"

"Nothing yet. He thinks I'm at a chef's convention," Christina confessed as their hands linked. "I need to deal with the mess I've made of our life and figure out what I'm going to do about it. Sam's still blissfully unaware I've betrayed him, and I can't look him in the eye right now."

Jeremy pressed his lips to her brow and shook his head. "We're in this together. And you haven't made a mess, *we've* made a baby. I won't deny the situation is complicated and the timing's even worse - but it's a child. Our child. And you didn't mean to hurt Sam, just like I didn't mean to hurt Emily."

"Something tells me they'll see this very differently."

Because it was true, Jeremy held her tight and closed his eyes. He'd had enough of pain - both the pain he felt and the pain he caused...but - God help him - there would be more to come.

~~

Linus accepted that his granddaughter was growing up - like it or not, he thought, as an ache set in around his heart. She was intelligent, watchful, and blisteringly blunt. But worse, and far more damaging, she was intuitive and adult enough to pick up on matters not of her concern.

Debra wasn't the little girl who once clutched his hand, which became painfully clear when they climbed out of the limo and her hand was now tucked through his arm instead. At sixteen, she carried herself like a young woman with purpose and nearly dragged him up the sidewalk to the entrance of Manhattan Special.

"I don't see why we couldn't eat at home, Grandpa," Debra pouted as the waiter disappeared into the kitchen with their orders and left them alone. "I don't like leaving Mama alone."

Linus sipped from his sparkling water and considered. As far as Debra was concerned, her father had left her mother to run off to an island paradise. But it wasn't that simple; in truth, it was a great deal more complicated. "Your mother isn't alone, sweetheart. Aunt Jamie and the nurse are with her. And you needed a change of scenery, and some fresh air, Debra. You can't sit vigil every minute of the day. That's not what she wants for you."

"Someone has to," Debra replied with a sting in her voice. "Daddy's too busy to do it, isn't he?"

He tuned into her poisonous tone and nearly winced. "The doctors told him there was nothing he could do for her right now. He still has business responsibilities. He'll be back in a few days."

Debra rolled her eyes. "Since when do you do business in Hawaii?"

Jarred by her overly-mature intellect, Linus stumbled over the question. "The family company is always looking to break new ground. Don't forget, the company's success puts those designer clothes on your back and allows your weekly shopping sprees."

"I read the gossip columns, too, Grandpa." Debra picked up a breadstick. "I'll bet Daddy hasn't even thought about business, much less done any."

Their conversation eventually turned to more comfortable subjects, and Debra seemed willing to drop the matter of her father's trip. That was why Debra's stunt as they were leaving stunned Linus like a fist between the eyes.

She turned to the head waitress as they were headed to the door and asked, "Where's Ms. Wagner? I want to tell her that her sundaes are the best in town."

"At a convention in Hawaii, poor thing. But I'll give her the message," the head waitress promised.

Debra shot her grandfather a seething look and stormed out into the street.

Linus cursed under his breath, gave the head waitress several twenties to pay their bill, and went after her.

~~

Maui, Hawaii
2:30am

She waited to hear the key in the door while she soaked in the over-sized bathtub. Surrounded by candlelight and covered in lavender scented bubbles, Christina pushed aside thoughts of right and wrong and drifted instead. She was exhausted and would have to become accustomed to it. A baby meant three a.m. feedings, diaper changes, and so much more. Tired was soon to become her middle name.

The warm, scented water soothed and relaxed her, and her mind quieted and drifted away to cozy bliss. Her hand rested protectively on the slight swell under her palm. As frightened as she was over the coming turmoil when the truth about her pregnancy came out, she was excited, too. Holding her tiny baby in her arms, knowing it was part her and part the man she loved would be unforgettable.

Jeremy found her covered in bubbles, sleeping. He stared; his eyes roaming over her, a depth of love welling up in his heart. He undressed, suddenly wanting to gather her close.

Christina was the most beautiful woman, and right or wrong, she was his. In her heart, where it most mattered, she was his, and he was hers. As he slipped into the water without a sound, he prayed she knew that as plain truth, and could never doubt it. When he slid behind her, she opened her eyes sleepily. His long, muscular legs glided along hers as he leaned back against the tub and settled her against him. He could feel her feather-light breath caressing his chest, and pressed his cheek against her hair.

It was then that she came awake. Awake and aroused, Christina lifted her chin to press soft, delicate kisses to the sensitive skin beneath his chin. Steam rose up off the water, giving his skin a moist, silky feel. Her mouth, her lips, her tongue trailed down to taste more, to linger over the pulse already quickening and losing control.

His scent was as familiar and intoxicating as it was the very first time she was in his arms. Memories played through her hazy mind, inviting her, inspiring her, torturing her. Christina had memorized every inch of his magnificent body. Sending water lapping over onto the floor, she shifted to straddle him and drive him deliciously mad.

Her heart raced as wildly as his at the wonder she always felt at his touch. This never got old. The passion that was, even now, demanding that she take instead of give, swallowing her up with its greed. Her hands ran over him as she traced the hard line of muscles in his back up to massage his shoulders.

He was amazed, though dimly, he knew he shouldn't be. She made him weak and had from the very first time. As she journeyed over his body with hungry lips, hungry hands, and her silky tongue, he became weaker still. It was a gift he treasured even while she meticulously drove him beyond thought. This kind of need, might consume him. This kind of want just might burn him alive - but he would die a happy man.

Will it always be this way? he wondered hazily, clinging to her, frantic and as hungry as she. *Yes*, her murmur and his moan replied as her arm snaked around his neck to capture him closer still.

Her long fingers skimmed, then fisted in his hair. With his gasp, she pulled him to her and crushed her mouth to his. Her tongue seduced and tormented to torture them both.

Now it was his hands fisting in her hair. Now he sought to pleasure as he was being pleasured. He ended the kiss, dizzy and desperate, and shifted to close his mouth greedily over her breast. Gasping, her head fell back limply as his tongue flicked over her nipple.

Darkly aroused, her breath hitched and his vision dimmed, but it wasn't enough, and would never be. His hands ravaged her, streaked over her, and took possession of her. His fingers skimmed over her, and - when they found her core - slipped into her.

Rocked to a peak, she went over the edge of oblivion and came with a vicious cry of triumph. She then could only tremble, digging her nails into his shoulders. Desperate for release himself, he lifted her and plunged into the only paradise he would ever need with a throaty groan of ecstasy. They found a rhythm and lost their minds.

Jeremy cradled Christina in his arms as she lay spent against him, her heart thudding wildly to match his, beat for beat. Later, when she was spooned against him in bed and her breath was feather light on his skin again, sleep wouldn't come for the joy he felt. For all the pain that would come of it, their baby was meant to be.

~~

Two days later Christina walked out of J.F.K airport and hailed a cab across town to Sam's firm. She couldn't wait any longer to face him. It wasn't fair to him and the sooner she set things right, the better it would be for everyone. Jeremy stayed behind in Hawaii and planned a late flight home the next night. Their time in Hawaii couldn't be linked together in any way by the press.

The cab made its way through the rush hour traffic in Manhattan at a slow crawl. She tried to relax and tune out the blaring horns of the irate drivers, but her nerves were raw. Hurting the man who had done nothing but love her, didn't sit well in her heart or her conscience.

~~

Sam could only gape at her from behind the chaos of his desk. Talk of the convention and her flight died quickly when he finally looked up from his deposition to see the sorrow in her eyes. Before he could even ask her what was wrong, she'd blurted it out - all of it - and destroyed him.

He sucked in a breath in disbelief as the weight of her confession registered. He hadn't heard her right...he couldn't have...but her eyes confirmed it. Beneath her tears, the truth was staring back at him, and the power of her words mercifully killed his love for her in an instant. Christina was having an affair with Jeremy Beckett, and she was pregnant with his child.

She wanted to go to him and lessen the pain she'd caused, but his eyes and the hard line of his jaw told her that he would never allow her to touch him again. "I'm so sorry, Sam." *So easy to say*, she thought, and she wanted to say more, but the undeniable glint of anger in his usually gentle eyes had her drawing in a deep breath.

Firmly, he placed his palms on his cherry wood desk and pushed himself to his feet. Damned if he'd let her walk away thinking she'd cut the legs out from under him, he told himself, steeling himself against the twin edges of pain and humiliation. "I guess the nasty rumors are true."

She started around the desk, but his raised hand had her reconsidering. "Sam, I did love you. I still do."

With contempt all over his face, Sam stared at her and jammed his hands into his pockets as his anger threatened to overrule reason. "Don't. I think we both know who you love, Chris - don't we?"

She wiped a tear from her cheek and steadied herself. Everything in her wanted to turn around and run, but she stayed because she owed him that much. "I never meant to hurt you. You have to know I hated lying to you."

His back ramrod straight, he turned away to look out his window. He told himself it was to control his anger, but he knew better. He couldn't face her pain as well as his own. "But you do it so well," he threw back. "How long have you been going behind my back to his bed?"

"That doesn't matter."

"It matters to me."

"More than a year."

He cringed, thinking about the times he'd made love to her while she was slipping between the sheets with Beckett. Visions of seedy afternoons in the city's finest hotels flashed in his mind. With considerable effort, he swallowed the bile rising in his throat. "And if not for this baby, I still wouldn't know. The sonofabitch thinks he's entitled to both a wife and a mistress. I thought your pride wouldn't allow you to be one over the other...guess I was wrong."

"Sam, please look at me." Even as she said the words, she felt the wall already between them.

In the ridged set of his shoulders, his arms crossed over his chest, he closed himself off from her. "Get out. Enjoy your life as a mistress."

~ 38 ~

Jeremy's mood soured over breakfast when he turned to the society page and saw a large color photo of Christina leaving her doctor's office. It was the caption underneath, though, that had him seeing red. Simple and very effective:

Baby Beckett on Board?

He shoved away from the breakfast table, struggling to hold an already fraying temper in check. When his coffee cup tumbled off the edge of the table and shattered on the hard oak floor, he cursed loudly. Stooping to gather the pieces, an image of strangling Rona Mitchell flashed in his mind.

A piece of bone china sliced into his finger. First came the sting of pain, then came more anger. "Fuck!" A ribbon of blood dribbled through his fingers before he could stand, and he hissed out a breath of frustration.

Jamie hurried into the room, having seen what happened from the doorway. "What've you done to yourself?" Grabbing a napkin from the table, she wrapped his hand to stop the bleeding. "You might need a few stitches; let me see."

"I'm fine," he snapped, meeting his sister's skeptical eyes. She knew him too well.

"You've seen Rona's latest jab, then?"

"Hard to miss. I'd love to cram it down her throat."

At the bar now, she opened a bottle of club soda. "I'm heading to Manhattan Special for breakfast." Crossing back to him, she unwrapped his hand and doused the wound with the soda, flinching herself when he hissed in pain. "Want me to give her a message?"

He clamped his fingers around the napkin to slow the bleeding. "Tell her I'm sorry," he said softly and left the room to deal with his injury.

Jamie watched as he moved up the stairs - a mixture of anger and pain contorting his face - and she wondered if he even realized how unhappy he was anymore.

~~

Manhattan was packed, and Christina couldn't chalk it up to appreciation for her cuisine. She knew the picture in the paper was worth more than a thousand words. Idle gossip brought droves of people through the door to whisper, point, stare, and - since they were here and the culinary critics have raved - to eat. But why throw them out to gossip on the street for free when she could let them wag their pretentious tongues in her restaurant and charge them outrageously for revenge?

There was a price for her pride, though, and it burned. Every time she served people who secretly delighted in her humiliation, it burned. She damned them all to hell with every swipe of their gold cards.

She was careful to ensure they never got what they really came for. Even allowing them a glimpse of her would be allowing them to win. *Let them look down their noses at me*, Christina thought, *even while they have the nerve to blather on about my food*. But she was not for public display.

Putting the finishing touches on a French toast/egg platter, she reminded herself what was important. At that very instant, her baby was kicking up a storm in her belly. Stress wasn't good for either of them, so she murmured words of comfort as she laid her hand over her belly.

She'd be damned if she'd let Rona Mitchell hold that much power over her. So what if the loose tongues around town were wagging about her? It was hardly the first time. She rang the bell for order pickup and sighed, supporting the small of her back with one hand while pulling up a stool with the other.

Standing in a chaotic kitchen over a hot stove was the last place she should be with only weeks left until her due date, but she needed to feel useful and wouldn't allow the appearance that she was hiding in shame. Christina did what came naturally when stress threatened to overwhelm her: she cooked. Her feet were swollen, and her back was aching under the strain, but busy hands and a busy mind were the only things keeping her from storming the New York Times building and committing an illegal, but very satisfying act.

~~

Alone in the kitchen of Manhattan Special, Christina waited. Hours after closing, when sleeping should have been the only thing on her mind, it was furthest from her thoughts. She was exhausted and desperate to escape being public fodder.

When the soft knock on the back door came, she breathed a sigh of relief. When Jeremy's silhouette filled the doorway in front of her, she sighed once more and pulled him inside. He pulled her to him, wrapped his arms around her in the darkness of the kitchen, and she never felt safer.

The mound of her belly was a welcomed obstacle as he drew in the scent of her hair. Without a word, he drew back to kiss her. Fully, deeply, their lips touched and offered, giving comfort and stoking a desire that never seemed to wane. At her soft moan of pleasure, his hands slid up her back to fist in her endless flow of auburn hair.

"You shouldn't be here." Her voice was a whisper against the curve of his neck.

"I needed to see for myself that you're alright," he said, drawing away to study her face.

Her hands kneaded his shoulders where tension had dug in permanently months before. She wasn't alone in this, she reminded herself. "I'm tougher than I look."

His hand on her stomach, he searched her eyes. "You shouldn't have to be. Sorry about the damned picture."

She pressed her cheek to his. "It's not your fault."

He sighed. "It sure as hell feels like it is." Wrapping his arms around her, they held each other close.

~~

Jeremy watched as the sun dawned, tired but more at ease after seeing for himself that Christina was holding up well under the constant strain of gossip and innuendo. He walked into the master bedroom as the shift change for Emily's nurse was happening. He listened to the night nurse briefing the day nurse on Emily's vitals, medications, and any changes throughout the night.

He nodded a greeting but said nothing as he crossed to the bed to lay his palm against his wife's cheek. He smiled when she stirred against his hand and opened her eyes in the dawn's first light. He crouched down and kissed her lightly on the lips, and she murmured in response.

Her body was frail and futile, but her eyes still revealed a spirit refusing to dim; so, he thought with a surge of affection, this would be a day when she remembered him. Their eyes met, held, and he tried to be grateful for this rare reprieve from the disease ravaging her brain. Stealing another, rare, lucid day from its cruel clutches would be a small victory in the face of so much loss.

He stayed with Emily, enjoying their easy banter and humor, catching her up with what Debra was up to. Little more than an hour later, she drifted to sleep as the morning course of medication began to take effect, so he settled in the chair next to the bed and read the report from the night nurse. His wife had an easy night, and he was grateful. The painful spasms assaulting her for weeks now seemed - for the moment at least - to be under control. She deserved better than what life had given her, but he'd long ago accepted that he was powerless to change it.

~ 39 ~

Linus found him asleep in the chair next to the bed. He looked from his son to his daughter-in-law and frowned. Both were worn down by her disease and the inability to change what fate held in store. Both were suffering, and the suffering would continue. He walked over to lay a gentle hand on Jeremy's shoulder and shook him gently to wake him.

Bleary eyed and stiff, Jeremy lifted his head with a groan. "Dad." He scrubbed his face with his hands and pushed himself to his feet. "What time is it?"

"After eight." Linus went to press a kiss to Emily's forehead before turning his attention back to his son. "You look like hell, son. Your mother's worried, and so am I. When was the last time you got a full night's sleep?"

"What year is it?" Jeremy made his way into the bathroom and splashed cold water on his face. Water dripping off his chin, he looked at his father's reflection in the mirror and sighed. Yanking a towel from the rack, he patted his face dry. "I'm okay, Dad."

Narrowing his eyes, he watched Jeremy shuffle back into the bedroom, legs heavy from fatigue. "Uh huh."

"I might be a little late for the Thompson meeting," Jeremy told Linus, shrugging out of one shirt and into another before heading into the hall. "The doctors are coming by in an hour, and I want to be here."

Linus tucked his hands into his pockets and looked through the doorway at Emily. "Of course. Your mother insists you come by for dinner tonight with Debra."

"I'd like to spend some time with Em tonight. If she's awake, I'll read to her. It cheers her up."

"Why don't we come here, then?"

"Sure."

"How was her night?" Linus asked, looking pained for his daughter-in-law.

Jeremy followed his gaze and sighed. "Better."

"Thank God." Linus watched as Jeremy tied his tie. "How's Christina handling the press situation?"

Jeremy's eyes flicked up to his father's and hardened. "Better than me. Fuckin' leeches, that's all they are. I don't want this shit to throw her into premature labor. I've been down that road before." He smoothed his tie and rolled his shoulders. "Don't care to do it again."

"She's a strong woman, son."

"Yeah. But strength doesn't last forever."

~~

Owen Harris boarded his private plane, fuming. The overt indiscretions of Jeremy Beckett and how easily he discarded his marriage to Emily would not be tolerated. The New York papers reveled in every sordid detail they could dig up. He plotted revenge as the plane took off and leveled off in the sky over Paris.

It was time to go home and deal with his worthless son-in-law. He had warned him, hadn't he? No one made a fool of Owen Harris or his daughter and escaped unscathed. And now, whatever happened, the blame could be laid squarely at Jeremy's feet.

Owen bit the inside of his cheek and focused on the dusky sky beyond the plane. He wasn't a man given to displays of emotion, but here, alone, the fear crept in, and a tear welled in his eye as he thought about Emily. She had become so weak, and he didn't need the doctors to tell him how close he was to losing her. He could sense it. The damn disease was winning, and all the money in the world couldn't stop it. The doctors had all but assured him she wouldn't survive another two years. The breakdown of her body would continue until one day her heart would stop and her pain would end.

And what had the great Jeremy Beckett done for her? Nothing but made her a fool. He carried on with his slut while his wife slipped away in their bedroom. He had done nothing to help or ease her pain. For that, Owen Harris would see that he and his slut paid dearly.

~~

In the state-of-the-art kitchen of Manhattan Special, Christina was in her element. No matter the spectacle her life had become, in this space of stainless steel and chrome she was unshakable. Adrenaline carried her through her days now as her delivery date neared - that, and the need to serve her clientele the very best.

Lucy swung into the kitchen as she was putting the finishing touches on a rack-of-lamb dinner and preparing to make a dessert of strawberries and chocolate over a bed of shortbread. The serenity on her boss' face made what she had to tell her even harder. The last thing she needed was a crisis in the middle of their dinner crowd, but a crisis was in the making.

An unscheduled visit by the New York State Health Department was anything but funny, but Lucy almost laughed when Mr. Levin served her with the notice of complaint - and Christina wouldn't find any humor in it either in her present condition. The very idea of Christina Wagner cutting corners and putting people at risk was laughable.

When Christina glanced up and saw her watching, she smiled. Lucy couldn't sugar coat it and didn't even try. When Christina learned Mr. Levin was out front on official business, she was curious but not concerned. It was a simple mistake; it had to be. So, Christina wiped her hands hurriedly and rushed out to speak to him.

Casting a watchful eye around at her clientele, she made her way out around the bar and noticed when several of her regulars waved in greeting. Others, only there for grist for the rumor mill, gawked as she flaunted her pregnancy in public. She ignored them and their whispers as she passed by, then spotted Mr. Levin giving one of her bartenders the once over.

With a deep, steadying breath, she made a bee line for what was bound to become a shouting match if she didn't intervene. *What in the hell is going on?* she wondered. Why in the world would Levin come in for an on-the-spot inspection during the crazy dinner rush? Her usually friendly barman was raising his voice and squaring his shoulders when she arrived, and she wisely stepped between them.

"Mr. Levin." She smiled sweetly, but they both knew of the steel underneath. He'd swallowed whatever crack was on the tip of his tongue and turned his attention to Christina. She motioned for her employee to go. "Lucy tells me we've got a problem. Would you mind lowering your voice and explaining?"

"We've had several complaints filed against your establishment here," he explained a bit too loudly and blandly. "I'm afraid I need to inspect the kitchen immediately."

Christina stared at him, stepping closer and lowering her voice, hoping he would do the same. She could imagine heads craning and tuning into every word. "On what grounds?"

"Unsanitary kitchen practices."

"You're joking."

Mr. Levin handed her the notice and waited while she read it over. "I'm sorry, but this is hardly a joking matter."

~~

The charges were ridiculous, and following the inspection of her kitchen by Levin, the charges proved to be exactly that: ridiculous. The scene he caused, however, was humiliating and embarrassing.

On the drive home, Christina was certain that by morning the accusations would be the talk of the town - and there would be no way to do damage control. Not with the tabloids and respectable papers alike paying handsomely for tips from suspected turncoats on her staff.

Loyalty. With her anger returning, Christina wondered where the loyalty among her family had gone - because that was how she thought of her staff: as family. If loyalty could be bought, then it could be sold as well - and money talked. If she couldn't trust the people around her, then she would truly be on her own.

Someone was out to cause trouble, and she had no idea who it could be, considering so many in the city viewed her as little more than a home wrecker. But someone - and someone powerful enough to lead Levin around by the nose - wanted her professional reputation to suffer as much as her personal one.

Christina could and would stake her reputation on the utmost and highest standards in her kitchen sanitary practices. Above reproach was how she maintained her kitchen; in fact, she was certain you could eat off any chosen surface and challenged anyone to prove differently.

It was just after midnight when she turned onto her street and spotted the light burning in the upstairs window of her cottage-style house. Jeremy was inside waiting for her. They had been using this system of clandestine meeting to steal a few hours together without fear of reprisal.

She pulled into the garage and waited for the door to roll closed behind her. He came through the door leading into the house before she opened her door. One look at him threatened to undo her. Why did they have to pay such a heavy price to follow their hearts?

Wasn't this the very same city that had once bathed their relationship in adoring approval all those years ago? She could remember a time when Emily had been the other woman and she the woman scorned. Times had changed, though, and if she ever forgot that, the constant sneers of disapproval reminded her quickly enough.

He helped her out of the car and wrapped an arm around her waist to support her. She knew he hadn't worn the sweat suit to work, so she thought he must have come from home. He smelled of the musk she loved so much, and in that moment she finally felt content.

She held on tight when he pulled her as close as her belly would allow. He was such a good man, she thought, and for him to be here could only mean Emily was asleep for the night - because he would never have left her otherwise.

~~

Jeremy spoke in a low, dangerous voice that made her regret telling him about the complaints with the board of health. "He's not going to get away with it." His gut told him where to lay the blame.

Owen Harris.

He had once promised Jeremy that he could make Christina's life 'uncomfortable' - that was the word he had used then - if he didn't keep his distance from her. And he had obviously followed through on his threat.

Christina listened to him fume. "You can't be sure it was him."

Her attempt at reason was laughable at best, and they both knew it. She saw the glint of derision in his eyes at the mere suggestion someone else might be responsible.

"Someone's trying to ruin you, Christina. Who wants that more than him?" he demanded.

"Half of New York thinks I'm a harlot or worse," she replied without pause. Fatigue and resignation had worn off the sharpest edge of her anger, but Jeremy was angry enough for both of them.

"But it's Owen who has the influence and the money to pull this off."

~ 40 ~

Jeremy met his father's questioning expression with firm determination. After hearing of Jeremy's suspicions concerning Owen Harris and the games being played with Christina's reputation, Linus couldn't blame him for being angry. He wrote off his son's demand as temper and waited a breath so he could reason with him.

Several seconds of tense silence passed, and the hard line of tension settling in Jeremy's jaw assured his father he had no intention of backing down. So, he agreed to green light his son's plan, recognizing resolve when he saw it. It was only business with a little revenge thrown in, and it was a chance to sweeten the victory by teaching an impudent, egotistical man a lesson in the dangers of meddling.

~~

December 1996

On shaky legs, Emily made her way to the French doors that led to the patio off the bedroom, stumbling through, she felt it a triumph, albeit a pitiful one. Despite the winter chill, she thought, the sun was warm on her face, and the air refreshing on her skin. This sensation made her smile even as others caused the burning, needling pain to take root behind her heavy-lidded eyes.

She wanted to feel the weight of her body on her legs again. She wanted to feel some control after too many months of helplessness, months when her thoughts were scattered and confusion muddled her mind. As she stood, weak-kneed and exhausted, Emily could feel the dark void threatening to swallow her up again, and it could at any moment.

She felt chilled to the bone, and she crossed her arms over herself for warmth. Drawing a deep breath into her lungs, Emily found herself wishing again. Wishing, she knew, was for children, but still she wished. She wished her body would stop betraying her, stop attacking her. But it was her failing mental capacity that caused her the most distress. When, of course, she was lucid enough to recognize how she felt at all. Her mind was little more than a jumble of disorderly and chaotic thoughts, and there were days when her daughter and husband were perfect strangers to her.

Shuffling to the edge of the patio, she looked down on the lush green lawn that was tended to by the gardener. She wondered if she would ever walk across it and feel the grass between her toes again. When a woman barely had the strength to walk to the bathroom, she reminded herself, she shouldn't ponder anything so frivolous as strolling through the vast expanse of grass below.

Her eyes closed against the sunlight when she heard Jeremy's car coming up the drive. He would be surprised to see her out of bed and standing up under her own power. She opened her eyes and worked to focus them on his imposing figure as he climbed out of the car and slammed the door.

He was agitated. She knew her husband well after so many years. Dealing with his moods was easy enough. He disappeared into the house, and she knew he would be coming up to see her momentarily.

Carefully, and considerably weaker than she had been only moments before, she turned and slowly carried herself back into the bedroom. She lifted her arms and brushed her fingers through her flat, limp hair. If she looked as poorly as she felt, then she would be a sight; Debra had left that morning without fixing her hair for her.

Emily managed to pull her hair into a careless ponytail and was working her way back to bed when Jeremy came through the door, carrying a tray with tea and crackers for her.

"You're up." He smiled, careful to mask what she had already seen easily enough when he hadn't been aware she was watching. He carried the tray to the bedside table and put it down. He then turned, and took her hand to help her to the bed. "Your color's better." He brought her into his arms.

"The pain's manageable today." Leaning back, she looked into his eyes. The anger, there only moments before, had vanished. He pressed his warm lips to hers and she framed his face in her hands when their kiss ended. "You're home early."

Jeremy covered her hands with his and felt their iciness in contrast to his own. He kept his concern masked and smiled instead. "Purely self-preservation. I had to get out of the office before Sarah lynched me," he said lightly. "Apparently, I've been a handful all day."

Emily smiled at the image that brought to mind. "Handful? You?" She let him help her back into bed. "I can't imagine."

"Very funny," he replied before tapping her nose playfully and covering her with the thick down comforter. He should tell her about her father's devious dealings, but this was his battle - not hers. He shrugged off his sour thoughts, toed-off his shoes, and climbed onto the bed to settle beside her.

He would handle Owen Harris the way he handled any adversary: with quick, deliberate action - and he would do so without remorse. He worried only about the heart of his wife and the illusions she carried about her father.

~~

Jeremy greeted the two men in his office with the cool politeness attributed to him. "Just give it to me straight," he said, cutting the need for any small talk by getting to the point.

"Thompson Electronics is going to be expensive," the shorter of the two men said. "Harris' offer is generous to the point of being foolish. If you're going to cut him out of the running, it's going to cost."

"He's offering three million above the highest bid," the other man offered when Jeremy's steely glare pinned him.

"Then offer ten million above Harris' price," Jeremy replied easily. "Harris may want this company, but I'll have it - and I'll have it before he knows what hit him."

"And your wife? I mean, she's Harris' daughter."

Jeremy fixed both men with a level stare. "There's no room for sentimentality in business, gentlemen. My wife knows that, and so should you. Now make the offer."

~~

Two Weeks Later
January 5, 1997, 3:30am
Christina Wagner's Residence

Christina recognized the stabbing back pain she was feeling as her first contraction and the beginning of labor. The pain struck with a fierceness that seemed to rip her out of a deep sleep and brought her fully awake with a gasp. In an instant she knew this was no false alarm, and it was time to get to the hospital. Carefully, her mind already shifting into crisis mode, she planted her feet on the floor, cradled her belly, and pushed herself to her feet.

As quickly as Christina could manage, she dressed and went to the closet for the bag that Jeremy had packed for her weeks ago. She thought of him as she phoned for a cab; he promised to be there for the delivery, but at this hour phoning him at home would be a delicate matter. She placed another call instead and was hanging up when the next contraction had her doubling over and focusing on her breathing techniques.

The cabby was hammering on the door when she finally made it down the stairs. Then, half way down the walkway, another contraction had her moaning and grabbing for the cabby's arm. He had taken her bag and helped her to the cab by the time the contraction eased. By her count, they were coming seven minutes apart, and time was of the essence.

The cabby jumped in, threw the car into drive, and gunned it down the street. His eyes darting from the street to the rearview mirror to be sure he didn't wind up with an extra passenger on the way. "You alright back there, lady?" his voice sounded as pained as her contractions.

Men, she thought miserably, were no good under pressure. Lifting her head, she managed a smile to put him at ease. "I'm okay. Get me to Manhattan General Hospital - and you'd better hurry."

~~

Her water broke in the backseat of the cab thanks to a poorly timed traffic light three blocks from the hospital. Her contractions were four minutes apart before the flow of traffic began to move again, and as the cab screeched to a halt outside of the emergency department, Christina was working her way through the latest when she was lifted out of the cab and onto a gurney.

Inside the maternity ward, her feet were placed in stirrups, and her obstetrician, Dr. Daniels, appeared out of nowhere as she panted through another contraction. He patted her arm and turned his attention to the baby monitor before he checked her dilation. Grinning, he looked up and dropped down onto a stool.

"Looks like show time to me, Christina," he said, his voice anxious and upbeat. "How'd you feel about giving me a nice big push?"

Too busy screaming and panting to answer, she pushed hard. Sweat ran like a river into her eyes as she moaned when they finally told her to rest, but before she was ready - she was pushing again. It seemed to go on forever before Jamie was at her side, holding her hand. She had never felt so bone tired in her life. She lay limp against a pillow when Dr. Daniels seemed to scream inside her head.

"Okay, Christina, we're almost there; the head and shoulders are out. I need a couple more good pushes, and you'll be holding your baby. Come on, you can do it. On three, okay?"

Christina pushed with all her strength with Jamie cheering her on. One push, and then another. She felt the moment her baby was pushed into the world, and the last sound she heard before exhaustion overtook her was the high pitched cry of her son.

~~

Jeremy pushed the accelerator to the floor and swore viciously when the traffic light at the next corner turned red. The fates were against him, no doubt about it; otherwise, why would Christina have gone into labor in the middle of the goddamned night?

He braked and brought his car to a jerking halt at the light. Raking his hand through his hair, he blew out a breath of frustration. He had to be grateful that she wasn't alone. It mattered, so much, that if he couldn't be there with Christina when she needed him most, someone he loved and who loved her was by her side. It mattered that the moment his son took his first breath of life, Jamie had been there to hear it.

~ 41 ~

Manhattan General Hospital
January 5, 1997
7:30am

With the window of Christina's hospital room at his back, Jeremy watched the sunlight slant across her sleeping face. He finally knew perfection in its purest form. She was already sleeping when he arrived an hour ago.

His son was wide awake, though, and gathered close in his arms now - and he could think of nothing that touched him as deeply as fatherhood. With a grin splitting his face, he ambled across the room, cooing to his baby boy. He went to her bedside and dropped quietly into the chair. Jamie had left in search of caffeine and a mirror to freshen her makeup.

Shifting the baby in one arm, Jeremy took Christina's hand in his and pressed his familiar kiss to her palm. She'd given him a son, strong and healthy and already so much like his mother that Jeremy fell in love the moment he saw him.

Patrick Joseph Avery Wagner. Seven pounds, ten ounces, with hair like his father's and a chin that was his great-grandfather's through and through. He wished Christina would wake up and see them together, father and son.

Then his eyes filled, and a sob choked him. He thought of Nathaniel. He'd been given a second chance to be a father to a son. Right or wrong, he was a grateful man for it. "Thank you for our son, my love," he whispered. "I'll do right by him. And you. I swear it."

~~

Jeremy and Christina couldn't hide from the outside world for long. News of Patrick's birth hit the papers a scant eight hours later, and media throughout the city were out to scoop each other, with little regard for the feelings or privacy of the people involved. By the evening news, word had spread, and a fresh burst of gossip began.

Debra flatly refused to speak to her father when he arrived home to tell her about the birth before she learned about it from a live network feed from the hospital. She retreated to her mother's bedside, ever loyal. His daughter was angry with everyone, but none more than he. So, he asked Jamie to come to the house to shield Debra from the reporters.

~~

Jeremy found his daughter curled up beside her mother in the master bedroom. Debra was sleeping, her hand protectively over Emily's stiff fingers. He stopped short, taken aback by how much his daughter had grown to look like her mother. He smiled, taken in by the peaceful expression on her face. Sleeping angels, he thought, moving to the bed to press a kiss to Emily's brow.

He sighed. Grateful to find that, though pale, she was pleasingly warm to the touch rather than burning with fever - or worse, cold as ice. Debra stirred beside her, and Jeremy stepped back, hoping she wouldn't wake and fix him with the glare of contempt to which he'd grown accustomed. What he needed was a shower and a change of clothes, not hostile words from his daughter.

When he stepped out of the bathroom freshly showered, he felt revived and infused to deal with the day. He was toweling his hair dry when he turned to find Debra watching him in silence. He smiled and tossed the towel aside before tightening his robe.

"Morning, sweetie." His tone was cautious, testing.

"Good morning," she replied, getting off the bed and straightening her mother's blankets.

He pulled a comb through his hair and watched her tend to her mother with loving ease; he couldn't remember the last time his daughter had so much as hugged him, but he was willing to play the bad guy in Debra's eyes, and he couldn't argue. He was a bad guy in this area of his life. In her version of ideal, fathers didn't have on-going affairs, children out-of-wedlock, or starring roles in the city's many gossip mills.

When Debra finally turned her attention to her father, it was with accusation written all over her face. She walked over to stand next to him so that they both were reflected in the mirror. "So, how's the new mother?"

The sarcasm in her tone was hard to miss, and he squared his jaw before their eyes met. "I know this is difficult for you, but this isn't the place for this conversation."

He was determined to try and reach out to her. He turned to her, cupped her chin, and looked in her eyes for a trace of the little girl who once adored him - but she wasn't about to soften, and he could only feel sadness over the rift that seemed to grow ever-wider between them.

"It must be inconvenient to have a wife and daughter complicating your new family."

"That's not true. I love you and your mother very much. Debra, you have no idea how complicated life can be. Someday you'll know; not everything is as you imagine it to be."

~ 42 ~

Jeremy did his best to put the conversation he'd had with his daughter the day before behind him. Still, the walls Debra placed between them seemed insurmountable, and worry gnawed at him. She was angry at the world and him. Her mother was bedridden, and on most days unaware of what was going on around her. Add that to her disillusionment with him, and Jeremy worried his little girl felt adrift and abandoned by her parents. Another failure, he supposed, sure the distance between his daughter and himself would only grow.

His parents were the only ones she allowed to reach out to her. With her grandparents, she was the warm, giving girl she had been as a child. He, on the other hand, saw only her fear and anger when - and if - she decided to acknowledge him at all.

Her fear her mother would die and leave her with a father she no longer trusted was real, but it pained him to know his daughter felt him to be more of an adversary than the loving father he was in reality. Her anger towards him because he wronged her mother and continued to was justified - he knew that, too - but he wished she were old enough, mature enough, to understand that sometimes life was far from simple. That sometimes the shades of grey in life were more plentiful than the black and white.

The buzzing of his phone pulled him out of his head and back to the business at hand. He picked up the phone and listened as the latest update on the takeover bid for Thompson Electronics was rattled off in his ear. It was proving difficult, but the payoff of sticking it to Owen Harris was worth the effort. His father-in-law was livid and ranting; Jeremy smiled victoriously.

~~

Emily was sitting in the sunroom, looking out through the glass walls to the day beyond. She was lounging in an overstuffed wicker chair when she heard Jeremy come up behind her and bend to kiss the back of her neck. They both ignored the icy feel to her skin as he came around to sit on the matching sofa.

"You look exhausted," she said with only a shadow of the smile that used to light up her face. "You home for the night?"

He thought of Christina and the baby at Cherry Hill. He'd planned on driving out to check on them, but now he wavered. Emily was out of bed and lucid, and he knew her too well to misinterpret her question. She wanted him to say yes, and looking into her eyes, he already knew he couldn't leave her. Christina would understand.

"I don't plan on moving from this spot. How're you feeling?" He took her chilly hand between his own and rubbed gently to warm it.

"The headaches are getting worse, more frequent." She squeezed his hand. "I was thinking we could spend the evening with Debra. She's been so down lately."

"She's home on a Friday night?"

"She's afraid to leave me, Jeremy."

~~

Cherry Hill
January 19, 1997

Jeremy was a man being pulled in two different directions, but he grinned like a fool when Christina settled their son in his arms. It was an incredible feeling being with the woman he loved and the child their love created. It was hard to believe the sweet smelling infant wrapping his tiny hand around his finger had arrived only a scant two weeks before.

Outside, snow was falling, piling up, making travel a risky business - but inside, Jeremy and Christina were warm, cozy, and happy. This was their time together as a family, and every minute was precious.

The week they would spend here together was a gift. The son they doted on would have uninterrupted time to bond with his proud father, and his proud father marveled over every inch of him.

Emily was well taken care of, and Jeremy could relax without watching the clock. He could feed Patrick at three a.m. and stub his toe making his way through the dark to the crib. He could hold Christina in his arms, sleep with her curled into him, and imagine he hadn't a care in the world. He could dream with Christina's scent mingling through his subliminal senses.

His baby would know him, no matter the whispers or the gossip, no matter the lenses out for fuzzy photos tabloids paid obscene amounts of money to print.

For a number of reasons, Patrick couldn't take his rightful name, but he would know that he was a Beckett and be proud of the name. Although it infuriated him, for the foreseeable future he would have to see his baby by clandestine means, but the insanity wouldn't touch him. Jeremy simply would not permit it; he would protect his son.

~~

The Eastside Inner-city Youth Program was to be the fourth and final center Jeremy opened in the city. The benefit dinner would coincide with the opening, and was expected to raise well over six figures in donations, and Jeremy, as founder and project CEO, was expected to attend. He had to shake hands, slap backs, and open checkbooks with no more than his wit and charm.

The engraved invitations were mailed one month in advance, and the R.S.V.P.'s were returned and cataloged. Three hundred socialites and financiers filled the guest list. They would turn out in droves and be generous, if only to outdo each other so they could crow about it later.

Jeremy spent the morning at the center, making sure the caterers were settled in the kitchen and the waiters set up the tables as he requested. When the time came to go home to get into his tux, he was surprised to see not only his daughter dressed to attend, but his wife as well. Emily smiled brightly from her electric wheelchair, and words, quite simply, failed him.

"Em, you look so lovely." He bent down in front of her and kissed her. "You're sure you're up to coming?"

"I missed the last opening; I don't want to miss this one, too." She cupped his cheek and smiled as his eyes filled with emotion. "I love you, you silly fool - and I'm proud of you. I want to see you take your well-deserved bow."

"Well, then, I'd better hurry up and get dressed. Dad wants us to come by for drinks first, and we'll all leave from there together." He stood up and smiled at Debra. "You look beautiful, honey. I'm glad you decided to come."

He turned, ran up the stairs, and disappeared down the hall to dress. He was happy Emily felt well enough to come, and he was grateful that Debra had begun to open up to him over the last few weeks. Dressed in his tux, he turned off the lights and started down the hall to the stairs. He was a lucky man to have such wonderful women in his life.

~~

When Jeremy, flanked by his entire family, cut the ribbon declaring Eastside Inner-city Youth Center open, the thunderous applause was overwhelming. He gripped both Emily's and Debra's hands and grinned for the pictures. Jeremy's charm even quieted the gossips in the crowd. The evening turned out to be a huge success. The money flowed in unabated, and the meal was divine.

~~

Six Days Later

Owen Harris didn't bother announcing himself to Jeremy's secretary, he simply stormed past her and threw open the door. Hatred coursed through him as heated as the blood in his veins and his face contorted into a sneer. He looked every bit like a man clinging to sanity by the thinnest of threads. Rage boiled his blood, and he crossed the room to stand toe-to-toe with his son-in-law.

Jeremy had been expecting this visit for nearly a week. The homicidal glint in Owen's hard stare provided enjoyment instead of the intended intimidation. He watched Owen's face deepen to crimson and met his anger with an unflinching air of calm. "Owen. To what do I owe the pleasure?"

"You sneaky little sonofabitch." Owen wanted desperately to wrap his hands around his neck and squeeze the life from him. "Goddamn pirate, that's what you are!"

Jeremy almost smiled. "Ah. So, you've heard about Beckett International's latest appropriation then?" He stepped back, wisely putting distance between them. "Well, you can't say I didn't warn you. Now you have to pay the consequences."

"Thompson Electronics was mine. You stole it right out from under me."

"Consider it the business equivalent of tit for tat, Owen." Jeremy laughed. "You think I'm going to allow you to play your petty little games with Christina?"

"I never laid a hand on your little slut," he spat.

Jeremy's humor disappeared. "I'd choose your words carefully." He turned to the window and savored Owen's defeat by his own hands. He turned back. "You're a liar, and not a very good one. We both know the filing of that complaint with the state health board has your slimy fingerprints all over it. You're not the only one who can make life difficult."

"Does my daughter know you screwed her own father on a lucrative business deal to protect your mistress?"

Jeremy blew out a disgusted breath and his eyes narrowed on Owen. "Do you know she slipped into another coma - two days ago? Of course not, but if you came around more you would. It's unwise to use Emily against me, or even to bring her into this conversation. She has far more important battles to fight at the moment."

Owen's anger quickly faded to fear. "What happened?" His tone was accusatory. "Her picture in the paper at your opening was radiant."

Jeremy's eyes softened at the memory. She'd had so much fun that night, but her condition often changed in the blink of an eye. "She woke up with a terrible headache, and by the time the doctor arrived, she'd lost consciousness. Might be another stroke. The tests aren't conclusive."

The two men stood in silence for an unbearably long moment. Owen turned the color of paste and sank into the sofa, dropping his head into his hands. News of his daughter had thrown him. Something with which Jeremy could identify, common ground, could be found even among enemies.

Incredibly, Jeremy felt for the father in Owen and offered some unsolicited advice. "Focus on Emily. Your daughter needs you."

~~

Owen went quietly to his daughter's bedside and sat down in the chair next to the bed. He touched his fingertips to her soft, cap of chestnut hair, and pulled in a trembling breath. Heartbreaking memories of his daughter as a healthy, vibrant woman played like a reel in his head. Her frail body spoke of the battle she'd been waging against an illness that would steal her future.

A sadness he'd been spared since his wife's death enveloped his soul. Jeremy had been right about one thing: he had been away from his little girl too long. What if she never woke up again? He took her hand and sobbed over her stiffened, bent fingers. Her disease ravaged her insides and even marred her once unquestionable beauty.

A man who wielded as much power and influence as he, was not comfortable with futility, but uselessness has become a constant shadow. Always just a step or two behind, to mock him, to remind him that in matters of life and death he was, and always would be, impotent. There was nothing he could do to save her. There was no one to buy or threaten to have his way.

His helplessness bore down on him and drove him to his knees on the floor. The ashen tint of her skin, the shallowness of her cheeks, and the blue tint to her lips was undeniable proof that the end was near. His daughter was dying, and as he wept, he struggled to find the strength or the courage to face it.

Debra watched her grandfather from the doorway and marveled at the depths of his pain and love. She walked in, wanting to comfort him and be comforted in return. He understood the pain she carried because he carried it as well, and - unlike her father - the tears he cried were genuine.

Owen glanced over his shoulder at her touch and smiled, despite his tears. His granddaughter wrapped her arms around him and pressed a kiss to his cheek. He turned and wrapped her in his arms, soothing her as she soothed him. They wept together, clinging to each other.

Owen framed her face in his hands, drawn to the depth he saw in her eyes, her mother's eyes, and in them he found hope. The only reason to go on, to endure his desolation was this child. The child who came from his child.

One Month Later

He stood in front of the living room window, looking out into the gathering darkness. His eyes, tired and heavy, strained to make out an image he'd seen countless times before. But there was no use. Jeremy sighed and squeezed them shut for relief; his eyes felt as grainy as sand, and his vision blurred from lack of sleep.

His day had been long, and his spirits were low. Scrubbing his hands over his face to clear his sluggish mind, he wondered if he would ever feel truly happy or at peace again. His life wasn't as it should be, but he'd managed to make it work. So why, he wondered, was he so ill at ease?

The sound of muffled footsteps on the stairs drew Jeremy's attention away from the window. Emily's nurse quietly came into the room while he moved to the bar and poured two fingers of scotch into a short glass. He looked across the room at her, the question clear in his taunt expression. She shook her head sadly in reply and watched his jaw tense up before he downed the drink in one, angry gulp.

For weeks now, everyone who loved Emily waited for her to wake from the coma, but there had been no improvement, and her body only grew weaker. Neither of her doctors held any hope of her regaining consciousness, and her organs were finally failing; death was finally coming to end her suffering.

Elise watched Jeremy from the hallway while he finished off another drink and hurled the empty glass into the fireplace, where it shattered against the hard wood of the logs inside. Raking an unsteady hand through his hair, he turned to find his mother watching him with tears streaming down her cheeks. When she came to him, he opened his arms wide and wrapped her tightly against him. There was comfort in the embrace, and only now did he allow himself to weep. For the woman who had been his wife for nearly eighteen years. For the young girl who would never have this same opportunity, of being wrapped in her mother's strong, loving embrace.

Upstairs in the master bedroom, Linus and Owen stood by their granddaughter and offered as much comfort as they could, struggling with their own heartbreak. Debra rarely left her mother's side. She was as stubborn in her resolve to stay by her side as the rest of them were in wishing she would get some fresh air.

But she couldn't leave her mother. Not for an hour, not for a minute. As she gripped her mother's hand tightly, she wanted to give her the will to live, the strength. Hoping to keep her from slipping from this life to the next.

Jamie arrived and insisted that both men go downstairs for awhile while she stayed with Debra and Emily, and Jeremy kept plenty of distance between himself and his father-in-law. Distracted conversation with his parents was all that kept him from buckling under the strain; feigning normalcy over lukewarm coffee and scones as they waited for the moment they'd all been dreading for years.

All the while, the press hovered outside at the end of the driveway like mosquitoes waiting for their first taste of blood. They waited for word of Emily's last breath with anticipation; after all, such a dramatic twist to a story as salacious as this would send circulation and ratings through the roof. The death of Jeremy Beckett's poor, put-upon wife would be the talk of the city soon - new life breathed into an old story even as Emily Beckett's life come to a tragic end.

Jeremy was tempted more than once to jump into his Jag and mow them all down like bowling pins. Reason always won over the fantasy, though; more important things occupied his thoughts now. His wife was slipping further and further away in their bedroom upstairs, and no matter appearances, he loved Emily. Not perfectly or to the exclusion of all others, but he loved her.

Regrettably, for nearly two years now he had been forced to withhold the truth about Christina with lies of omission. His and Emily's marriage was not the game the society pages and magazines made it out to be, though, and at its core was true and deep affection for each other.

The truth was complicated and always had been. His heart was breaking for his wife, not rejoicing over a chance for freedom. After nearly two decades in this marriage, his heart was breaking, though, few would believe it.

To the masses outside the high walls of their home and beyond, he was a cold and distant husband, a man merely biding his time with a wife who was a burden. That is, until time and her death gave him the chance to escape.

Late into the night, Jeremy managed to call Christina. She was awake, worrying about him, and her voice offered him a soothing reprieve from the growing despair filling up every inch of his home. He confessed that his mind was preoccupied with memories of a marriage where only his wife had loved truly and passionately.

Guilt weighed heavily on him and Emily grew weaker. Should he let her go without apologizing for his ineptness as her husband? Should he apologize for the whispers and gossip? For the ugliness of scandal that had marred her without her even being aware?

Yes, there was so much to be sorry about, so much for which he wouldn't have the chance to make up to Emily. But he couldn't be sorry or apologize for loving Christina – and he certainly couldn't be sorry for Patrick.

The phone call ended with pledges of love from both of them. Then he fixed another drink while his thoughts turned to Debra. He cursed the distance he'd allowed to grow between them. Out of loyalty to her mother, she'd put up a wall between them, and the tension between them left everyone in the house uncomfortable in an already impossible situation.

Lifting his glass to his lips, he gulped scotch and faced the grim truth. As the scotch burned its way down his throat, he grimaced and closed his eyes. The truth wasn't pretty. As her father, and hell, even as an adult, he shouldn't have permitted her withdrawal from him just because it was easier. Easier than looking his daughter in the eye and taking her brutal honesty, her distaste, and her disapproval.

He sat the empty high-ball glass on the mantel of the fireplace and rolled the knots out of his shoulders. Tomorrow would be soon enough to start on the long road back to his daughter. He was in no condition to try and win Debra's affection back tonight, not with liquor on his breath and guilt weighing so heavily on his heart.

So he left the living room on legs leaden with drink and too little sleep. He climbed the stairs taking a deep breath to steady his nerves on the way. And when he reached the top, he willed himself forward. Inside the bedroom, he winced from the palpable pain on the faces of the people scattered around the room. He went to the bed and the fragile form of his wife.

He lowered himself to his knees and took Emily's hand between his. The light in the room was dimmed to protect her eyes, but it set Jeremy's teeth on edge. The room was preparing for death instead of fighting for life. He kissed her and shuddered to find her lips cold.

Something inside him told him Emily could hear him.

Tears blurred his vision, and he let them fall without shame. "Don't go, Em. We need you too much."

Jamie slipped into the room in silence. She'd heard her brother pleading with Emily, and the grief in his voice nearly broke her heart. They had been friends, parents, and companions. He loved his wife - and they were a family - and now that family was splintering apart, threatening to undo those Emily was about to leave behind.

~~

The morning sun peaking through the curtains woke him; one strong ray of light zeroing in on his face had him wincing even before he opened his heavy lidded eyes. He felt the softness of the bed's comforter against his cheek and the bitter taste stale scotch and dead sleep had left in his mouth.

He sat up, rolling the stiffness from his shoulders and back and blinking the sleep from his eyes. He wasn't alone with Emily as he'd expected to be. He saw his sister and daughter across the bed from him, hovering. He pushed himself up and out of the chair and tried to stretch the stiffness from his legs.

He smiled sleepily and was rewarded with smiles in return. The genuine smile he received from Debra was unexpected but welcomed. Feeling hopeful for the small link between them, he scrubbed his hand over his face to roust himself fully from sleep. He turned at the sound of the nurse as she dictated changes on Emily's chart.

He looked at the monitors himself then, he could read them almost as well as the doctors and nurses now. Even to his untrained eye, he could read the marked change in her oxygen levels. He didn't have to be told her vitals were weakening. His eyes shifted to meet the nurse's, and in the look that passed between them, he knew to prepare for the worst.

Swallowing the lump in his throat, he cupped his wife's cheek and struggled to keep it together for Debra. He noticed that her skin had cooled and perhaps paled further during the night. She was dying. Maybe she would manage to hang on for another day, but she would die, whether they were prepared for it or not. He had to face it, for both his daughter and himself.

He felt the tug to reach out to his daughter. "Debra, why don't we go downstairs and grab some breakfast? Aunt Jamie will stay with mama for awhile."

Debra gaped at the suggestion. "I'm not hungry."

Jeremy walked around the bed to his daughter. "Come on now, you need to eat - and mama'd be the first one to tell you that."

Jamie recognized the pleading look she saw in her brother's eyes, even if his daughter did not. "Your dad's right. Don't worry, I'll stay right here until you come back."

~~

The maid served breakfast at the dining room table while Jeremy and Debra sat in their usual seats in awkward silence. He hoped to engage his daughter in conversation while they ate, but it was clear from the closed-off expression on her face that the conversation would be one-sided. So, when the maid sat his plate of eggs with a side of bacon and toast in front of him, he offered her an appreciative smile instead.

Forcing Debra into a corner was hardly the way to extend an olive branch. If she didn't want to talk to him, he wouldn't push the issue. If she wanted to talk, she'd talk, he decided, watching her attack her plate of pancakes like an enemy.

He had finished breakfast and was pouring himself his second glass of orange juice when she'd surprised him by breaking the silence.

"Mama's not going to wake up, is she?" Debra pushed her plate away and looked her father straight in the eye, waiting for an answer.

"I don't know, sweetie." It was part truth. The rest of it would devastate her. He couldn't take away her hope. "She's very weak."

She nodded silently, considering what he'd said. She was staring, but he wouldn't look away. He kept his eyes level with hers and waited. "You look tired. You didn't have to sleep in a chair last night. I was with her. You could have gone to bed."

"It wasn't a chore for me," he said. "I love her, too."

She watched him closely. If the deep set lines at the corners of his eyes and forehead were any indication, he was exhausted - and in those lines, she was forced to face a hard truth. "You do love Mama."

Jeremy felt the carefully constructed wall between them begin to crumble. "Of course I do. She's as important to me as you are. I'd trade places with her if I could."

She believed him, but still felt enough anger to fix him with a cold, hard stare. "And Christina Wagner?"

His daughter's directness was well timed. He flinched as if she struck him. She was waiting, his own judge and jury, to decide how much of a chance she wanted to give him. "I'm in love with her," he said quietly, "and have been for as long as I can remember. Before your mother, there was Christina - and I intended to marry her."

She hadn't expected his candor, and the weight of his honesty now shuddered through her, but she ignored it. "But you didn't." she said flatly. "You married my mother. You took vows, you made promises, and you broke them. Why even marry her at all?"

Jeremy was silent for a moment, considering how to answer the question. No good could come from the whole truth. There had already been enough damage. "Things happened...we broke up. The details aren't important anymore."

She pushed away from the table without another word. She wanted the truth and got it. The pain was expected but hardly welcome. Still, something made her turn around again. "If Mama meant enough to you, Christina Wagner would mean nothing at all."

Jeremy felt her anger, and had even come to accept it. It was always there, and maybe it always would be. He stood, meeting the coolness in her eyes with patience. He went to her, and she backed away to wrap her arms around herself in defense. He felt the stab of pain deep in his heart. "Debra...you don't always get to choose who you love," he began. "But I choose to love her - right or wrong."

He wasn't surprised when she turned and ran from the room. While everything in him wanted to go after her, he stood, unmoving. His timing might have been poor, but at least he'd been honest. Sighing, he went back to the table and dropped into his chair.

~ 43 ~

By mid-afternoon, more security arrived on the grounds of the estate to hold the accumulating press at bay. Linus had given strict instructions: if even one member of the press crossed the property line, they were to be removed and arrested.

His son and granddaughter deserved privacy so they could concentrate on Emily, the woman who held their family together. As head of the family, Linus had taken over, handling everything from security to the endless incoming phone calls. He'd left word at the office that neither he nor Jeremy would be coming into the office until further notice.

He sent Edward to the house for clothing and essentials for himself and Elise. They would remain with their son and his family. Because this was a time to stay close and pull together.

~~

Optimism was in Michael's nature, whether it was personal or professional, he preferred focusing on the positive in any given situation. He disliked dashing hope, and today, right now, this very minute, he was being turned to, counted on for the positive amidst the overwhelming negative unfolding around them. He could read the hope in everyone's eyes, their silent pleas for even a glimmer of hope. He hated to squash it with reality. but he had no choice. "Her death is imminent. A matter of hours, really. It's time to prepare ourselves to let her go."

Linus moved to his son's side and put a firm hand on his shoulder for support.

Dr. Nigel, who had been standing behind Michael, stepped up and spoke gravely, "We both concur."

Jeremy closed his eyes, felt them begin to tear, and sighed. His father had stepped away, and now brought him a drink, a Bourbon. He took a long drink, welcoming the burn from his throat to his stomach. "I'm going to be with her."

Linus and Jamie watched him walk slowly out of the room toward the stairs. They exchanged troubled looks and wrapped their arms around each other.

~~

Christina kept an eye on CNN throughout the evening. Minute by minute, word on Emily's condition was reported, dissected. Celebrity journalists now had the venue they loved the most, discussing the topic they loved the most. Nothing said ratings and round-the-clock airtime like a bed-side vigil. She could only think of Jeremy, and of Debra, of course, and what this prolonged agony was doing to them.

What she wouldn't give to be able to comfort them both. She needed to do something, to feel useful in some small way. But she pushed the need aside, knowing it was not only impossible but inappropriate. He would be grieving with his daughter and his family surrounding him. She had to be satisfied that he wouldn't be alone. Perhaps the need to be beside him was almost overwhelming, but it might also be selfish.

She looked down at Patrick, asleep, cuddled close in her arms, and knew she had so much to be grateful for - not to mention their son to protect while his father dealt with a horrendous loss. So why worry because she couldn't pick up the phone and tell him she loved him? He knew. His parents and Jamie were all there to support him, and he would be the rock his daughter needed, if she would only let him be.

Christina had never known her own mother, like Debra, she had lost her far too soon, so she felt a kinship with Jeremy's daughter, despite understanding she would only be met with hatred for it. The loss Debra was about to feel would stay with her forever. And it would be devastating for her, she only hoped Jeremy was strong enough to help her through it.

She went to put the baby in his crib and knew she would not sleep as well tonight. Her mind and her heart would be with Jeremy and the painful night ahead, and her heart would ache for him and his daughter.

The media could say what they wanted about Jeremy's marriage, but they had no idea about the relationship between Jeremy and Emily. There was affection, deep and permanent, and love - even without passion - is love. Jeremy held Emily in high regard, and he was now, and always had been, a loving, supportive husband in the face of a devastating illness. After eighteen years of marriage they had a bond, a deep friendship, and an abundance of affection between them.

Disgusted with the prying eye of the media, Christina shut off the television and tossed the remote on the cushion next to her. Nearly midnight now, she went to her home office down the hall from the living room to call

Lucy at Manhattan Special. The Avenue was of no concern at the moment, because it was still closed for renovations.

Lucy picked up the kitchen line after four rings, sounding out of breath and rushed. It was a busy night, and business was booming. This was where Christina's head needed to be. Somewhere useful and productive. Business would take care of the loneliness, and vanquish the heaviness of her thoughts.

~~

Jamie was certain she was dreaming because only in her wildest dreams would what she saw actually be happening. Where there had been a peaceful, reflective vigil, with whispers and murmurs and hugs and commissary there was now a sudden whirlwind of activity. The nurse flew into the room and frantically called for the doctors while checking vitals and various monitors. Then the nurse glanced over her shoulder, looking incredulously at Jamie.

Slowly, Emily opened her eyes and moaned softly. Jeremy burst through the door with Dr. Nigel and Michael right behind him. The looks on their faces showed they couldn't believe what was happening, and feared the worst.

"What...what's going on?" Jeremy demanded, panic clear in his tone.

Jeremy looked from his sister to the nurse and back again. Patience was not an option at the moment. "Say something, damnit!"

Jamie eyes filled with tears as she looked over Jeremy's shoulder to the bed. Turning, he followed her gaze and gaped in disbelief at Emily's open eyes.

He pushed past Michael, who was flipping through Emily's chart like a madman. He dropped to the edge of the bed and carefully took her hand. "Emily." He was crying now, too. "Dear God." He could see she was disoriented and stroked her hand reassuringly. "It's alright, Em. I'm here."

~~

Dr. Mark Nigel studied the latest brain scan carefully. Michael leaned against the large marble vanity and waited for Nigel's opinion. Little more than three weeks ago, they had turned the master bath into a makeshift functioning hospital conference room. Emily was conscious, but her vitals were far from stable.

Finally, Dr. Nigel looked up from the readout and shrugged at Michael. "I can't believe she's still alive, let alone awake." He put the readout down and pinched the bridge of his nose in exhaustion. "Her heart's weakening, her brain's swelling. She's got to be in severe pain."

Michael nodded. "She says the left side of her head hurts, but there's some numbness, too."

Dr. Nigel closed his eyes, the pronounced lines on his forehead his only outward sign of stress. "End of the road," he said quietly. "Twenty-four hours maybe."

"You're sure?"

"That she woke up at all's a miracle, but it's the only one Emily's going to get."

~~

Jeremy needed to be with Emily. As husband and wife, they needed the privacy, the chance to say what needed to be said before time ran out. Jeremy looked at Emily smiling when the door closed and they were finally alone. For a moment, he just stared; he wanted to remember every moment because there were too few moments left.

Her skin was so pale, so cold, but somehow she was radiant. Was it her acceptance of death that lit her from within? he wondered, as he wandered to her bedside to take her hand.

"You cold?" he asked, trying to sound fine. "Want another blanket?"

"I'm fine." She shifted to make herself more comfortable against the pillows and make room for him. "Sit down with me," she said, patting the mattress beside her. "We should talk, Jeremy, while there's still time."

He sat, kicked off his shoes, swung his legs up onto the bed, then leaned back against the headboard and gathered her close. When she grabbed his hand, he pressed it between his own and tried to ignore the panic coursing through him.

Suddenly, he was shaken, and it was an effort to keep his pain from adding to hers. "Maybe you should get some rest first," he offered.

Despite the sharpening pain in her head, she smiled. "All I've done is rest, honey. Rest isn't going to keep me from dying."

"God," he muttered, laying his head against the headboard. He wasn't sure if she were going for humor to lighten the mood or not. "You've always been too damn blunt, Emily, but damn if it doesn't make me want to laugh and cry."

She watched him pale and close his eyes. He wasn't ready to face it, but he would have to be. "Why cry when you can laugh, Jeremy? I'm tired. I'm so tired of the pain and the fight. I'm ready to let go - and you need to be ready to let me go too."

Jeremy felt her flinch and squeezed her hand. He held his breath when she winced and wished he could take some of her pain on himself. *This isn't fair, damn it*, he thought as she sucked in a sharp breath. "You want something more for the pain?"

It was a minute or so before she opened her eyes again and nodded. "Not yet. I want to be clearheaded for Debra."

The nurse came in and recorded the spike in Emily's heart rate. Jeremy waved her off, and the sadness in his eyes told her all she needed to know. Michael and Dr. Nigel came into the room, and the nurse shook her head and led them into the bathroom.

Jeremy carefully brought his arms more tightly around Emily. When her sigh became a shudder against him, his heart broke. He cursed himself for what he'd never been able to give her. Years of marriage, while she waited for a declaration from him that never came.

Emily was determined to enjoy this moment. She wouldn't allow even the vicious pain to steal the pleasure of feeling him so close. She looked at her husband: his weary, exhausted face, the tense set of his shoulders; this connection still mattered.

Even with death so close, it mattered. Exhausted, she laid her head against his chest to rest and gather her strength. Then she gathered his shirt in her hand and held on.

"Debra's going to need you now more than ever," she said, her voice a whisper and an effort. "She's pretending she doesn't right now, but she does - and she will when I'm gone. You can't let her push you away, Jeremy."

He pulled in a breath and tightened his arms around her. There was so much damage done with their daughter. He wondered if there was any hope for them at all. "She prefers the distance between us. and it's what I deserve, really. It seems fair, that since I couldn't give you my whole heart, she would give you all of hers. There's no room in it for me."

Emily lifted her hand shakily to his cheek. She needed to end his guilt. It was so important he not carry it with him the rest of his life. But she waited, and let him say what he needed.

With the reality of what was happening settling in, Jeremy's eyes filled. Emily was dying. The woman who'd shared his life for eighteen years and suffered nearly every day of those years was leaving him.

He sucked in a shallow breath and prayed this confession wouldn't come too late. "Our marriage wasn't what it should've been, and I'm sorry about that. But I want you to know I value it. You've been such a wonderful gift in my life, Emily, and a true friend." He brushed the backs of his fingers over her gaunt cheek and furrowed his brow. "I need to be truthful now."

Emily had let the pain of his affair go a long time ago, and it meant so much that he wanted truth between them before the end came, but she didn't need to hear it from him. "You want to unburden yourself, Jeremy, but I don't want confessions from you. There's not enough time for them. You want me to know you're having an affair; well, I've known for some time, so there's no need to rehash it."

His tears brought on more tears of her own as she lifted her weak hand to his wet cheek. While her vision doubled and danced, she sought to comfort him. "How?" he asked.

A slow, steadying breath was interrupted by her derisive chuckle. "I might live shut away, hiding here in this room, but I don't live in a bubble, Jeremy. I know about the stories in the papers. I watch the news and gossip shows.

He grappled for something to say. "You...you never said a word. Why?"

"What would've been the point? I always knew you'd find your way back to her. But for our one reckless night together a lifetime ago, you'd be her husband right now, not mine. And the truth is, I came between you both because I was spoiled and jealous and selfish."

"Em, don't make excuses for me, I don't deserve them." He smoothed his hand over her cap of chestnut hair. "I won't let you make this your fault."

"Don't misunderstand, Jeremy. I'm no martyr, I don't blame myself." With her chilled, weak hand, she squeezed his. "But I don't blame you either."

The guilt was a hard knot, twisting in his stomach. "You should've thrown me out on my ass," he muttered, raking his hand through his hair.

"I thought about it," she confessed, "and I'd've done it if you'd been cruel, thoughtless, or thrown it in my face. I kept waiting for you to leave, but you didn't. You stayed when you could've left so easily. I've never felt slighted or discarded by you, Jeremy - only cared for - and you've never once made me feel like a burden."

He looked at her and noticed the sincerity in her eyes. "I never wanted to hurt you."

"Because you don't have a vicious bone in your body."

"I know a few people who'd disagree about that."

"Don't let Daddy get to you. I'm going tell you a truth, too, Jeremy: our marriage never should've happened. Neither of us wanted it. We did it for our parents, and it was a mistake that, if not for my being pregnant, would have happened."

"You should hate me; you deserved better," Jeremy said.

"I can't hate you, and believe me, I've tried. We both deserved better. You were honest with me from the beginning. Any illusion of love was on my part, not yours. Oh, I hoped you'd fall madly in love with me again, but you couldn't because you were already madly in love with Christina."

"But I do love you, Emily. Deeply."

"Yes, I know you do - but just not passionately."

He felt relieved and small at the same time. Having her absolve him only made him feel more unworthy. "It might've been better for Debra if you'd tossed me out. Maybe divorce is kinder than betrayal."

"I don't know about that," Emily murmured simply. "I love you, and we both love her. We built a family together, and it's a good one - and a strong one. You always were - and are - a good husband to me, Jeremy. You've been by my side through sickness and health. You're a good, affectionate, loving, caring man, and our friendship and the love borne from it is a gift to me."

"I don't want to lose you like this," he whispered hoarsely. His tears were falling freely and wet her hair.

Emily lifted her face to the crook of his neck and breathed his scent into her memory. "And I don't want to lose you, but we don't always get what we want. Who knows that better than us?" The comfort she found in simplicity was fleeting. Pain made her draw a sharp breath; time was short.

With more effort than she could afford, Emily lifted her head to look at him; she really wanted to see him. In those few seconds, she memorized the face to which she'd grown so accustomed.

She took in his beautifully handsome features and character lines that so many years had left behind. His eyes, his sandy hair graying a bit at the temples, his mouth - always so tempting to her - she'd take the memory of his face with her too.

Then she gave him the only thing she had left to give. "Forgive yourself," she whispered, "because I forgave you a long time ago."

Profoundly moved, he cupped her gaunt face in his hands and burned the beauty there into his memory. "You amaze me," he murmured, tucking her head to his chest. "I wish I could do something other than let you go."

"You can. Let go of the guilt and be happy. Your children need you to be happy, Jeremy."

She only smiled when he turned her face up to him and gaped at her. His eyes filled, and he choked back a sob. She knew about his son, another painful betrayal.

The time to make Jeremy suffer had come and gone. There wasn't time for grudges or resentments, and she couldn't allow guilt to torment him forever. She loved him too much for that. "I won't say it didn't hurt, but I'm glad you have the chance to raise a son."

He wiped his eyes and was too shaken to speak.

"Debra will come around with time. You...have to be...patient. As for your son, I'm sure he already adores you, but our daughter needs more care. Let her get to know her brother. Make sure she knows she's important."

He shook his head. "She's not as forgiving as you."

Emily winced but laughed weakly. "She loves you, Jeremy. Her anger's proof of that, and she'll need you."

In the silence that followed, Emily drifted. Jeremy sat, holding her, rocked by the secrets he'd kept between them that weren't secrets at all. He kissed her softly and slid out from behind her. "I always loved you, Emily, maybe not perfectly - and certainly not faithfully - but always and forever."

The slight movement had her gripping his hand and looking deep into his eyes. "Even now, you manage to charm me." Pain shuddered through her. "It won't be long, Jeremy. I need to rest before I see Debra. I need to be stronger when she sees me."

He kissed the cool skin of her fragile hand. She drifted again, caught between the twilight of sleep and clarity of acceptance. Somewhere between life and death, Emily waited. To leave the pain that racked her body behind, to cross from this life into the next and be reunited with their son.

~ 44 ~

By sunrise, Emily's heart rate and pressure dropped and her skin took on a sickly blue hue. Jeremy left her shortly after she had slipped into sleep, and Owen took his place at her side. She needed to gather her strength before her time with Debra. The nurse stood vigil while the family struggled to come to terms with the impending death of a precious member of a tightly knit family.

Jeremy, who had been keeping a watchful eye on his daughter, put his strong cup of coffee aside and cleared his throat. Debra looked down the long table at her father but kept her face was unreadable.

"You really need to try and eat something, sweetheart." His voice was weary but loving, a hint of the man she remembered, and idolized in childhood. "I don't want you getting sick."

Debra wanted to snap back at him, but she was just too tired, too emotional to hold on to her angry resolve - and maybe part of her felt - and could believe the concern she heard in his voice. "I'm not hungry."

An hour later, with the pretense of breakfast over and Jamie and Elise in the kitchen desperate to keep their minds and hands busy, Debra and her father climbed the stairs together holding hands. She wanted to be with her mother, and Jeremy wanted, needed to be with them both. He opened the door quietly and stuck his head in. To his surprise, Emily was awake and offered him a faint smile.

He led Debra to the bed with a smile. "You've a visitor, honey."

Emily's eyes brightened at the sight of her daughter. She lifted her hand and smiled when Debra took hold and sat beside her. "Hello, sweetheart."

She was determined not to cry and let the sadness overwhelm her. "Want me to fix your hair?"

"You look so scared," Emily said and lifted a hand to her cheek. "You don't have to be afraid, sweetheart; death's a natural part of life."

Determination to be strong fled, and childlike fear rose to the surface. "I don't care. I don't want you to die," she sobbed. "I need you."

Emily looked past her to Jeremy, and he understood. She wanted some time alone with their daughter to reconcile her with her death. "I'll be back in a bit," he said quietly. He kissed Debra on the head and left them, the two people he'd let down most in his life, with a heaviness around his heart.

Debra was a stunning beauty, even while pain was plain on her face, Emily thought she was beautiful inside and out. She wasn't too weak, or too muddled in mind to feel pride in her daughter's strength. Tall, regal, sure of herself, and nearly a woman, Emily was grateful to have survived long enough to see hints of the woman she would become. Resting her head on her pillow, she smiled while Debra fussed with her hair and tried so hard to be strong for her; even at seventeen, the little girl still hid inside and clung to hope. "You're growing into a beautiful young woman."

"You look great too, Mom," Debra said lightly, holding up a handheld mirror so her mother could see her creation.

"You work miracles, sweetheart," Emily agreed. It was becoming more difficult to breathe, and the vision in her left eye was gone. She felt her daughter take her hand and forced herself to focus on this last and most important thing she would do. "I love you, sweetie."

Debra swallowed hard and looked into her mother's eyes with tears overflowing from her own. "I love you, too, Mama."

"We need to talk about someone important."

"Who?"

"Your father. He loves you so much."

"He loves someone else more."

"No," Emily replied, squeezing her daughter's hand, closing her eyes against a burst of pain behind her eyes. "He loves no one more than he loves his children."

The color drained from Debra's face, and her annoyance gave way to shock; her mother knew. About her bastard brother, about the continued infidelity of her husband. Her voice turned cold, almost of its own accord. "What'd he do, confess his disgusting behavior so you'd absolve him of his sins?"

Debra wasn't the only one shocked. *Where*, she wondered, *did all the disdain come from?* She had to set things right before it was too late."You're too hard on him," Emily said firmly. "He's been a wonderful father to you, Debra. How can you speak of him with such disrespect?"

"And you're not hard enough," Debra countered. "How can you give respect to someone who has disrespected you?"

"You've no right to punish him because of me. It's not your place. You've never been slighted or pushed aside by him. Has he missed even one birthday, one holiday with you? How many baths, bedtime stories, and countless other things did he manage when I was too weak to get out of this bed? When have you ever needed him that he wasn't there for you, young lady?" Emily watched the stubborn line of Debra's mouth and the harsh glint in her eyes and sighed. "You don't know everything you think you do, Debra, but it's time you do. You need to know your father's not the only one to blame."

~~

Owen found his daughter so pale, she seemed to be disappearing into the stark white sheets beneath her. Her face was drawn, without the usually rosy cheeks he recalled from her childhood, she was in obvious pain. He knelt at her side and worked up a smile for his little girl. She managed a smile in return before a new wave of pain washed over her. Gritting her teeth, she sucked in a steadying breath before pushing the button to the morphine drip the doctor had ordered that morning.

"How are you, baby?"

She followed her instincts and lied, telling him what she knew he needed to hear. "I'm fine, Daddy." The pull to let go was strong, but she needed to set things right before she gave in. "I want you to leave Jeremy be. He's been a good husband, and he's a good man."

Owen shook his head, and his eyes hardened. "He's treated-"

With strength in her voice that surprised them both, she cut him off. "What he's done, Daddy, he's done to *me* - not you - and it's between *us*. He's never deliberately hurt me, and he loved me the best he could." She pulled his eyes back to her. "He loves her, Daddy. I knew that from the beginning."

~~

Emily Beckett died twenty one hours later; on February twenty-fourth, 1997 at 7:15 p.m. With her family gathered around her, she slipped into unconsciousness while the pain loosened its fierce grip. With her last breath, a look of serenity transformed her face, assuring them all that she'd finally left the pain behind.

Debra lay next to her for nearly an hour before Jeremy could pull her away. She wept with him, and Jeremy's heart ached with every sob. Eventually, she cried herself to sleep, but it was hours before he could leave her alone in her room.

It was Linus who came for him after Emily's body had been taken to the mortuary. Few would be as keenly aware of the emptiness left behind with her passing as he. After all, it is just this sort of scenario, that has always been his greatest fear. He could imagine, and often does, just how devoid of meaning his life would become if his wife were ripped away from him, if he had to surrender the fight with death to keep her. He helped Jeremy down the stairs to the living room, shaken with fatigue and grief, his son's movements were sluggish and clumsy.

Elise wrapped her arms around her son and felt his body sag against her. She hurt more from his pain than her own. One look at her eldest child, and she knew he was numb, already somewhere else in his mind. In a way the parasitic press and tabloid sleaze would never understand, he was devastated, and would never be the same again. Grief has changed him, just as the years of Emily's illness had changed him; from the boy he had been when he married her, to the man who had found the strength to let her go.

The press would want a statement, but with his son safe in the company of his wife and daughter, Linus slipped away to the study and set to work. Jeremy was in no frame of mind to see to details; no, silencing the gossip mongers would be a task Linus Beckett could sink his teeth into.

His son needed time, time to grieve and let go of the woman with whom he'd built a life. He had to come to terms with what remained: an angry and nearly grown daughter, a void where Emily had once been, a son and the life he had to make for him.

Jeremy insisted on seeing to the funeral arrangements himself. It was, he said, the very least he owed Emily. When the time came, the service he'd arranged was beautiful and poignant. With sprays of roses and all her favorite flowers filling the church and surrounding her coffin, he hoped she would approve. When the choir began singing her favorite hymns, everyone was in tears.

Jeremy sat in the front pew throughout the service with his arm around his daughter while his parents and sister formed a protective shield around them both. Debra's sobs were nearly more than he could bear. His pain wouldn't ease; in fact it felt like it was consuming him, threatening to pull him under. He wept genuine tears and let them fall freely.

He stayed at the cemetery long after Emily was laid to rest next to their son, Nathan. Long after the earth was packed into place, he sat on the marble bench next to the graves and mourned. Privately, he wept even more and vowed to Emily that he would be the kind of father their daughter needed him to be.

Pictures of he and his family leaving the church revealed Jeremy to be ashen faced behind dark sunglasses. The puffy redness he worked to conceal hadn't been there since he'd buried his son. He flanked his daughter, shielding her from camera lenses, and the crowd gathered to watch their pain. The car ride back to the estate was quiet and somber. Once inside the gates, they were closed off from all the prying eyes of the world.

~ 45 ~

For a fleeting moment, Christina thought about attending the funeral, but respect and common sense kept her from following through. It would be entirely inappropriate. The press would have a field day, and she loved Jeremy too much to add to his pain.

She hadn't seen him in more than a week. His time had been spent with his wife and daughter, but the glimpse she caught of him on the evening news concerned her. He was pale, thin, and lost. She wanted to close her arms around him and protect him.

He called her every night; he said that hearing her voice was one of the few things that got him through, but he thought it best that Christina didn't see him. On the phone, she couldn't see his ragged appearance, count the lines on his face, or see the bags under his eyes. Emily had forgiven his affair but she couldn't appease his guilt over her knowing and keeping silent.

~~

Christina woke with a start, expecting to hear the baby, but she heard the doorbell instead. She jumped from the bed and ran down the stairs to the door before the bell could wake him. Through the peephole, she saw him: Jeremy. With his head down, swaying back and forth on unsteady feet, he had come to her. She opened the door and let him inside.

"I didn't wake the baby, did I?" His voice was a slurred whisper, and his eyes - red from drinking and grief - looked bleakly at her. Unsteady, he righted himself by leaning against the wall behind the door.

She could smell the alcohol. Scotch was his drink of choice, and she wondered how it was that he'd made it to her door in his current condition.

"No," she said softly, looking out the window to see where he'd parked his car. She then realized that Edward must have dropped him off.

Slipping her arm around his waist, she walked with him into the living room and eased him onto the sofa. "I'd ask why you didn't use your key, but I think I know the answer."

Slumping back into the deep cushions, he gave her a lopsided grin, but his heart wasn't in it, and it vanished as quickly as it appeared. "I know I said I couldn't come over tonight, but Debra's better off with me out of her way. Dad and Mom are staying with us for awhile, in any case." He sighed and ran his fingers through his hair in a nervous habit both of them hardly noticed any more. "And the truth is, my daughter has no use for me right now anyway."

Sadness was rooted deep in his eyes, and she sat next to him and pressed her lips to his unshaven cheek. "Of course she does."

He shrugged, seeming not to hear her. "I needed you," he said, pulling her into his arms and inhaling deeply, his nose pressed to her hair, "and I need, Patrick too. I need to hold him, Christina, and you."

She held him as tightly as he held her. "It's okay."

"The funeral was so hard, harder than I thought it would be. I thought I'd be relieved her suffering was over. Debra's inconsolable. And, well, you know the press."

She did. All too well, she knew there were photographers waiting somewhere outside to snap the most inappropriate picture. "Try not to think about it now." She pulled away and took his pained face in her hands to kiss him softly. "It's almost time for Patrick's feeding. Let's go up and see him; I know he misses you."

"I miss him, too." As if on cue, a loud, determined cry broke the silence in the house, and together they climbed the stairs to go to their son.

~~

Linus walked up the flower-lined sidewalk with sunglasses shielding his eyes from the bright early morning sun. A gentle breeze blew his mostly gray hair about his head in tuffs. In all the years he'd known Christina, it shocked him to realize he had never once come here to her home. He walked onto the quaint porch, and a smile bloomed; this was just what he'd imagined her home would be.

The woman, he thought warmly, had impeccable taste. After all, she'd chosen his son to love. He knocked on the door and shoved his hands into his pockets to wait.

Christina opened the door, flushed and out of breath. She smiled at Linus as easily as if she'd been expecting him. "Hi," she said brightly. Then, out of habit, she stepped over the threshold and shrewdly began surveying the area for the tell-tale signs of telephoto lenses, reporters and cameras.

Linus quickly put her at ease. "Don't worry; I've handled the press."

Christina looked at him mischievously. "Do I want to know how?" she asked, moving aside to let him in with her eyes still sweeping the street.

Linus grinned and stepped into the house. "I've planted misinformation," he replied, leaning in to kiss her cheek. "You're out of town at another convention, you - or someone who will most definitely be mistaken for you - left late last night to avoid the paparazzi. You'll be happy to know you're staying in the penthouse suite at the Royal Elms in the Cayman Islands. It'll be a few days before they get close enough to realize they been duped, so until then you won't have to worry about them."

She laughed and threw her arms around him in a hug. "Thank you, Linus. With everything Jeremy's been dealing with, we could use some privacy."

"I agree." He returned the hug. "How is he this morning? Edward told me he was drinking before he dropped him off last night."

"Have a look for yourself," she replied, taking his hand and leading him into the kitchen.

Patrick was the center of Jeremy's attention. And while Jeremy looked a little rough around the edges, Linus could see that Elise had been right: Christina and his son were the only ones who could help Jeremy right now.

~~

Six Months Later
August, 1997

Traffic in Manhattan during midday rush was a lot like trying to gain distance in the ocean by walking into a tidal wave, or so Jeremy thought as he slid into a lane he'd picked in a moment of rash temper. It flowed no more quickly than the one he'd just escaped, and he muttered an oath that would have made his mother blush.

In his nightmares, this was how he would die. Awash in gridlock, gray haired and slack-jawed from the daily grind, his heart would give out on his way to somewhere. But not today, he reminded himself with satisfaction when the car in front of him picked up speed. Within seconds, he could see his destination up ahead.

He was having lunch with his daughter - a young woman now, as she was constantly reminding him. A smile played over his lips as he remembered her insistence that she was no longer a child. He could have sworn it was just yesterday when she was the little girl who smiled at him for no other reason than his walking into the room.

In fact, she was very nearly the young woman she proclaimed to be. She was growing into a mirror image of the mother she so adored, and in her, he saw very little of the girl who wrapped him around her finger; instead, he saw more of what Emily's death had forced upon her. Maturity and the loss of innocence were often causalities of grief and loss. Jeremy was working hard to heal the rift between them, just as he knew Emily wanted, and he - just as surely - needed.

With a feeling of triumph, he pulled his Jaguar into the first parking space he spotted across from Spago and shut off the engine. All too familiar with his daughter's impatience, he got out and crossed the street against traffic, ignoring the blaring horns, to get to Debra without further delay. A smart man did his best to avoid the temper she had inherited - especially the man she inherited it from.

~~

When he strolled into his office after lunch, Jeremy found Linus sitting on his sofa waiting for him. He smiled and hung up his coat, preoccupied with thoughts of Debra. "What's up, Dad?"

Linus knew from Jeremy's expression that his lunch date with his granddaughter hadn't gone entirely as he had hoped. "Lunch didn't go well?"

"Well, she didn't throw any drinks in my face," he said, dropping down on the sofa next to his father and slapping his knee affectionately.

"You should reconsider therapy."

Jeremy got up and crossed to his desk to check his messages. "She's angry with me, Dad. But she's finally listening to me, meeting me half way." He thumbed through them, picking out the most urgent. "Hawkins wants a call back."

Linus lifted a brow, the obvious change of subject meant the topic of his granddaughter was closed. Taking the bait, he said, "I thought the deal was sealed?"

Jeremy shrugged and buzzed Sarah. "As good as. Sarah, please get Michael Hawkins on the line." He glanced up at Linus and gestured to the tray on the corner of his desk. "Look for yourself."

Linus picked up the contract and turned away to look it over. The fine print blurred his vision and made it nearly impossible for him to read. From his breast pocket, he took out his glasses and perched them on his nose.

"Hand holding's part of it at this stage. It's a family-run company; it's gotta hurt losing it."

Linus turned back and dropped the contract on his desk. "Sentimentality is a liability in this business."

"End of the week, it'll be ours," Jeremy replied. As always, Linus was a no-nonsense businessman; no room for sentiment. "And I'm still serious about breaking it up and selling it off in pieces. I'm not interested in restructuring, Dad."

Frustration was easily read in his eyes. Linus knew his son was like a dog with a bone on this point. "I know where you stand."

"It just makes good business sense, Dad. The company's not viable as a whole. It's a money pit. That's why we got it at the price we did."

Linus gave him a wry look and started to pace. "You call a hundred and seven million low?"

"It is when I'll break it up and pull in a half-billion. That's a three hundred and ninety-three million dollar profit, Dad."

"You're awfully confident on the numbers."

"Because I know what I'm doing."

Linus couldn't argue with him. His son was at the top of his game, so he relented. "I'll talk to Tim this afternoon and see if he shares your confidence."

~ 46 ~

Christina was busily preparing dinner when Jeremy walked into the kitchen, scooped up Patrick from his playpen, and gave him a tired smile. "I didn't hear your key in the door."

He walked over and breathed in the aroma of roasting garlic. "Wasn't locked." Patrick was tugging on his loosened tie as Jeremy tipped up her face for a kiss. "Need to be more careful. What if - instead of me - some crazed lunatic came in here?"

"Cheerful thought, honey." At the sober look in his eye, she took him seriously. "Won't happen again, I promise."

"Good." Patrick had drooled down the front of his linen shirt and was pinching his cheek with his tiny fingers. Jeremy clucked his tongue and received a delighted squeal from his son.

"Avery called." She added chopped parsley to the sizzling garlic and stirred it briskly to avoid scorching. "I told him we'd be there around ten."

"Sounds good. I'm gonna change, throw some things in a bag."

"I already packed for us."

"You're too good to me." He winked at Christina and lifted Patrick in the air, walking out of the kitchen. "Come on, little one, and hang out with your old man."

~~

Owen Harris waited impatiently with a sour expression on his face. Memories of his unhappy childhood were clicking through his mind like a sickening slide show. Much to his dismay, Brooklyn was the place of his birth and his upbringing, and he had spent much of his youth trying to escape the dirty streets and grimy stoops of his childhood.

Long gone were the days when his afternoons consisted of stick ball with his friends. And then trying, and most times failing, to avoid the heavy hand of a mother lost in an abyss of fast living and the hard knocks of reality. Now, he was more than the troubled youth the county social workers had called a "lost cause." Now he was a well respected businessman, and a man with which to be reckoned.

He sat in his Lexus, pulled discreetly into an alley in a dingy part of Brooklyn where only drug addicts and vagrants reside. Uneasy with his trip down memory lane and wishing the man he was there to meet would finally arrive, he opened his window to be sure his presence hadn't attracted unwanted attention.

In his immediate line of sight, he could see a discarded syringe some junkie had probably been too high to dispose of properly, and he turned up his nose in disgust.

There was, he decided with disgust, a certain haze hanging over this part of New York. A pall so thick with the odor of alcohol and garbage that there was no more apt nickname than the one he heard so often: "Hell's Kitchen." Grateful for his escape and ascent to greatness, he closed his window and imagined himself to be anywhere else but here.

When the door across from him finally opened, Owen could only be grateful to take care of business.

"You're late," Owen said sharply, casting an appraising eye on the man who looked back in amusement. It grated his nerves to let the likes of this thug anywhere near him, but some things were more important. Some things were *this* important.

"Watch must'a stopped," the man replied. He slumped into the lush leather seat, unimpressed. Flicking a weathered toothpick from one side of his mouth to the other, he watched as carefully as he was being watched. "I'm here now. Sure you still want to go through with it?"

Owen shifted and faced the man, careful to keep his herring bone suit from rubbing up against his visitor's dirty leather jacket. "I'm sure." He handed the man a large padded envelope. "Half now, then the other half when it's done. There are step-by-step instructions inside as well. Follow them to the letter, and you won't have a problem. But whatever happens, there's no link whatsoever back to me."

"Goes without saying, man."

Owen doubted that very much. This man would finger his own mother if it suited him. "It bears repeating."

"You're the boss," the man replied with a sly smile when he opened the envelope and got an eyeful of his cash.

"You can go." Owen instructed. This would be their last contact until the job was done. He just wanted this greasy punk gone. "Don't screw this up," he warned, shoving his sunglasses over his eyes. "Call me when it's taken care of."

The man planted a leather-booted foot on the ground and stepped out of the car. Tucking the envelope into his coat, he watched the Lexus inch its way out of the alley before he disappeared into the shadows. By this time tomorrow, the job would be done, and more money than he'd ever seen would be his for the spending.

~ 47 ~

Albany, New York
Christina's Residence
9:30pm

Bess Wagner sat the baby monitor at her feet, which are presently propped on the glass-topped coffee table in her niece's living room. A quiet night closed in around her. Her great nephew was fighting a nasty cold and, after being fed and given his medicine, was likely down for the night so, she settled in and clicked on the TV. Flipping through the channels, she decided on a rerun of "The X-Files," and settled a bowl of popcorn in her lap.

Outside the window behind her, the street light at the end of the driveway winked out, and a widening stretch of darkness spread out over the area; from the blacktopped drive to the thick bushes that loomed on the other side of the street. A car passed by in the inky dark, but didn't notice the subtle trembling of the tallest bush among them. Down the block, it turned into an identical drive and the headlights fade out in the night. Inside Christina's home, Bess was too drawn into the program she was watching to notice the security system's lighted panel shutting down from deactivation.

Cherry Hill
10:45pm

Avery was still wide awake when Jeremy and Christina found him sitting in the living room. His hair was more silver and his profile a bit more wrinkled, but his nurse, Lissy, assured them he was right as rain and as quick as ever. Jeremy and Christina watched him, comfortably perched in his wheelchair, staring into the flames licking and crackling in the fireplace to warm his aging bones. Even in late summer in Vermont, a bite could still be felt in the air coming in off the lake.

He sat straight, his face more charming by firelight. The deep love and affection Jeremy always felt so strongly when he saw his grandfather, rose up inside him once more.

"Grandpa," Jeremy said, waiting until Avery turned from the fire before he crossed the worn oak floor of the den. He watched his grandfather's face transform into a smile; the ease he always felt in his grandfather's presence returned when he embraced him.

Christina joined Jeremy by the fireplace and slipped her arm around his waist, reveling in the warmth and coziness she always felt here; and the chance to be completely at ease. She watched Avery's face; the wrinkles earned during a lifetime of business and living and his wonderfully weathered face seemed aglow in the firelight. Realizing just how much she'd missed him, she bent down for a hug and pressed a kiss to both of his cheeks.

"Sorry we're so late," she said. "Aunt Bess felt compelled to wander the house, gossiping, before settling in to dote on Patrick."

"Don't give it another thought, dear," Avery replied, "though I'm disappointed you had to leave my great grandson behind."

"I hoped he'd be over his cold by now," Christina said with affection.

"Next time, then. I'm glad for the company. Come on, sit and tell me what I've been missing in the city."

~ 48 ~

Christina's Residence
Midnight

Within the bushes, he crouched. Alert, watchful, he lifted his wrist in the darkness, and the face of his watch lit as he checked the time. It was vital that he stick to the schedule. When he arrived, he wasted no time putting things in motion.

With the simple wielding of a palm-sized rock from his gloved hand, the street light that would make him most vulnerable to discovery went out. The barely discernable tickling of the broken light bulb falling to the pavement was the only sound to break the stillness of the night. What happens next must happen in stealthy silence, if he is to succeed.

The passing car had spooked him momentarily, but, hidden in the bushes with the darkness as cover, he knew it was impossible to be seen. With what could have been a disaster averted, he needed to get back to the task at hand, and do the job he'd been paid to do. Disabling the security had been easier than he thought it would be. He followed the line from the box and dug up the shallow-buried wires to snip them with the wire cutters he carried in his back pocket.

Then it was back to the bushes to wait. Patience - and he hated patience - was the next important step. He waited for more than an hour for the old lady to turn in, then more than another hour longer after the lights went out to be sure she was asleep.

Stiffly, he unfolded his legs and swallowed the groan of pain when he straightened and the needles shot up his thigh. He quickly rolled up onto his toes and back to wake his sleeping muscles. Once he felt his blood moving again, he pulled the knit mask over his head and covered his face.

It was time to go for the prize. He crossed the street in a crouched run, then moved across the small front yard before disappearing around back.

~ 49 ~

Jeremy lay content with Christina in his arms; as was so easy for him to do, he lost himself in her. Carried away by pleasure in her, he made love to her in the quaint den in front of what had been a thriving fire, with the lovely, quiet night outside embracing the house, embracing them. Her breath was light on his chest while she slept tucked so close to him.

A chill drifted into the room, the fire, now banked and dying in the late hour, can no longer warm them. With some regret, he slipped out from under her and into his boxers. Then, with his jeans tossed over his shoulder, he stooped and gathered her into his arms. Kicking the blankets they used aside, he carried her through the doorway and down the carpeted hall to the wide staircase.

Climbing the stairs with Christina murmuring against his neck, Jeremy thought about his children. Debra was away with Owen on an overnight shopping trip in Chicago, and Patrick was at home with Bess, hopefully getting a restful night's sleep despite his cold.

He was a lucky man, he thought, shuffling through their bedroom door and crossing in the darkness to lay Christina on the bed. He carefully tugged the down comforter from under her and pulled it over her for warmth. With a beam of moonlight draping her face, he watched her sleep. It never ceased to amaze him just how breathtaking she remained. Time and the years behind them had been kind to her. He went to his side of the bed, slid in next to her, and pulling her close, drifted off to sleep.

Christina's Residence
12:10 am

His choice of entry was simply pragmatic. The kitchen door faced the woods beyond the yard and offered him cover and a quick getaway. And, now, he'd moved through the spacious professional-style kitchen with ease - thanks to the blueprints provided for him to lead the way. The soft soled shoes on his feet were silent as he made his way to the stairs. Looking around the moon-kissed living room to his left, he decided the restaurant business and the wealthy lover had been very good to Christina Wagner.

He started up the stairs, smug and confident and convinced the lady's luck had just took a drastic turn for the worse.

~~

In the upstairs hall, he paused outside what he knew was the guest bedroom. Putting his ear to the door, he listened for - and heard - the silence he needed. Knowing the old lady wouldn't be a problem, he crossed the hall to the nursery. The door stood open, and he could see the crib in the center of the room. A slow smile crossed his face as he walked inside.

As he expected, the baby was sleeping. Though time was at a premium, he lingered, looking down at the tow-headed infant he'd come for. As rug rats went, he supposed the baby boy was cute enough; he couldn't imagine why anyone would want the trouble that came with kids.

Oh well, he thought, *not my problem, and not why I'm here*.

Taking a quick survey of the nursery, he found the diapers and stuffed them into a nearby diaper bag. He then grabbed a blanket draped over the back of a rocker. It was time to grab the kid and bolt, time to put distance between him and this house, and time to deliver the goods.

He turned to the crib and reached for the baby with awkward hands more suited to handling guns than an innocent child. Carefully lifting the baby into his arms, he took only a step or two when the silence was broken by the baby's sharp, fussy cries. He flinched, panic crawled up his throat, and he knew he only had an instant to react.

Instinct made him bolt, and he'd nearly made it past the guest room when the door opened and a disoriented voice stopped him in his tracks. In the instant when he knew she'd seen him, his mind clicked through his options. She blinked in the darkness and clutched the front of her nightgown, when her thoughts disconnected by sleep suddenly began to form reason.

Bess took a shaky step forward and instinctively reached for her great nephew. She never uttered a word, and suddenly she lay sprawled on the floor. Her last thought was to protect the baby, so she tried to get up - but a sudden, sharp blow to her head made the attempt futile as darkness closed in around her.

~~

With his heart hammering in his chest, he took off down the stairs and out the front door. Thanks to his discovery of a pacifier as he cut across the lawn, the baby was quiet while his hard-pumping legs furiously ate up the road to the car he had stashed a half-block away. As he did his best to secure the baby in the car seat, he worried that the old lady was dead; he feared a simple scoop-and-run job had turned him into a murderer, and a clumsy one at that.

As he jumped behind the wheel of his getaway car and cranked the sluggish ignition to life, Bess, dizzy and bleeding from the head, crawled to the phone by her bed and dialed 911.

~ 50 ~

12:40am
Cherry Hill

Christina bolted upright in bed just as the shrill ringing of the phone broke through the peaceful silence. Something was terribly wrong, and the certainty of it brought a rush of panic that stole her breath. Suddenly frightened, she gripped Jeremy's shoulder as he rolled over and answered the phone.

"Hello?" he mumbled with a tongue thick from sleep.

The voice on the line was that of a stranger, and he wasted no time. "Mr. Beckett, this is Detective Williams with NYPD. I'm afraid I have some difficult news."

Fumbling with the bedside lamp, he sat up in the harsh light and turned to Christina to grip her hand. "What is it, Detective?" His first thought was of Debra, so the answer to his question caught him totally unprepared.

"I'm calling from Christina Wagner's residence." He paused for a moment, searching for the best way to deliver the coming blow. "I'm sorry to have to tell you this, but your son, Patrick, has been taken; it looks like a kidnapping."

Christina's heart stopped as she watched the color drain from Jeremy's face. "What is it? Jeremy, what's happened?"

Swinging his feet to the floor, his whole body stiffened. "Kidnapping? What the hell're you talking about? My son's with Bess Wagner. Where the hell is she? I want to speak to her."

Detective Williams cleared his throat and told him the rest. "Ms. Wagner can't talk right now, Mr. Beckett. She's on her way to the hospital with a nasty blow to the head."

Christina's high-pitched wailing snapped him out of the fog of disbelief. Taking Christina into his arms, he swallowed the urge to vomit and replied, "We've got a helicopter on the grounds. We'll see you in thirty minutes." He hung up.

Avery arrived, concern obvious on his face. "Call the pilot, Grandpa," Jeremy said flatly. "Patrick's gone." He raked a shaky hand through his hair, he couldn't make himself believe it. "They said he's been kidnapped." His eyes, filled with worry, locked on Avery's while he tried to quiet Christina. "We need to get home."

~ 51 ~

The quiet street was under siege with flashing police lights and patrol cars when Edward turned onto the street and slowly drove them up to the barricade. They were waved through and continued on up the road until the limo stopped in front of the house. Jeremy stepped out with a shaken Christina clinging to him in shock. They made their way up the drive, relieved the press had yet to pick up the story.

He saw Linus standing outside the front door, talking to a uniformed policeman. He called out to him, "Dad!"

Linus looked up and saw Jeremy and Christina making their way to him and he started across the cemented sidewalk in a jog to meet them. "Son," he said quietly before pulling him into his arms. "Christina, dear, let's get you inside," he continued, and draped his arm around her shoulder to lead her inside.

Inside the house, the activity and lights and countless uniforms were jarring. It was not yet two in the morning, but the living room was filled with too many people; it appeared her home was under siege.

Outside, the street was beginning to line with curious neighbors - and Jeremy knew the press wouldn't be far behind. They would be intent on making the nightmare he and Christina were living that much worse.

Jeremy followed Linus to Christina's office and waited until he sat Christina down on the sofa before he demanded answers. "Where's this Detective Williams? I want to know what's being done to find Patrick - right now."

Linus squeezed his son's shoulder. "I think he's upstairs in the nursery with the crime scene unit. I'll take you up."

Jeremy shook his head and turned to Christina. "Bring him down here, Dad; I'm not leaving her." He went to her and dropped to a crouch in front of her. "I think she's in shock."

"I'll call Michael after I tell Williams you're here."

"Thanks Dad." When they were alone, he touched Christina's face. "Sweetheart, look at me." It felt like an eternity before her wet, terror-filled eyes focused on him. "I'll find Patrick. I'll find our boy - I promise." She leaned forward and wrapped her arms around his neck to sob. He held her close in comfort and murmured to her. "I promise."

~~

He didn't trust cell phones, in fact he didn't trust much in life, so he cast a weary glance to the back seat and sighed with relief to find the baby was sleeping and mercifully quiet. He pulled off the street into an alley and stopped next to a beat up phone booth. He got out, eased the door closed, and ducked inside the booth to make the call.

~~

"I'm terribly sorry we're meeting again under these circumstances, Mr. Beckett." Though they had crossed paths before through his foundation, but Williams couldn't claim to know Jeremy Beckett well.

"Me too, Detective," Jeremy said, raking his hand through his hair. "What do we know so far?"

Detective Williams stood in the kitchen doorway with Jeremy in front of him, but his attention was directed over his shoulder. "The CSI unit found the wiring to the security system dug up and cut," he said, nodding to the door across the room. "We found a footprint in the flower garden outside the backdoor. That was his point of entry."

"What else do we have to go on?"

"Just a vague description from Ms. Wagner," he said, silently cursing the very little they had to go on. "Height and build, but not much else, unfortunately. We're enacting all SOP's for abduction. Uniforms are blanketing the immediate area, questioning neighbors and securing the block as a crime scene."

"I want the FBI brought in," Jeremy said.

"Already done due to your high profile; a couple agents should be here momentarily. But first things first. I hate to ask this, but we need you to leave the premises until the investigative and CSI officers clear it. This house is a crime scene, and we can't have it compromised. You can gather some things together and make other arrangements."

"We can't go anywhere. What if the sonofabitch tries to make contact?"

"We've tapped the phone lines here, and we can put a tap on your cell, or reroute any incoming calls to whatever number you give us. Besides, you'll be back here as soon as possible."

"I don't have a cell phone." Jeremy said. "I've always found them to be too intrusive. You can do whatever else you think is necessary. We'll clear out, that's not a problem." He didn't want Christina there right now anyway

- not while her home was being invaded. First by whoever had stolen their son, and now by armed policemen and investigators scouring every inch of the house for clues. "But before I go, I want to know what needs to be done. Should I pull together a ransom? Make a public plea for his return? What? What can I do to help my baby?"

"Let's just take this one step at a time, Mr. Beckett. Now, is there anyone you can think of who's got a grudge against you?"

"No."

"Business associates?"

"Of course not. Detective, disagreements in business are dealt with in the boardroom," Jeremy snapped, "not with assaults and kidnappings."

"Family members?" the detective said, easing back a bit with his tone.

"No," he answered, frustrated. "No one in my family or Christina's would ever do this. Why would they? What would possibly be their reason?" Jeremy could feel his fierce grip on his control slipping. He backed away, then started down the hall before turning back. "You're headed down the wrong road-" he said, falling silent when his mind honed in on a dark thought. He pinched the bridge of his nose in mounting frustration. He had to be wrong, but he couldn't take any chances. "Owen Harris."

Detective Williams flipped through his notes. "Your father-in-law?"

"Former father-in-law," he corrected. "He's in Chicago with my daughter. He's the only one sick enough to pull this - and God knows he hates us both enough."

Before Williams could respond, the front door opened and a uniformed officer brought in a man and woman with badges hanging from chains around their necks. The expected FBI agents, Williams presumed. He and Jeremy watched them approach.

"Detective Williams," the man spoke first and offered his hand in greeting. "I'm Special Agent Mick Wallace, FBI," the two men shook hands, "and this is Agent Jensen Brice, my partner."

Jensen Brice offered Williams a slight smile and shook his hand firmly. "Detective. We're here to assist in any way we can."

"Agents, thanks for coming," Williams said. "This is Jeremy Beckett."

Jeremy shook hands with them but wasted no more time with small talk. "What's our next move?"

Agent Wallace understood the sense of urgency and met it head on. "We'll be conducting interviews, and we're canvassing for witnesses, as well as using the federal labs for evidence analysis. Mr. Beckett, the FBI and NYPD will work together to find your son. We'll leave no stone unturned until we bring Patrick home."

Jeremy shook his head. "I don't want handholding, Agent Wallace. I just want my son back. Now, if you'll excuse me, I need to check on Bess; Christina's very worried." he said, turning away and heading for the office.

~~

Michael was sitting next to Christina on the sofa when Jeremy came in. Closing the door behind him, Jeremy went to her, then smoothed his palm over her hair and spoke to Michael. "How is she?"

Michael was checking her pulse and looked up over his glasses at Jeremy. "Stubborn," he replied before laying his stethoscope against her chest. "Beyond that, she's in mild shock, but she's refusing to be medicated - even mildly. I still think it would help her sleep."

Jeremy sighed. He could feel her panic right along with his own. "Well, she may change her mind. Detective Williams want us to clear out of here. They don't want us contaminating the crime scene or any evidence that might have been left behind. Besides, this place's gonna be crawling with people, cops. We'll have no privacy - not with press outside and nosy neighbors craning their necks for a better look, and God knows who else."

"This is our home," Christina mumbled, agitated. "Patrick's, yours, and mine." Christina closed her eyes, focusing on what she could control. "I'm just supposed to leave them here and go? Where?"

Jeremy exchanged looks with Michael and then his father. He pulled in a breath and went to calm her. "We'll stay with my parents, sweetheart."

"Of course you will," Linus said with a reassuring smile.

"I don't belong there," she murmured, clutching the front of Jeremy's shirt. "The press will torment them, and they don't deserve it."

"Then we'll go to the Waldorf. We'll get a suite - our suite," Jeremy decided. "The press can't crowd us there." He pulled back and took her face in his hands. "But we need to go, Christina."

"And what if there's a ransom demand? What if they call? What if they kill him when we're not here to talk to them?"

"The police have that all worked out."

"I need to call the hospital and check on Aunt Bess."

"I have, sweetheart," Jeremy said, lifting her hand to kiss it. "She has a concussion, but she'll be fine in a few days."

~~

Half an hour later, Jeremy and Christina walked into their old suite in the Waldorf - but they were not alone. Linus and Elise were with them, and so were Agents Brice and Wallace. They set up a tapping and taping device on the suite phone, then walked Jeremy through how to handle the call if one came.

By two a.m., there were two uniforms outside the suite door, standing guard. Agents Brice and Wallace were gone, and only Jeremy, his parents, and Christina remained. No one spoke for long periods of time; too many fears occupied their thoughts for small talk.

Christina wandered through the suite aimlessly, but Jeremy was never more than two steps away from her. He liked to think the memories the two of them shared here might comfort her when nothing else could. Their life and their love began here. They dared to dream of a lifetime together here. This place had once been a home and a refuge for them.

Now it was a refuge again, and for the worst possible reason, from the intrusive press and the public - and Jeremy was quite simply ready to climb the walls. His son was out there somewhere...with a stranger? he wondered. Or Owen Harris? He couldn't decide which was worse, all he knew for sure was that his baby boy was probably terrified and crying for his mother.

And he could do nothing.

The woman he loved more than his life was terrified and struggling to hold it together. As was he, but he had to be strong for them both; so, he did what he could do. He quietly went to her, eased her back against him, pressed a kiss to the back of her head and wrapped his arms around her for warmth and solace.

Minutes stretched to hours without any word, and the silence was heavy and maddening. Jamie arrived, but no one could reach Debra. Time stood still while Jeremy and Christina feared the worst.

~ 52 ~

Stone-faced, he listened while the man from whom he took orders prattled on in his ear. "What the hell am I supposed to do with this kid?"

"You'll just have to sit tight. Your sloppiness has complicated the situation. I'll call when I have all the details."

Striding around the limited space of his RV, he squeezed the phone at his ear until his knuckles whitened. "I didn't sign on to be a fuckin' babysitter. I met my end of this deal, and now it's your turn - and don't even think about double crossing me, or you'll regret it."

~~

The sun was coming up by the time Jeremy and his sister convinced Christina to take one of the mild sedatives Michael left for her and lie down on the sofa. Through the hours crawling by, she roamed the suite, afraid to stand still and let the despair overtake her. She moved from room to room with memories of Patrick for company.

Jeremy found her weeping in the spacious bathroom suite, and his knees nearly buckled as his own grief finally caught up with him. The grief combined with his anger ate away at him in the quiet moments. He hadn't been able to protect his son, and he would never be able to forgive himself for it. He had to pull himself together, though, so he could be the strength Christina needed to survive whatever lay ahead.

The phone remained silent through the wee hours of the morning, and his thoughts of what could be happening to Patrick tormented him. He tried to busy himself, to think of anything other than his precious son's safety. He felt useless, but he couldn't dwell on it or he'd be just as useless to Christina.

He hoped the house offered some clue for Detective Williams and the FBI to follow. The home he shared with his son and Christina would forever be changed now; such a lovely home now sullied by the violence unleashed inside.

Their lives were turned upside down now, and it made Jeremy crazy because there was nothing he could do but wait; wait for word, wait for a demand, wait for a price to be put on his innocent son's head.

As a father, Jeremy would do whatever it took to bring his son home safe, but the man in him, the angry man who thirsted for revenge, wanted to strangle the person responsible. He could feel it welling, gathering inside him. The rage. He could feel himself becoming blinded by it.

Some time later, he wandered into the bedroom and found Christina finally sleeping, though fitfully. Jamie watched him from the corner of the room in silence. It was obvious he didn't know she was there, and perhaps it was intrusive, perhaps it was wrong not to let him know he was being watched. But she remained silent.

It hurt to see him like this; awash in fear, guilt, and self-torment because there was nothing else to do but blame himself. As usual, he is putting others before himself, even though he looks like he is about to drop from exhaustion. She watched him, doing what comes so naturally, murmuring to Christina softly; soothing her in her sleep.

Movement outside the window caught her attention. With dread, she saw a TV helicopter coming close for a better look. Discreetly, Jamie stepped away from the window and closed the blinds. Turning to her brother, she sought to comfort him.

She walked to him and feathered her fingers through his hair. "How're you holding up, honey?"

"I didn't know you were in here." he said softly, but it was a moment before he reacted to her touch. "I'm about to start climbing the walls, I think."

"You look exhausted. Maybe you should try to sleep, too?"

Jeremy finally turned around to look at his sister, taking her hand he kissed it, and gave her a tired smile, then he stepped over and pulled the cotton comforter over Christina. "You're joking, right?"

Jamie watched him stand and begin to pace the floor. "You have to take care of yourself, too. I know what you're thinking, Jeremy, but this is not your fault."

Jeremy shook his head, releasing a breath. "Maybe it is, and maybe it's not, Jamie. But Patrick's still gone, he's not here with his mother where he belongs. And that's damn hard to deal with."

"The police will find him," Jamie replied, believing it. "You have to believe that."

Jeremy closed his eyes and prayed for that. "If Harris is behind this, we have no idea what he's capable of. If he's got my son, it's because of me." he muttered. "If you want to help, find Debra. Tell her I need her. Ask her to come home."

~ 53 ~

Julie Harmon plodded along behind her pudgy bulldog, huffing out the air she was greedily sucking into her lungs. She was in a valiant effort to stave off the effects of living her fifty-nine years with little concern for heart disease or high cholesterol. It was more than improved health bringing her out on such a chilly afternoon, though; curiosity and her reputation as the block gossip, had her wanting to follow up on what she'd heard on her scanner over coffee that morning.

In the wee hours of the morning, while walking the same pudgy bulldog, she'd experienced a sort of close call. Of course, it could be, and likely was, a whole lot of nothing - but didn't she have a duty to inform the police? Wasn't it up to the authorities to decide what was important and what was not? It was her civic duty, after all.

But, she hadn't been expecting the barricade or the young officer manning it, and watching her with a shrewd eye. With an internal pout, she had to accept that her pursuit of fresh grease for the rumor mill had just stopped cold. Disappointed, Julie and her bulldog made their way back down the block to her home. Still pouting, she nearly missed the crushed face of the water meter next to the steps leading to the house.

When she walked close enough to examine the damage, her disappointment turned to anger. She then sent the dog up the steps and through the dog door, bellowing for her husband. "George! George! Get out here and look at this - and bring the cordless; we need to call the water company!"

~~

FBI Agent Mick Wallace drove slowly up the street and parked in front of the Wagner residence. He studied the immediate environment and considered. In the wee hours of the morning, he'd arrived on the scene with his partner. The moonlight and broken streetlight obscured the nuances that were easily seen in the light of day.

So he looked around with a scrutiny acquired years before at the FBI academy in Quantico, Virginia; scrutiny honed through years of seeing the worst acts of inhumanity. His gut clutched as he frowned...something didn't feel right.

From the moment he arrived on the scene at one-thirty that morning, Mick hit the ground running. By two a.m., he was walking the grid with the CSI unit, and by two-eighteen he was bagging and vouchering evidence to be analyzed at the Bureau lab downtown. By two-thirty, he was on the street, canvassing for potential witnesses.

At home in the thick of things, Mick stayed alert and most useful in the field. He wasn't great with the hand holding - as Beckett bluntly pointed out - that was required when it came to dealing with the family. It was a task better left to his partner, Jensen Brice - one he gladly left to her.

With a narrow, intense gaze sweeping from one neighboring yard to another, he scoped out his surroundings, choosing the easiest, most direct route to the house. Thinking like the perpetrator he was hunting, he was making mental notes. The bushes on the other side of the picturesque street drew his pensive gaze. Could those bushes be where the kidnapper lay-in-wait until the perfect time came to make his move?

The rock the perp used to shatter the bulbs in the streetlight was thrown from the trajectory and distance of the bushes. The discarded cigarette butts CSI discovered confirmed he'd waited there; an hour, maybe more. And while he waited in the dark, he planned without fear of discovery or detection. So Mick figured the perp knew the parents were away. He knew an old woman was all that stood between him and Patrick Beckett.

With patience and knowledge the first obstacle was out of his way, he moved on to gaining entry and spiriting the infant away. It was only because of the unforeseen complication of Bess Wagner that he couldn't slip away as invisibly as he'd entered.

Mick's thoughts turned to the neighbors on either side of the Wagner residence. Both couples were elderly and had been sleeping soundly at the time the kidnapping took place. It had been the sirens and lights of the responding police cruisers stirred them from their sleep.

His radio pulled him out of his thoughts. Answering it, he received the first glimmer of hope in the investigation. Mick climbed out of his car and dug out his sunglasses on his way to the door. Finally, he could be the messenger of progress in the case. He had what looked like the first promising lead in Patrick Beckett's abduction.

~~

Wallace wanted to bring the family up to speed, so he sent his partner to conduct a couple follow-up interviews while he followed up on the potential lead. Williams let him into the suite, and he wasted no time getting to the point. "We might've caught a break," he said, coming further into the foyer. "I need you to check it out with me. In the meantime, Brice is doing a couple follow-up interviews and trying to flush out more details."

Williams nodded. "Everyone is in the living room," he said, heading for the living room with Wallace a step behind him.

Mick couldn't miss the expectation on the family's faces, hell, he could even feel it, like a presence in the room, and he hoped he wouldn't have to let them down. "We might have something," he began tentatively.

Jeremy was on his feet before he could say more. "What is it?" Christina clutched his hand and held her breath.

"I'd rather not get into it until Detective Williams and I look into it." With that, Williams was going for the door. "We'll get back as soon as we can," Mick said before turning and disappearing into the foyer to catch up with Williams.

Williams waited until they were inside the car before he broke his silence. "So what've we got?"

Mick shrugged and turned the key in the ignition. Then he pulled away from the curb and headed down the street. "Could be nothing, but my gut says different. A half a block down from the Wagner residence, a lady found her water meter smashed."

Williams wasn't following him. "So?"

"So a tech from the water company says it met up with the back end of a car." Mick began. "And the time clock on this meter stopped at 12:23 a.m. Turns out this Harmon lady was out with her dog a little after midnight, and when she doubled back she saw a car pulling into the street near her house in a real hurry. It nearly ran her down, gunning past her."

"Jesus," Williams said. "Could we get this lucky?"

"Let's find out."

~~

When they stopped across the street from the Harmon residence, both Wallace and Williams could see one of the responding uniforms engaged in a very animated discussion. Crossing the street, they walked up the steps, careful to sidestep the soft piece of ground that bordered them. The woman occupying most of the conversation was Mrs. Harmon.

Coming up behind the officer with Mrs. Harmon, Detective Williams rescued him. Mick hung back to get a better look at the taped-off square of muddy ground.

"Thanks, officer," Williams said with a slap on the guy's shoulder, "we'll take it from here. Better call in and see what's keeping forensics."

Grateful, the officer took off down the steps, leaving the woman well out of earshot.

Williams started with a charming smile. "Mrs. Harmon?"

"Yes, but please call me Julie."

Obligingly, Williams pulled out his note pad from the breast pocket of his jacket as Mick came up beside him. "Okay, Julie. This is Agent Wallace,

FBI, and I'm Detective Williams, NYPD. We'd like to ask you a few questions."

Wallace jumped in with the first one. "I understand you told 911 you think you might have information regarding Patrick Beckett?"

Julie's face seemed to light up with excitement. "I think I might. I was out with Merlin - that's my bulldog - after midnight, and on our way back I heard a car start and then pull into the street like a madman. The crazy sonofabitch nearly hit me when he flew by. I didn't think much of it beyond being thankful the car missed me. Wish I could say the car did the same for my meter. Anyway, thought a bunch of high-schoolers were out for kicks until I heard about the kidnapping on my scanner this morning."

"The car? Did you get a look at it? Can you describe it?"

"Well, it happened so fast, and it was dark. Maybe black or blue, four doors."

"Large model or small?"

Julie narrowed her eyes as if visualizing it in her mind. "Small, I guess; the doors were closer together than on one of those luxury models."

"Thanks." Williams and Wallace digested everything they'd learned and turned back to the street to wait for forensics to arrive. "If we need anything more we'll be in touch."

~~

An hour later, Agent Wallace and Detective Williams were in a department interrogation room, smelling of stale coffee and sweat. Spread out on the table in front of them were dozens of color pictures of the smashed meter and the tire tracks left behind in the grass by the car when it jumped the curb and clobbered the Harmon's water meter.

It wasn't much to go on. In fact, it was practically nothing at all. A speeding car and broken water meter didn't have to mean a damn thing. Or, it could be, mean everything. The timing had to be more than coincidence. When half a block up the street, a stone's throw, really, a baby is abducted literally moments before, there had to be a link.

Like, maybe a kidnapper needing to get the hell out of Dodge? Instinct and common sense told them to follow this lead, however flimsy, to run it down, to follow where it might take them. Their perp couldn't go far with an infant on foot, and the location made sense, so they rolled the dice and operated on the assumption that the car in question was a link to Patrick Beckett and his abductor.

Other members of the squad were spread out in the room, ready to do whatever they could to bring Patrick Beckett home safe and sound and close this case. Many among them were parents themselves and were uncomfortable even imagining what Christina Wagner and Jeremy Beckett were going through. If there were a clue or a lead to be found - however small - they were determined to find it.

Detective Williams sat at the end of the table with his tie tugged loose and his shirt collar open. It didn't matter that he was tired and needed sleep - not when a baby's fate lay in the balance.

Williams broke the tense silence after a gulp of coffee cleared the cobwebs from his mind. "We don't have a tag number, model, or a description of the driver, but what we do have is unique and telling." He tapped the photo in front of him. "There's a break in the tread pattern of the left rear wheel, which leaves a pronounced gouge in the track left behind. Considering the damage to the water meter and the skinned paint transferred at impact, we're looking for a black four-door with noticeable damage to the rear of the vehicle, probably at or near the trunk."

Standing silent behind the door, Mick Wallace spoke up. "We're eleven hours into this. No one here needs to be reminded of the statistics for recovery beyond the first twenty-four hours. We've got an APB out, but we need more. Detective Williams and I think it's time to approach the family about a press conference. The more eyes we have peeled on this, the better. If we're lucky, our perp's already screwed himself, and we might bring this baby home in time for breakfast tomorrow."

~~

As morning stretched into early afternoon and a ransom demand seemed more and more unlikely, Jeremy knew Wallace and Williams were right: waiting could do more harm than good. He'd been doing his own research, and he didn't care for the outcomes in the majority of the abduction cases he'd read about. Besides, he had to do *something*.

The time for waiting was over if they wanted their son back. But the irony of a press conference wasn't lost on him. Turning to the press after a lifetime of animosity toward them meant only that they were desperate to bring Patrick home. He would face the devil himself to hold his son again.

Together with the authorities, Jeremy and Christina decided the press conference should be held on the front lawn at twelve-thirty. It would be brief and conclude with the release of a picture of Patrick to be carried nationwide numerous times throughout the day. Linus worked out all the details and coordinated with the NYPD on the statement released to the public.

Christina and Jeremy arrived back at the house and stood bravely before the television cameras. The long night's ordeal was etched in their faces for all to see. Together, the renowned Beckett family stood, showing a united front. The statement was read by Agent Wallace; with Detective Williams on one side and the family on the other. Cameras were snapping continuously but silence fell among them as Williams stepped before the microphones.

"First, let me convey the Beckett's appreciation for your cooperation during this difficult time. I have a prepared statement after which there will be no questions at this time. Early this morning, at approximately 12:20 a.m., seven-month-old infant, Patrick Beckett, was abducted from the Wagner home. His whereabouts at this time are unknown."

Detective Williams paused, turned to Agent Wallace, and took the chosen picture in his hand. "This is a current picture of Patrick Beckett," he continued, holding the photo up for the cameras to zoom in on. "His abductor is believed to be a white male, approximately 5'11" inches tall, between 25 and 40 years old with a solid, athletic build. He might possibly be driving a black, four-door car with likely damage to the rear of the vehicle. Anyone with any information that could offer assistance in our search is asked to contact the authorities. Thank you."

~~

From the back seat of her grandfather's limo, Debra turned off the TV at the conclusion of the press conference. It all seemed so unreal; her half-brother, the one she rarely acknowledged, was stolen from his crib in the dead of night. A sweet woman she'd only begun to know was violently assaulted and hospitalized. Her father's and his lover's world had been turned upside down.

The street was lined with reporters and curiosity seekers on both sides. The long ride in from the airport gave Debra time to imagine the worst of what she could find here. She was relieved to find the police presence ample enough to avoid chaos and overt invasion of privacy; like perfect strangers crossing the property line and surrounding Christina Wagner's house. Another dose of madness that Debra felt the family didn't need to have shoved in their face.

When the limo slowed to turn into the drive, Debra heard the hurried shuffle of competing photographers vying for the best angle. Giving into a rare indulgence in vanity, she checked her face and hair in her compact before dropping it back into her purse just as the driver opened the door. With undeniable grace, she lifted her long legs and spiked heels out and stepped into view.

Tall, regal, and strikingly beautiful, she walked briskly to the front door without so much as a backward glance. Debra ignored the crude, cruel questions being flung at her as she slipped inside the house. When her father seemed to appear out of nowhere, she saw the lines exhaustion had etched on his face; she looked into his eyes and saw the sadness settled there.

"Oh, Daddy," she said when he came to her. After a moment's hesitation, she went into his arms. "We flew back as soon as Aunt Jamie called. You must be going out of your mind."

"Are you alright?" he asked, grateful she was holding him as tightly as he was holding her. "I tried to reach you myself, but there was no answer in your hotel room. And then...well...things got crazy."

"I'm fine, Daddy, really." The veneer of cool disinterest she usually displayed to her father wavered. Debra felt his pain: in his somber, quiet tone and the palpable, taut tension in his muscles, his pain couldn't be denied. So she held him, comforting him. "How's Christina?"

"She's hanging in there." Jeremy pulled back and kissed her forehead. "I can't seem to keep her from wandering into the nursery. She's out of her mind because Patrick's medication was left behind. Any link to Patrick is a lifeline for us right now."

"I'd like to see her."

"Sure," he said. "She's right in here." He took her hand and walked with her into the living room.

Christina turned when she heard them come in. A brief smile passed between she and Debra before she spoke. "It was good of you to come, Debra."

In the months since her mother's death, she'd kept her distance from Christina Wagner; though she was never rude, never antagonistic, and never able to maintain anger towards her, she stayed distant out of loyalty to her mother. One look at the woman now, though, and compassion carried her across the room to take Christina's hand and kiss her cheek.

~ 54 ~

Under a glass domed ceiling, Owen Harris lounged in the conservatory of his palatial home with summer's colorful blooms all around him. He thought very little of the pain he was inflicting and concentrated only on the small measure of justice he secured for his late daughter. The overnight trip to Chicago had accomplished everything he'd hoped it would: time with his granddaughter and the refuge of plausible denial - if it were needed.

Guilt didn't weigh on his conscience, nor did it distort the precious memories of his Emily. Her honor had been soiled, sullied by the carelessness of others, and he had to make it right; what he'd set in motion was just in his mind.

~~

Jeremy went to Christina, and from behind wrapped his arms around her. Their combined nightmare; barely seventeen hours old, already felt like a lifetime. The crippling helplessness - a palpable presence in the room - seemed to smother any feelings of the hope fighting against it. It was like being held in suspended animation. Debra watched them, witnessing - what up until this moment - jealousy had blinded her to. It was suddenly so obvious, the unmistakably strong bond of love between two people standing together against the world.

~~

On the outskirts of rural New York, miles from nowhere, he waited. The RV was well hidden among the massive oaks in a one-time park forgotten by most at this time of year. This remote area had been the right place to choose to be invisible. Civilization, and the people who populated it, were the enemy now.

So imagine his surprise to find himself the subject of a press conference and to learn that the baby he'd kidnapped belonged to one of the wealthiest and most renowned men in the country. This wasn't good news, and he started to sweat. *Billy*, he mused, growing angrier by the second. Why should he be surprised to realize he had left out essential information?

"A simple scoop-and-run job."

He could still hear Billy telling him that, promising him that. He should have known better, of course it would turn into an all out manhunt, because everything Billy touched turned to shit. The stakes were a whole lot higher now. He was cursing his gullibility and warming a bottle of formula when the little brat woke up, crying.

It was his own misguided loyalty that brought him to the predicament in which he now found himself. He couldn't claim to be a new player in the game by which he lived. A smart man like himself knew the rules and knew them well.

The first rule was so simple and basic, it was an embarrassment to admit he'd broken it: ask questions. Which was quickly followed by the second rule: know the in's and out's of a job before signing on. Billy talked a good game, though, so he'd let a lifetime of friendship cloud his judgment and slit his own throat at the same time.

With the baby finally quiet after a diaper change and now contentedly sucking his bottle and fighting sleep, he tried to relax - but only a little. He laid the squirming infant on the middle of the bed and picked up the cell phone Billy had forced on him. For emergencies only. For a moment he regarded the phone the same way he would regard dog shit on his shoe. Then he punched in Billy's pager number and disconnected, impatiently waiting for Billy to call him back. If this debacle didn't qualify as an emergency - nothing would.

~~

Jeremy and Christina walked into the private hospital room where Bess lay sleeping with an IV in her arm. Pale and fragile, her head wrapped in white gauze, Bess looked awful. Christina picked up her aunt's hand and covered it with her own.

"She's cold," Christina whispered, struggling to keep her voice even. "Can't we get her another blanket? I don't want her to catch a chill."

Jeremy touched Bess' cheek with the back of his hand. "I'll go ask a nurse to bring one in." He softly kissed Christina's cheek as he left.

Bess then stirred in her sleep, moaning before her eyes fluttered open and brought Christina's face into focus. The dull ache at the base of her skull was threatening to make her vomit, but she swallowed hard and tried to speak. "I'm...sooo...sorry."

"Sshh, there's nothing for you to be sorry about," Christina soothed.

Fuzzy images filled the dark corners of her memory, and tears overflowed. "Patrick."

"You risked your life trying to protect him, Aunt Bess." Christina leaned over the bed and pressed her cheek to her aunt's chilled one to comfort her. "It's not your fault."

Jeremy came into the room with a nurse. "I heard her crying in the hall." He tried to comfort the old woman he'd come to so adore. "Bess, I won't let you blame yourself."

"But you trusted me to take care of him."

"And I still do," Jeremy replied, kissing her carefully on the head. "The only thing I want you to worry about is getting back on your feet."

They stayed until she was sleeping calmly before leaving her in the care of her doctor. She would be fine physically, her doctor reassured them, but emotionally there could be difficulty to come.

In the car, Jeremy thought about what he wanted to do to the man who'd stolen his child and assaulted a harmless old woman. Violence wasn't in his nature, but he could envision doing serious bodily harm. And if it was Owen pulling the strings? Well, he'd simply kill him with his own two hands.

Meanwhile, Christina was praying for Patrick's safety, wondering - and not for the first time - if this nightmare were a punishment from God. Is this what it feels like to be out of God's favor? She's heard the phrase often, growing up. Aunt Bess had never missed an opportunity to make an impression on a young, impressible girl.

~ 55 ~

Two hours after the press conference, the phones at the station were ringing with dozens of sightings, and every lead was being painstakingly investigated. Agent Brice was following up on Owen's activities in Chicago, looking for any link to the abduction, while Detective Williams and Agent Wallace returned to the house and gathered everyone in the living room to bring them up to date on the latest information.

"We've had nothing from the airports, train stations, or bus depots, all of which were notified with pertinent information within thirty minutes of the 911 notification," Williams began. "No demands for ransom have been made, so we're confident this is personal, efficient, and professional."

Christina's wry laugh surprised everyone. "It's personal!" Her bitter tone silenced the room. "Of course it's personal!" she snapped, her voice taking on a hysterical edge as she got to her feet. "He came into this house - my house - and took my baby, Detective. It's about hate, and that's as personal as it gets. And no one hates me more than Owen Harris." She turned to Jeremy as a sob broke through her. "I've felt it from the moment we knew Patrick was gone. He took our baby, and we all know it."

Jeremy had known this moment would come, and he watched her stride around the room, oblivious to all the troubled eyes drawn to her. With her faith shaken and her strength gone, it was yet another blow to realize there was nothing he could say that would comfort her. Everyone had a breaking point, a line inside themselves - and once it's crossed, no amount of courage could protect them.

Still, he went to her, determined to be strong enough for them both. "Sweetheart-"

"No!" Christina screamed, shoving away from him. "Why are you here telling us nothing instead of questioning him?" she demanded, whirling around to pin Williams and Wallace with her frantic eyes. "He swore he'd make me suffer, and he's doing it." She stormed out of the room without waiting for an answer, leaving everyone shocked in her wake.

No one moved or even breathed for a moment. Jeremy stood frozen, caught between giving her the space she wanted and his need to be by her side. It was Debra who broke the uncomfortable silence first.

"She can't really believe that." Her tone was one of disbelief. "Daddy, tell me *you* don't believe that!"

Jeremy looked at his daughter, knowing what she wanted to hear, but he couldn't say the words - not when every word Christina said was what he believed to be the truth. So, he turned to Wallace and Williams instead. "Just how long do you intend to wait before you question him?"

The answer was interrupted by Debra brushing past her father without another word. He reached for her, but she jerked her arm away and left the room. When he heard the door slam behind her, he could only sigh and let his sister go after her.

"Within the hour, hopefully," Detective Williams answered, uncomfortable witnessing a family's private pain. "We started checking him out the moment you mentioned him. I'm looking into his activities in Chicago. He's been less than cooperative, and he's an old college friend of the mayor's - need I say more? His alibi's iron clad, and while you and I know that doesn't mean dick, the mayor is of another opinion."

"I don't give a shit if he's the President, alright? He's behind this, but he wouldn't risk fucking up his manicure by handling it personally. But it's him pulling the strings." Jeremy closed his eyes and blew out a frustrated breath. "Put the screws to him - or I will," he snapped. "Now, if you'll excuse me, I need to check on Christina."

~~

Detective Williams was back in Interrogation Room 1 as the investigation continued into its eighteenth hour. He glanced at the clock above the door with a grim face; the lack of any real progress as the hours passed was eating away at morale.

Agents Wallace and Brice stopped pacing the tight space of the room to fill paper cups with coffee. Before taking their place at the long, battered table that was as old as Williams' gold shield, they conferred. Fatigue was as heavy in the room as the aroma of stale coffee and cigarette smoke, but sleep was the last thing on anyone's mind. No one in the room had been home in nearly two days.

Gathered around them lay the few tips from the hotline that seemed most promising. They searched for information that might break the case wide open. Something, anything to buoy the faltering hopes of the baby's parents - who were already past the breaking point if Christina Wagner's outburst an hour ago was any indication. Fear and the mounting hours without word on their son stretched their nerves and their faith.

Now, Williams had nagging doubts of his own. He'd been a cop too long and had seen too much ugliness to cling to a rose-colored view of the world. And, since money wasn't the motivation behind the abduction, the remaining motivations coiled fear in the pit of his stomach.

Revenge was among the most dangerous motivation, and, unfortunately, it now seemed the most likely. To settle some score, either real or imagined, might drive an unstable mind to do the unthinkable.

The sweetest revenge for a twisted mind just might be a dead baby. He closed his eyes, sucked in a steadying breath. He needed to be focused on what was tangible and right in front of him. Dark thoughts of recovering Patrick Beckett's lifeless body, served no purpose at all.

Clearing his throat, he drew all the attention in the room. "Until Harris convinces me otherwise, he's our best suspect," he began.

"He sure hates Beckett enough," Williams offered, "but he didn't get where he is today by being stupid. He'd have to know we'd look at him for this."

"Maybe he just didn't care."

"What we know is he arrived back in the city from Chicago at one this afternoon with his granddaughter, and they were in their suite at the Imperial Arms in the heart of downtown Chicago from just after seven last night until their wake-up call at eight this morning. Room service receipts confirm it. They delivered to the suite at 11:36 p.m. Harris answered the door."

"What's interesting," Agent Wallace continued from the far end of the table, "is hotel records confirm three direct dialed calls to the suite between eleven p.m. and one a.m."

~ 56 ~

Billy listened while orders were being barked in his ear. He already regretted getting involved in this man's madness, but it was too late to do anything other than follow it through to the end. *So much for easy money*, he thought, feeling the reassuring bulge of cash in his inside jacket pocket. So long to his dreams of an endless flow of green to pad his wallet, he thought viciously.

"Yeah, I got it," he muttered, sticking a coke-covered pinky in his nostril and sniffing his way to oblivion. "I ain't stupid, man - but my guy ain't Mary Poppins, and he wants the kid off his hands, like yesterday."

"Well, you'll just have to convince him to hang on to the kid until I've finished with the arrangements."

Billy sniffed another nostril full and sighed. "He's not gonna like it."

"He doesn't have to like it, asshole, he just has to do it. What's another dozen hours with the money I'm paying?" he snapped.

"Take it easy, man. Chill out, I'll take care of it."

"See that you do."

~~

Detective Williams was unimpressed with the grand estate belonging to Owen Harris. He pulled up along side the wide terra cotta steps and got out paying no attention to the ostentatious grandeur around him. What was it but brick and plaster and vanity? And the true measure of the man who lived inside playing God was telling if Jeremy Beckett's suspicions proved to be right.

He climbed the steps, rang the bell, and wasn't surprised when a stately servant opened the door with a dour expression.

"May I help you?" he said in a voice without inflection.

"I'd like to speak with Mr. Harris, please," Williams replied, showing the man his badge.

"Please come in." He moved aside to let Williams into a long terra cotta hall before closing the door and leading him into a side room. "I'll let Mr. Harris know you're here."

Williams used the time alone to get a feel for the man who had, up until this moment, evaded questioning in the Beckett kidnapping. Harris' reputation was one of ruthlessness. Could he really rip a child from his mother's arms? Was he a man capable of such a heinous act?

~~

For a man accustomed to adapting to whatever the situation called for, this unsettling feeling in his gut made the hair on the back of his neck stand on end. He was untouchable, he reminded himself. He was a man without a name, and because of it he could disappear - if need be - as freely as a gust of wind.

He was confident enough in his ability to blend, another twelve hours either way could be managed. It would just be a pain in his ass, and Billy's jerking him around grated like a rock in his shoe. Sediment couldn't be allowed to make him soft. Soft in his occupation could get a man - even a nameless, faceless man like himself - very dead or very much screwed.

"Let me tell you the difference a dozen hours can make, you stupid sonofabitch," he argued, casting a wary glance to the sleeping baby on his bed. "This baby's as hot as a Saturday night special. The longer I've got him, the greater the odds of my getting away clean, vanish. The difference could mean jail time - and if I go down, you go down."

Billy cursed under his breath. "Listen, pal, you think I'd screw you? You think I'd play you like that? Have a little faith, man! I'm talking twelve fuckin' hours - not a lifetime."

He knew when his ass was being kissed and drew in a slow breath for patience. "Twelve hours, Billy. Twelve hours - and not a second longer." He hung up his cell and tossed it aside with a string of whispered expletives. He caught his reflection in the high shine of a glass-fronted cabinet. "Guess Billy's not the only stupid sonofabitch around here."

~~

Owen walked into the room to greet his most unwelcome visitor with a smile and a handshake. The nerve of this common civil servant was enough to have his stomach rolling with disgust. "Detective Williams." He flashed gleaming white teeth and clasped the working man's hand in his own. "This is a surprise. I thought we'd settled our business with the confirmation of my whereabouts."

Williams read a lot in the slightly sneering smile, the overly firm handshake, the charm oozing from every pore. Owen Harris was trying to work him and read him as easily as he was being read. "Just a few follow-up questions."

Owen blinked and gestured to the sofa behind them. Once they were sitting down, he nodded. "Concerning?"

"Your relationship with your son-in-law," he said and watched Owen's eyes harden. Clearly, the animosity in Jeremy ran just as strongly through Harris.

"Jeremy Beckett and I have no relationship."

"You share a common bond."

"You're referring to Debra, I assume?"

"And his bond to your daughter, sir."

"Hardly, Detective," he said with contempt. "A bond implies love. Unfortunately, only one of us loved Emily - and that's me."

He would have had to be blind to miss the loathing or the blatant hatred in the cool, slate-colored eyes gazing intensely at him. "You believe Jeremy Beckett never loved his wife?"

"I not only believe it, Detective Williams, I know it."

Williams saw the truth in those cold, hard eyes. Hate was a powerful motivator, and hate combined with wealth could be a dangerous combination.

~~

Mick Wallace had been denied sleep for too long. Coming off a twenty-four hour stakeout only to step neck deep into a round-the-clock abduction case did little to improve his already bristling personality. His determination could overcome any flaw, though, and he was working this case until it was solved - come hell or high water.

He was monitoring the calls coming in on the hotline while nearly everyone else on the case was refueling on burnt coffee and day-old donuts. A half dozen calls later, Mick was about to move on and leave the tedious logging of all incoming calls to those with more patience. Pushing himself to his leaded feet, he moved sluggishly away from the banks of phones.

"Agent Wallace!"

The sound of his name being bellowed snapped him out of his fog. He turned back and zeroed his bloodshot eyes in on the uniform on the other side of the table. "Yeah."

"I think we might've caught a break," he replied. "A black four-door sedan's been reported abandoned in the warehouse district. The back bumper and rear quarter panel's damaged."

"Get an address and radio me in the car," he barked, already running for the stairs. "Get Williams. Tell him I'll meet him there."

~ 57 ~

Wallace sped through the streets to the strip of weatherworn warehouses adjacent to the waterfront district. The only light came from the rusted old lamplights lining the edge of the docks, and the darkness pressing against their yellow glow looked eerie as he passed one warehouse after another.

He saw the tale-tell signs of a police presence lighting the inky blackness. He slowed and came to a stop behind a patrol car. He wasn't a praying man, but he said a prayer as he grabbed a flashlight from the glove box. He gathered his fraying patience and stepped out to join the ordered chaos of the scene.

The breeze off the water was heated and sticky as he made his way along the dock. Crime scene tape wound its way around the abandoned car and two uniformed officers secured the area. He aimed the beam of his flashlight at the rear bumper and quarter panel as he closed the distance. The damage to the trunk was just as forensics had predicted.

He crouched down for a closer look and ran a gloved hand over the gray paint-skinned bumper. His pulse picked up as he trained the light lower to the left rear tire. He didn't need to see the gouge in the tread to know they had the car they were looking for. "You run the plate?"

The uniform nodded. "Yep, came up registered to a William Rutledge. Reported stolen two days ago."

"Of course," he replied sarcastically, pushing himself to his feet. "Who spotted it?"

"An old-timer still fishes off the pier, if you can believe that. He saw it, phoned it in. I asked him to stick around. He's over there with my partner."

Mick looked across the pier and saw the man sitting on a bench. Detective Williams came up beside him. He took the flashlight and looked over the back of the car himself. "Looks like our car," he said. "Anything inside?"Mick pulled out another pair of latex gloves and handed them over. "Let's find out."

~~

A simple 'scoop-and-run,' then he would drive off into the sunset. Because he took pride in his work, he'd consider it a job well done - and the one hundred and twenty five grand for his trouble was just a nice bonus.

Fat chance. Nothing involving Billy was ever simple, and knowing him as well as he did, this nameless, faceless man should have known better. Now, he found himself up to his eyebrows in the high profile kidnapping of the state's most sought after infant.

And now the kid was congested and coughing up a lung.

What the hell was he supposed to do with a sick baby?

Awkwardly, he picked up the baby and did what a guy like him had never done and never wanted to: he cuddled the infant high on his shoulder and patted his back, trying to quiet his fussy cries. He cooed and hummed and swayed, but that accomplished nothing. So, he did what he did best: he paced the narrow walkway in the RV until the Beckett brat cried himself to sleep.

When his cell rang, he cursed and answered it before it woke the baby.

"I'm going to kill you." he said in a harsh whisper.

"Whoa. It's Billy, man. What the hell's eating you?"

"You screwed me six ways to Sunday, MAN!" he snapped, moving away from the bed and the sleeping baby on it. "That's what's eatin' me. First you sucker me into this mess, then you leave me holding the bag, and now this kid's sick on me."

Billy didn't like the sound of that. "Sick? How the shit did that happen?"

He rolled his eyes and imagined strangling his old school chum with his bare hands. "How the hell do I know?"

"Chill out. It's not important now anyway; it's time to move. A couple hours' time, he'll be nothing but a bad memory for both of us. The man's ready to take the kid."

He breathed an audible groan of relief. "'Bout time. When and where?"

"There's an airstrip about two hours north of you; if you leave now you'll make it before the plane. Grab a pen, and I'll give you directions."

~~

Together, they went over every inch of the interior, Williams in the front seat and Wallace in the back; and it was Wallace who found the proof that Patrick Beckett had been in the car. Crammed under the backseat, tangled in a green fleece baby blanket, he found a tiny sock with the initials 'PAB' on the cuff.

"Pay dirt," he said, holding up the blanket and sock to Williams."Baby Beckett's been in this car. I saw a drawer full of these monogrammed socks when the CSI went over the nursery."

~~

Owen strode around his bedroom, throwing odds and ends into a small overnight bag. His temper still raged with every angry step. The unmitigated nerve of that Detective infuriated him; to come into his home with his presumptions and look at him as if he were something to be scraped from the bottom of his dreadfully worn loafers.

Just who the hell did they think they were dealing with?

There was no more time. He was a man with much to do, and he wouldn't allow his attention to be diverted any longer. There was business to attend to half a world away. Lifting his bag off the bed, he checked his Rolex as he stalked from the room. Through the hall and down the stairs, he knew he'd won - whatever the cost.

~~

Jeremy crossed the back lawn using the light of the moon as his guide. She drew him to her; probably without even realizing it, he mused. With his eyes never leaving her, he marveled at her strength. Here she stood, exhausted and frightened, but she wouldn't allow herself to fall apart. His admiration and love for her, always strong, grew immeasurably. He wanted to hold her, and he needed to.

Christina sensed him and turned before he could drape his arms over her shoulders. His easy smile cracked the shield of anger she'd been hiding behind since her outburst. She cupped his cheek in her palm and pulled in a deep steadying breath. "I'm okay," she said, answering the question in his eyes.

Her hands were like ice, and for an instant he felt a strong - and fleeting - sense of Emily presence. He met Christina's eyes with his own to judge for himself. He'd given her space, but it had cost him. Letting her go went against his every instinct. So, he watched her from the kitchen window when she fled for fresh air and the calming clarity she needed to pull herself together.

"You're freezing," he said. "I could get you a jacket." He took her chilled hands in his, and rubbed them for warmth.

"I don't know why, in this heat." She took the last step between them, and they embraced. "Just hold me instead."

"I was afraid you'd never ask." Jeremy arms tightened around her and he chuckled. "Your temper is an extraordinary beast when you unleash it."

Her smile was half-hearted at best. "I'm sorry Debra had to hear it," she said quietly. "She'll punish you for it."

"You said what most of us are thinking. It's only self-control keeping me from going to Owen and ripping him limb from limb."

She pulled back, and laying her hand against his chest, she waited for him to look at her. "Do you think he'll hurt him?"

Jeremy drew her head to the crook of his neck and was silent too long for either of their comfort. "I think it's about hurting us, not Patrick. He hates me, he blames me because of Emily, and there's enough blame to go around. Hell, I blame myself for this entire mess."

"Jeremy." Christina eased back to look at him, and when he resisted, she simply framed his face in her hands and forced him to look at her.

"Why don't *you* blame me, Christina? God knows you've got plenty of reason."

"Because you're not to blame. If it's Owen, then he's to blame."

They held on to each other in the moonlight; Christina holding on to Jeremy's belief as tightly as she held on to him, and Jeremy praying that his read on his former father-in-law was right. Surely, he wouldn't harm an innocent child. Surely, Owen Harris wasn't capable of murder...or was he?

~~

The old-timer's name was Benny, and he was delighted to be the center of attention. "I didn't think anything of it until the wife mentioned the press conference today. It ain't unusual to see all kinds of vehicles down here. Kids party and cut loose down here every night of the week."

"You didn't see who ditched it here?" Williams asked.

"Nope; wasn't really looking, though."

Mick Wallace ran his hand through his hair and sighed. "So you didn't see anything out of place, odd?"

"Well," Benny scratched his whiskered chin and looked thoughtful. "An RV was parked here a day or so ago."

~ 58 ~

Debra didn't know where she was going when she fled Christina's home, but the need for escape was vital. To keep from saying things she might regret later, distance was vital, too. She could understand Christina's outburst. She could even understand her need to lay blame and accuse.

Her baby had been stolen away in the middle of the night. She had to cling to something in her despair. Her contempt for a man that Debra knew to be the total opposite of Christina's perception of him was all she had to hold on to when she couldn't hold on to Patrick.

What Debra couldn't understand was why her father had said nothing, done nothing to defend her grandfather. She knew there was no love loss between them, but did he really think Owen Harris capable of such a cruel act? It was this question that brought her to where she'd thought she'd never return again: to the hillside where her mother lay buried. Maybe her mother could provide the answer.

Debra sat next to her mother's grand marble headstone, tracing the letters on the stone with her fingertip. The moonlight lessened the darkness, and being so near her mother lessened her fear and her loneliness; and she knew this was the place where she felt safest in the world.

A voice she barely recognized as her own broke the silence. "Grandpa couldn't do this, could he, Momma?"

~~

A truck from forensics readied the black sedan for towing to police impound while Wallace and Williams looked on. Luck was finally with them, and it was time to turn it to their advantage. Mick held the bagged sock and blanket in his hand as they headed for their cars. There was finally something to do besides wait.

"I might've known Billy the Rut couldn't keep his nose clean for long," Williams muttered.

Wallace shrugged, confused. "Billy the Rut?"

"Rutledge's street name," Williams explained, his jacket collar flapping in the warm gusts coming in off the water. "Only one still calling him 'William' is probably his mother. He's a small time thug with a nasty coke habit and a record as long as your arm. If the money's right, there's nothing too low for him to do."

"If Harris's pulling the strings, you can bet he's paying top dollar," Mick said.

Williams opened his car door and dropped inside to start the car. "Yeah, and Billy'd be counting the cash, eager to please."

"Know where to find him?"

"Shouldn't be too hard; he's predictable," Williams replied. "If he's got cash, he'll be spending it - on drugs, women and drink. I'll go looking under rocks in his favorite dives. Go back to the house, bring the family up to speed, and confirm the sock and blanket belong to Patrick."

Agent Wallace nodded. "Call when you grab'em."

"You bet," Williams said shifting into drive. "We'll work him together. A little 'good cop, bad cop."'

"Can't wait."

~~

Billy was cruising. A little coke and whiskey were keeping him high and humming as he sat on a grimy bar stool in the Eagle's Nest. With his buzz the only thing keeping him upright, he worried about the meet at the airport. He was nervous, and even his favorite bar, favorite hooker, and a free flowing supply of cash couldn't ease his nerves.

Through his blurry eyes, he watched the clock hanging above the bar and felt a little better. It'd be behind him in another hour. In another hour, the baby would be someone else's problem. Then he could slip away with the busty Randy, the best lay his money could buy, and do what came naturally. She sat next to him, sipping the glass of wine he'd bought her when he sealed the deal for her company.

Hell, he was getting hard just thinking about it.

When the Beckett baby was long gone, life would be normal again - and Randy would work her magic. Then, Billy the Rut would think up how to spend his ill-gotten gains.

~~

Williams saw Billy through the neon lit window of the Eagle's Nest. From the street, he watched a well known prostitute working the Rut with her best moves. And, unless his eyes were playing tricks on him, she was giving him a hand job right there at the bar.

Making a mental note never to come here without a shot of penicillin, he decided it was time to bring an abrupt end to Billy's wet dream. *Oh, you'll get screwed tonight Billy*, Williams thought while pulling open the door, *but not by who you think*. The stench of cheap alcohol, stale cigarette smoke, and deep fried food hit him full force as he went across the sticky wooden floor.

He'd ditched his jacket and tie but felt all the eyes in the dim, dingy bar slide over him, pinning him as a cop. Fleetingly, he wondered how many scattered throughout the bar were friends of Billy's and might come to his defense, but he couldn't let the thought distract him as he spun Billy around to face him.

Billy teetered and cursed. "What the fuck, man!" He lifted his head and sneered.

Williams chuckled and looked over the sad specimen in front of him. "Oh, Billy, Billy, Billy," he chided, sweeping his eyes over an obvious erection. "Sorry to interrupt."

Billy glared and finished off the last of his whiskey. "Shit, Williams! What the hell do you want?" he demanded.

Williams dragged him off the stool and shoved him against the bar. "I'm just performing my civic duty," he said, patting him down. "Thought you might like to know we found your car - you know, the one you reported stolen?"

Billy laughed. "Oh yeah." Williams went over every inch of him, paying special attention to his jacket. Billy began slapping at Williams' hands. "Got a warrant?"

"Don't need one when your dick's hanging out for public view, man," Williams replied, discovering the bulge inside Billy's jacket. "What do we have here?" He opened an envelope and whistled.

Billy tucked and zipped up. "I won the lottery," he quipped. "What can I say? I'm a lucky guy."

Williams pulled out his cuffs. "Beat it, Randy, before I haul your ass in, too." He yanked Billy's hands behind his back and cuffed him just a bit too tightly. "Let's go for a little ride downtown, Billy. I'd say your luck's just run out."

~~

Agent Wallace stood with Jeremy and Christina in silence. He looked on while Christina clutched the bag of evidence to her chest, and Jeremy lowered them both to the sofa when her legs went out from under her. She sobbed uncontrollably as Jeremy cradled her against him. Neither of them had to say a word; the sock and blanket did indeed belong to their son.

Minutes passed before Christina quieted and Jeremy turned his attention back to Agent Wallace. "What's this mean?" he asked tightly.

"It means we're getting close. We've got a real lead to your son."

Christina's broken voice asked the question everyone else was afraid to: "How do we know he's safe?"

Wallace wavered, afraid to offer false hope. "There's absolutely no indication of violence in the car, Ms. Wagner. We're confident he's unharmed."

Jeremy locked eyes with Linus across the room, and they both knew what the other was thinking. "I want to know the moment you learn anything, Agent Wallace, particularly if there's any link to Owen Harris."

"Let the authorities handle this." But then he nodded, "Having said that, the moment we know more, you will."

~~

Pensive, anxious and alone with his thoughts, Owen drove down a dirt road not found on any map. It had been a wise decision to stash this car and send his limo back to the estate once he'd been seen at Logan airport. As far as anyone knew, Owen Harris was taking a midnight flight to Japan. Countless people would confirm seeing him checking his baggage, buying a paper at a newsstand, and entering the VIP lounge.

His plane would be flying to Japan. He would not.

A smile spread across his face. By the time anyone knew that, he would be gone, and his debt to his daughter would be paid. Revenge, while sweet, still left him wanting as he negotiated a pothole in the middle of the road. It would be better to see the pain he inflicted face to face, but he was wise enough to see the folly in granting that wish.

No. He would have to be content knowing he had done what he set out to do. Better to relish what was accomplished than to belabor what could not be attained. It was nearly over now. End game. Checkmate.

When the sun came up, Owen would give birth to his coup d'état. He could imagine it all as his destination came into view and he slowed to make the turn off the road. His chariot awaited him.

~ 59 ~

Jensen Brice studied the banded one-hundred dollar bills closely. "It's legitimate currency. I'm running the serial numbers to get a point of origin," she said to Detective Williams.

"I'll bet a C-note the bank it came from holds an account in Harris' name." Williams shrugged and drank from his almost cold cup of coffee. "I'm letting Billy sweat for awhile."

Mick Wallace barreled into the squad room. His face taunt from tension, he nearly strode by his partner and Williams without a word. Suddenly, he stopped and blew out a hard breath. "Where the hell is he?"

Williams watched Wallace flex and relax the hand holding the sock and recognized the signs of a man about to blow. It was the strain, the frayed nerves, the pressure, and the lack of sleep he felt steeping in himself. "Interrogation Room 1." He took the sock from Wallace. "It's Patrick's?"

He sighed. Jensen brought him a cup of coffee, and he breathed in the rich, strong scent. "They confirmed it."

"Good. Let's go wave this under Billy's nose and see how long it takes for him to crack."

~~

Billy was coming down hard. Cut off from his whiskey and coke, the buzz he was counting on to get him through the dwindling hours of a felony was winding down. He was about to crash, and he would hit hard. When the door opened and Detective Williams walked in with another seriously hardnosed guy behind him, Billy knew the shit was about to hit the fan.

Williams didn't waste any time with introductions; instead, he tossed the evidence bag down in front of Billy the Rut and waited for a reaction.

"You've done some stupid shit in your days, Billy, but this stunt tops the list." He leaned in close across the table, putting his face mere inches from Billy's. "You're pretty flush with cash, Billy. Where'd it come from?"

The Rut shrugged, he might be stupid, but his survival instinct was strong. "Paper route."

It took tremendous effort not to smack the greasy grin from his face. "We're talking almost a hundred and twenty-five grand, Billy. You're a small-time drug dealer; you don't have the stash to bring a hundred and twenty five large, and we both know it. Do yourself a favor, use whatever brain cells you haven't toasted and help yourself."

Billy didn't blink, but the sheen of sweat on his forehead betrayed him. "What the fuck you talkin' about Williams?" He met him eye-to-eye and sneered. "I'm just here to get my car."

Mick moved around the table behind Billy. He had been silent because he didn't have the history with this guy that Williams did. He preferred to hang back, let Williams work the grimy piece of shit in front of him. He was calculating, reading Rutledge's demeanor, judging his words as truth or lies.

But no more, he thought, his patience was finally gone. Now it was time to knock the cocky swagger out of this little pissant's attitude. Good cop, bad cop, right?

Without warning - and taking Billy the Rut by complete surprise - he grabbed hold of his dirty leather jacket at the shoulders, yanked him from his chair, and sent him careening into the wall. "Your car's a crime scene, ass-hole!" He straddled the overturned chair and pinned Billy between himself and the wall. "You think we're playing? You're the only one playing here kid, playing big boy games, and you're way out of your league."

Between heaving breaths, Billy only glared.

In another surge of temper, Mick jerked him around, lifted him off his feet and shoved him flat against the table. "What's a small time piece of shit like you want with a baby? I mean, what's in it for you? Babies aren't your thing, right - they're messy, loud, more trouble than they're worth."

Billy didn't like what he saw in this guy's eyes. This dude was fucking-out-there. "You're crazy, man. Crazy. What the hell would I want with the rugrat?" Billy argued, struggling to get out from under the viselike arms. "That's a good question, Billy." Williams interjected, but he made no move to get between Wallace and the Rut. "How you answer it, well, now, that's really important. Could mean the difference between cutting a deal or cutting your own worthless throat."

"We can put your car near the Wagner house, damn near. You understand what I'm saying?" Mick Wallace's face was stone, his tone a warning. "The jig is up, Billy, believe me when I tell you, you're not smart enough to pull this off. You're too fucking sloppy. We found Patrick Beckett's sock and blanket in the backseat, jack-off." He smashed Billy's face against the plastic bag until he was sure he'd gotten a good look.

"You got dick on me." Billy grimaced, his reply was muffled, and telling.

Williams let it go as far as he was comfortable, then stepped in and peeled Agent Wallace off. He waited while Billy pushed himself off the table and shrugged his jacket back in place. "That's where you're wrong, Billy." Williams told him quietly, reasonably. "We've got plenty, starting with a large cut of cocaine in your trunk and an unregistered Glock in your glove box. I've got two words for you Billy: Parole violation."

"You get one chance to help yourself here, Billy - and only one. We're running the serial numbers on the money; it'll only be a matter of time before things fall into place. You help us, maybe we'll help you," Agent Wallace offered. "Maybe we didn't find coke in your car or the gun either. Maybe we were mistaken."

Billy the Rut was quiet while he looked at the clock on the wall and considered his options. He could stall for time, and the kid would be out of their reach. "Car was stolen, right? I'm supposed to know where some fuckin' sock came from?"

Williams was reaching his limit with Billy the Rut. "Let's review, Billy," he said, coming around the table to sit in front of him. "We got you by the short hairs. The felony amount of coke alone'll put you back in Rikers for five. Throw in the weapons charge and conspiracy, and you'll pull a long stretch, maybe even double digits." He let the hard truth hang in the air and watched the Rut's veneer of cock sureness start to crumble. "You're up to your neck in this, Billy. Even you're not stupid enough to not do the smart thing, here."

He gave Billy Rutledge time to consider. Time to weigh the consequences of holding out and keeping his mouth shut. He saw first doubt, then fear move into Billy's eyes - and he went for broke.

"Spill it, Billy. Where's Patrick Beckett?"

~ 60 ~

He made the two-hour drive in silence and now sat in the RV, waiting for this madness to end. Billy assured him the moment he handed off the baby he could hit the open road and leave New York behind him in the dust, and that was just what he planned to do.

By daybreak, he'd be well on his way to California. He checked his watch and settled in to wait for the headlights to signal the imminent arrival of the plane, his vehicle of escape. The man pulling his strings would use it in the final leg of his plan.

Looking over his shoulder, he was pleased the baby was still asleep. The cough syrup he'd bought at a Quick Mart when he stopped to fill both tanks with fuel had done the trick and quieted the kid's nasty cough. Now, both of them could benefit from the medicine's effects.

Another look at his watch, and he could already feel the sense of relief filling him. He was almost out from under Billy's idiotic influence with his hard earned half of a two-hundred and fifty grand fee. Whatever happened after the plane was airborne would be somebody else's problem.

A half hour later, headlights lit up the darkness, straightening him in his seat. The car approached as the distinct sound of an airplane and bright lights of the landing gear appeared over head. Then he felt home free.

~~

As he stepped on the brake, bringing the car to a jerky stop in the rough and dusty field, Owen smiled. Releasing his seatbelt, he turned and glimpsed the plane as the landing gear dropped and it closed the distance between itself and the narrow landing strip. Pleased with himself, he got out of the car, wincing when he felt his Italian loafers sink into the soft earth.

Forgetting his shoes, he walked to the RV and rapped sharply on the door. When the door opened, he leveled his eyes on the muscular man filling the doorway. Neither man said a word, but Owen stepped up into the looming vehicle with an air of superiority that irritated the man who'd been waiting for him. He stepped aside, out of the way, and allowed the man to lead the way through the RV.

When he stopped at the man's side, he could see the contempt with which he looked down on the baby. While he held no feelings for the baby himself, the hatred in the man's eyes made his blood run cold. Owen stooped, picked up the baby without any change in his ominous expression, and turned to the man at his side.

"He's got a fever," Owen mentioned without concern.

"He's sick," he replied. "Medicine's in his bag."

Owen shrugged and shouldered his way past the man. "Very well, then. Bring his things, and we'll not inconvenience you any longer."

In an effort to move things along, he did as he was told without comment. As far as he was concerned, any annoyance was worth a speedy exit. He grabbed the car seat and diaper bag and caught up with them at the door. In the dark, they moved through the field without speaking further; the less they knew about each other, the better, Owen decided.

Patrick slept on his shoulder, but to Owen Harris he was just a vivid reminder of his daughter's cruel treatment at the hands of her husband. He looked ahead and saw the plane roll to a smooth stop across the distance. Soon, he would have this blight to his daughter's memory a world away. Then, he would watch with utter delight as Jeremy Beckett and his whore tried to live happily ever after without their child.

~~

Agent Wallace pressed the gas pedal to the floor and cursed under his breath. Detective Williams was on the radio, communicating with the three patrol cars on their tale, coordinating their plan of action once they arrived at the airfield. Burning up the roadway, Wallace tried not to think of the odds of reaching the plane before it lifted off.

Billy the Rut cracked, but he took his own sweet time doing so.

There hadn't been time to call Jeremy Beckett and tell him his suspicions were right all along. Owen Harris masterminded his son's abduction and was at this very moment trying to spirit him out of the country. Wallace checked his watch and set his jaw. If Billy was right and they were sticking to a strict schedule, the plane would lift off in minutes.

"Two miles out," Jensen Brice spoke up from the back seat, eyeing her laptop and looking over a map of the area on the screen. "We're closing in, but better get the lead out, Mick."

Williams signed off and turned to Wallace. "Okay, we're ready. When we turn off into the field, unit 22 and 36 will cut across the field and try to cut off the plane and surround it. Unit 12 is with us. We'll take the plane."

Wallace glanced at Williams. "And if we don't make it?" Wallace asked. "We don't know where he's going."

Williams grimaced and stared into the night. "We'll make it," he said with determination. "We have to."

~~

Midnight came without word from the police. Jeremy stood by the living room window looking up at the moon. He was wondering if any news - good or bad - was better than no news at all. Christina was busying herself in the kitchen with his parents for company. She was brewing tea, serving the decadent desserts that were trademarks in her restaurants. Anything to keep from thinking about their boy, anything at all to keep her fear at bay.

He worried about Debra, too. Wondering where she'd gone, consumed with anger and disappointment with him, and this held another kind of fear for him. Jamie had gone after her and hadn't yet returned. Jeremy turned away from the window, smoothing his thumb over the deep creases in his forehead, damning himself for letting his daughter leave.

In the quiet moments like this, his faith deserted him. What if Patrick was already dead? It was unimaginable for him, preparing to lose another son. Hell on earth, for him, would be to outlive another son. But, he couldn't stop the dark flow of his thoughts, as hour passed into hour. And that's when he felt the dam inside him finally break. Alone with such terrible thoughts, he no longer had the strength to hold himself together. Tears burned in his throat and filled his eyes, but his sob caught him unprepared; shuddering through his body, then brought him to his knees.

~~

Owen climbed the steps to the plane without as much as a glance over his shoulder. The man on his heels was no one for the great Owen Harris to consider, and he would do his bidding because everyone did.

The man in question was only concerned with putting distance between him and the bad decision he'd made at the request of a dimwitted friend. If either of them had been paying attention to their surroundings, they might have seen the red and blue lights approaching in the distance - a mistake they would both soon regret for the rest of their lives.

Inside the plane, Patrick was discarded to his car seat without a second thought by either man. Owen used the intercom to tell the pilot to prepare for takeoff. A slow, satisfied smile transformed his face as he looked to the man he no longer had any use for.

"I'll assume you've been compensated?" Owen asked.

"Well enough."

"Then you may go so we can go," Owen finished and turned to take his seat.

Unease filled the man with no name, but he turned without another word and exited the plane. By the time he put his feet on the ground, something drew his attention - and in the next instant his eyes stared into the unbelievable sight ahead.

His only thought then was to survive, so he cut across the field at an angle, running full out. He'd damned himself, he knew. This couldn't end well, and he knew that, too.

~~

Everything that came next seemed to happen in slow motion. The plane lurching to a chaotic halt as the patrol cars slid haphazardly into position at the nose of the aircraft, making it impossible to continue down the airstrip. Uniforms exiting the units and surrounding the aircraft, guns drawn and ready. And then the unit with Wallace, Williams, and Brice speeding past to run down a fleeing suspect.

Owen Harris could only gape as he watched his plan crumble before his eyes. He heard the shouts of the police and cursed. He realized there would be no escape, and panic surged through him. A man so self-important was unaccustomed to being trapped. Wide-eyed, he watched helplessly as law enforcement jumped from their cars on a dead run for his plane.

He was defeated, beaten - and he was a man used to neither. Until now. Until this moment in a dusty field with his revenge now all but gone.

So, he waited for the inevitable to come. He looked on glassy-eyed as Williams, Wallace, and Brice stormed, guns drawn, into his plane. He made no move, only met the eyes and guns trained on him with contempt and defiance.

Detective Williams crossed to him, pulling him to his feet. "Owen Harris, you're under arrest for conspiracy and the kidnapping of Patrick Avery Beckett. You have the right to remain silent..."

Harris was shoved out of his plane in silence, while Brice went to check the baby and Wallace holstered his weapon and used his phone.

~ 61 ~

Radio silence was maintained en route to the hospital. The last thing anybody wanted was a parking lot full of press vans and journalists when Mr. Beckett and Ms. Wagner were reunited with their son. Upon arrival, Patrick was whisked away to be thoroughly examined while Agent Brice waited at the door for his parents. Her partner and Detective Williams were headed back to the station to supervise Harris' processing.

Thirty minutes later, Jeremy and Christina burst through the emergency room doors. Jensen tried to calm them as she led them to the cubicle where Patrick was being examined. Christina rushed to him the moment the curtain was pulled back and she saw him. Jeremy only stared at his son while his vision blurred with tears.

Attempting to pull himself together, he turned to Agent Brice and clasped her hand. "Thank you," he managed, choking up again.

Christina covered Patrick's face with kisses. "Mommy's here now, baby," she whispered through tears, "and Daddy, too," she said, reaching for him.

Jeremy came to the bed and lay his forehead against his son's. He kissed both of his round cheeks and grinned foolishly. "Welcome back, little man. We missed you."

~~

Patrick was released from the hospital after a course of IV antibiotics. The beginning of a respiratory infection was threatening. Under other circumstances, the baby would have been admitted for observation, but the physician decided mother and child had been separated long enough. So, he prescribed oral antibiotics, rest, and plenty of fluids, then he sent the family home with assurances he would come to the house to check on his patient in a couple days.

During the drive to the house, Christina sat in the back seat with Patrick. Her cheek was pressed to the top of his head, his tiny fingers wrapped her thumb. She could finally breathe again, her heart could beat because her worst fear had come to pass. But she couldn't take her eyes off him and didn't want to. He slept soundly as she counted fingers and toes and took in the wonderful baby scent of his fine hair.

Words seemed to fail them on the drive home, and the baby's breathing was the only sound in the car. Christina couldn't speak without dissolving into tears, and Jeremy couldn't speak because his utter joy at his son's return had shifted to a burning fury; he had every intention of strangling the life from Owen Harris.

He looked in the rearview mirror at Patrick more times than he could count and was relieved to finally see Christina whole again. When she finally met his eyes in the mirror, their bond felt as strong as ever. Their connection was more powerful than he could have dreamt possible all those years ago as he waited for her in O'Donnell's.

He'd known nothing about her then except her temper, and yet he'd been drawn to her. So he stayed - and in doing only that, he'd sealed his fate with hers. He risked his ego for the chance to know her better, and it paid off and changed his life. He was every bit as drawn to her now.

~~

Linus and Elise heard Jeremy's car and embraced. A soft kiss and tears of thankfulness ended the hell of the past twenty-four hours. Arm-in-arm, they went to the foyer and opened the door to welcome their grandson home.

~~

Jamie arrived a short time later and was moved to tears to find her nephew safe in her brother's arms. She returned alone, though, and Jeremy's happiness was lessened a bit to think his daughter preferred anywhere else to being with him. Everyone who mattered was there. Everyone who made this family whole. Everyone but Debra. She was out there alone at such a late hour - one a.m. - but that couldn't stop the smiles and laughter. Or the wine and celebration. There were hugs and more tears as their nightmare began to release them all from its hold.

~~

Debra woke with the rising sun peaking over the hill. She had fallen asleep and spent the night next to her mother. Stiffly, she uncurled her long legs and felt the cold marble beneath her.

She reached out to her mother's stone and smiled. Her mother had comforted her through the night, just the way she always had - the way her father never could.

When she finally stood to leave and made her way down the hill, her thoughts turned from the mother she loved to the father she had never understood. Disagreements of all kinds managed to erode their relationship over the years, but never had she thought them as insurmountable as she did now.

Was she supposed to choose between them, her father and her grandfather? Did her father really believe, as Christina did, that her grandfather was capable of such a heartless act as stealing a baby from his mother? It was inconceivable to her, and she couldn't believe it. She wouldn't believe him capable of such a monstrous act.

Debra got into her Aunt Jamie's car and left the cemetery, determined to stand by her grandfather. She drove in silence, strong-willed and focused, already sure of what she had to do next. She ended up at the place from which she'd fled the night before; and cut the engine with a half-laugh.

Christina Wagner's home.

She thought of Christina as she sat staring at her house, and an incredible change of perspective moved through her. This house was her brother's home. And, surprisingly, even oddly, it meant something to her too. With all its quaintness and charm, it was inviting - as inviting as the woman who lived inside, she realized. If nothing else, Debra respected and admired her and knew her love for her father was true, no matter how she felt about it.

~~

As for Owen Harris, he was having problems the likes of which his granddaughter couldn't imagine. He'd had to endure the humiliation of being fingerprinted and photographed. He watched the sun rise from his four-by-six-foot cell in the isolation wing of the NYPD jail. His lawyer was unable to work his well-paid magic and secure a speedy arraignment and reasonable bail, and the result had been six hours behind bars.

Compared to his crime, his reputation meant nothing. Stripped of his tie, his belt, his shoe laces, and his dignity, Owen was reduced to a common man. And as such, he was reduced to suffering the common man's punishment as well.

There had been a sleepless night to add to his haggard appearance. His arraignment was in less than an hour, and it gnawed at him. He'd stand before a judge with whom he probably golfed, as a beaten down, bested man.

~~

It was Jamie who came to the door when Debra knocked. Before she could speak, she was pulled inside, kissed, and wrapped in her aunt's arms. "We found him. Oh, Debra, we found him. Patrick's safe - and he's home."

Debra pulled away to look incredulously at her aunt. "He is?" She stepped back and smiled. "Really?"

Jamie laughed and cast her eyes to the ceiling. "Really. He's upstairs in the nursery with Jeremy and Christina; they're trying to get his medicine into him."

She lifted a brow as concern for her brother caught her off guard. "Medicine?"

"It's nothing too serious, but the doctor wanted to be careful. His cold's turned into a minor respiratory infection, so he's on antibiotics. Other than that, he's a real trooper."

"I should go up and see him."

"And your father. He's been worried about you."

Debra tried not sigh. "When isn't he?" She handed over the car keys. "Thanks for lending me your car." Turning to the stairs and starting up, she added, "Now we can find and punish the real culprit."

Jamie frowned, wondering how Debra would handle the truth. Not well, she was sure. Not well at all.

~~

She paused outside the nursery door, watching her father and Christina deal with a very unhappy Patrick after a dose of his medicine. There could be no denying that the three of them were a family. She couldn't help but feel like an outsider, but she put a smile on her face and cleared her throat to announce her presence.

Jeremy turned around, wiping at his shirt where Patrick had spit the first dose of medicine. He was tired but relieved, and the easy smile he gave Debra was genuine. "Morning, sweetheart," he said, coming to her and kissing her cheek warmly. "You're alright?" he asked, stepping back to get a good look at her.

Debra smiled and touched her father's cheek. The depth of his love for her was unmistakable. "I'm fine, Daddy." She looked him over and saw the tension was gone and was happy to see it. "You missed some," she said and took the wet wipe in his hand and scrubbed at the front of his shirt.

Jeremy chuckled. "Little bugger's got amazing aim."

Christina came to his side, holding Patrick and smiling. "He's a mess right now, but he's wonderful."

Debra laughed and ran a fingertip along her brother's sticky cheek. "Yes, he is." She met Christina's eyes and saw the joy in them, then stepped closer to press her cheek to Christina's. "I'm so happy he's safe, Christina. Truly."

"I know that, Debra," she assured her. "Well, I'm going to get him into a bath." She paused to let Jeremy press a kiss on the baby's head and her own. "We won't be long."

They watched Christina walk out the door and laughed when they heard Patrick's unmistakable squeal echo down the hall. Jeremy covered his face and released a heavy, grateful breath he hadn't realized he was holding. Debra reached for him and wrapped her arms around his broad shoulders. He could say nothing; only hold her as tightly as he could.

She hadn't expected the tears, but they came, and with her choked up voice she soothed her father. "I really am so happy to have him back," she managed. "Maybe now I can make up for being a lousy big sister."

Jeremy drew away and winked. "You'll find your brother's impossible to resist."

Debra's face changed, grew serious. "Who did this Daddy? Who did such a horrible thing to your family?"

"Our family," he corrected. Her eyes bore into his, and he faltered. How could he tell her? "The police found him at an airstrip a couple hours outside the city on a private plane headed God knows where." He paused to take her hand. "I'm so sorry, honey. We found him with Owen. Your grandfather planned every last detail."

She pulled away as if she'd been struck. Whirling away with her back to Jeremy, she shook her head in disbelief. "I don't believe that."

He went to her to lay his hands on her shoulders. "I know, sweetie, but it's the truth." He turned her around to face him. "Look at me." And when she did, he continued. "The police arrested him at the airstrip. Inside the plane, with Patrick strapped in right beside him. He paid an obscene amount of money to get his hands on your brother, Debra. It was Owen from the beginning."

Tears ran down her face, and she nearly collapsed against her father. "No, Daddy, don't say anymore. Please," she pleaded.

His heart broke for her, but he needed her to face the truth, no matter how painful. "It's true Debra. I know it hurts, baby, but it is true."

Wiping at her tears, she pulled herself together and moved away from him. "I can't believe it!" she exclaimed, her tears drying and fire taking their place in her eyes. "Not until I hear it from him." Without another word, she left the room on shaky, unsteady legs.

Jeremy damned Owen Harris to hell. He wanted to kill him with his bare hands. He needed to end his crusade of terror in their lives; if Owen were allowed to buy his freedom, Jeremy knew they would never be safe.

~ 62 ~

Her hands on her hips, Christina stood defiant in a stance Jeremy knew better than to question. She had made up her mind - long experience with her stubbornness convinced him of that- and there would be no swaying her. So, he inhaled a leveling breath and relented.

"You're sure you want to do this?" he inquired skeptically. "You want to see him?"

His question made her reconsider - but only briefly. The last forty-eight hours were too fresh in her mind, and she remembered what was at stake. "It not a matter of want; it's a matter of need. I want to look the bastard in the eye. I don't want him to think for a second that he got even a fraction of what he wanted."

"If it's that important to you, we'll go." He went to her and cupped her face in his hands. "I just want to take care of you. We've just been put through the ringer. No one will blame you if you want to focus on Patrick and leave Harris to the legal system."

She kissed him, loving him all the more for his protectiveness. "I love you, but I need to face him, honey." She pulled him close. "We both do."

"I love you, too. So, we best get a move on, or we'll be late."

~~

Owen Harris was livid as he paced the witness room from corner to corner, annoyance written all over his face. His attorney had gotten off to a poor start, and a long night in a cramped cell fit for the repugnant had put him in an uncooperative mood.

"Sit down, Owen," Kenneth Breen advised sharply, peering over the top of his glasses, "and pull yourself together."

"You wouldn't be so cavalier had it been you locked up like an animal," Owen muttered as he lowered himself into a hard oak chair and sighed.

"What the hell were you thinking? How could you be so brainless?"

"Watch your mouth, Ken - you're on thin ice already," Owen advised. "I'd expect even a green lawyer to get me bail."

Kenneth pursed his lips and removed his glasses with a quick jerk. "Then you're a fool. Do you have any clue how much evidence there is against you?" he asked, dropping his glasses on the table in front of him. "The money used to pay for your ill-advised scheme has been traced to your bank. And your fuckin' prints are on the money, Owen, not to mention the exact amount of which was withdrawn from your account. Then there's the phone records tying you to the thug you hired...but the topper is he's pointing fingers to save his ass - and he's pointing them at you."

"Who'll believe Rutledge over me?"

"All it'll take is one juror. Add them to the rest of the evidence, and you're screwed."

"I won't spend another night in jail."

"Don't bet on it," Ken warned. "You're an enormous flight risk, as you've already vividly demonstrated. And you've shown flagrant disregard for the law, which judges tend to frown upon."

"I want bail."

"And I want you to see reason, but we don't always get what we want, Owen."

Owen was about to lose his temper when a knock on the door made him hold his tongue. Both men glared at each other, stewing in tempers both were well used to seeing over twenty years of attorney/ client relations. When the door opened, a security officer stepped inside.

"Mr. Harris has a visitor," the security officer said. "I'll give you five minutes."

"Thank you," Kenneth Breen replied.

In another moment, Debra appeared in the doorway. Owen paled as she walked in. He watched her eyes sweeping over him and knew she saw him as a stranger. Kenneth wisely cleared his throat and excused himself. Once they were alone, a gulf opened between them.

"You look tired," she said, and her voice felt as hollow and strained as it sounded. She crossed the room and sat down across from him.

"I didn't sleep well."

"How could you do it?"

He considered feigning innocence, but she was the only one to whom he owed the truth. He shrugged indifferently. "How could I not?"

Debra closed her eyes and shook her head, wanting so badly to cling to denial. She couldn't look at him. Her grandfather had shattered her heart with four little words, and the utter lack of apology in his tone and eyes was too painful. "What're you saying, Grandpa?"

"I did it for your mother. I'm not ashamed, and I'm not sorry," he answered. "That child's a slap in the face to her. Beckett sired a bastard with a whore. I'm just grateful she died without knowing the fool her husband had made her out to be."

"Patrick isn't a bastard, Grandpa, he's a child," Debra said with an edge, "and he's my brother."

Owen blinked. "An accident of birth."

"You think this stunt honors my mother?"

"I do."

She wanted to be sick, but instead she stood and stared at the man she had set on a pedestal and thought could do no wrong. It was a crushing blow to know he was a stranger, and even a monster. "Then you never really knew her." She'd heard enough to see his true nature, and it scared her. "And I guess I never knew you." Looking away, her eyes filling, she left without another word.

Owen would remember forever how it ripped him apart inside to watch Debra's eyes - really his daughter's eyes - fill with disappointment and tears because of him.

~~

The bubble of secrecy the family was counting on had burst. The story of Patrick's return and Owen's involvement in the abduction had broken, and signs of the coming media storm were all around them. Jeremy weaved in and out of the gathering press caravan lining the street outside the house and cursed every one of them. He turned off the street and scowled at this constant invasion of their privacy.

At the courthouse, Jeremy was disgusted to find several media vans behind him. They had to get inside with as little uproar as possible; he would not have his son further traumatized.

Christina turned in the passenger seat and cast a protective glance to Patrick. He was sleeping in his car seat between Jamie and Elise. Perhaps she should have left him at home, but she couldn't. The need to keep him with her, to keep him safe was paramount.

As thoughts of the cameras and microphones surrounding them outside the courthouse made her cringe, she cast wary eyes to the rearview mirror. "Why can't they just leave us alone?"

Jeremy took her hand in his and put her at ease. "Don't worry. I've arranged it with security to enter through the underground garage. It's off-limits to the press, so there'll be no reporters or cameras to dodge."

She smiled with relief. "Thank God."

~~

They managed to slip into the courtroom without being accosted just as Owen was led in through a side door next to the judge's bench. It didn't take long for him to seek out Jeremy in the gallery and lock eyes with him. He wanted to taunt, to provoke. He wanted to cause his former son-in-law to lose control.

Owen shuffled to the defense table with a smirk, forgetting the shackles on his ankles and hands. Shackles were for animals, and he was no animal; he was simply a father doing right by his daughter.

That Jeremy was free to come and go as he pleased may have grated, but Owen fooled himself into believing he had still won. He had struck where Jeremy was most vulnerable and bested him in his daughter's name. He had caused pain - and there was no pain too great - for the whore and Emily's faithless husband.

Jeremy watched Owen with a dangerous mix of rage and contempt heating his blood. Even while feeling Christina's hand squeezing his, he was tuned into the man he wanted so desperately to pay for his heinous crime. He wanted to leap over the polished oak separating them and beat the smirk off his face.

A strong-voiced white haired judge took the bench and rapped his gavel to call the room to order. "In the matter of the state vs. Owen Harris - charges of kidnapping, aggravated assault, and conspiracy," Judge Lane Thompson began. "Mr. Harris, how do you plead?"

Owen stood and lifted his chin. "I plead not guilty, your honor."

~~

To no one's surprise but Owen's, bail was denied, and he was taken back to his cell in gaping disbelief. Linus appeared at the back of the courtroom as Owen exited the courtroom, flanked by security. He took Jeremy aside as the family made their way out into the corridor.

"Bail was denied, then?" he asked.

"Yes."

Linus nodded. "I've called in a favor. You can have ten minutes with Owen before he's transferred to county jail."

"Thank you, Dad," he said. "I'll just tell Christina, and we'll be on our way."

Linus laid a hand on Jeremy's arm. "Christina's going with you?"

"She's insisted, and I've agreed."

"Is that wise?"

"She's determined, and I'm not going to stand in her way," he replied, then changed the subject. "You and mom take Patrick back to your house with you."

Linus looked at Christina, worrying. "Of course. Since the press is already circling, maybe you, Christina, and the baby should plan to stay with us tonight."

"You read my mind," Jeremy said. "We'll be back in time for lunch."

~ 63 ~

In a small conference room in the basement of the 55th district of the NYPD, Owen sat, staring into space. Stripped of his impeccability tailored suit, he was forced into an overly bright orange jumpsuit. A faceless part of the masses now, an unimportant among the unimportant, he mused. His transfer to the county jail was imminent, but not before one last visit from the outside.

When the door opened and Jeremy and Christina walked in, he scoffed. When the door closed and the three of them were left alone, Owen's laugh died and his cold gaze narrowed as they faced him. With the table between them, it was Christina who spoke, breaking the chilly silence in the room.

"Was this one-sided war of yours worth your freedom?"

"My daughter's worth any price I pay," he replied with an icy glint in his eye.

Christina looked hard at the man who had waged a quiet campaign of torment against her for far too many years. Face-to-face, he was nothing but a pathetic bully. He was not the sinister manipulator set on destroying her from behind the scenes any longer; he was just a pathetic and bitter man, and seeing him without the veil of fear set her free.

"I didn't know Emily, but I'm sure she would be ashamed of what you've done in her name," Christina said.

At the mention of his daughter name, his face twisted into a mask of blind rage that brought him out of his chair. "How dare you speak her name, you little slut!" He lunged for her then, craving the feel of her flesh under his hands when he snapped her whoring neck. But Jeremy had yanked her out of the way and put himself in reach instead.

"You sick sonofabitch!" Jeremy exclaimed, grabbing a fistful of Owen's jumpsuit and jerking him over the table. Deadly rage blinded him to reason as he drew back and drove a fist into Owen's face with a dark kind of pleasure. The distinct sound of bone breaking had Owen crying out in agony as blood spurted from his broken nose all over Jeremy's shirt.

In the next instant, the door flew open, and both men were being pulled apart as Christina was hurried from the room. It took three officers to gain control over them.

Owen, refusing to be stopped, continued to scream. "The maniac broke my damn nose!" He then tried to break away to lunge for Jeremy again. For his trouble, he was taken to the floor under the weight of two angry cops. Pinned under a knee, he began to rant. "I want to press charges! You hear me, I want to press charges!"

"It was self defense," Jeremy interrupted calmly as he straightened the collar of his bloody shirt. "He went after Christina, the crazy bastard. I was protecting her."

Owen was cuffed and warned. "Don't worry, the security camera recorded the whole thing," the bigger of the two officers handling Owen said. "I saw the whole thing," he added, dragging Owen to his feet, then from the room.

~~

One Week Later
County Jail

Judge Lane Thompson never came down to the hollows, the nickname of the cellblock in his county's overpopulated jail. The darkness never left this block, no matter the time of day. Sunlight will never reach, neither cell nor man, because this cellblock stretches far and wide, it also runs underground.

No, Lane Thompson didn't care for these surroundings, but he thought if he owed nothing else to his one time cribbage partner, he owed him the benefit of some sage advice. Harris had further screwed himself with his attempted assault of Christina Wagner; so here he stood, peering into Owen Harris' cell, waiting for the cell door to slide open.

He excused the officer, and the two men were left alone. Owen glared at Thompson from behind blackened eyes and a splinted, purple nose. Lane couldn't recognize the man slumped against the cement wall at his back, he couldn't recognize the man with whom he'd shared cognac and cigars on countless occasions.

"What's happened to you?" Thompson began, slipping his hands into his pockets. "When was it you deemed yourself all-powerful?"

Owen said nothing at first; he only seemed to stare right through Lane Thompson as if he weren't there. Then, he just as quickly met the pair of worried eyes with angry ones. "I've always been powerful," he muttered.

"From the day I left that stinking gutter my mother had the audacity to call home to this moment, I've leveled anyone stupid enough to cross me or stand in my way."

Lane shook his head in dismay. "An eight-month-old child stood in your way? An infant crossed you? Do you know how insane that sounds, Owen?"

Owen laughed. "Please," he jeered. "Don't look at me like that. That infant is nothing more than an abomination, a disgrace to my Emily, while his father parades around this city with his whore, living a life my daughter deserved."

"Emily's death was unfair, that's true," Lane agreed, "but it was no one's fault; only fate's. You allowed grief to cloud your judgment, old friend. Making a child suffer because you hate his father is foolish."

"The sins of the fathers should be revisited on the sons."

Lane Thompson could only shake his head sadly. "I can't decide if you're slap-ass crazy," he muttered, "or just bone-deep mean." There would be no reasoning with him. "But it'll cost you."

Owen slid off the bed to his feet and shrugged. "That remains to be seen."

"Yes, Mr. Breen advised me of your insistence in going to trial when I suggested a plea bargain yesterday. You made too many mistakes, and your attempted assault on Christina Wagner compounds it. No jury will excuse your actions, and a guilty verdict could put you behind bars for twenty-five years to life. My advice: take a deal."

"I don't take deals, Lane." Owen replied with arrogance. "I make them, remember?"

Lane Thompson frowned. "I won't be in a position to help you, Owen."

"I figured that out when you screwed me on bail," he shot back. "I'll risk it."

"It's a fool's risk."

"Risks are my business."

~~

Cherry Hill

Jeremy chose to see Debra's accompanying him, Christina, and the baby to visit Avery as a good sign. He extended the invitation and was thrilled when she accepted. It seemed the visit she paid to Owen in jail ripped away the blinders she wore and softened her. While he was furious when she told him about her confrontation with Owen, he understood her reasons for it.

She stood by her promise to get to know her baby brother, even hauling him out of his car seat herself when they arrived on the hill and tickling giggles from him with abandon. Avery was waiting to greet them, and his eyes filled at the sight of his great-granddaughter. Too many years had passed since she'd visited, and he missed her terribly.

The ease his family longed for was felt the moment Jeremy planted his booted foot on the soft earth. Zoom lenses and press intrusions would not be a worry here; here, they could heal as a family in private.

He pulled in a deep breath and smelled the country air. Grinning, he carried Patrick down to the stables to see the horses. How his boy loved the horses. So, he took off with the baby for private father-son time.

The horses whinnied and swished their tails to Patrick's unabashed enjoyment, and Jeremy wanted to freeze this moment. If there were a sweeter sound than his son's laughter, he had yet to hear it. He drew the baby boy close and smelled the sweetness of powder and lotion and thanked God for protecting him.

He'd nearly lost him to a mad man, but with a gentle kiss on Patrick's head he pushed the horrible thought from his mind. That was over and done. And hadn't they come here to keep from dwelling on it? He held the boy out to let him feel the texture of horse's mane with his tiny fingers.

In a few days, the rest of his family, and Aunt Bess too, would join them here at Cherry Hill, and there would be fewer opportunities for this quiet time with his son. With the wonder in his innocent eyes, Jeremy suddenly felt reborn, renewed. Second chances, he mused, where presented for a reason, and he wouldn't be foolish enough to squander his.

~ 64 ~

County Jail
September 1, 1997

Looking out the wire meshed tempered glass window at the far end of the recreation room, Linus focused on the fenced-in yard below. He thought long and hard about paying this visit. In the end, he decided it might be the only way to end this nightmare of Owen Harris' making. The sound of the door buzzing open turned him around to see Owen being led in, shackled at his ankles and cuffed at his wrists.

Little more than two weeks in jail had transformed him into a gaunt, graying, wild-eyed and aging man. His broken nose was healing, but his eyes were still slightly discolored and the swollen bridge of it, still cut. When Owen was seated at a table in the middle of the room, Linus walked over to join him. For a brief time, neither man spoke.

"You're looking..." Linus began hesitantly.

"Like hell," Owen finished for him. "Your son has a hard right, goddamn him. What do you want?"

Linus marveled at the open contempt in Owen's bruised eyes and decided to get to the point. "I'm here to talk about our granddaughter."

"Debra," Owen replied, leaning back in his chair. "Is there a problem?"

"No, but that'll change with your trial."

"I'm not following you."

Linus set his jaw when he realized Owen was being purposely obtuse. "Then I'll be specific. This circus of a trial you're determined to put us all through will be difficult for Debra; humiliating, actually."

Owen's eyes hardened. "Ah." he said, reading Linus perfectly. "You want me to spare her such a cruel fate?"

Linus nodded. "The press will hound her. The particulars of your actions will destroy her and any hope of your salvaging a relationship with her. Take the deal."

"You mean admit guilt," Owen shot back.

"You are guilty."

"Jeremy's guilty," he said flatly, "of cruelty and adultery and neglect."

"He loved Emily," Linus said sincerely. "As for guilt, it's you and I who're guilty. We insisted on the marriage of our children, and they both suffered. The sins of the fathers are visited on their children." His face softened, he sighed. "Don't make our granddaughter suffer for our mistakes, too. Take the deal."

~~

Once he'd made the choice, a strange calm moved through him. His decision crystallized his thinking and directed his next actions. It was really so simple - and oh, the damage simplicity can do with a deepening madness to guide it.

Fresh from the shower, Owen sat on his bunk, not a hair out of place as he went about his business. A whirl of thoughts spun in his head...this was just business, after all, and in business you didn't achieve greatness without knowing how to read the writing on the wall. With a tine of his fork; hidden from dinner and a steady hand, he poked a hole through the damp towel from his shower, he tore the fabric enough to be useful but still strong enough for the task ahead...

...leaving the game when nothing useful would be gained by playing was only prudent. The fork abandoned, he now used his own hands and ripped the towel into long strips, then tested their strength. Satisfied, he tied them together. Particularly when leaving on your own terms meant exiting without admitting defeat.

The noose was tight around his neck, and he stepped on his mattress with a strong sense of anticipation buoying him. By the time bed check was made, the end - his end - will be complete - and final. When he took that final step off the mattress, his life drained out of his body with his last thoughts turning to Debra. Before the darkness overtook him, he wondered, *would she miss him at all?*

~ 65 ~

Four Years Later
September 2001

Jeremy Beckett should have been in his office by now, but he was on a much deserved vacation instead. He would finally marry the woman of his dreams. It was hard to believe that, after so long, in four short days he would finally be a husband again.

He sat in the kitchen, enjoying his second cup of coffee with Christina behind him at the stove and Patrick in the booster seat beside him, waiting for his mother's French toast. His attention was tuned to the newspaper and the Today Show on the television across the room. His hair was still damp from his shower, and his long sleeve denim shirt was still unbuttoned. He was relaxed and, he decided, ready to deal with the finicky caterer, and the rest of the last minute details expected with impending wedded bliss.

After that meeting, there were others, but none that could annoy half as much; yet, he was willing to endure it all if it meant giving Christina the wedding she deserved. She had waited so long, so anything and everything she wanted was exactly what he would give her.

She had just brought a tray of fresh, steaming French toast to the table when the world as they knew it was changed forever. Suddenly, live coverage from the Today Show is interrupted, and muffled conversation is heard between the morning anchors. Camera footage changes, and together, Christina and Jeremy watch in horror as a plane careens into a World Trade tower and explodes. In the first few seconds after impact it is thought to be a horrible accident, but bad turns to awful as another plane comes in low and crashes through a second World Trade tower in a fiery ball of devastation.

"God Almighty," Jeremy gasped, stumbling out of his chair to the phone.

Christina fumbled, stunned by what she'd witnessed. She managed to feed Patrick while Jeremy tracked down his family to be sure of their safety. She switched off the television as her son ate, she wanted to shut out the grim reality unfolding in the city. Mercifully, Jeremy's parents and sister were safe, but he would lose many friends.

Events only grew more tragic as the day wore on. Towers One and Two of the Trade Center collapsed, the Pentagon was hit, and a fourth plane crashed into a field in Pennsylvania.

Within the first hour it is believed to be a terrorist attack on American soil. Planes had been hijacked and flown into the mighty towers and the Pentagon symbols of American greed and commerce and might.

So much grief and destruction, so much pain and loss. The city looked like a war zone - and even Manhattan Special was one of its many casualties.

Christina knew windows and brick could be replaced, but the thousands of lives lost could not. Time froze, and the country struggled to come to grips with the attacks - and their wedding was postponed while the city faced the long and daunting road to recovery.

Three Years Later
September 2004

Jeremy held on to his youth by being a full participant in his son's life. Though he was hardly an old man, his forty-seventh birthday was a wake-up call, and he could see signs revealing every year. The hair graying at his temples, the eight pounds he couldn't shake that no one noticed but him, reading glasses for his daily dealings with fine print.

It was thanks to Patrick that he thought more about kite flying in the park or playing catch in the back yard than of board meetings and white-knuckled takeovers. He was a healthy, energetic, thriving little boy whose zest for life demanded a father who could match his pace; gone were the twelve-hour work days and stresses he carried home at the end of the day.

More than two years ago now, he'd put his priorities in order. His family came first, and his painting a close second; the business of Beckett International came in a distant third, so, a three-day week with regular hours became the norm, with him home every night by six.

The simple pleasure of sharing dinner with Patrick and Christina and tucking his son in bed with a story were memories he would hold dear. There had been far too little of those sort of memories in Debra's childhood - a lesson he'd learned too late. And he was determined to not make the same mistakes again.

So, his life was finally headed in the right direction; really coming together in every regard except one. Because of one disaster after another, he had yet to marry the woman he loved.

It grated, especially went the gossips drew their own conclusions as to why the wedding was put off again and again. Christina had even begun thinking that fate was conspiring against them. *Well, damn if I let her doubt our shared destiny*, he thought.

First 9/11, then six months later, in March of 2002, Aunt Bess suffered a stroke in the middle of Manhattan Special's renovation and reopening. Then, in May 2002, three weeks before their rescheduled wedding, his grandfather, Avery, passed away peacefully in his sleep. His grief was so great, he couldn't even think about the wedding. Hell, he thought back now, he could hardly function after such an emotional blow.

But their time has finally come, he thought, putting the finishing touches on a painting - and it was about time, too. Come November, he would make Christina his wife - come hell or high water. She would take his name, and they would have each other till death do they part.

~~

Christina moved about the large kitchen of The Mirage, the third in her now trio of restaurants, smack in the heart of Greenwich Village. A new recipe had her full attention, and she didn't hear Jeremy come in with Patrick chattering away on his shoulders. Jeremy, realizing she hadn't a clue she now had an audience, stopped and appreciated the lovely view of the most amazing woman he had ever known.

"Mooommmmy," Patrick called out in a sing-song voice.

His was, she knew, her favorite voice in the world. She looked up from the mixing bowl, all distraction and consumption with her dish forgotten, and smiled at both of the men in her life with love and pleasure at seeing them blooming on her face.

"Well, if it isn't my two favorite guys," she said, wiping her hands on the towel hanging from her waist before going to them and lifting her face for a kiss hello.

"And if it isn't our favorite girl." Jeremy kissed her thoroughly. He then stooped, allowing Patrick to kiss his mother noisily on the cheek. "Ready for our date?"

"Absolutely. So what have the two of you been up to?" she asked, turning back to the oven to check her pastry.

Patrick patted his father's cheeks, exclaiming, "Daddy let me throw whole quarters in the fountain at the park!"

Christina winked at Jeremy. "Whole quarters, huh?"

"Yeah," he proclaimed wide-eyed. "It was sooo cool."

Unable to resist, she delayed removing the pastries from the oven to open her arms to her son. He was so much like Jeremy, in personality and looks. His hair was the strawberry blonde of her youth, and his eyes had come to mirror hers as well. A perfect mix of the two of them, they agreed.

The affectionate little boy leapt into the hug. His giggle brought out a giggle of her own. He wrapped his arms around her neck and cuddled. "What's to eat?"

"Your favorite."

"Meatballs and fries!" he said with delight.

"You know it," Christina replied. "Now why don't you and Daddy go out to the table, and I'll be out in a sec." She bent down to set him on his feet.

"Let's go, pal," Jeremy said.

"Okay, pal," Patrick mimicked, taking his father's hand.

~~

Later, when Patrick was finally asleep in bed, his parents collapsed together on the couch to discuss their day. "...I swear to god, I thought I'd die right there on the spot," Christina was saying incredulously.

Jeremy laughed uproariously until tears filled his eyes. "So what'd you do?"

Christina was now laughing herself. "The only thing I could. Helped him fish his toupee out of his soup and gave him his dessert on the house."

"With a straight face?"

"I was the very essence of tact and professionalism."

"And for that, my love, you deserve a beer."

He was up off the couch and heading for the kitchen when she wondered out loud if he'd given any thought to her suggestion of two days earlier. "Have you thought at all about what we talked about?" Christina asked loud enough to be sure she was heard.

Jeremy stuck his head out to smile at her. "You mean a public show of my paintings?"

"So you have thought about it?"

He didn't say anything more until he came back into the living room, carrying two bottles of beer. He was smiling thoughtfully. "I'm no Picasso, Christina," he said, dropping down next to her and taking a long pull on his beer before he finished. "I'll just be making myself a target for all manner of shit."

She took a drink of her own beer. "I'm not suggesting a career change, Jeremy. Give them something more to write about than our sex life, for a change. Show them you're more than a rich, spoiled heir apparent."

He lifted a brow. "You've given this a lot of thought."

Christina skimmed her fingers over his chin and made him look at her. "You're so talented; why hide it?"

"They'll have plenty to wag their tongues about when we're married and respectable. I paint for me sweetheart, not for the public," he said simply. "For my own enjoyment. Not public recognition."

She gave him a look that said 'who are you trying to kid?' "We both know better. A small showing? Jamie knows the perfect gallery for your style."

Jeremy took another drink and nearly choked on her last words. "My style," he chuckled. "I have a style now?"

Stretching her long legs out over his, she rolled her eyes. "Of course you do, darling."

He shook his head and winked, loving Christina for the compliment. "I dabble."

Christina winked back. "Ah. But you dabble with style," she countered with another drink of beer.

This woman never ceased to amaze him. Her beauty, her still lush flowing hair cascading around her shoulders, the depth in her eyes - always so easy to fall into. She had faith enough for both of them, he supposed.

He was beginning to consider the idea, when only days before he'd never allowed himself to think about it. "How're we going to pull together a show with our wedding in November?"

"Well......"

"Ah huh," he said doubtfully. "Don't even think about delaying our wedding. We've tolerated one delay or disaster after another until months of putting off turned into years. You read the papers. Everyone in this damn city's calling us a permanent engagement. We're not getting any younger," he teased.

She hit him. "Speak for yourself." And, scooting closer, she slid them into a kiss that scattered senses and stirred their desire. "I wouldn't dare."

October 1, 2004

Jeremy signed the contract for his art show debut, but he insisted on a month-long preparation period. So, with the ink drying on the dotted line, he became a man possessed. His determination to show only the very best he had to offer; and the confidence to stand behind what came from his soul was absolute. And time flew by, well, in no time at all.

For the past three weeks, he'd done nothing but eat, sleep, and surround himself with his paintings. He scoped out the most comfortable spot in Christies Gallery and chose from nearly two hundred paintings in his studio for the strongest eighteen contenders. Now, he looked at his life in vivid color, on canvas.

He was alone in the gallery, and he was nervous. All that stood between the debut of Jeremy Beckett the artist, a man very different from Jeremy Beckett the heir apparent, was a sliver of time, and it made his gut clench. A mere twenty-four hours from now, his passion - his true passion - would be on display for the entire city, entire world to see.

And while the man in him was thinking: *Up yours, New York.* The artist in him was, quite simply and definitely, scared to death. And he had to ask himself why. Ridicule from the upper-crust in society would be nothing new to him, and he'd never let it bother him before. Nerves. That's all this surge of panic was. Nerves.

And that is where Debra found him, standing back from his art as if he were waiting for the canvases to leap out and take a bite of him. Her early arrival from Paris wasn't expected, but she jumped at the chance for an earlier flight and the chance to spend more time with her family.

She watched him for a moment. His intense eyes bore into his paintings, and somehow she could feel his doubts warring with his resolve to succeed. She could see the beauty he created - even if he could not. And so, too, would everyone else.

She admired the courage it took for him to lay himself open to the world. But this wouldn't be the first time he would take such a risk, and this, likely, wouldn't be the last. Seeing him, Debra hadn't known she missed him. Until this moment, she hadn't known she was capable of it, but she felt something inside her give. She looked at his paintings, then back at him, and to her surprise, she felt unmistakable pride.

Her two years in Paris had changed her; forced her to become self-sufficient. Perhaps, it even gave her the chance to come to grips with the betrayal she felt she suffered from within her own family, and then to let it go.

Suddenly, all she wanted was her father's arms around her. For too long, she held him responsible for so much, for too much. And it wasn't fair. It had taken Owen Harris and the nightmare he'd thrust them into to make her see she was wrong, and it had taken his suicide to set her free. She could love her father for the wonderful, caring man he had always been. She could forgive the rest, just as her mother had asked her to do.

~~

"Dad." When he turned and saw her, he grinned. She flew into his arms, laughing. As always, his cologne was familiar, and she held him close to breathe it in.

After indulging in a moment of pure pleasure, Jeremy drew away and held her out at arm's length. "You look amazing sweetheart. Paris agrees with you."

"And you look exhausted."

"Couldn't sleep right now if you paid me."

Debra smiled and kissed his cheek. "You're nervous." She stepped around him and looked at his exhibit with a critical eye.

"Petrified," he corrected, watching her look over each painting.

Finally, she turned back to him with an odd look in her eyes. "I don't know why," she said. "They're terrific, Daddy. Really."

He laughed. "You sound like Christina," he mumbled, his attention pulled back to his canvases, "and you're both biased."

She walked over and tucked her arm through his. "Oh, ye of little faith." She turned him away from the exhibit and started for the door. "I've been sent to drag you out of here, kicking and screaming if necessary."

"Christina or your brother?" he asked, flipping the lights off as they passed the switch.

"Both, actually. Besides, Christina's fixed a mouthwatering dinner."

Jeremy's eyes brightened as he waved goodnight to the security officer who buzzed them out. He covered his daughter's hand as they walked through the door to the street. "And I wonder why I can't drop five lousy pounds."

"You look fit, so don't be vain."

Together, they walked down the block to the waiting limo. He opened the door for her himself. "I'm glad you're home, sweetie. I missed you; we all did."

"I missed you, too, Daddy, and I wouldn't miss your big night for the world. You'll be a smash."

He shook his head ruefully as she slid into the seat beside her. "From your lips to God's ears, Debra," he said, and pulled the door shut.

~~

Jeremy was pleasantly surprised to find his parents and sister at home when he and Debra arrived. Patrick ran to his father, wearing the sweatshirt his sister had brought him from Paris. He lifted the boy into his arms, preparing to be entertained. Debra had moved off to help her grandmother set the table while Jeremy followed the sound of Linus' voice into the kitchen.

"Well, what smells so incredible in here?" he asked, coming through the swinging door.

"You'll have to wait and see," Christina teased, coming and taking Patrick from his father. "Time to wash up for dinner, honey." She sent the boy along with a pat on the head. "I see Debra was able to accomplish what the rest of us couldn't. See, Linus, I told you he was still alive, though you wouldn't know it to look at him."

"You're great for a man's ego," he quipped and dropped his head for a kiss. "How are you Dad?" he asked with a slap on his father's back. He watched Christina vanish through the door, when the familiar sound of Patrick whining drifted in from the other room.

Linus popped a baby carrot into his mouth and sat down on a bar stool at the counter. "Old," he replied with a wink.

"You? Hardly."

"Everything ready at the gallery?"

Jeremy shrugged and picked up a carrot, too. "Hope so."

"Your mother's bubbling with excitement. Ever since you walked her through the exhibit yesterday, it's all she can talk about," Linus said, biting into another carrot. "I have to say, I think it's great Jeremy. You should be very proud."

Jeremy gaped at his father. "You saw it?"

"Went down this morning while you were tied up in the board meeting," Linus explained. "It's something. I don't have a creative bone in my body, so I figure you get it from your mother."

"Thank you, Dad."

Linus looked at his son and smiled. "You're surprised I like your work, but I do. I've never doubted your talent, son. I just didn't understand your need for it. I do now. It's your passion, the way business is mine."

"I enjoy business."

"But you love painting. And a grown man should be able to do what he loves, Jeremy. I'm sorry I didn't see that before."

"You firing me?"

Linus laughed heartily. "Hell, no. I need your killer instinct to carry Beckett International through the decade at least. But I don't want to see you in your office more than a couple days a week. Focus on your passion the way I focused on mine. I'll call you if I need you."

Christina walked in and knew from the looks on their faces that they were in a deep discussion. The love between them was obvious. "Okay, boys, dinner is served."

~ 66 ~

Christies was filled with curious art lovers by the time Jeremy Beckett arrived. Cool and collected on the surface, he was a jangle of nerves and nausea underneath. The cameras zoomed in on him the moment he and Christina walked in the door. He smiled easily for the pictures, but he waited for his family to all but surround him before he made his way through the crowd to his exhibit.

Champagne-topped trays circulated in the expert hands of waiters and waitresses as he mingled. Christina never left his side as he moved through the throngs of people. He was the artist and man of the hour, after all, so he had to work the room.

When he discussed business with colleagues who came to please their wives, it was with Linus as a buffer. He charmed more than one critic with his knowledge of art. Debra was on his arm from time to time, and his sainted mother kept an antsy six-year-old who was perpetually tugging at his tie, from becoming bored.

His self-effacing view of his painting dispelled the rumors that his debut was just another attempt to feed his ego. He spoke with everyone in the room. He shared his views on color and composition when asked; and patiently answered endless questions about his opinion on the importance of style in art. Jeremy was more in his element than he realized, and his debut proved to be a big success.

~~

A week later, the positive reviews of his debut were the talk of the town, but for Jeremy they were pleasant memories. He found himself behind his desk, thinking he may have dreamt it all. Laying the groundwork for a merger between one of Beckett International's subsidiaries and a struggling computer software company required his full attention, and if it were to be a successful business move he had to keep his head in the game. Linus was counting on him down to the last detail.

When his phone buzzed, he dropped his pen, took off his glasses, and tossed them aside. "Yes?"

"Mr. Beckett, it's Madeline. I'm sorry to bother you at work-"

He cut her off; even when distracted, Jeremy picked up on his son's nanny's tone. "What is it, Madeline?"

"I don't mean to alarm you, but I couldn't reach Ms. Wagner on her cell phone. I took Patrick to the park for a play date, and I think one of the boys must have said something to hurt his feelings because I found him crying in the sandbox alone."

Jeremy could hear Patrick crying in the background. Something major would have happened for him to cry like that. "Is he hurt?"

Madeline Richards sighed. "No, no, not physically, but I can't get a word out of him. He's just gone into his room and slammed the door. He's inconsolable, Mr. Beckett. What should I do?"

Jeremy stood up and grabbed his jacket. "Try to calm him down," he suggested, searching his desk for his car keys. "I'm on my way home."

~~

Midday traffic had slowed to a crawl, so the drive home stretched to thirty minutes before he pulled into the drive. It was quiet when he walked into the house. He didn't know if that was a good or bad sign as he headed for the stairs.

"Madeline?" he called.

"We're in here." Madeline's voice carried out from the living room.

Jeremy appeared in the doorway and found Patrick curled up on his nanny's lap. He could see the boy was sniffling and his eyes were pooled with tears. "Sorry, I got caught in traffic."

"He's calmer now."

Jeremy came in and bent down to bring his son into his arms. "Has he said what happened yet?" he asked.

"Not a word," she said, getting to her feet, "and I still haven't reached Ms. Wagner."

Jeremy rubbed Patrick's back soothingly when the boy wrapped himself around his father and tucked his hot, wet face in the crook of Jeremy's neck. "She's in Napa with my mother and sister for the final fitting."

When they were alone, Jeremy lowered them both to the couch. "Want to tell Dad what's wrong, pal?"

Patrick lifted his head and leaned back to look at his father. Still sniffling with his face heated to pink and his hair matted with sweat against his forehead, he dropped his eyes and mumbled, "I'm a bastard."

Jeremy was stunned. It was a beat in time, but his anger worked its way through fast. "Where'd you here that word?"

"From Tony," Patrick answered meekly, as if sensing the shame the word induced. "He says his mommy and daddy say that's what I am cause my mommy and daddy aren't married."

"So that's what made you cry?" The gossip and lies were a fact of life for he and Christina, but he'd be damned if he let them touch his son.

Patrick nodded, tracing the stripes in his father's tie with his finger. "It's a bad word, isn't it?" he asked, frowning. "I know 'cause Tony told Billy and Marissa and they all started pointing and laughing at me. They said I'm bad, too."

It was a testament of Jeremy's strength that the hands that wanted to do damage were gentle instead as he wiped the fresh tears from his son's cheek. "You're not bad, Patrick, you're perfect. You're our perfect little boy, and Mommy and I love you very, very much."

With the innocence of childhood, he humbled his father. "Do you love each other?"

"Very, very, very much."

"Then why aren't you and Mommy married?"

He opened his mouth, then closed it to weigh his reply. The simplicity of the question belied the complicated answer. How could he explain it to a six-year-old? "We will be very soon."

"Tomorrow?" Patrick asked, his mood brightening.

"No, not tomorrow, but soon. I promise." Jeremy said seriously, brushing the boy's sweaty hair away from his face.

"Can I come?" the little boy asked excitedly.

"You'd better," Jeremy said, tickling the boy's nose. "You're my best man."

"Really?" Patrick asked wide-eyed.

"You bet!"

"Then we'll be a family?"

A piece of him broke hearing Patrick's innocent question. Had he failed to provide his son with a sense of family? Was Patrick being made an outcast because of a piece of paper? It was lost on him how anyone could look at his sweet little boy and see anything less than magnificence.

Jeremy kissed his son's brow, then pulled him into a fierce hug and spoke the truth, "We are a family, son."

~ 67 ~

Jeremy lay memorizing the wood beamed ceiling while he listened to Christina move about downstairs. Then he listened moments later as she climbed the stairs on her way to him. He was still awake when she crept into the bedroom just after midnight. Her routine, as predictable as the setting sun, remained unchanged.

He could see her easing Patrick's door open and slipping inside to kiss him goodnight. She'd fuss with the disarray of his bed, then brush her fingertips through his hair before slipping out again. She'd leave a light on in the hallway, and then come to their bed.

As he watched Christina in the darkness, he knew that she was exhausted. He could see it in her sagging shoulders and hear it in her quiet sigh when she pulled her hair free from the pins that she styled it with when she cooked. He watched her undress and listened to the thudding of his heart.

"You're awake," she said, unzipping her skirt and letting it drop to the floor at her feet. "Were you going to say anything, or just leer at me in silence?"

He was surprised by her constantly, and in moments like these, he knew he always would be. Her ability to sense him, read his mind, and see into him had never wavered.

"Leering at you is one of my favorite things to do," he said.

With a sultry laugh, Christina shuffled to the bathroom and flipped on the light. The light slanted over the bed and revealed his face. "Why are you still up? Didn't Patrick exhaust you? He exhausts me on a nightly basis."

Jeremy slid up in the bed as she came and sat next to him. She dropped her head to press a kiss to his chest. "He zonked out by eight, and I was left to entertain myself. How was Napa? Did the fitting go well?"

"Great, actually," Christina replied, turning around to let Jeremy undo the clasp on her necklace. "Your mother's really enjoying helping out, and Jamie finally found a dress she could, and this is a quote, 'live with.'"

"Will wonders never cease?" he said playfully.

"Can't sleep?" she asked, touching his cheek and effectively changing the subject. "Is it the merger?"

"No, it's fine." He knew he would have to tell her about what happened with Patrick, so he saw no reason to put it off. "Patrick had a rough day."

Christina lifted a brow and waited for him to continue. When he didn't, she prodded him. "Define 'rough day,' please."

"Tony seems to have broadened his vocabulary. He called Patrick a 'bastard,' and then proceeded to explain why."

"He called him what?" she demanded, her eyes bright with anger. Furious, she shot to her feet.

Jeremy grabbed her hand. "He's okay now." She looked into his eyes, and she believed him. "He was inconsolable when Madeline called me, so I came home and got him through it."

Christina's anger drained away to pain. "I should've been here." Sitting back down on the mattress, she sighed. "When is this going to become easier?" she wondered, already grown weary from the fight of slings and arrows.

It was a question he asked himself many times throughout the evening, and it was a question without a simple answer. As was his habit, he sought to take her pain away, just as he'd done for their son earlier. Reaching out, he ran his fingers through her hair to relax them both, then began to work on the knots in her shoulders.

"He wanted to know why we weren't married," he replied thoughtfully. "I didn't know where to begin."

"I don't blame you."

"Time has a way of sneaking by on you, I suppose." Jeremy kneaded his way across her shoulder blades and down her back. "First, there was Debra's grief to consider and the reality of Emily's death. Then, your full plate once you opened the new restaurant..." His voice trailed off, and he grew quiet.

Christina knew what he was thinking and the fresh wave of pain it brought to them both. "Then we lost Avery."

"Yeah." His voice, husky with emotion, faltered. The pain was still new, his grandfather had been gone nearly a year, and yet the swift stab of pain ran deep.

"For every one of those snobs who sees us as a couple, there are two more who think we're a disgrace," Christina muttered. "But they have no problem coming into my restaurants, being smooth as silk to my face, and then eating my food even while they plunge a knife in my back." She sank back against Jeremy with a sigh. "Of course, their venom will spill onto our child. Where do children learn to be so cruel?"

"From their cruel, morally bankrupt parents?"

"Maybe once we're sanctioned by God and the state, we'll be absolved of our sins."

"Don't count on it, baby." Jeremy laughed as a thought popped into his head. "I think I know the perfect revenge: raise your prices," he quipped. "Hit'em where it'll really hurt."

Despite herself, Christina laughed. Of course, he would make her see the humor in it. She tugged his head down to her face and captured his mouth with a kiss. "You're terrible," she said, feathering his hair with her fingers and falling in love with him all over again. "But I do love you."

~~

Jeremy signed off on the final drafts of the contracts for the merger and turned his attention to paying the bills of his foundations. He cut the checks, returned a few pressing phone calls, dropped several inter-office memos off with his secretary, and left the office for the day. He was heading to *The Mirage* for lunch with Christina. He lucked into a parking space right across the street, hopped out, and made a quick dash across two lanes of traffic stopped at the light.

The midday sun beat down as he trotted his way to the sidewalk. Tugging his tie free, he stuffed it into his pocket as he pushed through the door and felt instantly relaxed. He smiled and waved to the bartender as he headed to Christina's office in the back. He couldn't wait to see her or hear the sound of her voice.

Jeremy imagined her at her desk, worry lines creasing her lovely, milky skin. He opened the door and stuck his head in. "You know what they say about all work and no play," he offered, coming in and closing the door behind him.

She didn't need to look up from the mound of receipts on her desk to know he was smiling. "Yeah, it keeps the IRS away," she answered easily, glancing up in time to meet his kiss. She pulled off her glasses and stretched before slipping her heels back on and standing. "What's your pleasure?"

Jeremy lifted a brow and grinned wickedly. "Well..."

"Down, boy," she countered. "I'm talking lunch."

"What do you suggest?"

"Poached salmon salad," she said coming around her desk. "I'll just go tell Henry. Be right back."

"I'll be here," Jeremy said. He slipped his hands into his pockets and meandered about her office. He closed his eyes and caught her scent. Her perfume. Her many flower arrangements scattered here and there were fragrant and beautiful.

He opened his eyes and was drawn to the bay window and the panoramic view beyond. Christina had built a hugely successful business with sweat, heart, and drive, and she'd done so on her own terms as her own boss. He loved her all the more for it. Most important, he respected her need to stand on her own professionally.

Smiling as a new idea popped into his head, Jeremy crossed the room to Christina's desk. As he picked up the phone, his gaze caught sight of the large, colorful canvas commanding the wall space behind her chair, and he smiled once more. His canvas. The one he'd painted a lifetime ago for her birthday - that she'd returned.

Now, a lifetime later, it hung here in her own private space. For her own private enjoyment. It was a sign of her love for him and her pride in his work.

He picked up the phone to set his plans in motion. Imagining Christina's surprised face made his smile widen - and Jamie would be thrilled to be his partner in crime.

~ 68 ~

Jeremy was thinking about her, of course. Being honest with himself, he could admit the moments were few when she wasn't in the foreground of his thoughts. This day would prove to be no different, he knew, crossing West 52nd street on a mad rush to meet Jamie at Harry Winston. A potent mixture of excitement and anticipation kept him awake last night and carried him through his morning meetings.

The streets and sidewalks were crowded with midday traffic, but Jeremy found his sister easily among the throngs of people. She was loitering, of course, and smoking one of her high-priced cigarettes, looking bored and restless. Closing the gap between them, he whistled and cat called, and as he knew it would, her head whipped around, her brow lifted in annoyance.

When she realized the offensive remark came from her brother, her annoyance gave way to amused irritation. "You kiss your mother with that mouth?" Jamie cracked, tapping his cheek before she kissed him.

"And my sister, too," he teased. Grinning, he leaned in to kiss her perfectly blushed cheek. "Thanks for this."

She let him guide her to the door and stepped in ahead of him, grateful to escape the crowded sidewalk. "No biggie. But I find it hysterical you trust your judgment in billion-dollar business deals but not in choosing jewelry."

"It's more than jewelry," he corrected. "It's an engagement ring." Together, they spotted Harry across the room behind a massive glass encasement.

"And because I think you're an adorable puddle of goo right now, I won't mention you've given Christina a perfectly stunning rock already."

Jeremy sighed. Catching Harry's eye, he waved. "Decades ago, little sister, and for an engagement that came to an abrupt end. She gave it back, if you'll remember."

Jamie looked at his anxious face and softened. "A new page then? A fresh start?"

"Exactly. And it has to be perfect."

~~

While Jamie and Jeremy were going over every stone in Winston's vault, Christina put the finishing touches on an order of broiled sea bass. Her kitchen, as always during the lunchtime rush, was a whirl of activity that might have driven anyone else crazy. But, she was in her element, and she thrived. The smell of the divine dishes for which she was renowned stimulated her senses and fed her need to create. The many sounds and voices filling her kitchen was music to her ears.

Order after order kept her busy until well after two. Then, she was finally able to take a moment and sit down to catch her breath. She was tired lately, and she was becoming concerned. Christina knew herself too well to think that all there was to her fatigue was overwork.

Handling chef duties four nights a week and alternating between her three restaurants each night would make anyone tired. Add to that raising a six-year-old boy and planning a wedding, and the average person would be exhausted. So, she shrugged away her concern.

Among her responsibilities at the moment was to go to the dining room and mingle. To introduce herself to any new faces in the crowd. Business was booming, and she had her patrons to thank for it. Personal attention meant repeat patronage While it still made her blood boil to know hiding in plain sight or behind kind smiles and enthusiastic praise, were gossips and rumor mongers.

As long as they paid their bills and tipped the waiters and waitresses well, she would take their money and curse them to hell. She had more than she ever thought she would. She had a child she cherished with the man she loved more than anything, and in a matter of weeks she would be Christina Wagner Beckett - and be damn proud of it.

She made her way through the crowded dining room with a smile. Stopping here and there to share a word with the most loyal of her patrons, she charmed. Touching a hand here or a shoulder there, asking if their meals were prepared to their liking. She impressed even the most suspicious.

Christina was confident, considerate, and cunning in her ability to sidestep the rare awkward stare. Christina Wagner worked the room without a care in the world.

**One Week Later
October 15, 2004**

A man who had made his mistakes didn't have a right to be this happy - or so Jeremy thought. Standing in his studio and opening the gold velvet box for another look at the perfect ring for the perfect woman, he grinned. Even his carefully planned proposal would be perfect.

Three carats and square cut. The emerald was the same vivid shade of green in her eyes and was encircled with small square diamonds. Jamie and his mother pronounced it stunning; as beautiful as the woman who would wear it. He had to agree with them as he stood grinning with smears of paint drying on both cheeks.

Only two more days, he told himself. Just two more days, and he could whisk her away for romance and charm and his undivided attention. He hoped the surprise would be one Christina would never forget.

He had planned everything down to the last detail with the help of his sister and the groundskeeper at Cherry Hill. All that was left to do was to drag her away from work on one of the busiest nights of the week. This feat would be the most difficult of all, but under the guise of a catastrophe at Cherry Hill, he thought he could pull it off. Nothing less would pry her out of the kitchen at the *Manhattan Special* on a Friday night.

Except for this chance to propose in a way worthy of her, Jeremy would never infringe on her business in any way. But this mattered. This night alone on Cherry Hill mattered more than anything. The moment he slipped this ring on her finger and spoke from his heart would never be relived, the look in her eyes when she knew beyond all doubt that the gossip, the rumors, the snide remarks aside, she owned his heart from the beginning and would forever.

October 17, 2004

Christina walked into the house just after midnight, still wearing a chef's jacket stained with spaghetti sauce. She'd put a load of clothes in the washer with her jacket and then turned in. Through the archway, she could see that Jeremy had left the living room light on for her.

It moved her, how such a simple gesture made her feel so loved. With Jeremy upstairs sleeping in their bed and Patrick in his room down the hall, this house was a home. From the moment Jeremy moved in three years ago, it became a home, and so much more.

There were traces of him everywhere. A discarded tie, a money clip tossed casually onto the dresser. A pair of his running shoes tossed into the closet next to the backdoor. It was here that he came after a long day at the office, here where he felt the most at ease.

With the washer started, Christina walked out of the laundry room. She made her way through the dining room and stopped in the doorway of the living room. The new addition to the décor stopped her cold.

She saw Jeremy's latest canvas. It was a lake scene at night, under the white glow of a moon high in the sky. Large weeping willows closed in around the black water. Deep purples and blues with kisses of pink throughout. He'd left it against the sofa, and in the lamp light it glowed and soothed.

The scene stirred her, drawing her into the scene's serenity. Even without being properly displayed, it dominated the room. As it should, she thought, crossing to it for a closer look. It revealed more than just his talent, she decided, it displayed a truth few knew existed: Jeremy Beckett possessed a passionate soul.

She found it affecting. Every stroke in this painting affected her, as it would affect anyone who really took the time to see. It wasn't business that defined him, as it had his father and grandfather before him. It was something deeper, though Christina doubted even Jeremy himself could define it.

With a smile, Christina imagined Jeremy's hands working, blending oils for the perfect shades. Filling the brush, and then making the bristles flow and float to his whim. This was a glimpse into his soul and into the man he so rarely revealed to anyone but her.

Tired and touched, Christina cast one last glance at the painting before she turned out the light and moved through the room on her way to the foyer. Automatically, she checked to make sure the state-of-the-art security system was armed, then she climbed the stairs, unbuttoning her blouse as she went.

By the time she was shuffling down the hall, she was undressed except for her silk slip. As she went about her nightly routine, she never felt happier in her life. When she saw Patrick asleep in his tousled bed, her heart warmed.

Tucking him in was such a gift. Simple, and some would say ordinary, but it was a gift to her. When she entered her bedroom, letting the silk fall free from her shoulders, she climbed into bed and spooned Jeremy.

~ 69 ~

In her office at The Mirage, Christina kicked off her flats and prepared to spend the next few hours at her desk. The mountain of receipts amassed through the week would keep her occupied until late afternoon. But she would enter into the busy weekend with a cleared desk and a balanced book, she decided, beginning to work the calculator, hoping she would make it back to Manhattan Special in time to supervise her junior chef through the dinner crowd.

This weekend, like all weekends, would be hectic. And not just at The Mirage, but at The Avenue and Manhattan Special, respectively, as well. It seemed everyone in the city had a craving for the ambience and food in her restaurants at the end of a trying week. The coming fifty-four hours would be nonstop madness, but she could handle it.

An hour into the receipts, she was interrupted by a knock on her door. A quick glance at the clock told her she was on a roll and shouldn't stop now. When another more persistent knock had her stumbling with her numbers, she sighed and admitted defeat.

Slipping into her flats and taking off her glasses to pinch the bridge of her nose, Christina pushed back from her desk and closed her eyes to gather patience. "Yes?" she answered, making no attempt to mask her irritation.

When the door opened and the familiar face of her maître d' appeared, Christina motioned him inside. He seemed bothered and spoke in a rushed whisper. "I'm sorry to bother you, Ms. Wagner, but it seems you have a rather persistent visitor who insists on seeing you."

"Does this visitor have a name, Joel?" Christina asked, sure it was just another of the many people who liked to gush over a favorite dish.

Joel came closer to her desk and nodded. "Sam. He says he's sure you'll see him."

Christina couldn't help but gape in surprise. She hadn't see Sam in almost...she had to stop and think. Had it really been more than six years? After their breakup, he took a transfer to his firm's London office. Now he was back in New York and decided to look her up.

Shaken, she stood up and came around her desk. "Is he alone?" Christina asked Joel with a voice that belied her calm.

Joel nodded. "Yes. He came in, had a sandwich at the bar, and then asked to see you."

Christina blew out a steadying breath and assembled her frayed nerves. It would have been her pastrami on rye. He had always raved about her pastrami on rye, she thought, trying to gather herself. "Ah, tell him I'll be right out."

"He'd like to see you in here."

So he wanted a private reunion? The thought made her stomach twist, but it was a reasonable request. "Alright," she told Joel. "Show him back."

Joel glanced over his shoulder, then back to his boss. "You're sure?" he asked taking in her pale color.

Christina fixed a smile on her face. "Of course."

~~

Sam Radcliff took his first hesitant steps into Christina's office in silence. Suddenly, coming face to face with a very painful part of his past didn't seem as harmless as it had when the idea came to mind on the long flight from London. Too late to back out now, he thought, coming further into the room so the man who showed him in could close the door.

Christina watched him pull his hands out of his pockets and caught sight of the wedding band on his left hand. Though she couldn't explain her reaction to such a natural progression, her equilibrium shifted, realizing it came as such a surprise. Nothing else about him, at least on the surface, had changed.

He looked like life in London suited him. Fit, trim, and successful, if the Rolex on his wrist was any indication. And married, she reminded herself. She could see no lines etched in his face earned from life's ups and downs, no deep furrows in his forehead.

His eyes were as kind as she remembered, and his posture as straight. The solidness she always counted on, found so admirable remained as well. To look at him, it seemed no time had passed at all.

When he finally looked at her, Christina could see his nerves clearly in those kind eyes, and she was grateful. It was nice to see she wasn't the only one at the mercy of a queasy stomach and regrets. With a smile, she found her voice. "You look just the same," she said, taking a tentative step from out behind her desk.

Then he went on instinct and went to her. When he took the chance to hug her, she returned his embrace with a nervous laugh, one he recognized even after all this time. "And you're as beautiful as ever, damn you," he said softly stepping back.

His uncomfortable laughter brought her uncomfortable laughter back. "Are you in New York on a case?" she asked.

Sam stared at her, and his intense gaze unnerved them both enough that he finally broke eye contact. "No, I'm on vacation, actually," he replied.

While she didn't sense anger in him, she didn't sense the ease of bygones and friendship either. "With your wife?"

Thrown off balance, Sam's eyes flicked back to hers.

Christina could see she caught him off guard. "Your wedding ring," she explained.

He lifted his hand and looked at the gold band sheepishly. "Oh. Yes, Amelia's with me," he answered with an easy, relaxed smile. "She's off shopping. We're in the city for a Broadway revival. An old school friend of Amelia's has the lead."

Christina let the name sink in. Amelia. So he had found someone and settled down. Somewhere inside, the guilt she'd carried for so long about Sam faded away. "You're happy, then?"

"Very," Sam answered. "Are you happy, Christina?"

"Very."

"Well, you've made a name for yourself, no doubt about it," Sam mused, looking around her plush office before dropping into the chair opposite her desk. "How's Patrick?"

Now it was her turn to be thrown. Somehow, he knew her son's name. "He's wonderful and the best thing that's ever happened to me." With the tension gone, she leaned on the edge of her desk.

The sting of what might have been had lessened over the years, but it had left an indelible mark on him. "And Jeremy's well, I assume?" Sam wondered aloud, keeping the edge from his voice as he wished for the painful memory to fade.

"He's busy, but otherwise, he's fine."

"Too busy to marry you?" Sam regretted the words the instant he spoke them, but the pain was inflicted, the damage done, so he got the rest off his chest. "He's been free for years, and you're still waiting Christina-"

Christina pushed herself to her feet and went around her desk. She needed the distance and the barrier between them. "So, I guess I have my answer," she said tightly.

In an effort to diffuse the situation, he flicked his hand through his hair and sucked in a calming breath. He was better than such a cheap shot made him seem. "What's the question?"

"Why you're here," she snapped, making a vain attempt to organize the mess on her desk. "You came to take cheap shots at Jeremy?"

"You deserve better," Sam countered and sighed. "It might be a cheap shot, but it's also the truth."

"I'll decide what I deserve, Sam - and who," Christina shot back. "We're engaged. The wedding's next month, actually."

"Yeah? Guess there's nothing like being backed into a corner to make you feel all warm and fuzzy!" Sam didn't bother to veil his mocking tone. "But you're right. Whatever makes you happy, you should have. Though for the life of me, I don't understand why it's Beckett."

"You don't have to understand it," she argued back, "but you could accept it."

He came around the desk and grabbed her busy hands, lifting her left hand up to see her ring finger was naked. "He hasn't even bothered to give you a ring, Christina. Dammit!" Frustrated with himself, he dropped her hands and backed away. She looked like she wanted to slap him, and he knew he deserved it. "I didn't come here for this. I came to give you some advice. You were forbidden fruit for him in the beginning, and you're forbidden now. If he loved you, really loved you, Christina, he'd have moved heaven and earth to be with you."

Her green eyes blazed with fury as she rounded her desk for the door. "That's exactly what he did, you idiot! I love him, and I'll be damned if I'll justify why to you or anyone else. You don't have the first clue about Jeremy and me."

"I know he's a free man, Chris, and he's been free for years now. So why aren't you married? Why didn't he marry you the minute Emily was out of the way?" Sam went to her. "I want what's best for you, and I just don't happen to think it's Jeremy."

Christina's eyes glittered furiously. "There were very good reasons to wait. September 11th for one, and there're others - but there none of your damn business. So let me give *you* some unsolicited advice Sam: worry about your own life - not mine. I know I hurt you and I'll be sorry for it for the rest of my life, but you have no right to invade my relationship in an attempt to undermine it."

Sam smiled wanly. "He's all you've ever wanted, isn't he?" he asked, mystified. "It was over for us before it ever began," he continued, answering his own question. Shaking his head, he jerked open the door and turned back. "I do wish you all the best. I mean that. Have a good life."

She believed him, but couldn't let go of her anger. "I will."

~ 70 ~

October 17, 2004
8:00pm

Christina pulled into her driveway, planning to do nothing more than crawl into bed. She was still unnerved by Sam's surprise visit, and queasy from skipping both lunch and dinner, but the fragrant aroma of eggplant parmesan when she walked in the door changed her mind. She would eat first, and then go to bed.

When she found the note on the counter from Jeremy, saying he had to run an errand and would be back soon, she was grateful. Having the chance to pull herself out of her mood before he saw her was a good thing. Then the intoxicating ring of Patrick's laughter drew her up the stairs to find him playing with his boats in the bathtub under his nanny's watchful eye.

As tired and unsettled as she was, her son brought a smile to her face. "Don't forget to wash behind your ears," she reminded him, leaning against the door frame.

Happily sending a boat crashing into the water, Patrick said, "Daddy says I'm clean as a whistle."

Christina winked. "Alright then, time to get out," she said, straightening up and pulling her hair free from its ponytail. "I can take over here, Madeline, if you want to escape." Then she turned her attention back to her water-logged son. "Lights out in ten minutes."

Patrick filled up a cup with bubbles and dumped them over his head. "Aw, Mommy," he whined, sputtering bubbles from his lips.

"Aw, nothing," came his mother's reply when she handed over a towel and turned away to give him privacy.

~~

8:30pm

Jeremy walked through the door just as Christina was coming down from tucking Patrick into bed. His grin told her his day had been far better than hers. He met her at the bottom of the stairs and kissed her soundly on the mouth.

"You look pleased with yourself," she said when he let her up for air. All she needed to do was look into his eyes to see, and be sure of his love. All he needed was to look into hers, and he melted. "I love you."

"Good. I'm crazy in love with you." Jeremy read the tension in her brow and kissed her forehead before wrapping her in a hug. "Long day?" he asked, leading her into the living room.

"Endless," Christina said on a sigh.

"I know what you need," he said, lowering them both onto the sofa.

"Me, too," she murmured. "A good night's sleep."

"Or a change of scenery," he countered.

Willing to play along, Christina rested her head against Jeremy's chest. "Tahiti?" she quipped.

"Cherry Hill," Jeremy began. "We've missed the weekend traffic, so we'll make good time."

"Much as I'd love to escape with you, we can't."

"Why not? Jamie's already agreed to come and stay with Patrick, and we can be back in time for Sunday dinner."

"I've got too much on my plate this weekend. I'm booked solid through, and I've had an awful day," Christina explained, pulling away and closing her eyes against the pain building at her temples. "All I want to do is crawl in bed."

One look at her, and he could see all his plans for romance and commitment crumbling. "You can sleep through the drive, sweetheart. I've planned a surprise."

Pushing herself off the couch, Christina felt a twinge of annoyance building. "I've had enough surprises for one day, Jeremy, believe me."

"Please. It's important to me, to us."

She turned around and drew in an exasperated breath. "What is it with men thinking they know better than me what's important?"

Jeremy lifted a brow and got off the couch. Someone had ruffled her feathers, and, as always, he wanted to soothe. "I'm feeling a little out of the loop."

"Join the club," she said shortly.

He went to her and waited. "Alright, tell me what's got you so worked up."

"Surprises, for one thing." At her wits end, she strode to the bar and poured water, then rifled through the cabinet underneath for an aspirin. "I received a rather nasty blast from the not-too-distant past this afternoon."

Jeremy watched her tearing the cabinet apart and spared her. "In the cabinet above the bar, sweetheart. Anyone I know?"

After chasing down three aspirin, Christina slammed the empty glass on the bar and gave a derisive laugh. "Sam."

"Sam?" Jeremy's eyes narrowed in thought. "Sam Radcliff?"

"Know any others?"

"And he upset you?"

"Pissed me right off."

Wisely, he fought off the smile that threatened. "In what way?"

"Every way imaginable," she answered. "Came all the way from London with his wife to tell me I'd be making a mistake marrying you, among other things."

"Really?" He'd never had a fan in Sam Radcliff, so his opinion came as no surprise; what did however, was Christina's reaction to it. "And you're angry with him?"

"Oh yes."

Jeremy shrugged, studying her posture, her mood curiously. "Why does it matter to you? Don't let it get to you, don't give him the satisfaction."

Christina turned her narrow, angry eyes on Jeremy. How.......rationale, she mused, and how infuriating."Gee, why didn't I think of that?"

Jeremy wasn't sure why she was so angry, but he wanted to put her mind on something positive. "Cherry Hill will chase away old ghosts with big mouths."

"Aren't you listening? I'm not going to Cherry Hill or anywhere else, dammit!" Her tone was sharp, and she sighed to regain control. "I'm going to bed."

Jeremy had had enough and was willing to match her, temper for temper. "So Sam Radcliff blows into town, pushes your buttons, and I'm paying for it."

Christina lifted her chin and narrowed her eyes. If he wanted to fight, she'd oblige him. "Not yet, but keep it up."

"Christ." Jeremy could see she had her back up. "What's this really about, Christina? Why do Sam's half-ass opinions bother you so much? We both see worse in print about us three times a week. Are they his doubts or yours?"

He might have slapped her, given the look that crossed her face. "Go to hell."

"I'm sorry," he muttered, he started to go to her. "That was unfair."

"I'm going to bed before the urge to strangle you gets the better of me." Christina meant to stride past him, but he stopped her.

"Jamie's on her way, let's just go to Cherry Hill. We need to do this. You need this right now, trust me, and everything will make sense once we're there. Trust me."

"I have responsibilities here, Jeremy. To my business, to our son. I can't pick up on a whim and disappear whenever I like." And with that, she walked out, and the next sound he heard was the bedroom door slamming behind her.

Jeremy left the house with anger a tidal wave inside him. Maybe she was jealous because Sam was no longer pining for her. Maybe she had doubts of her own and he made her face them. Maybe she didn't trust his love.

He sped off, holding the ring box in a death grip. So much for proposing and lovemaking by midnight, he thought. She wanted to strangle him. Well, he knew just how she felt. He had the urge to strangle her, too, but he'd give her the night to cool off and use the long drive to Vermont to settle his temper.

Ten minutes later, Jeremy turned onto the interstate ramp that would lead him away from Albany and flipped on his low beams. He was still angry, and he drove with the echo of their words ringing in his ears. He tried to relax and settle in for the long drive...........

~ 71 ~

Albany General Hospital
12:30am
Jeremy's Bedside

When Christina woke, the argument with Jeremy still resonated keenly within her mind, but the fog of her disquieting sleep vanished with the touch of a reassuring hand. Through heavy-lidded eyes, Elise Beckett's kind face came into focus, and she gripped the gentle hand on her shoulder.

Holding fast to each other's hands, the two women looked at Jeremy in an understanding silence. Each held an invaluable place in his heart and soul. One gave him life, and the other completed it.

Stiffly, Christina pulled herself up in the chair and reached for Jeremy's hand and covered it with hers. "He's so still," she said softly. "I'm not used to seeing him so still."

Elise moved closer to her son and looked over every inch of his face. She surveyed the abrasions and bruising and the deep cut above his brow with a mother's concern. She worried for him, about him, fearing the worst when the hospital's call propelled her and Linus into a panic.

Seeing him, knowing his strength, her hope buoyed her spirit. "It's the body's way of helping him heal," Elise replied, "and it's probably a good thing. When he does wake up, we'll have our hands full trying to keep him in this bed."

The thought of Jeremy stubbornly insisting he didn't need all this fuss made Christina smile in spite of the unsettling paleness to his skin. "I wish I could relive the last four hours. I was looking for a fight, and dammit if he didn't just walk in at the wrong time and give it to me. It was so stupid."

Turning to Christina, Elise refused to allow her to take the blame. "You didn't put that deer in the road, and you didn't make him drive too fast for his own good. Temper and bad luck put him here, Christina - not you."

With a sigh, Christina leaned in close to Jeremy. "Wake up for me, honey." The plea came from her soul. The last time she'd looked into his eyes - those beautiful eyes - they had been brightening with anger. Anger she put there, because she had enough of men telling her what was right, what was wrong.

Watching such a pained expression on Christina's face, Elise knew the reason her son was in this bed meant nothing. She noticed her future daughter-in-law's ring finger was still bare and was sorry for it. Because of an argument and her son's bullheadedness, he'd stormed out, taking his pride and the ring with him.

The door opened, and Linus ushered his daughter into the privacy of the dimly lit room. "Damnable press packs are at it again," he muttered, stopping long enough on his way to the windows to touch his son's foot. "Always out for blood." He yanked the blinds down as far as he could.

Jamie kissed her brother's forehead and tried not to cry. "The doctors think you can pull through this, and so do I, in fact, I know you can." She cupped Jeremy's battered cheek with her manicured hand. "Don't let me down, big brother."

The monitor alarm went off, and chaos ensued. Christina jolted to her feet. Elise clutched her husband's arm while Linus fought the panic bubbling up in his throat. Before anyone could think beyond their terror, the door burst open, and Dr. Montgomery and a resident crossed to the bed and flew into action.

"Pressure's crashing." Dr. Montgomery's clipped voice commanded the scene.

"Internal bleeding?" the resident inquired, gingerly probing Jeremy's abdomen.

A nurse arrived and opened his IV wide while the other phoned ahead to the OR. "Yep. Damn. I need to open him up right now." Montgomery and the resident yanked the bed away from the wall and steered it through the open door into the corridor. "Get him up to OR 1 and prep him for surgery," he ordered. "I'll be right behind you."

Salvador Montgomery turned to the family and acknowledged them and the palpable fear written all over their faces as the elevator carried Jeremy to surgery. It was Linus who asked the question everyone else was avoiding. "It's the bleeding in his stomach you were worried about?"

"Yes," he confirmed. "I won't know how serious it is until I get a look inside."

Linus felt Elise shuddering against him and wrapped a reassuring arm around her to steady them both. "You can repair the damage?"

Montgomery hesitated long enough to make them all uncomfortable. "I'll do my absolute best, Mr. Beckett."

Christina spoke. "You have to," she said bluntly. "My son and I need him."

Salvador laid his hand on her shoulder. "Try not to worry, he's very strong, and that counts for a lot." he said with sympathy. "Maybe it'll help you all to head down to the blood bank and donate."

"Will my brother need blood?" Jamie asked.

"It's volume versus loss; most likely he will."

"We're both B-positive. I'd like to give him a transfusion from me."

"Then we better get moving, Ms. Beckett," Dr. Montgomery replied, humbled by the obvious love that bound this family together.

An instant later, Dr. Montgomery and Jamie took off for the bank of elevators at a run. When Christina watched the elevator doors close, her resolve crumbled. Linus embraced her, and, flanking the two women who loved his son the most, he took them to the private waiting room at the end of the corridor.

The space was vast, quaint, bright in a way meant to distract from the reason people would occupy the room in the first place. Privacy was needed to focus on Jeremy and his injuries. And it would offer a shield from the press while they waited. There would be no chance for obtrusive observations from those who ascribed to no moral base.

Linus settled his wife and Christina on the sofa and went to pour coffee. Hours lay ahead of them, to wait and worry, he thought grimly. He needed to prepare himself and his family for the long wait ahead.

~~

Elise couldn't rest as Linus would have preferred. Rest was the very last thing on her mind as the seconds ticked away to minutes and the minutes ticked into hours. Her child was not supposed to be fighting for his life. He was not supposed to need his battered body further traumatized to save his life. It wasn't supposed to be this way.

The irony of this situation left a bitter taste in her mouth as she stood to pace the waiting room. After decades of frail health and mystery symptoms, should it not be her who is so close to death's door? After years upon years of illness and tests, there was finally a diagnosis, a name for her fragile condition: Chronic Fatigue Syndrome.

Medications and a new diet were already making a difference in her energy and pain levels. She was feeling better than she had in too many years to count. Was her child's suffering the price fate demanded because of it?

It wasn't fair, and she wanted to scream at God for his cruelty. Wasn't it the cruelest kind of anguish to watch her son slip away just as she was finally feeling that she could start living again? She wanted to fall to her knees and pray that God would spare her son. *Take me*, she pleaded silently. *Take me if someone has to be taken - not my Jeremy*. She lifted her face up, and her prayer became a plea.

Then she felt the strong, sure hands of her first and truest love on her tense shoulders. He felt her pain and misery just as intensely as he felt his own. She leaned into him and swallowed the sob threatening in her throat. When his arms came around her, she felt safe, protected, and loved.

~~

Jamie found them in the waiting room with her father's anxious demeanor adding to an already charged environment. Concern was evident, and the fear underneath was palpable. She felt it and wanted to put them all at ease. "Well, they took me for a pint and forced juice down my throat."

Linus looked to his daughter and said the thought uppermost in his mind. "We still haven't reached Debra. We need to before a sleazy reporter does it for us."

"I've been calling her cell and her flat for more than an hour," Jamie said, crossing the room to pour herself some coffee.

Elise sighed heavily, awash in the verity of her family in upheaval again. But there was no time to hand wring over the unfairness of the situation; she was no longer a young woman, and her health was precarious at best - but Elise would find the strength to guide her family through.

When she spoke, it was with steel in her voice. "We have friends in Paris, darling," Elise said to Linus. "Call someone to track her down and get her on a plane."

Why he hadn't thought of it before? "Of course; I don't know where my head is," Linus replied. "I'll call Pierre right now."

~ 72 ~

Jeremy was feeling no pain. Sensation - good or bad - was absent. He heard the voices of the surgical team working to save his life, and he watched from above as feverish hands moved inside his open abdomen to repair the still-seeping tear. His little sister's blood was flowing into him as his own continued spurting out.

He thought of his children and of Christina, of his parents and his sister. Of how much more living he wanted to do. And yet the thought of crossing over to whatever lay beyond didn't frighten him. The chance to see his firstborn son filled him with longing. To see Avery and Emily now freed from their physical pain was tempting as well.

But the truth of it was that he couldn't leave. He wouldn't go and leave Christina behind to mourn. He wouldn't abandon Patrick to a fatherless childhood, and he wouldn't allow Debra to suffer the loss of another parent. So he drifted back into his body, and felt the pain come rushing back; determined to survive.

~~

4:15am

Following what Dr. Montgomery assured her was a successful surgery, Christina was at Jeremy's side in recovery. The damage had been repaired, and as a result the pale tint to his skin was gone and his vitals improved dramatically. He would live. She wept now for what she almost lost. Wept for what she'd allowed herself, however briefly, to doubt.

An unshakable love was rooted inside them both. Built and strengthened over a lifetime, given and received - despite separation and pain.

"I love you," Christina whispered.

Having heard Christina's words from the door, Linus came up quietly behind her. She was breathtaking in her beauty and kind and devoted to Jeremy. He could easily see why his son loved her so much. This woman was an indispensable member of the family.

Bending over, Linus kissed her cheek. "You haven't so much as moved your baby finger in more than a hour," he chided, smiling at the tired confusion in her eyes. "Go and stretch your legs, honey; I'll stay with him."

Christina let go of Jeremy's hand long enough to unfold her legs and stand to get her blood moving again. "I'm fine, Linus; really."

Linus looked skeptical. "Uh huh." He went around to the other side of the bed and kissed Jeremy's brow. "Come on, son; wake up," he pleaded.

Usually reserved and buttoned up in his three-piece suits, Linus kept a vigil for his son as constant as hers. Christina was touched by the scene. It was rare; this window into a complicated relationship between Jeremy and Linus, and it did her heart good to witness it.

Older and wiser, his thick hair gone snow white, he doted on his son. The misery he felt for Jeremy was evident on his caring face. His feeling of helplessness and the torment must be eating him alive. She could recognize the quiet suffering because she felt it, too.

~~

Jamie had stayed by her mother's side until she was certain she was asleep. The stubborn resolve of a mother determined to suffer along with her son could be an awesome obstacle to overcome. Outside the waiting room, she walked off the cramping in her legs from the stiletto heels she favored. She paced up and down the corridor and caught sight of the approaching policemen as she turned to make another pass.

When he seemed to be heading straight for the waiting room where her exhausted mother finally slept, Jamie stepped directly in his path to stop him. "Can I help you, officer?"

He was about to excuse himself and move around her, but she had backed herself into the doorway to block access to the room. "I'm looking for the Beckett family," he answered.

Jamie's heart skipped a beat. "Regarding?"

"I have some property belonging to Jeremy Beckett from his accident scene."

"I don't want them bothered right now," Jamie replied, not moving an inch. "You can leave it with me; I'm Jeremy's sister."

The officer studied the tenacious woman in front of him and shrugged. It was too damned late, and he was too damned tired to argue. "Alright. But I'll need to see some I.D., and you'll have to sign this waver as proof of receipt of property." He thrust the clipboard that had been tucked under his arm at her.

With barely a glance at what she was signing, Jamie scrolled her signature on the line and handed it back. Then, from her purse she pulled out her wallet and passed it over for scrutiny. Apparently satisfied, the officer gave her a small padded envelope.

When she opened it and looked inside, she knew why this cop had been leery about trusting her with it. She recognized the velvet box immediately. Inside would be Christina's engagement ring. "Thanks," she said with a little more consideration in her voice. "I'll be sure my brother gets it."

~~

It was the soft, audible moan from Jeremy that yanked Linus and Christina from the edges of sleep; a sound not much more than a whisper, and yet to the two of them it might have been a scream. When he stirred, trying to move his battered and bruised body beneath the sheet that covered him, he moaned again, clear and distinct, and proved it wasn't a dream.

Linus hit the call button for the nurse and urged his son on. "That's it, son. Open your eyes."

Christina grasped his hand between hers and smiled through her tears. "I'm here, baby. Wake up and talk to me."

Jeremy forced his heavy eyelids open and squeezed the hand holding his so tightly. When he could see her and focus clearly, he tried to smile. The pain of that simple act was great, so great, he sucked in a breath as his eyes filled. When Christina moved close to soothe him, he croaked out the thought foremost in his mind. "Don't...even think...about putting...off the wedding."

6:00am
Three Days Later

There was nothing quite like teetering on the edge between life and death to solidify a man's desire to live life to its fullest. Fully awake now and alert - and after being prodded and probed by well-intentioned medical staff - Jeremy lay propped upright by pillows with Christina by his side. Although his broken ribs throbbed and his head thumped in time with his heartbeat, grateful was the only word he would use to describe how he was feeling.

He survived an accident many would not have, and his family surrounding him with unfailing love and support reminded him of just how lucky he was. There was more good news: Debra was home with plans to stay throughout the Christmas - and she was so happy and beautiful and loving. She stayed with him late into the night, reading aloud from the latest bestseller. Best of all, he watched a true closeness develop between her and Christina.

He remembered nothing about the accident, and his only recollection of the argument with Christina was that he'd allowed it to escalate unnecessarily. He only needed to see her bare hand to be reminded of the real failure of the evening: a ring not offered, a proposal not proposed.

He decided not a moment more could be wasted. It was time to do what should have been done long before now. Jeremy wished for a more romantic setting, but this would have to do. He wanted his ring on her finger, but his mind blanked when he tried to remember what had happened to the ring.

Christina was at home, sleeping, he hoped. After nearly seventy-two hours at his side, her chair as close to the lowered bed rail as possible, immovable, she needed to rest as much as he did. In the end, it had taken a joint effort by his parents and himself to convince her to go home to get some fresh clothes and a shower, but it was the mention of Patrick that finally sent her home.

Jeremy pressed the call button, knowing his family would track down the ring for him before Christina returned.

~ 73 ~

Christina wanted to cry for the agony so easily read in Jeremy's wrecked appearance. Shallow cuts from the shattered windshield and abrasions from the exploded airbag had inflicted painful damage. Jeremy's face was almost entirely bruised, with eyes so blackened, he said it actually hurt to blink, and in his hand he clutched a single, long-stemmed red rose.

To complete the sorrowful picture, the deep wound above his left eye was closed with three staples; yet, when he handed her the rose, and a velvet box that seemed to appear out of nowhere, she found the shimmering ring inside, and Christina was suddenly speechless. She watched as his abused face bloomed into a smile that surely must have hurt.

"The moment I saw it," Jeremy began, "I knew this had to be your ring. It matches your eyes, my love, and that's when I knew. God knows you deserve it and so much more for all the time you've spent waiting for me. For our life to truly begin-"

"Oh, sweetheart-" Christina tried to interrupt him, but he wouldn't be silenced.

"I need to say this." With effort, he reached for the sparkling ring, ignoring the pain it caused him. "You need to know you've never been anything less than first in my heart. You've claimed my soul from the moment we met, and I've wanted you as my wife from the instant I knew I loved you. We're meant to be, Christina. Very soon, you'll take my name and become my wife. This ring is beautiful, but it can't compare to your beauty - and it could never equal the depth of my love for you."

Her tears flowed, and words failed her. Weeping, she helped slide the stunning emerald onto her finger. Her eyes met his, and she saw his filling with tears, too. Swept up in the love she felt for him, she pulled him close, ever so gently, and kissed him as passionately as his battered face would allow. "You wonderfully articulate man."

He shut his eyes against the sharp shocks of pain from his stomach to his rib cage. Her joy was worth the agony. "You inspire me." With a sharp intake of breath, Jeremy pulled away slowly and collapsed against his pillows. "Though I sounded like Shakespeare, I never imagined bedpans and disinfectant would be the backdrop for this moment. Maybe a fire if the air off the lake was cold. Maybe some champagne and candlelight while I danced with you, but never this. We'll just have to make do with the flickering fluorescent lighting and IVs instead."

Christina sighed and closed her eyes, understanding everything now and feeling incredibly small for her behavior nights before when he was only trying to be romantic. "This is why you wanted to go to Cherry Hill, to give me this ring in our special place. And I let Sam ruin it for you, for us."

Sliding his legs into a more comfortable position, Jeremy dismissed her self-scolding. "Christina, all that matters is right now. If I've learned nothing else from this knock to my brain, I've learned that."

~~

After seven days in the hospital, Jeremy was released to go home. Linus assured Dr. Montgomery that Jeremy would not lift so much as a pen for at least another week, and Jeremy knew that if he wanted to be on his feet in time for his wedding he would have to follow Dr. Montgomery's orders to the letter.

So he took to the guestroom next to Christina's office so he wouldn't have to navigate the stairs and made Patrick happy by letting him think he was taking care of daddy. His internal injuries were healing nicely, and the black bruising and cuts on his face were finally beginning to show the first signs of healing.

Pain killers and a sense of humor made the slow process of healing easier, but it wasn't long before Jeremy was feeling restless and itching to do anything. Christina reluctantly went back to work, but it had taken serious arm twisting to chase her out the door and back into everyday life.

~~

Part of everyday life was running her restaurants. Left in the capable hands of her staffs, Christina had scarcely thought of work during Jeremy's time in the hospital. But, with him on the mend and home under the watchful eye of Madeline Richardson, even she agreed it was time to see to her other responsibilities.

Her first stop was The Avenue. Her morning would consist of returning phone calls and going over vendor invoices and supplies. Then checking in with staff and VIPs and choosing the specials for the week.

The lunch rush found her in Manhattan Special, running the kitchen like a finely honed machine. Cooking, baking, and mingling with her patrons while gracefully sidestepping their questions about the accident. It wouldn't be the first time Christina walked a tightrope of propriety, nor would it be the last.

To Christina's surprise, it wasn't Jeremy's accident that she heard about in the murmurs and hushed voices in the dining room. When she heard their names at all, it was in talk of the wedding. The society columns speculated over every detail. Why so and so was excluded from the guest list, why other so and so's were not. Who would walk the bride down the aisle since her father had passed?

The questions never seemed to end, but the venomous undercurrent in the delivery had. The smiles greeting her as she presented one signature dish after another were genuine. The concern felt for Jeremy's health was true. The compliments were sincere.

Christina was still puzzling over the abrupt change in mood when she breezed into the house and found Debra fussing over her father. Over a sumptuous dinner of baked chicken with oyster stuffing, Waldorf salad, and asparagus tips with crème quiche for dessert, their discussion turned to the sudden attention their wedding was receiving.

"Imagine my surprise to hear my patrons practically gushing about our getting married," Christina declared as she served dessert. "The tide seems to have turned in our favor."

Jeremy finished his glass of white wine. "And to think; I only had to nearly die to earn the public's good graces."

Debra rolled her eyes and spooned up a huge gob of toasted cream topping. "Daddy," she admonished. "It's hardly something to joke about. I suppose it would be too much to hope all the busybodies started paying attention to their own lives."

"Don't make me laugh," Jeremy replied, diving into the rich dessert Christina sat in front of him. "It's much more likely they've found someone else to crucify in our place."

Patrick, hearing a word he was unfamiliar with, decided to join in the conversation. "What're 'busybodies?'"

Christina exchanged a look with Jeremy before she answered him. "People with nothing better to do than talk badly about others, sweetheart. Now finish your dessert before Madeline calls you for your bath."

~~

November 10
2004

Jeremy came into the sunroom to say hello to his mother. He limped as he walked, guarding his injured leg and his tender ribs. The thin cut above his eye was raw but healing. A thin pink scar would remain to remind him how fragile life could be.

The green tints of his bruises were becoming less noticeable by the day. Although he'd never been accused of being a vain man, he wanted his wedding pictures to be memorable for very different reasons besides his hellish appearance. So, he was grateful only slight traces of the damage from the accident would be visible on his wedding day.

He found his lovely mother among her pansies and peonies. Her sunhat was pulled low to shield her eyes from the bright morning sun, and her gloves were snug on her hands, no doubt, he thought, to protect her manicure. To hear her humming old standards made him want to take her dancing on the spot, and brought a smile to his face. Seeing her up to her wrists in her pampered soil made him immeasurable happy.

He chuckled and offered a hand when she looked over her shoulder to find him standing there, watching her. "Good morning, fair lady," he teased, helping her to her feet.

Chagrinned at being caught unaware, she kissed him and dusted off her gloved hands. "You're looking well, dear." She let him usher her inside to the table and pour her a cup of tea. "How're you feeling?"

Jeremy shrugged. "Almost as good as new," he said, settling in the chair next to his mother with a cup of tea for himself.

Elise looked him over and was satisfied. "So, are you nervous yet?" she inquired, picking through a bowl of diced fruit the maid placed on the table between them. "Just two more weeks of freedom left."

Jeremy laughed and bit into a juicy piece of cantaloupe. "Eighteen days, actually - but who's counting? If I'm nervous at all, it's about something happening to throw a wrench in the works. But am I nervous about marrying Christina? Not possible."

"You're finally happy."

Jeremy took his mother's hand and kissed it affectionately. "I am. Happier than I thought was possible."

~~

Napa Valley,
California

The three dressing assistants linked curved, floor-to-ceiling mirrors together and revealed Christina in all her beauty. She was adorned in white, the classic streaming of two very important lines for every woman: waistline and breast line. Hand-stitched Victorian lace drew the eye to a V-bosom cut that subtly revealed her breast line, then drew the eye lower still to a snug, trim waist. And still more lace accented a five-foot train which fell, in sweeping layers behind her to the floor; eight mirrors encircled and flattered her and the dress she had helped to create.

It was finally happening. Her dream of marrying the man she loved for more than half her life was finally coming true. She seemed to shine, glow, even radiate light from within; and she felt every inch a princess. Her perfect gown was finally complete, and Christina finally felt like a bride for the first time in her life.

Happy tears made her sea green eyes shimmer. She had to draw in a calming breath to regain control. It wouldn't do to weep like a starry-eyed school girl, but staring at her reflection completed the dream every little girl wished for when she grew up. She'd carried this very picture of herself in her mind since she was a child.

Debra's voice pulled her back into the moment. "You look amazing," she said, coming into view in the mirror, smiling. "Beautiful, really. Daddy's gonna fall through the floor when he sees you."

Wiping away tears, she laughed. "You're sweet." Stepping down from the pedestal, she turned to Debra. "I'm so glad you could fly out with me today. It means so much that you're here."

Debra took Christina's hand, still smiling. "I'm glad you asked." Stepping back, she gave one last shrewd, appraising look. "It's a good thing this was designed with you in mind, Christina, because no one else could do it justice." With a pause, she chose her next words with care. "I haven't always been kind to you," Debra confessed, stepping behind Christina to unzip her gown.

Surprised by the bluntness of the admission, Christina met Debra's eyes in the mirror. "Considering my place in your father's life, I understood - and still understand - your feelings," she said, slipping her arms out of the sleeves and stepping out of the dress. "Your loyalty is to your mother. And that's how it should be."

Debra shook her head with a rueful grin and handed off the dress to a nearby assistant. "Loyalty is one thing," she countered, "cruelty is another. I was terrible to you."

"That was a long time ago, Debra."

"Which shouldn't excuse my treatment of you. I think I saw you differently once I'd grown. Momma explained things about you and Dad, and her total lack of animosity towards you was amazing. And then when Patrick was taken and I saw your strength and the deep love between you two, I couldn't doubt how much you loved each other."

"Jeremy and I never meant to cause the pain our being together brought you and Emily."

"I know," Debra said with confidence. "Momma called you two destined. And she was right."

Christina gave no thought to what happened next. She simply hugged Debra with appreciation. "Thank you."

~ 74 ~

With the wedding only one week away, Jeremy walked into his office to tie up a few loose ends with his father's latest merger. His strides were smoother, and his limp was less pronounced. His bruises were fading, which improved his battered appearance.

During his month-long absence from his office and all things business related, Jeremy was pleased to find Linus and Tim had managed quite well without him. For the first time in twenty-five years, Jeremy's finesse hadn't been necessary for a successful end result, and it made his decision to scale back on his time spent on business there easier.

Linus asked him to go over the final drafts of the contracts with a critical eye, and he'd agreed without hesitation because his mind was crying out for an outlet. He'd ambled up Madison Avenue in no hurry, weaving in and out of the foot traffic, drawing the city air deep into his lungs. He was almost used to his ribs' painful protests.

The fresh air had done him a world of good, he thought, settling in, putting on his glasses, and picking up the Pitney merger contracts lying in the center of his desk. It took no more than skimming the first paragraph for Jeremy to know that Tim had done exactly as he would have had he drawn up the contracts himself. He was halfway through his reading when his intercom buzzed, interrupting his train of thought.

"What is it, Sarah?" he asked, finding his place in the fine print again to initial a clause he thought too vague.

"I'm sorry to disturb you, Jeremy, but a gentleman's here to see you."

He wasn't prepared to see anyone; he hadn't shaved in two days and he was dressed casually. "I'm not seeing anyone today, Sarah."

"I've told him, but he's insistent."

With a sigh, Jeremy tossed his glasses aside. "Does this insistent man have a name?"

"Sam Radcliff."

Jeremy was shocked into silence, but his brow lifted, and his curiosity peaked. "Send him in," he replied, pushing himself carefully out of his chair. He would meet Christina's former lover eye-to-eye.

When the door opened, Sarah came in with Sam at her heels. The two men took each other's measure before either of them drew their next breath. Sarah felt the tension and spoke up. "Would you like coffee or tea, Mr. Beckett?" she asked out of formality.

Jeremy's intense gaze shifted, coming to rest on Sam. "Would you care for either, Mr. Radcliff?" he asked.

Sam took in the bruises, the cut above the eye that would scar his almost pretty face, yet somehow leave it more handsome. He'd expected to find Beckett in a pretentiously overpriced suit, but he wore faded, well worn jeans and a white tee shirt. Hate swelled anew, but he smiled anyway. "No, thank you," he replied.

Jeremy returned the thin, false smile and turned to his secretary. "That's all, Sarah," he said, excusing her.

With her hand on the door knob, she turned. "I'll hold your calls," she said, and then was gone.

"Well, sit down, Mr. Radcliff." Jeremy offered the chair to the right of the front of his desk. Once both of them were settled, he got to the point. "To what do I owe this visit?"

"Call me Sam," was the reply. "We don't need to stand on ceremony, surely not with what we have in common."

Jeremy smirked at the dig and pinned the man across from him with a level stare. "We're not going to be friends, so you should get to the point, Sam."

"You must feel very fortunate. It's not every man who survives a brush with death."

"You sound disappointed."

Sam shrugged. "Some are just luckier than others," he said, "no matter how undeserving they might be. Christina deserved better than the famed playboy she pined for even after you'd publicly humiliated her, and she deserves better now - but she's too stubborn for her own good."

"It's interesting you still devote so much time worrying about Christina's choices. Your wife must really appreciate it."

"Did yours?" Sam countered.

Jeremy's hard eyes narrowed. Evoking Emily was one of many ways Radcliff could earn a fist in the mouth. "Be careful, Sam, or this playboy just might kick your ass."

"Yes, I can see where my pointing out that, under all your manicured glitz the true man is one who cheats on his wife with a woman he tossed aside like garbage, might rub you the wrong way." Sam grinned and threw up his hands in surrender. "But why let this deteriorate into a pissing contest? So I'll leave you with this warning and go."

Jeremy bit back his rising anger and lifted a brow. "Warning?" he stood and looked down at Sam. "Should I be quaking in my shoes, Sam?"

Sam got to his feet, damned if he would let scum like Beckett look down his nose at him. "If you hurt her again," he said, moving closer until they could feel each other's breath on their faces, "you'll answer to me."

"Go home to your wife, you dumb sonofabitch," Jeremy advised tightly. "Christina's my concern, not yours."

"Well, it's about damn time." Satisfied to have the last word, Sam turned and left without another word. There was no need; he'd made the point he'd come there to make.

~~

Jeremy followed the unmistakable gales of laughter and found his son playing in the gated back yard. His irritation over his face-to-face with Sam was forgotten at the sight of Patrick pushing his toy bulldozer across the grass. When the boy looked up, grinning, Jeremy couldn't help but do the same.

"Hi, Daddy!" Patrick called brightly, jumping to his feet for a mad dash at his father for a hug. "Mom's making a pecan pie for dessert."

Jeremy swept the hair out of Patrick's eyes. "Wow. Did Mommy help you try on your tuxedo?"

Patrick groaned. "Yeeeeesss," he grumbled, keeping up with his father's wide strides across the yard to door. "Mommy says I look sweet."

"I'm sure you do." Pushing the door open, the two of them walked into the kitchen just as Christina was putting the pie in the oven.

Christina fixed Jeremy with a disapproving glance but went willingly into his arms when he opened them. "So you finally escaped?"

He wiggled his eyebrows playfully and kissed her. "Call me crafty."

"I think you mean pigheaded, honey," she said, winding her arms around his neck.

"Tenacious."

"Mulish."

He held her tight, then pulled back to look her in the eye. "I was revising contracts, not climbing Everest," he said seriously, though there was still laughter in his eyes. "The fresh air and the work recharged my brain."

She skimmed the fine lined scar over his brow and sighed. "I just don't want you over doing it."

"I'm fine sweetheart, really." He, in turn, pulled the pin in her hair and watched her lush hair tumble to her shoulders. "How was your day?" he asked, changing the subject and going to the refrigerator for a beer. "Was Henry a lamb or a lion?"

Christina chuckled and moved to the counter to prepare shrimp salad and crab cakes for dinner. "My day was busy, and Henry was very lamblike, which scared me."

Twisting the cap off a Coors, Jeremy guzzled. "He's probably still riding high because you've left the rehearsal dinner and reception in his hands."

Putting fresh crab into a large mixing bowl, she smiled. "And no doubt his oversized ego sees it as a validation of his culinary skills. So, how was it? Being back in the office?"

Leaning casually against the far end of the counter, Jeremy shrugged. "Good." he said. "Dad made it sound like I'd find a mess, but Tim handled everything like I would have. A few subtle modifications, and crisis averted."

"Anything else exciting happen?"

He ran through his options. He could tell her about Sam's impromptu visit, or he could forget it ever happened. When he saw the puzzled look on her face, he knew he owed her the same honesty she'd given him.

She cracked an egg and added a generous amount of dill, celery salt, fresh onions, and grated garlic.

Deciding to forgo tiptoeing up to the subject, Jeremy instead jumped right in. "I had a visit from Sam today."

Christina's hand stilled. "You're not kidding," she replied after seeing annoyance come over his face.

"Wish I was," Jeremy quipped after another long pull on his beer. "It was quite enlightening."

"What do you mean? What did he want?"

"To throw down the gauntlet and warn me that if I hurt you again there'll be consequences. He still loves you."

"That's ridiculous."

"I couldn't agree more. But it's true."

She sighed. Forgetting about the crab, she dropped her head. "I hurt him."

Of course, she would blame herself, he thought, setting his beer down and going to knead the knots the mention of Sam's name put in her shoulders. "Don't blame yourself because he doesn't. He lays the blame with me, and I can see why. I did pursue you."

No matter what Jeremy said, Christina knew better. Sam had trusted her and her love, and she betrayed him. "I don't know why he keeps rehashing our past," she said. "He has a wonderful, successful life, and a wife who loves him."

"Well, speaking from experience, you're a hard woman to get out of one's system. You get into our blood."

Turning around, she smiled. "I should have been more careful with his feelings."

"Hindsight," Jeremy reminded her. "And he's right. About how badly I hurt you, though I didn't enjoy having it thrown in my face." He framed her face in his hands and looked into the sea green storms in her eyes. "I'd cut off my arm before I'd hurt you again. You know that?"

She pressed her face to his. "Yes."

~ 75 ~

November 24th
Manhattan Special
Rehearsal Dinner

The week flew by as days of anticipation were reduced to dwindling hours. Surrounded by family and friends, good music, fine wine, and sumptuous food, Christina welcomed the butterflies fluttering in her stomach. The nausea accompanying them, though, made her pass on the rich dessert and choose club soda over the delicate merlot- over which everyone was raving.

This was what she'd been waiting for: the moment she and Jeremy became husband and wife and would no longer have to make excuses or apologize for their love. She would have Jeremy's name and receive it proudly. By this time tomorrow, she and Jeremy would be safely tucked away at Cherry Hill, celebrating their wedding night, followed by a honeymoon flight to a private island in Hawaii for a week of fun in paradise.

They danced and laughed with people who loved them and had waited for this day almost as anxiously as they had. Jeremy seemed a boy again as he twirled and dipped the woman who would finally become his wife, and Christina pressed as close to him as she could manage. She felt like the girl who had been charmed and seduced by him from the moment they met.

When the evening was over and everyone scattered to hotel rooms and homes alike, Jeremy found Christina where he expected her to be.

In the backyard of his family estate, Christina stood silhouetted in the moonlight. Her attention was drawn to the large gazebo centered in the vast lawn for the wedding, she didn't notice him at all. Come morning, the gazebo would be transformed to a thing of beauty as pink and white roses adorned with baby's breath twined around the latticed wood and tulips flanked the outside chairs and lined the paper runner serving as the aisle.

It would be a thing of beauty, Jeremy knew, but it would still pale next to Christina in the moment she walked down the aisle toward him, and their long-overdue future together. He didn't speak because he wanted this chance to see her in this unguarded moment; instead, he went to her in awed silence and pressed his face into her lush, tumbled hair, drawing in a breath of her scent.

She wasn't surprised that he'd come to her, and she couldn't resist when his arms snaked around her waist and he molded them together hip to hip. Without a word, she placed her hands on his and tilted her head up to let his mouth trail kisses along the hollow of her jaw. For a moment, she considered sneaking him into her room at the top of the stairs, but she wouldn't chance the bad luck.

"If your mother finds you here, she'll skin you alive," Christina murmured, turning around to look at him in the darkness.

"It's only eleven-thirty," he argued. "You're not off limits until midnight."

"A technicality she'll ignore if she catches us together."

"She's fast asleep."

"Jamie's not, and she'll come looking for me if I'm gone much longer."

Jeremy pulled Christina close and chuckled. "So I wanted a few stolen moments with you, big deal. I'm not scared of my sister."

"You should be." Jamie's voice broke the quiet solitude and had Jeremy flinching. "It's bad luck to see the bride on your wedding day."

"It's not our wedding day yet," Jeremy defended.

"Twenty minutes, big brother. Now clear out; Debra's waiting for you."

Relenting, Jeremy kissed Christina, drawing out the goodbye. When he pulled away, his eyes were moist. "I won't sleep tonight for thinking about you. I love you."

"I love you, too. Now get before Debra starts to worry." Together, she and Jamie watched him disappear into the darkness, then went inside to remove temptation.

~ 76 ~

November 25, 2004
Wedding Day

The Beckett estate was a whirl of activity by the time the sun broke through the remnants of the night sky. The white glowed moon was but a sweet memory for Christina as she embraced this new day made for promises fulfilled and new promises vowed. At the window of the room she'd shared with Jamie the night before, she watched as the florists worked their magic on the lawn below.

Christina smiled, realizing her wedding day was finally here. Flowers and lace, ribbon and baby's breath complemented each other, turning a rolling sweep of manicured grass into a fairytale brought to life. Rows and rows of white wicker-backed chairs were being set up with efficient precision, enough for their seventy-five invited guests.

Jamie breezed into the room, a fine silk robe billowing around her, breaking into her thoughts and filling the room with an energy that could only belong to her. "Mom's put out a buffet in the garden. Anything you could think of for breakfast is yours."

Christina instinctively put her hand to her stomach. "I couldn't eat a thing right now."

Jamie laughed and opened a bottle of pale pink fingernail polish. "Good." she patted the mattress next to her. "We'll start with your nails."

~~

In contrast, Jeremy lingered over a fruit plate, cold cereal, black coffee, and the company of his daughter. He liked spending his last night as an unmarried man in the home he had made for Debra and her mother. Oddly, he still felt comfortable here, even though more than six years had passed since he'd considered it home.

He sat in the breakfast nook tucked into the corner of the kitchen he'd rarely spent any time in during the eighteen years he lived there. Debra sat across from him, chattering on the phone to her flat mate in Paris. Patrick had vanished upstairs for his bath after plowing through his oatmeal. Letting his gaze wonder, he saw obvious touches of Emily anywhere his eyes settled.

He knew then why Debra spent so much time here alone; of course, she would feel her mother within these walls and yearn for any link with her. As for himself, he missed Emily's laughter and her charm, and he felt her presence as surely as if she were right next to him.

His eyes fell, then, on her raven hair and lovely face. For Debra, this house would always be home. The decision he'd made the night before when he walked this house with his memories was right, and only natural.

~~

By ten a.m., Jeremy was alone, drifting on the excitement that in three short hours he would be bound to Christina for the rest of his life.

Debra and Patrick had left for the estate, leaving him - and the nerves he was certain wouldn't be a problem - behind to settle in. The face in the mirror as he shaved was an anxious one. In the shower, he realized he was shaking, but he wasn't the least bit chilled. Damnable nerves betraying him, he thought happily. He was about to marry his soul mate and wouldn't let jitters take away from his happiness.

If his hands were trembling unzipping the heavy linen bag and removing his custom-tailored midnight blue tuxedo, so be it. A giddy laugh bubbled up his throat when, stepping into his pants, he found he couldn't get his thick fingers to fasten the clasp at his waist. Problems such as these could make a man's day.

Finally dressed, he snapped on his Rolex - an engagement gift from Christina - and fumbled in his overnight bag for the cufflinks Avery had given him on their last Christmas together. He made quite a picture, even if he did say so himself. The pearl colored shirt under the deep midnight blue vest was a wonderful choice.

With his tie hanging loosely at his neck and dressed to impress his bride, Jeremy hurried down the hall and trotted down the stairs. A silly grin plastered his face, even while the jitters in his stomach made him queasy. Then he was out the door, keys in hand, and he nearly ran Edward over in his mad dash for the car.

"Good morning, Jeremy," Edward said brightly. "Your father decided it would be wise to have me pick you up in the limo and be your driver for the entire day."

"Did he now?" Tongue-in-cheek, Jeremy clapped a hand on Edward's shoulder and headed them both for the stretch at the curb. "Then let's get rolling. I refuse to be late, fashionably or otherwise."

~~

Dressed in her gown and stunning, Christina was a thing of beauty. Hair swept up into a French twist, her eyes were aglow. Debra, Jamie, and Elise gasped as she stood before them, as if she walked out of the pages of a fairy-tale. 'Classic Christina' was the first thought that came to the minds of the women surrounding the bride.

Patrick broke the spell of silence with an honest pronouncement all his own. "Mommy, you're the most beautiful woman I know! Let's get married," he proclaimed as laughter from all the women in his life filled the room.

~ 77 ~

At precisely one o'clock, the opening notes of a classical rendition of the Beatles' "And I Love Her" began. Jeremy stood at the steps of the gazebo with a proud smile on his face, and Patrick stood to his left with a tight grip on the ring in his coat pocket. Elise was already crying when he winked at her, so he nearly cried himself.

Debra was first down the aisle, looking stunning in a backless pink Versace gown, followed by Jamie in a shimmering pink creation of her own. Jeremy was humbled by the gift of each of them, and was feeling blessed to have such women in his life. When Christina appeared, to be escorted down the aisle by Linus, everyone stood, and she walked down the aisle toward a new life.

Jeremy would always remember her walk down the aisle, as if she were gliding slowly on air wanting to make the moment last forever. Closing the distance between her and Jeremy, she'd never felt happier. When she locked eyes with him and smiled, they were alone in the moment.

When at last she took his hand and they stepped into the gazebo, Jeremy realized that both of them were crying. They wept with happiness at the realization of this dream coming true, wept for the road traveled to bring them to this moment, this day. Before the priest and God, family and friends, vows were pledged, then rings were given and received, and two lives locked together to become one.

~~

By dusk, the celebration was still going strong with no signs of stopping. Having shared divine food, rich creamy cake, champagne, and dozens of wedding gifts through the afternoon, all that remained was dancing and the laughter - and such laughter and happiness would not soon be forgotten.

God blessed their union, and as if to prove it, He gifted them with perfect weather to celebrate their day. This late in the fall, the air should have been too chilled for an outdoor wedding and reception, but it was unseasonably warm from sunup to sunset. Even when the chill finally moved in the air under the moonlight, no one even seemed to notice. With the cooling of the air, a heated tent was opened, and the dining tables were moved off to the edges of the lawn.

Jeremy and Christina christened the enormous dance floor with their first dance as husband and wife. If neither of them could stop smiling, what did it matter? Waltzing, they covered every inch of the floor and opened the floor for everyone to join them.

Christina danced with Patrick and then Linus while Jeremy danced first a slow waltz with his mother and then his sister and daughter in turn. Eventually, Christina and Jeremy wound up back in each other's arms. One dance after another, kisses and whispering secrets throughout, with smiles and waves for the only two press photographers invited.

Still, they did mingle with their guests. Together and separately, they accepted the well wishes given so freely by some of the same people who years before condemned their relationship. It had taken Jeremy's near death and Debra's open acceptance for the society to turn over a new leaf.

As the night sky lit up with stars, Jeremy stole Debra away for a quiet moment. Arm in arm, moving through the crowd of guests, father and daughter moved outside for privacy. This moment wasn't for anyone but the two of them.

Debra tilted her head up and took in the beauty of the starlit sky above them. She liked to think her mother was one of those stars - the brightest - and perhaps she was looking down on this night. She'd be happy for Christina and her father, and Debra realized that she was too. Then her gaze moved to her father. She saw the obvious joy on her father's face and was moved. "You're so happy," she said simply.

Skimming her cheek with the back of his fingers, he nodded with eyes bright with elation. "I am. And I want the same for you."

Touched, she raised up on her toes to kiss his cheek. "I'm very happy at the moment, Daddy. For you and Christina and Patrick and me, I'm so happy."

"We're a family, all of us. And you'll always have a home with us, no matter where your life takes you."

She jerked up a brow and reminded Jeremy instantly of Emily. "Is one of us going somewhere?"

A contented laugh and a kiss would be her only answer. "I have something for you," he said, reaching into his inside vest pocket and pulling out a thick envelope.

Debra looked at the envelope warily. "Just tell me it's not a copy of your will," she retorted, only half joking.

"Hell, no. I plan on being around another forty, fifty years, at least." he assured her, then handed it to her. "It's not my will. Go ahead, open it," he urged when she hesitated.

Slowly, Debra opened the envelope and pulled a thick fold of papers free. Unfolding them, she skimmed the pages with confusion. "The deed to our house?"

"The deed to your house now," Jeremy corrected.

"You're giving me the house?"

"Lock, stock, and garage."

"But..." Her eyes widened in surprise. "I don't know what to say."

"You don't have to say anything, honey. Just take the house and make it your own. Your mother loved the home we made there, and I know you do, too. So, it's yours, and that's just as it should be."

Clutching the deed, she looked at her father through tears. "Thank you, Daddy," was all she could manage before stepping into his open arms.

Enfolding her in his strong arms, he tucked her head under his chin and cleared the emotion from his voice. "I love you, baby."

"I love you, too, Daddy."

~~

When the newlyweds finally said their goodbyes, leaving a sleeping Patrick in the care of his grandparents, it was almost ten-thirty. Exhausted, they escaped to the house to change out of their wedding clothes and take the company helicopter for the thirty-minute flight to Cherry Hill. Only immediate family saw them off, waving and smiling as they lifted off and flew into the night.

They noticed the trail of candlelight leading from the helipad to the house from the sky. When the helicopter touched down on Cherry Hill property, Jeremy swept Christina off her feet and carried her along the light-ed path and over the threshold. The foyer was a sight to behold as four-foot tapered candles cast the quaint space in a warm glow.

It was the living room that was the true masterpiece of seduction and romance. The sheer curtains on the windows were open to let in the moon-light, as were the curtains on the patio doors. Pale light poured through, and the room seemed to shiver with a glow that flowed through to the wrap-around back porch. Lavender scented candles were burning everywhere, while a roaring fire crackled in the hearth. Romantic light, meant to embrace them as they embrace each other.

Chilled strawberries and whipping cream sat on a sterling silver cart, and champagne stood chilling in an ice bucket. His gaze swept the room, taking in the setting Jamie must have created for them, in this special place, as a sur-prise. He knew the mark of his sister when he saw it. He could only imag-ine what lay in store for them in the bedroom. Jeremy set Christina on her feet and watched as she wandered through the room with a smile of approval.

Although neither of them had slept in the last twenty-four hours, neither wanted to sleep. Christina kicked off her heels and slipped off the earrings dangling from her ears. Jeremy tossed aside his winter weight linen sports coat and drew her into his arms.

Then he did as he'd been dying to do from the moment he saw her at the end of the aisle. With a feather light kiss to the hollow below her earlobe, he tugged the pins from her hair and let it fall free. With a satisfied groan, he mumbled. "I've wanted to do this all day, Mrs. Beckett."

Hearing her name on his lips thrilled her, and her laugh was seductive, rich. She sought his mouth with hers. Found, she took them both under with a kiss that spread searing heat through them both. She wanted. She needed. And taking them under again, demanded. "Make love to me, Jeremy. Make love to your wife."

~ 78 ~

Hawaii
Maui Island

The white sand at their feet lay before them like a vast blanket warmed and coddled by the sun. The often heard calls of tropical birds lifted their gaze skyward to see many of them in flight. Hand in hand, Jeremy and Christina strolled along the beach, towels slung over their shoulders, sunglasses shielding their eyes against the bright, but welcome sun.

They came to an abandoned cove and settled in for their picnic lunch. On top of a large blanket, Christina unpacked the basket with Jeremy lying beside her. Her eyes swept the scene around them. She watched the waves crashing against the rocks worn down by time and Mother Nature. The sun shined down warmly, unblocked by clouds or smog as it was at home.

Jeremy lay back, and as his wife watched paradise, he watched her. A few days in the warm sea air had freed her from the responsibilities she was a slave to in the city. Her beauty was enough to render him senseless, and here and now he would have done her bidding.

"Hey, where are you?" he murmured as he skimmed a path from the small of her back to her neck with his fingers. "You seem a world away."

An easy smile crossed her face as she turned her head provocatively to look over her shoulder at him. "Not that far." Happy as she was to be here with her husband - her husband, she thought again - it still felt too much like a dream to be real. "I'm just so...happy here."

"Me, too," he said. "I think we should send for Patrick and become Hawaiian beach bums."

"Tempting, honey. Impractical, but tempting." She offered him a thick slice of melon, and with the plate between them she stretched out on the blanket and kicked off her sandals.

"Think of it, I'll spend my days picking pineapples, and you can make grass skirts for the tourists."

"Grass skirts? Me?" she gave a rueful laugh at the picture that formed in her mind. "Can't I just cater the luaus?"

~~

Later, when the picnic was over and the beach forgotten, they locked themselves away in the honeymoon suite, content to leave the world outside the door. Making love and plans, evening turned to night, but time was unimportant. Phone calls to Patrick was the only link allowed to their life in New York.

Sated and satisfied, Christina was wide awake. On the pillow next to her, Jeremy drifted off not long after making love. His deep breathing might have lulled her to sleep if her mind weren't working overtime.

How had she missed it? Very easily, she mused, when dealing with the craziness that seemed to define her life these last two months. Was it possible? Of course, it was. Was it likely? Of course, it wasn't. But the signs were all there, and there was only one way to know for sure.

Gently, she slipped out from under Jeremy's arm and decided to end her uncertainty. When she closed herself in the bathroom, she was grateful for room service and discreet staff. With a deep breath, she steadied her nerve...in five minutes, she would know.

~~

Breakfast was ready and waiting for her when she opened her eyes. She had slept eventually, but not nearly enough. On the patio, Jeremy was putting the finishing touches on a romantic morning meal. Slipping into her robe, she let the aroma of pineapple drizzled pancakes tempt her out to join her husband, even as her stomach rolled at the thought of food.

~~

Jeremy found Christina on the edge of the bed, waiting for him. The odd expression on her face amused him. The long, slim velvet bowed box in her hands intrigued him. Willing to play along, he ambled over to her with mischief and seduction in mind.

"Want to skip the sail and have a bath instead?" he quipped with a grin.

"I have something else in mind," Christina said, tentative at first. "I have a surprise for you. Here."

He looked at the box, and then at his wife. "A good surprise or a bad one?"

"A bad surprise? Would I give you a bad surprise on our honeymoon? It's a great one."

"Ooooh, a great surprise. You spoil me."

She handed him the long velvet box. "Open it," she prompted while a foolish grin covered her face.

With a wink, he lifted the lid and stared. "What's this?"

"A pregnancy test."

"A pregnancy test?" He looked at the thin blue line as realization dawned. "You're pregnant?"

"Yes."

He tossed the box on the bed and pulled her into a passionate kiss. Twirling her, elation soaring, he laughed and cried at the same time. "We're having a baby?"

"We're having a baby."

Epilogue

July 10, 2005
3:08 am
St. Vincent's Hospital

"Come on, baby, you can do this!" Jeremy encouraged, wiping her forehead with a cool cloth. "Just one more good push."

Christina, beyond exhaustion, fought to bare down. Hours of labor had sapped her strength and determination for a drug-free delivery. "I'm so tired...I need to rest."

"One more push, and you can." He looked into her eyes and winked. "You want to see her don't you?"

Where she found the energy, she didn't know, but she pushed as hard as she could with Jeremy bracing her from behind. Her reward was hearing the sharp cry of her daughter. Jeremy kissed her with more love than he thought possible and watched, welling up as the doctor lay the squalling infant across her mother's chest.

"She's beautiful," Christina cried, kissing her daughter and suddenly feeling like she could take on the world.

"She is." Jeremy Beckett just beamed, as proud as any father could be. "Welcome to the world, Gabrielle Sophia Beckett. We've been waiting for you."

* * * * *